ALSO BY MARY RENAULT

The Last of the Wine

THE KING
MUST DIE

Mary Renault

POCKET BOOKS, INC.
NEW YORK

THE KING MUST DIE

Pantheon edition published July, 1958

Book-of-the-Month Club edition published July, 1958

CARDINAL GIANT edition published January, 1960
1st printing..................November, 1959

CARDINAL GIANT editions are distributed in the U.S. by Affiliated Publishers, Inc., 630 Fifth Avenue, New York 20, N.Y.

CONTENTS

Oh, Mother! I was born to die soon;
but Olympian Zeus the Thunderer
owes me some honor for it.

—Achilles, in the *Iliad*

BOOK ONE

TROIZEN

1.

THE Citadel of Troizen, where the Palace stands, was built by giants before anyone remembers. But the Palace was built by my great-grandfather. At sunrise, if you look at it from Kalauria across the strait, the columns glow fire-red and the walls are golden. It shines bright against the dark woods on the mountainside.

Our house is Hellene, sprung from the seed of Ever-Living Zeus. We worship the Sky Gods before Mother Dia and the gods of earth. And we have never mixed our blood with the blood of the Shore People, who had the land before us.

My grandfather had about fifteen children in his household, when I was born. But his queen and her sons were dead, leaving only my mother born in wedlock. As for my father, it was said in the Palace that I had been fathered by a god. By the time I was five, I had perceived that some people doubted this. But my mother never spoke of it; and I cannot remember a time when I should have cared to ask her.

When I was seven, the Horse Sacrifice came due, a great day in Troizen.

It is held four-yearly, so I remembered nothing of the last one. I knew it concerned the King Horse, but thought it was some act of homage to him. To my mind, nothing could have been more fitting. I knew him well.

He lived in the great horse field, down on the plain. From the Palace roof I had often watched him, snuffing the wind with his white mane flying, or leaping on his mares. And only last year I had seen him do battle for his kingdom. One of the House Barons, seeing from afar the duel begin, rode down to the olive slopes for a nearer sight, and took me on his

3

crupper. I watched the great stallions rake the earth with their forefeet, arch their necks, and shout their war cries; then charge in with streaming manes and teeth laid bare. At last the loser foundered; the King Horse snorted over him, threw up his head neighing, and trotted off toward his wives. He had never been haltered, and was as wild as the sea. Not the King himself would ever throw a leg across him. He belonged to the god.

His valor alone would have made me love him. But I had another cause as well. I thought he was my brother.

Poseidon, as I knew, can look like a man or like a horse, whichever he chooses. In his man shape, it was said, he had begotten me. But there were songs in which he had horse sons too, swift as the north wind, and immortal. The King Horse, who was his own, must surely be one of these. It seemed clear to me, therefore, that we ought to meet. I had heard he was only five years old. "So," I thought, "though he is the bigger, I am the elder. It is for me to speak first."

Next time the Master of the Horse went down to choose colts for the chariots, I got him to take me. While he did his work, he left me with a groom; who presently drew in the dust a gambling board, and fell to play with a friend. Soon they forgot me. I climbed the palisade, and went seeking the King Horse.

The horses of Troizen are pure-bred Hellene. We have never crossed them with the little strain of the Shore People, whom we took the land from. When I was in with them, they looked very tall. As I reached up to pat one, I heard the Horse Master shout behind me; but I closed my ears. "Everyone gives me orders," I thought. "It comes of having no father. I wish I were the King Horse; no one gives them to him." Then I saw him, standing by himself on a little knoll, watching the end of the pasture where they were choosing colts. I went nearer, thinking, as every child thinks once for the first time, "Here is beauty."

He had heard me, and turned to look. I held out my hand, as I did in the stables, and called, "Son of Poseidon!" On this he came trotting up to me, just as the stable horses did. I had brought a lump of salt, and held it out to him.

There was some commotion behind me. The groom bawled out, and looking round I saw the Horse Master beating him. My turn would be next, I thought; men were waving at me from the railings, and cursing each other. I felt safer where I was. The King Horse was so near that I could see the lashes of his dark eyes. His forelock fell between them like a white waterfall between shining stones. His teeth were as big as the ivory plates upon a war helm; but his lip, when he licked the salt out of my palm, felt softer than my mother's breast. When the salt was finished, he brushed my cheek with his, and snuffed at my hair. Then he trotted back to his hillock, whisking his long tail. His feet, with which as I learned later he had killed a mountain lion, sounded neat on the meadow, like a dancer's.

Now I found myself snatched from all sides, and hustled from the pasture. It surprised me to see the Horse Master as pale as a sick man. He heaved me on his mount in silence, and hardly spoke all the way home. After so much to-do, I feared my grandfather himself would beat me. He gave me a long look as I came near; but all he said was, "Theseus, you went to the horse field as Peiros' guest. It was unmannerly to give him trouble. A nursing mare might have bitten your arm off. I forbid you to go again."

This happened when I was six years old; and the Horse Feast fell next year.

It was the chief of all feasts at Troizen. The Palace was a week getting ready. First my mother took the women down to the river Hyllikos, to wash the clothes. They were loaded on mules and brought down to the clearest water, the basin under the fall. Even in drought the Hyllikos never fails or muddies; but now in summer it was low. The old women rubbed light things at the water's edge, and beat them on the stones; the girls picked up their petticoats and trod the heavy mantles and blankets in midstream. One played a pipe, which they kept time to, splashing and laughing. When the wash was drying on the sunny boulders, they stripped

and bathed, taking me in with them. That was the last time
I was allowed there; my mother saw that I understood the
jokes.

On the feast day I woke at dawn. My old nurse dressed
me in my best: my new doeskin drawers with braided borders, my red belt rolled upon rope and clasped with crystal,
and my necklace of gold beads. When she had combed my
hair, I went to see my mother dressing. She was just out of
her bath, and they were dropping her petticoat over her
head. The seven-tiered flounces, sewn with gold drops and
pendants, clinked and glittered as she shook them out. When
they clipped together her gold-worked girdle and her bodice
waist, she held her breath in hard and let it out laughing.
Her breasts were as smooth as milk, and the tips so rosy that
she never painted them, though she was still wearing them
bare, not being, at that time, much above three and twenty.

They took her hair out of the crimping-plaits (it was darker
than mine, about the color of polished bronze) and began to
comb it. I ran outside on the terrace, which runs all round
the royal rooms, for they stand on the roof of the Great Hall.
Morning was red, and the crimson-painted columns burned in
it. I could hear, down in the courtyard, the House Barons
assembling in their war dress. This was what I had waited
for.

They came in by twos and threes, the bearded warriors
talking, the young men laughing and scuffling, shouting to
friends, or feinting at each other with the butts of their
spears. They had on their tall-plumed leather helmets, circled
with bronze or strengthened with rolls of hide. Their broad
breasts and shoulders, sleekly oiled, shone russet in the rosy
light; their wide leather drawers stood stiffly out from the
thigh, making their lean waists, pulled in with the thick
rolled sword-belts, look slenderer still. They waited, ex-
changing news and chaff, and striking poses for the women,
the young men lounging with the tops of their tall shields
propping their left armpits, their right arms stretched out
grasping their spears. Their upper lips were all fresh shaved,
to make their new beards show clearer. I scanned the shield

devices, birds or fish or serpents worked upon the hide, picking out friends to hail, who raised their spears in greeting.
Seven or eight of them were uncles of mine. My grandfather
had got them in the Palace on various women of good blood,
prizes of his old wars, or gifts of compliment from neighbor
kings.

The land barons were coming in from their horses or their
chariots; they too bare to the waist, for the day was warm,
but wearing all their jewels; even their boot tops had golden
tassels. The sound of men's voices grew louder and deeper
and filled the air above the courtyard. I squared back my
shoulders, and nipped my belt in; gazed at a youth whose
beard was starting, and counted years on my fingers.

Talaos came in, the War Leader; a son of my grandfather's
youth, got upon a chief's wife taken in battle. He had on his
finest things: his prize helmet from the High King of Mycenae's funeral games, all plated, head and cheeks, with the
carved teeth of boars, and both his swords, the long one with
the crystal pommel which he sometimes let me draw, the
short one with a leopard hunt inlaid in gold. The men touched
their spear shafts to their brows; he numbered them off with
his eye, and went in to tell my grandfather they were ready.
Soon he came out, and standing on the great steps before the
king-column that carried the lintel, his beard jutting like a
warship's prow, shouted, "The god goes forth!"

They all trooped out of the courtyard. As I craned to see,
my grandfather's body servant came and asked my mother's
maid if the Lord Theseus was ready to go with the King.

I had supposed I should be going with my mother. So I
think had she. But she sent word that I was ready whenever
her father wished.

She was Chief Priestess of Mother Dia in Troizen. In the
time of the Shore People before us, that would have made
her sovereign queen; and if we ourselves had been sacrificing
at the Navel Stone, no one would have walked before her.
But Poseidon is husband and lord of the Mother, and on
his feast day the men go first. So, when I heard I was going
with my grandfather, I saw myself a man already.

I ran to the battlements, and looked out between their teeth. Now I saw what god it was the men were following. They had let loose the King Horse, and he was running free across the plain.

The village too, it seemed, had turned out to welcome him. He went through standing corn in the common fields, and no one raised a hand to stop him. He crossed the beans and the barley, and would have gone up to the olive slopes; but some of the men were there and he turned away. While I was watching, down in the empty court a chariot rattled. It was my grandfather's; and I remembered I was to ride in it. By myself on the terrace I danced for joy.

They fetched me down. Eurytos the charioteer was up already, standing still as an image in his short white tunic and leather greaves, his long hair bound in a club; only his arm muscles moved, from holding the horses. He lifted me in, to await my grandfather. I was eager to see him in his war things, for in those days he was tall. Last time I was in Troizen, when he was turned eighty, he had grown light and dry as an old grasshopper, piping by the hearth. I could have lifted him in my hands. He died a month after my son, having I suppose nothing to hold him longer. But he was a big man then.

He came out, after all, in his priestly robe and fillet, with a scepter instead of a spear. He heaved himself in by the chariot rail, set his feet in the bracers, and gave the word to go. As we clattered down the cobbled road, you could not have taken him for anything but a warrior, fillet or no. He rode with the broad rolling war straddle a man learns driving cross-country with weapons in his hands. Whenever I rode with him, I had to stand on his left; it would have set his teeth on edge to have anything in front of his spear arm. Always I seemed to feel thrown over me the shelter of his absent shield.

Seeing the road deserted, I was surprised, and asked him where the people were. "At Sphairia," he said, grasping my shoulder to steady me over a pothole. "I am taking you to see the rite, because soon you will be waiting on the god there, as one of his servants."

The news startled me. I wondered what service a horse god wanted, and pictured myself combing his forelock, or putting ambrosia before him in golden bowls. But he was also Poseidon Bluehair, who raises storms; and the great black Earth Bull whom, as I had heard, the Cretans fed with youths and girls. After some time I asked my grandfather, "How long shall I stay?"

He looked at my face and laughed, and ruffled my hair with his big hand. "A month at a time," he said. "You will only serve the shrine, and the holy spring. It is time you did your duties to Poseidon, who is your birth-god. So today I shall dedicate you, after the sacrifice. Behave respectfully, and stand still till you are told; remember, you are with me."

We had reached the shore of the strait, where the ford was. I had looked forward to splashing through it in the chariot; but a boat was waiting, to save our best clothes. On the other side we mounted again, and skirted for a while the Kalaurian shore, looking across at Troizen. Then we turned inward, through pines. The horses' feet drummed on a wooden bridge and stopped. We had come to the little holy island at the big one's toe; and kings must walk in the presence of the gods.

The people were waiting. Their clothes and garlands, the warriors' plumes, looked bright in the clearing beyond the trees. My grandfather took my hand and led me up the rocky path. On either side a row of youths was standing, the tallest lads of Troizen and Kalauria, their long hair tied up to crest their heads like manes. They were singing, stamping the beat with their right feet all together, a hymn to Poseidon Hippios. It said how the Horse Father is like the fruitful earth; like the seaway whose broad back bears the ships safe home; his plumed head and bright eye are like daybreak over the mountains, his back and loins like the ripple in the barley field; his mane is like the surf when it blows streaming off the wave crests; and when he stamps the ground, men and cities tremble, and kings' houses fall.

I knew this was true, for the roof of the sanctuary had been rebuilt in my own lifetime; Poseidon had overthrown its wooden columns, and several houses, and made a crack in the Palace walls. I had not felt myself that morning; they had asked me if I was sick, at which I only cried. But after the shock I was better. I had been four years old then, and had almost forgotten.

Our part of the world had always been sacred to Earth-Shaker; the youths had many of his deeds to sing about. Even the ford, their hymn said, was of his making; he had stamped in the strait, and the sea had sunk to a trickle, then risen to flood the plain. Up till that time, ships had passed through it; there was a prophecy that one day he would strike it with his fish-spear, and it would sink again.

As we walked between the boys, my grandfather ran his eye along them, for likely warriors. But I had seen ahead, in the midst of the sacred clearing, the King Horse himself, browsing quietly from a tripod.

He had been hand-broken this last year, not for work but for this occasion, and today he had had the drugged feed at dawn. But without knowing this, I was not surprised he should put up with the people round him; I had been taught it was the mark of a king to receive homage with grace.

The shrine was garlanded with pine boughs. The summer air bore scents of resin and flowers and incense, of sweat from the horse and the young men's bodies, of salt from the sea. The priests came forward, crowned with pine, to salute my grandfather as chief priest of the god. Old Kannadis, whose beard was as white as the King Horse's forelock, laid his hand on my head nodding and smiling. My grandfather beckoned to Diokles, my favorite uncle; a big young man eighteen years old, with the skin of a leopard, which he had killed himself, hanging on his shoulder. "Look after the boy," said my grandfather, "till we are ready for him."

Diokles said, "Yes, sir," and led me to the steps before the shrine, away from where he had been standing with his friends. He had on his gold snake arm-ring with crystal eyes, and his hair was bound with a purple ribbon. My grandfather had won his mother at Pylos, second prize in the chariot race, and had always valued her highly; she was the best embroidress in the Palace. He was a bold gay youth, who used to let me ride on his wolfhound. But today he looked at me solemnly, and I feared I was a burden to him.

Old Kannadis brought my grandfather a pine wreath bound with wool, which should have been ready, but had been found after some delay. There is always some small hitch at Troizen; we do not do these things with the smoothness of Athens. The King Horse munched from the tripod, and flicked off flies with his tail.

There were two more tripods; one bowl held water, the other water and wine. In the first my grandfather washed his hands, and a young server dried them. The King Horse lifted his head from the feed, and it seemed they looked at one another. My grandfather set his hand on the white muzzle, and stroked down hard; the head dipped, and rose with a gentle toss. Diokles leaned down to me and said, "Look, he consents."

I looked up at him. This year his beard showed clearly against the light. He said, "It means a good omen. A lucky year." I nodded, thinking the purpose of the rite accomplished; now we would go home. But my grandfather sprinkled meal on the horse's back from a golden dish; then took up a little knife bright with grinding, and cut a lock from his mane. He gave a small piece to Talaos, who was standing near, and some to the first of the barons. Then he turned my way, and beckoned. Diokles' hand on my shoulder pushed me forward. "Go up," he whispered. "Go and take it."

I stepped out, hearing men whisper, and women coo like mating pigeons. I knew already that the son of the Queen's own daughter ranked before the sons of the Palace women; but I had never had it noticed publicly. I thought I was being honored like this because the King Horse was my brother.

Five or six strong white hairs were put in my hand. I had meant to thank my grandfather; but now I felt come out of him the presence of the King, solemn as a sacred oak wood. So, like the others, I touched the lock to my brow in silence. Then I went back, and Diokles said, "Well done."

My grandfather raised his hands and invoked the god. He hailed him as Earth-Shaker, Wave-Gatherer, brother of King Zeus and husband of the Mother; Shepherd of Ships, Horse-Lover. I heard a whinny from beyond the pine woods, where the chariot teams were tethered, ready to race in honor of the god. The King Horse raised his noble head, and softly answered.

The prayer was long, and my mind wandered, till I heard by the note that the end was coming. "Be it so, Lord Poseidon, according to our prayer; and do you accept the offering." He held out his hand, and someone put in it a great cleaver with a bright-ground edge. There were tall men standing with ropes of oxhide in their hands. My grandfather felt the cleaver's edge and, as in his chariot, braced his feet apart.

It was a good clean killing. I myself, with all Athens watching, am content to do no worse. Yet, even now, I still remember. How he reared up like a tower, feeling his death, dragging the men like children; the scarlet cleft in the white throat, the rank hot smell; the ruin of beauty, the fall of strength, the ebb of valor; and the grief, the burning pity as he sank upon his knees and laid his bright head in the dust. That blood seemed to tear the soul out of my breast, as if my own heart had shed it.

As the newborn babe, who has been rocked day and night in his soft cave knowing no other, is thrust forth where the harsh air pierces him and the fierce light stabs his eyes, so it was with me. But between me and my mother, where she stood among the women, was the felled carcass twitching in blood, and my grandfather with the crimson cleaver. I looked up; but Diokles was watching the death-throe, leaning easily on his spear. I met only the empty eye-slits of the leopard-skin, and the arm-snake's jewelled stare.

My grandfather dipped a cup into the offering bowl, and poured the wine upon the ground. I seemed to see blood stream from his hand. The smell of dressed hide from

Diokles' shield, and the man's smell of his body, came to me mixed with the smell of death. My grandfather gave the server the cup, and beckoned. Diokles shifted his spear to his shield arm, and took my hand. "Come," he said. "Father wants you. You have to be dedicated now."

I thought, "So was the King Horse." The bright day rippled before my eyes, which tears of grief and terror blinded. Diokles swung round his shield on its shoulder sling to cover me like a house of hide, and wiped his hard young hand across my eyelids. "Behave," he said. "The people are watching. Come, where's the warrior? It's only blood."

He took the shield away; and I saw the people staring.

At the sight of all their eyes, memories came back to me. "Gods' sons fear nothing," I thought. "Now they will know, one way or the other." And though within me was all dark and crying, yet my foot stepped forward.

Then it was that I heard a sea-sound in my ears; a pulse and a surging, going with me, bearing me on. I heard it then for the first time.

I moved with the wave, as if it broke down a wall before me; and Diokles led me forward. At least, I know that I was led; by him, or one who took his shape as the Immortals may. And I know that having been alone, I was alone no longer.

My grandfather dipped his finger in the blood of the sacrifice, and made the sign of the trident on my brow. Then he and old Kannadis took me under the cool thatch that roofed the holy spring, and dropped in a votive for me, a bronze bull with gilded horns. When we came out, the priests had cut off the god's portion from the carcass, and the smell of burned fat filled the air. But it was not till I got home, and my mother asked, "What is it?" that at last I wept.

Between her breasts, entangled in her shining hair, I wept as if to purge away my soul in water. She put me to bed, and sang to me, and said when I was quiet, "Don't grieve for the King Horse; he has gone to the Earth Mother, who made us all. She has a thousand thousand children, and knows each one of them. He was too good for anyone here

to ride; but she will find him some great hero, a child of the
sun or the north wind, to be his friend and master; they will
gallop all day, and never be tired. Tomorrow you shall take
her a present for him, and I will tell her it comes from you."

Next day we went down together to the Navel Stone. It
had fallen from heaven long ago, before anyone remembers.
The walls of its sunken court were mossy, and the Palace
noises fell quiet around. The sacred House Snake had his
hole between the stones; but he only showed himself to my
mother, when she brought him his milk. She laid my honey-
cake on the altar, and told the Goddess whom it was for. As
we went, I looked back and saw it lying on the cold stone,
and remembered the horse's living breath upon my hand, his
soft lip warm and moving.

I was sitting among the house dogs, at the doorway end
of the Great Hall, when my grandfather passed through, and
spoke to me in greeting.

I got up, and answered; for one did not forget he was the
King. But I stood looking down, and stroking my toe along
a crack in the flagstones. Because of the dogs, I had not
heard him coming, or I would have been gone. "If he could
do this," I had been thinking, "how can one trust the gods?"

He spoke again, but I only said "Yes," and would not look
at him. I could feel him high above me, standing in thought.
Presently he said, "Come with me."

I followed him up the corner stairs to his own room above.
He had been born there, and got my mother and his sons,
and it was the room he died in. Then I had been there
seldom; in his old age he lived all day in it, for it faced
south, and the chimney of the Great Hall went through to
warm it. The royal bed at the far end was seven feet long
by six feet wide, made of polished cypress, inlaid and
carved. The blue wool cover with its border of flying cranes
had taken my grandmother half a year on the great loom.
There was a bronze-bound chest by it, for his clothes; and
for his jewels an ivory coffer on a painted stand. His arms
hung on the wall: shield, bow, longsword and dagger, his
hunting knife, and his tall-plumed helmet of quilted hide,

lined with crimson leather the worse for wear. There was not much else, except the skins on the floor and a chair. He sat, and motioned me to the footstool.

Muffled up the stairway came the noises of the Hall: women scrubbing the long trestles with sand, and scolding men out of their way; a scuffle and a laugh. My grandfather's head cocked, like an old dog's at a footstep. Then he rested his hands on the chair-arms carved with lions, and said, "Well, Theseus? Why are you angry?"

I looked up as far as his hand. His fingers curved into a lion's open mouth; on his forefinger was the royal ring of Troizen, with the Mother being worshipped on a pillar. I pulled at the bearskin on the floor, and was silent.

"When you are a king," he said, "you will do better than we do here. Only the ugly and the base shall die; what is brave and beautiful shall live for ever. That is how you will rule your kingdom?"

To see if he was mocking me, I looked at his face. Then it was as if I had only dreamed the priest with the cleaver. He reached out and drew me in against his knees, and dug his fingers in my hair as he did with his dogs when they came up to be noticed.

"You knew the King Horse; he was your friend. So you know if it was his own choice to be King, or not." I sat silent, remembering the great horse-fight and the war calls. "You know he lived like a king, with first pick of the feed, and any mare he wanted; and no one asked him to work for it."

I opened my mouth, and said, "He had to fight for it."

"Yes, that is true. Later, when he was past his best, a younger stallion would have come, and won the fight, and taken his kingdom. He would have died hard, or been driven from his people and his wives to grow old without honor. You saw that he was proud."

I asked, "Was he so old?"

"No." His big wrinkled hand lay quietly on the lion mask. "No older for a horse than Talaos for a man. He died for another cause. But if I tell you why, then you must listen, even if you do not understand. When you are older, if I am here, I will tell it you again; if not you will have heard it once, and some of it you will remember."

While he spoke, a bee flew in and buzzed among the painted rafters. To this day, that sound will bring it back to me.

"When I was a boy," he said, "I knew an old man, as you know me. But he was older; the father of my grandfather. His strength was gone, and he sat in the sun or by the hearth-side. He told me this tale, which I shall tell you now, and you, perhaps, will tell one day to your son." I remember I looked up then, to see if he was smiling.

"Long ago, so he said, our people lived in the northland, beyond Olympos. He said, and he was angry when I doubted it, that they never saw the sea. Instead of water they had a sea of grass, which stretched as far as the swallow flies, from the rising to the setting sun. They lived by the increase of their herds, and built no cities; when the grass was eaten, they moved where there was more. They did not grieve for the sea, as we should, or for the good things earth brings forth with tilling; they had never known them; and they had few skills, because they were wandering men. But they saw a wide sky, which draws men's mind to the gods; and they gave their firstfruits to Ever-Living Zeus, who sends the rain.

"When they journeyed, the barons in their chariots rode round about, guarding the flocks and the women. They bore the burden of danger, then as now; it is the price men pay for honor. And to this very day, though we live in the Isle of Pelops and build walls, planting olives and barley, still for the theft of cattle there is always blood. But the horse is more. With horses we took these lands from the Shore People who were here before us. The horse will be the victor's sign, as long as our blood remembers.

"The folk came south by little and little, leaving their first lands. Perhaps Zeus sent no rain, or the people grew too many, or they were pressed by enemies. But my great-grand-father said to me that they came by the will of All-Knowing Zeus, because this was the place of their moira."

He paused in thought. I said to him, "What is that?"

"Moira?" he said. "The finished shape of our fate, the line drawn round it. It is the task the gods allot us, and the share of glory they allow; the limits we must not pass; and our appointed end. Moira is all these."

I thought about this, but it was too big for me. I asked, "Who told them where to come?"

"The Lord Poseidon, who rules everything that stretches under the sky, the land and the sea. He told the King Horse; and the King Horse led them."

I sat up; this I could understand.

"When they needed new pastures, they let him loose; and he, taking care of his people as the god advised him, would smell the air seeking food and water. Here in Troizen, when he goes out for the god, they guide him round the fields and over the ford. We do it in memory. But in those days he ran free. The barons followed him, to give battle if his passage was disputed; but only the god told him where to go.

"And so, before he was loosed, he was always dedicated. The god only inspires his own. Can you understand this, Theseus? You know that when Diokles hunts, Argo will drive the game to him; but he would not do it for you, and by himself he would only hunt small game. But because he is Diokles' dog, he knows his mind.

"The King Horse showed the way; the barons cleared it; and the King led the people. When the work of the King Horse was done, he was given to the god, as you saw yesterday. And in those days, said my great-grandfather, as with the King Horse, so with the King."

I looked up in wonder; and yet, not in astonishment. Something within me did not find it strange. He nodded at me, and ran down his fingers through my hair, so that my neck shivered.

"Horses go blindly to the sacrifice; but the gods give knowledge to men. When the King was dedicated, he knew his moira. In three years, or seven, or nine, or whenever the custom was, his term would end and the god would call him. And he went consenting, or else he was no king, and power would not fall on him to lead the people. When they came to choose among the Royal Kin, this was his sign: that he chose short life with glory, and to walk with the god, rather than live long, unknown like the stall-fed ox. And the custom changes, Theseus, but this token never. Remember, even if you do not understand."

I wanted to say I understood him. But I was silent, as in the sacred oak wood.

"Later the custom altered. Perhaps they had a King they could not spare, when war or plague had thinned the Kindred. Or perhaps Apollo showed them a hidden thing. But they ceased to offer the King at a set time. They kept him for the extreme sacrifice, to appease the gods in their great angers, when they had sent no rain, or the cattle died, or in a hard war. And it was no one's place to say to him, 'It is time to make the offering.' He was the nearest to the god, because he consented to his moira; and he himself received the god's commandment."

He paused; and I said, "How?"

"In different ways. By an oracle, or an omen, or some prophecy being fulfilled; or, if the god came close to him, by some sign between them, something seen, or a sound. And so it is still, Theseus. We know our time."

I neither spoke nor wept, but laid my head against his knee. He saw that I understood him.

"Listen, and do not forget, and I will show you a mystery. It is not the sacrifice, whether it comes in youth or age, or the god remits it; it is not the bloodletting that calls down power. It is the consenting, Theseus. The readiness is all. It washes heart and mind from things of no account, and leaves them open to the god. But one washing does not last a lifetime; we must renew it, or the dust returns to cover us. And so with this. Twenty years I have ruled in Troizen, and four times sent the King Horse to Poseidon. When I lay my hand on his head to make him nod, it is not only to bless the people with the omen. I greet him as my brother before the god, and renew my moira."

He ceased. Looking up, I saw him staring out between

the red pillars of the window, at the dark-blue line of the sea. We sat some while, he playing with my hair as a man will scratch his dog to quiet it, lest its importunities disturb his thoughts. But I had no word to say to him. The seed is still, when first it falls into the furrow.

At last he sat up with a start, and looked at me. "Well, well, child, the omens said I should reign long. But sometimes they talk double; and too early's better than too late. All this is heavy for you. But the man in you challenged it, and the man will bear it." He got up rather stiffly from his chair, and stretched, and strode to the doorway; his shout echoed down the twisted stair. Presently Diokles running up from below said, "Here I am, sir."

"Look at this great lad here," my grandfather said, "growing out of his clothes, and nothing to do but sit with the house dogs, scratching. Take him away, and teach him to ride."

2.

NEXT year, I began my service to Poseidon. For three years I went to Sphairia one month out of four, living with Kannadis and his fat old wife in their little house at the edge of the grove. My mother used to complain that I came back spoiled past bearing.

It was true I came home rough and noisy. But I was only breaking out after the quiet. When you serve a holy place, you can never forget, even in sleep, that the god is there. You cannot keep from listening. Even on a bright morning, with birds in song, there are hushing whispers. Except at the festival, no one cares to be too loud in a precinct of Poseidon. It is like whistling at sea. You might start more than you bargained for.

I remember many days like one: the hush of noonday; the shadow of the thatch falling straight and sharp; no sound but a cicada out in the hot grass, the restless pine-tops, and a far-off sea-hum like the echo in a shell. I swept the floor round the sacred spring, and scattered clean sand; then took the offerings laid on the rock beside it, and put them in a dish for the priests and servers to eat. I wheeled out the great bronze tripod, and filled its bowl from the spring, dipping the water out in a jug shaped like a horse's head. When I had washed the sacred vessels, and dried them in clean linen, and set them out for the evening offerings, I poured off the water into an earthen jar that stood under the eaves. It is healing, especially for tainted wounds, and people come a long way to get it.

There was a wooden image of Poseidon on the rock, blue-bearded, holding a fish-spear and a horse's head. But I soon came not to notice it. Like the old Shore Folk who worshipped the Sea Mother under the open sky there, killing their victims on the bare rock, I knew where the deity lived. I used to listen in the deep noon shadow, quiet as the lizards on the pine trunks; sometimes there would be nothing but a wood-dove's coo; but on another day, when the hush was deepest, there would sound far down in the spring a great throat swallowing, or a great mouth smacking its lips together; or sometimes only a long thick breath.

The first time I heard, I dropped the cup back in the bowl, and ran out between the painted columns into the hot sun, and stood panting. Then came old Kannadis, and put his hand on my shoulder. "What is it, child? Did you hear the spring?" I nodded. He ruffled my hair and smiled. "What's this? You don't fear your grandfather, when he stirs in his sleep? Why fear Father Poseidon, who is nearer yet?" Soon I grew to know the sounds, and listened with my courage on tiptoe, in the way of boys; till the days of silence came to seem flat. And when a year had passed, bringing me trouble I could tell no one, I used to lean over the hollow rock and whisper it to the god; if he answered I would be comforted.

That year, another boy came to the sanctuary. I came and went, but he was there to stay; he had been offered as a slave to the god, to serve the precinct all his days. His father,

being wronged by some enemy, had promised him before his
birth in exchange for this man's life. He got home dragging
the body at his chariot tail, on the day Simo was born. I was
there when he was dedicated, with a lock of the dead man's
hair bound round his wrist.

Next day I took him round the sanctuary to show him what
to do. He was so much bigger than I, I wondered they had
not sent him sooner. He did not like learning from a smaller
boy, and made light of all I told him; he was not a Troizenian, but came from up the coast near Epidauros. As I saw
more of him I liked him less. By his own story, there was
nothing he could not do. He was thick and red, and if he
caught a bird would pluck it alive and make it run about
bare. I said he should let them be, or Apollo would be after
him with an arrow, because birds bring his omens. But he
said sneering that I was too squeamish to make a warrior.
I hated even his smell.

One day in the grove, he said, "Who is your father, tow-
head?"

With a bold front and sinking belly, I answered, "Poseidon. That's why I am here." He laughed, and made a rude
sign with his fingers. "Who told you that? Your mother?"

It was like a black wave breaking over me. No one had
ever said it openly. I was a spoiled child still; nothing much
worse had come my way than justice from those who loved
me. He said, "Son of Poseidon, a little runt like you! Don't
you know the gods' sons are a head taller than other men?"

I was shaking all over, being too young to hide my heart.
I had felt safe from this, in the sacred precinct. "So shall I
be tall, as tall as Herakles, when I'm a man. Everyone has to
grow, and I shan't be nine till spring."

He gave me a push that tumbled me over backwards.
After a year in the holy place, I gasped at the impiety. He
thought it was him I was afraid of. "Eight and a half!" he
said, pointing his blunt finger. "Here I am not turned eight,
and big enough to push you down. Run away home, little
bastard! Ask Mother for a better tale."

There was a bursting in my head. What I next remember

is hearing him yell in my ear. My legs were knotted round
him, and I had both fists full of his hair, trying to crack his
head upon the ground. When he put up an arm to beat me
away, I sank my teeth in it and held fast. The priests got me
off him by prizing my jaws with a stick.

When we had been scrubbed and beaten, we were brought
to beg the god's pardon, burning our suppers before him to
purge our impiety. At the moment of the sacrifice, the throat
of the spring gave a great belch and gurgle. Simo jumped
a foot in the air; he had more respect for the god's presence
thereafter.

Kannadis cured his arm, when it festered, with the holy
salt water. My wound was inward, and slow to heal.

I was the youngest of the Palace children; I had never
thought to measure myself with any others. Next time I went
home, I began to look about, and to ask people's ages. I
found seven boys born in my year and season. Only one of
them was smaller than I. There were even girls who were
taller. I began to be silent, and to brood.

All these six boys, as I saw it, were threats to my honor.
If I could not outgrow them, I must prove myself some other
way. So I would challenge them to dive between steep rocks,
to poke wild bees' nests and run, to ride the kicking mule or
steal eggs from eagles. If they said no, I would make them
fight. These contests I won, having more at stake than the
others, though I never said so. Thereafter we could be
friends, for me. But their fathers complained of me, that I
led them into danger; and I was never two days running out
of a scrape.

One day I saw old Kannadis walking home from Troizen,
and overtook him near the ford. He shook his head and said
he heard sad tales of me; but I could see he was pleased I
had run after him. Taking heart from this, I said, "Kannadis,
how tall are the sons of the gods?"

He peered at me sharply with old blue eyes, then patted
my shoulder. "Who can say? That would be making laws
for our betters. The gods themselves can be what size they
choose; Paian Apollo once passed as a shepherd lad. And

King Zeus himself, who got mighty Herakles, another time went courting as a swan. His wife had swan-children, curled up in eggs, as little as that."

"Then," I said, "how do men know if they are god-begotten?"

He brought down his white brows. "No man can know. Still less may he claim it. Certainly the gods would punish his pride. He could only seek for honor as if it might be true, and wait upon the god. Men are not asked to know such things; heaven sends a sign."

"What sign?" I asked. But he shook his head. "The gods will be known, when they are ready."

I thought much about this matter of honor. Talaos' son, climbing out on a limb which bore my weight but not his, got a broken arm, and I a beating. The god sent no sign; so it seemed he was not satisfied.

Behind the stables was the pen of the Palace bull. He was red as a pot, with short straight horns and a look of Simo. We boys liked teasing him through the palings, though the bailiff would clip us if he caught us at it. One day we had been watching him serve a cow and the show was over, when it came into my head to jump down in the bull pen and dodge across.

He was quiet after his pleasure, and I got away easily; but it made a stir among the boys, which was enough to send me back next day. The life I had been living had made me hard and wiry and quick-footed; and when other boys out of emulation joined the game, I was still the master. I chose my band from those who were slight and spry; we would play the bull two or three together, the envy of the rest, while someone watched out for the bailiff.

The bull too was learning. Soon before we were on the fence he would be pawing the ground. My troop grew shy, till at last the only boy who would go in with me was Dexios, the Horse Master's son, who feared nothing four-footed. Even we two liked to have the others drawing off the bull's eye before we jumped. One day, waiting his mo-

ment, young Dexios slipped, and fell in while the beast was
watching.

He was a boy younger than I, who followed my lead and
liked me. I saw what must happen, and all through my fault.
Being at my wits' end what else to do, I leaped down on the
bull's head.

What happened I don't well remember, or how it felt, or
if I expected to die. By luck I grasped him by the horns; and,
being as new to this as I was, he rid himself of me carelessly. I flew up, struck my belly on the top of the fence and
hung, felt the boys grab me, and was down on the other
side. Meanwhile Dexios had climbed out, and the noise had
brought the bailiff.

My grandfather had promised me the thrashing of my
life. But seeing, when he had me stripped, that I was black
and blue as if I had had it already, he felt me over, and
found two broken ribs. My mother cried, and asked what
had possessed me. But she was not the one I could tell that
to.

By the time my bones were mended, it was time for the
shrine again. Simo had now learned some manners; but he
remembered his bitten arm. Now he never used my name,
but always "Son of Poseidon." He said it too smoothly, and
we both knew what he meant.

When it was my turn to cleanse the sanctuary, I used to
kneel afterwards by the spring, and whisper the god's name;
and if any murmur answered, I would say softly, "Father,
send me a sign."

One day of midsummer, when I was ten years old, the
noon stillness seemed heavier than I had ever known it.
The grass of the grove was pale with drought; the mat of
pine needles muffled every sound. No bird was singing; even
the cicadas were dumb; the pine-tops stood unmoving against
the deep blue sky, as stiff as bronze. When I wheeled in the
tripod, its rattling seemed like thunder, and made me uneasy, I could not tell why. I trod soft-footed, and kept the
vessels from clinking. And all the while I was thinking, "I
have felt this before."

I was glad to have done, and did not go to the spring, but straight outside, where I stood with my skin prickling. Kannadis' fat wife greeted me as she shook her blankets, and I was feeling better; when up came Simo and said to me, "Well, son of Poseidon? Have you been talking to Father?"

So he had spied on me. Yet even this did not move me as at another time. What rubbed me raw was that he had not lowered his voice, though all the world seemed to be saying "Hush." It rasped me as if all my hair were being combed backwards; I said, "Be quiet."

He kicked a stone, which set my teeth on edge. "I looked through the shutter," he said, "and saw the old woman naked. There's a wart on her belly."

I could not endure his voice sawing at the stillness. The offended silence seemed to brood around us. "Go away!" I said. "Can't you feel Poseidon is angry?"

He stared at me; then gave a jeering whinny. As it left his mouth, the air above us was loud with whirring wings. All the birds in the grove had left their trees, and hung above uttering their warning calls. At the sound I tingled all over, body, limbs, and head. I did not know what oppressed me so; but Simo's laughter was past bearing. I shouted, "Get out!" and stamped my foot.

My foot struck the earth; and the earth moved.

I felt a rumbling, and a sideways ripple, such as some huge horse's flank might give to shake off flies. There was a great noise of cracking timber, and the roof of the shrine came leaning down toward us. Men shouted, women shrieked, dogs barked and howled; the old cracked voice of Kannadis called on the god; and suddenly there was cold water all about my feet. It was pouring out from the sanctuary, from the rocks of the holy spring.

I stood half dazed. In all the din, I felt my head clear and lighten, like the air after thunder. "It was this," I thought. "I felt it coming." Then I remembered how I had felt strange, and cried, when I was four years old.

Everywhere in the precinct and beyond, people invoked Poseidon Earth-Shaker, and vowed him offerings if he would be still. Then close at hand I heard a voice weeping and bawling. Simo was walking backwards, his clenched fist pressed in homage to his brow, and crying, "I believe! I believe! Don't let him kill me!"

As he blubbered, he backed into a slab of rock, and went down flat, and started to roar, so that the priests came running, thinking he was hurt. He went on babbling and pointing at me, while I stood too shaken to be glad, swallowing tears and wishing for my mother. The water was turning to mud about my toes. I stood in it, hearing the cries of the wheeling birds and Simo's sobbing, till old Kannadis came up and made the sign of homage. Then he stroked the hair from my forehead, and led me off by the hand.

No one was killed in the earthquake; and of the houses cracked or broken, none fell right down. My grandfather sent the Palace workmen with two new columns for the shrine; they mended the conduit of the holy spring, and the water returned to its course again. He came out himself to see the work, and called me to him.

"I hear," he said, "that the god sent you a warning."

I had been long alone with my thought, till I hardly knew the truth any longer; but this came as true to me. He knew such things, because he was priest as well as king. My mind rested.

"Henceforth," he said, "you will know it again. If it comes to you, run out of doors, and call to the people that Poseidon is angry. Then they can save themselves, before the houses fall. Such warnings are a favor of the god. Try to be worthy."

I said I would. I would have promised anything to the kind Horse Father, who had answered my long prayers with a sign.

Next day in the grove Simo sidled up to me, and thrust something warm into my hands. "For you," he said, and ran away. It was a ring-dove. He had kept it to pluck, I suppose, and changed his mind. It trembled between my palms, while I chewed on the thought that Simo had done me sacrifice, as if I were divine.

I looked at its bright jewelled eye, its feet like dusky

coral; the bloom of the back feathers, and the magic changing rainbow around its neck. A saying of my mother's came
into my mind, that we offer to the gods from their own
creation; I remembered the birds and bulls I used to pinch
from wet clay, and looked at the workmanship in my hand.
It was Simo, after all, who taught me how far man is, even
at his height of fortune, below the Immortals.

I wondered if I should sacrifice it to Poseidon. But he does
not much care for birds, and I thought I would give it back
to Apollo. So I held up my hands and opened them, and
let it fly.

3.

AFTER the god's sign, I no longer doubted I should grow tall.
Season after season I waited, trusting. I had seen other boys
shoot up all in a year or two, even without a god to help
them. Seven feet, I thought, had been good enough for
Herakles and would do for me; but I would settle for six, if
Earth-Shaker required.

I turned eleven, and finished my service to Poseidon, and
loosed a half-grown boar, whose tusks were showing, in the
Great Hall when the King of Tiryns was dining there. Being
younger than he had looked to me, he joined whooping in
the chase, and said he had never spent an evening better;
but my grandfather whipped me all the same, saying it
might as easily have been the High King of Mycenae.

I turned twelve, and played in the thicket with a land
baron's daughter, who was thirteen. This came to nothing;
she scolded me off, saying I hurt her. I argued that from all
I heard, it was only to her credit; but she said she was sure
I must be doing it wrong.

None the less, I was coming into manhood. In that way, I
was better grown than boys much older. But I was still the
smallest of my year but one; and when Simo brought a
message from the shrine, I saw he was a whole hand taller.

My uncle Diokles could comb his beard to a point now, and would soon be married. He laughed at my scrapes when I was in disgrace with everyone else, taught me the skills of war and hunting, and tried to make me spend my spirits usefully. But one day when I was thirteen, finding me out of heart beside the wrestling ground, he said to me, "See, now, Theseus, no one can do everything. Some things need a light man, others a heavy one. Why can't you take yourself as you are? You are doing well enough. You're the best jumper about here, long or high; you nearly always win the foot race; as for riding, you can stay on anything; you are better than Dexios, who is better than all the rest. And you have a very straight eye, both for the bow and javelin; I know Maleus throws further, but how often does he hit? You will make a warrior, if you go on as you are; you're not frightened, you are quick, and you've a grip like a grown man's. If you are sensible, and get to know yourself, you'll seldom come away from the games without two or three prizes. That should be enough for anyone. It's time you stopped fretting your heart out, and wasting time, over contests where only weight will do. You will never make a wrestler, Theseus. Face it once for all."

I had never seen him so serious; and I knew he was really fond of me. So I only said, "Yes, Diokles. I suppose you are right." I was too old now to cry. I thought, "He has even forgotten why I should be big. It is not that he wants to hurt me, like Simo; not at all. Simply he never thinks of such a thing. It never enters his head."

Poseidon's sign was four years behind me. In youth, four years is long. And even the people thought less about it, now they saw I had not the stature of god-got men.

I was fourteen; the Corn Moon shone, and it was harvest home. My mother received the Goddess' offerings, or read her the pledges written on leaves of clay. At evening she went down to the Navel Court, and following as far as the cloister walk, I heard her soft voice, telling the House Snake all about the harvest; for, as she said, if we kept anything from him we should have no luck next year. I lingered in

the shadow thinking how she must once have told him who
my father was. Perhaps she was talking of me now. But it is
death for men to spy on women's mysteries. Lest I should
hear a word of what she was saying, I slipped away.

Next day was the Corn Feast. In the morning she offered
to the Mother at the sacred pillar, standing before it straight
as the shaft, and graceful as the rising smoke. No one would
have thought her sacred dress was so heavy, the flounces
clashing with ivory lozenges and disks of gold. "Why does she
not tell me?" I thought. "Does she need to be told I suffer?"
And anger burned me like a red-hot rod, striking on my
heart where it was tender with love.

Later we had the Games. I watched the wrestling, the big
men grasping each other round the middle, straining and
heaving to lift each other off the ground. Nowadays you will
have to go far in the back hills to see Old Hellene style; but
in those days, there was no other in the Isle of Pelops, and
as much skill in it as in a tug of war.

In the boys' events I won the jumping, and the foot race,
and the javelin-throwing, just as Diokles had said. When the
prizes were given on the threshing floor, I got a bag of
arrowheads, a pair of javelins, and a belt sewn with scarlet.
As I came away with them, I heard a voice say in the crowd,
"He is blue-eyed and flaxen like a Hellene; but he is built
like the Shore People, wiry and quick and small." And someone answered softly, "Well, who can say?"

I went outside. The Corn Moon shone great and golden.
I laid my prizes on the ground, and walked down to the sea.

The night was calm. Moonlight lay on the strait, and a
night bird called, soft and bubbling, like water from a narrow
jar. From uphill I heard the singing, and hands clapping to
the dance.

I walked straight into the water as I was, in my belt and
drawers. I wanted to be far from men and their voices. As
I struck out with the current to the open sea, I said within
me, "If I am the god's he will look after me. If not I shall
drown, and I do not care."

Beyond the narrows and the headland, the strait opened

to the sea. Then over on Kalauria I heard music and saw torches weaving; and boylike I wanted to go and see. I turned, and struck for the island shore; but the lights grew smaller whenever I looked. I saw I might truly die; and I wanted life.

The current had borne me easily; but when I fought it, it was cruel and strong. I began to be tired, and cold; my leather breeches dragged at my thighs, my wet belt pinched my breathing. A wave slapped me head-on, and I went under.

I could not right myself; I seemed to sink to the very bottom of the sea. My head and my chest felt bursting. I thought, "The god rejects me. I have lived for a lie and there is nothing left. Oh that I could be dead without dying! It is hard to die, harder than I know." My eyes flashed and saw pictures: my mother in her bath; a hunchback the children laughed at; the shrine in the noon stillness; the youths in their horse-dance stamping for the god; and the sacrifice, my grandfather beckoning with his bloodstained hand. And then, just as when I was seven years old, I heard within me the sea-surge, bearing me up and on. It seemed to say to me, "Be quiet, my son, and let me carry you. Am I not strong enough?"

My fear left me. I ceased to struggle, and my face broke water. I lay on the sea, as easy as the lost child the father finds on the mountain, and brings home in his arms. Once round the point, the current always sets for land again. But I should never have lived to remember it but for Poseidon, Shepherd of Ships.

In the hills' shelter the sea was calm and the air gentle. Climbing to the torches I lost the last of the chill. I felt light and lucky, full of the god. Soon I saw light through apple leaves, and dancers whirling; there were pipes and singing and the thud of feet.

It was a little village feast, on a slope of orchards. The torches were fixed on poles around the floor, for the torch-dance was over. The men were doing the Dance of the Quails, with feathered masks and wings, wheeling and hobbling and dipping and giving quail-calls; the women stood round singing the song, clapping and tapping their feet. When I came out into the torchlight, they broke off singing; and the tallest girl, the village beauty the men were whistling and calling to, cried out, "Here is the Kouros of Poseidon! Look at his hair all wet from the sea!" Then she laughed. But when I looked, I saw she was not mocking me.

After the dancing we ran away, and lay hidden close in the deep wet grass among the apple trees, stifling each other's laughter when one of her suitors came crashing and roaring past. Afterwards she held me away from her; but it was only while she got out a windfall from under her back.

That was my first girl, and I had my first war not long after. The men of Hermione came north over the hills, and lifted thirty head of cattle. When I heard my uncles shouting to each other, and calling for their horses and their arms, I slipped away and helped myself from the armory and the stable. I stole out by the postern, and joined them up on the hill road. Diokles thought it a good joke. It was the last he ever laughed at; one of the raiders speared him. When he was dead, I rode after the man who did it, and dragged him from his horse across the neck of mine, and killed him with my dagger. My grandfather had been angry at my going without leave; but he did not rebuke me after, saying it was only proper I should avenge Diokles, who had always been good to me. I had been so angry I could not even feel I was killing my first man; only that I wanted him dead, like a wolf or a boar. We got back all the cattle before nightfall, except for two which fell down a steep place on the mountain.

A few months after this, the time of King Minos' tribute came round again.

The tax goods were gathering at the harbor: hides and oil, wool and copper and boarhound bitches in whelp. People looked sour; but I had other trouble. I knew this was when the small boys were taken out from the tall ones, and sent to the hills to hide. I made offerings to Poseidon, and Zeus, and the Mother, praying in secret to be spared this shame.

But soon after, my grandfather said to me, "Theseus, when you are up in the mountains, if there are broken necks, or cattle stolen, I am telling you now you will be the first to answer for it. There is your warning."

My heart reproached the thankless gods. "Must I go, sir? Surely it's beneath the house, for me to hide away. They would never take me; they can't think so meanly of us as that." He looked at me testily. "They will think you are just the build of boy they like for the bull-dance; that and nothing more. Don't talk when you know nothing." I thought, "Well, that is blunt enough."

"Who is King Minos," I said, "to treat kings' houses like a victor? Why do we pay him? Why not go to war?"

He tapped his fingers on his belt. "Come back later," he said, "when I have less to do. Meanwhile, we pay Minos tribute because he commands the sea. If he stopped the tin-ships we could make no bronze, and should have to make swords of stone, like the first Earth Men. As for war, he has ships enough to bring five thousand men here in a day. Remember also that he keeps the seaways clear of pirates, who would cost us more than he does."

"A tax is all very well," I said. "But to take people, that is treating Hellenes like slaves." "All the more reason to avoid it. In Corinth and Athens, likely boys were allowed to be seen; now other kingdoms know better. To talk of a war with Crete, as if it were a cattle raid! You try my patience. Behave yourself in the mountains. And next time I send for you, wash your face."

All this was bitter to my new-found manhood. "We ought to hide some girls too," I said. "Can we pick our own?" He gave me a hard look. "It's a young dog that barks over his bone. You have leave to go."

It was my bitter hour, when the big lads swaggered free in Troizen, while the small and slender, bear-led by two unwilling House Barons, were led away. Even though the cripples and the sickly stayed in Troizen too, we all felt disgraced for ever. Five days we were in the mountains, sleeping in a barn, hunting and climbing and fist-fighting and coursing hares on foot, a plague to our guardians, trying to prove to ourselves we were good for something. Someone got an eye pecked by a raven, and one or two of us, as we learned later, got sons or daughters; they are wild but willing, those girls in the back hills. Then someone rode out on muleback to say the Cretans had sailed for Tiryns, and we could come home.

Time passed, and I grew taller, but never overtook the others; and the wrestling court was a place of grief to me, for there were boys a year younger who could lift me off the ground. I no longer hoped to be seven feet tall; I wanted a foot even of six, and I was rising sixteen.

When there was dancing, my troubles always lifted; and I came to music through the dance. I loved the winter evenings in the Hall, when the lyre was passed about, and was glad when I began to be called on for my turn. On one such evening, a guest was there, a baron from Pylos. He sang well, and in compliment gave us the tale of Pelops, the founder hero of our line. It was not the same song as the one favored in Troizen, which was of Pelops' chariot race for the hand of the Earth King's daughter; how the King speared all her suitors as their chariots turned the end stone, till the trick with the waxen linchpin threw him first. This song was about Pelops' youth: how Blue-Haired Poseidon loved him, and would warn him of the coming earthquake when he laid his ear to the ground; he was called Pelops, so said the song, from the earth-smear on his cheek.

I kept my thoughts to myself. This, then, was where my warning came from. Not a pledge straight from the god to me, but an inborn skill, like this man's sweet voice who sang. It came to me in my mother's blood.

Next day, still sick at heart, I went to look for my friends; but all the youths were wrestling. I stood beside the ground, seeing the white dust fly up to the poplar leaves; too proud to take a turn with the boys of my own weight, for those who were worth a match were all younger than I.

I watched them straining and grunting, heaving each other up and tossing each other down; and a thought came to me, how easily a man is thrown if something strikes the side of his foot just when his weight is coming on it. It puts him off balance and down he goes; it had happened to me with a wayside stone. I watched the feet, and then the bodies, and thought about it.

Just then Maleus, a great shambling youth, called out, "Come on, Theseus, give me a match!" Then he bawled with laughter; not that he hated me, it was his way. I said, "Why not?" which made him slap his knees and roar. When we were closing, and he reached out to lift me, I moved and made him lean a little. Then I backheeled him. He went down like a boulder.

For some time, helped by the dust-cloud and by being quick, I threw the youths of Troizen with this one chip alone; till a day when I woke feeling lucky, and went for no reason down to the harbor. There was a small trader in from Egypt, buying hides and horns. Two little brown boys, as lithe as snakes, were scuffling naked on the deck. They were wrestling, not fighting; and though they were only half-taught children, I saw what they were up to. I got sweet figs and honey, and climbed aboard; and came away with half a dozen chips as good as my backheel, all fit to throw a heavier man. It was news to me in those days that the Egyptians know all about this matter. I thought it a portent straight from the god.

Nowadays, it is all Athenian style wherever you go; so once again you must match with your own weight, if you want to go far. But I still umpire at the Games of Poseidon, because it pleases the people. Sometimes I wonder who will umpire at my funeral games. I thought once it would be my son; but he is dead.

Soon, in Troizen, even men were coming to see me wrestle, and I took some on. Though they learned a few of my holds, I kept a few ahead, for one thought leads to another. And people began to say there was surely something between the god and me; for how could I keep it up against men so much bigger, unless Earth-Shaker put out a hand to pull them to the ground?

So, as I neared seventeen, I was in better content with myself, even though I had not grown beyond five feet and a half. It had not stood in my way with girls; and the children I got were fair and Hellene. Only one was small and dark; but so was the girl's brother.

My birth month came, when I should be seventeen. And on the day of my birth, in the moon's second quarter, my mother said to me alone, "Theseus, come with me; I have something to show you."

My heart paused in its beating. A secret so long kept is like a lyre-string stretched near breaking, which a feather will sound, or a breath of air. Silence held me, as it had before the earthquake.

I went with her; and she led me through the postern, up the road to the hills. I walked half a pace behind her, going softly. The path skirted a gorge, where the mountain stream ran deep, green with ferns below and woods above; we crossed it by a great flat boulder, put there by giants before anyone remembers. And all the while I thought my mother looked quiet and sad, and my heart was chilled; this was not the countenance, I thought, of women whom gods have favored.

We turned up from the stream, and came into the holy Grove of Zeus. It had been old already on the hillside in the time of the Shore People who had the land before us. And even they can only say it has been there time out of mind.

It is so quiet there, you can hear an acorn dropping. Now it was spring; the leaves were tender on the great gnarled boughs; and about the trunks which two men's arms together could hardly span, faint starry shade-flowers grew. Last year's oak leaves smelled musty underfoot, soft and black, or brown and rustling. All the way we had not spoken, and now the snapping of a twig seemed loud.

In the midst of the wood was the most sacred spot, where Zeus had hurled his thunderbolt. The ancient oak it had blasted had almost rotted into the ground, it was so long ago. But though the huge limbs were perishing among the brambles, a stump like a tooth still stood, with a secret life

in it; faint buds of green showed on the roots where they
humped like knees above the earth. The spot is so sacred
that no sapling has dared to grow there since Cloud-Gatherer
struck it; through the hole in the green roof one can see
the sea.

My mother walked on in her gold-clasped sandals, lifting
her skirt in front to clear the slope. Fawn-spots of sun fell
on her fine bronze hair, and on the thin shift under her
bodice which showed the pink tips of her moving breasts.
Her forehead was broad, her gray eyes widely set, with
soft brows nearly meeting above her straight proud nose;
the arch over the eye was her greatest beauty, and the
smooth clear curve up from the eyelid. Like any priestess,
she had a mouth for secrets; but it was serious, not sly like
some one sees. Though I could never see it when people said
I was like her, I was always glad if they said I had her eyes.
Mine looked bluer because I was tanned, and my chin was
my own, or else my father's. But to me, this long time now,
she was the priestess no one dares question, more than she
was anything else. She seemed armored in the Goddess; so
that if she were to tell me my father was Thyestes the lame
stillman who brewed her bath scent, or a swineherd from the
back hills, it would not touch nor shame her, but only me.

She led me up to the sacred oak, and stopped; and I saw
at her feet a stone.

I knew it. I had found it as a boy, when Dexios and I first
went tiptoe to the oak wood, daring each other under the
gaze of the trees; the dryads who live there stare harder into
one's back than anywhere else I know. It was an old gray
slab; put there for an altar, I suppose, when Zeus first hurled
his thunder. I had never met anyone there, yet often there
were fresh ashes, as if someone had been offering. Now they
were there again, looking almost warm. Suddenly I wondered
if it was my mother who came. Perhaps she had had some
omen she meant to tell me of. I turned to her, feeling gooseflesh on my arms.

"Theseus," she said. Her voice sounded hoarse, and I
looked at her surprised. She blinked, and I saw her eyes were

wet. "Do not be angry with me; it is no choice of mine. I swore your father the oath gods dare not break; or I would not do it. I promised him by the River, and the Daughters of Night, not to tell you who you are, unless by yourself you could lift this stone."

For a moment my heart leaped up; royal priestesses do not take such vows at the bidding of base-born men. Then I looked again, and saw why she had wept.

She swallowed so hard that I heard it. "The proofs he left for you are buried there. He said I should try you at sixteen, but I saw it was too soon. But now I must." Her tears ran down, and she wiped her face with her hands.

Presently I said, "Very well, Mother. But sit over there, and do not watch me."

She went away, and I stripped off my arm-rings. They were all I had on above the belt; I went bare in nearly all weather, to keep hard. But, I thought, much good that had done me.

I crouched by the stone, and dug with my hands to find the lower edge. Then I loosened it round, scraping like a dog the earth away, hoping to find it thinner at the other end. But it was thicker there. So I went back, and straddled it, and hooked my fingers under it, and pulled. I could not even stir it.

I stopped, panting and beaten, like the half-broke horse who still finds the chariot tied behind him. I had been beaten before I had begun. It was a task for a youth like Maleus, as big as a bear; or for Herakles, Zeus-begot in a threefold night. It was a task for a god's son; and now I saw it all. "It must be with the gods as with men; a son may be lawful, but take all after the mother's side. My veins have only one part ichor to nine parts blood; this is the touchstone of the god, and the god rejects me." I looked back on all I had endured and dared; it had gone for nothing from the beginning, and my mother had wept for shame.

It put me in a rage. I seized the stone and worried at it, more like a beast than a man, feeling my hands bleed and my sinews cracking. I had forgotten even my mother, till

I heard the sound of her skirt and her running feet, and her voice crying, "Stop!"

I turned to her with my face dripping sweat. I was so beside myself that I shouted at her, as if she had been a peasant, "I told you to stay away!"

"Are you mad, Theseus?" she said. "You will kill yourself."

"Why not?" I said.

She cried, "I knew how it would be!" and pressed her hand to her brow. I did not speak; I could almost have hated her. She said, "He should have trusted me. Yes, even though I was young." Then she saw me staring and waiting, and closed her mouth with two fingers. I turned to walk off, and cried out with pain; I had torn a back muscle, and it took me by surprise. She came over and felt it gently; but I looked away.

"Theseus, my son," she said. Her gentleness almost undid me; I had to shut my teeth together. "Nothing forbids me to tell you this: it is not I who find you wanting. And I think I am fit to judge." She was silent, looking out through the gap in the oak leaves at the blue sea. Then she said, "The Shore People were ignorant; they thought Ever-Living Zeus dies every year. So they could not worship the Mother rightly, as we Hellenes know. But at least they understood that some things are better left to women." She paused a moment; but she saw I was only waiting for her to go away. So she went; and I threw myself upon the ground.

The black oak soil, rich with the scents of spring, drank down my tears into the fallen leaves of ages. The Grove of Zeus is not a place where one can defy the gods. I had been angry with Poseidon, who had broken my pride like some column tossed down for a whim. But presently I saw he had done me no harm, but many favors. It would be hubris to affront him; and not even worthy of a gentleman, who ought never to be outdone, either in cruelty by an enemy or in kindness by a friend. So I limped home, and got into the hot bath my mother had ready. She rubbed me down after with oil of herbs; but we did not speak.

I could not wrestle for a fortnight, and told the other

youths I had fallen on the mountain. For the rest, life went on as before; except that the light had been put out. Those to whom this has happened will understand me; not many, I daresay, for such men die easily.

For a man in darkness, there is only one god to pray to.

I had never before singled out Apollo for worship. But of course I had always prayed to him before stringing a lyre or a bow; and when I went shooting, I was never mean with his share. He had given me good bags time and again. Though he is very deep, and knows all mysteries, even those of the women, he is a Hellene and a gentleman. Keeping that in mind, it is easier than it seems not to offend him. He does not like tears intruded on his presence, any more than the sun likes rain. Yet he understands grief: bring it to him in a song, and he will take it away.

In the small laurel grove near the Palace, where he had an altar, I gave him offerings, and played to him every day. At night in Hall, I used to sing of war; but alone in the grove, with only the god to listen, I sang of sorrow: young maidens sacrificed on their wedding eve, ladies of burned cities weeping their fallen lords, or the old laments which have come down from the Shore People, of young heroes who love a goddess for a year, and foreknow their deaths.

But one could not always be singing. Then melancholy would fall black upon me, like a winter cloud heavy with snow. Then I could bear no people. Those days I took myself into the hills, alone with my bow and my dog.

One day in summer I had wandered far, loosing at small game and taking up my arrows; but the wind had tricked me, and I had got nothing but one hare. I was still on the heights in the last light, and looking down saw the shadows of the hills thrown right across to the island. From the foot slopes hidden by trees and dusk, the smoke of Troizen rose faint and blue. They would be trimming the lamps there. But on the tops, birds still gave softly their evening calls, and a deep light carved the edges of the grass blades.

I came out upon the bare round summit ridge, where the sun strikes first at morning, and Apollo has his altar. On

two sides you can see the sea, and to the west the mountains
about Mycenae. There is a house for the priests, built of
stone because up there the winds are strong; and a little
stone sanctuary for the holy things. Underfoot are springy
heath and thyme; and against the sky is the altar.

My black mood was still on me. I had resolved not to go
and eat in Hall; I should only affront someone and make
enemies. There was a girl by the harbor who would put up
with me, because it was her trade.

A dim curl of old smoke rose from the altar, and I paused
to salute the god. The hare I had shot was in my hand. I
thought, "It is not worth cutting. One can't be paltry with
Apollo. Let him have it all; he has given me something for
nothing, often enough."

The altar stood black against a clear sunset sky, yellow
as primroses. It smoldered still from the evening sacrifice,
and the smell of burnt meat quenched with wine hung on
the air. The priests' house was silent, lampless and without
smoke. They were fetching wood, perhaps, or water. There
was no human creature to be seen in all the world; only
the thin pure light, and great blue spaces stretching away,
mountains and seas and islands. Even the dog was daunted
by the solitude; the hair darkened on its back, and I heard
it whimper. The evening breeze touched my bowstring, and
a humming came from it, high and strange. And suddenly
the place overwhelmed my soul, as an ant drowns in a river.
I would have given anything for the sight of an old woman
gathering sticks, or any living thing. But nothing stirred in
all that vastness; only the bow still sang, small like a gnat.
My nape shuddered, and my breath came thick. Almost I
fled headlong into the hillside forest, like a hunted stag,
crashing down through the woods till the thicket held me.
I stood at stretch, my hair stirring like the dog's hackles;
and a clear voice said in my ear, "Do not be late tonight,
or you will miss the harper."

I knew the voice. It was my mother's. The words too I
knew, for she had spoken them that morning, when I set
out. I had answered heedlessly, my mind on my troubles,

and had at once forgotten. Now, like an echo, the sound returned.

I went up to the sanctuary, and laid the hare on the offering table for the priests to find. Then I walked home through the dusky woodland. The black mood that drove me out had lifted; I felt hungry for supper, for wine and company.

Though I made good haste, I was still rather late; my grandfather raised his brows at me, and I saw the harper already at his meat. I went down to the foot of the table, where he sat among the House Barons, and they made room for me beside him.

He was a middle-sized man, dark and spare, with eyes deepset and a thinking mouth. His life had made him at home at kings' tables; he set himself neither too high nor too low, and was easy to talk to. He told me he came from Thrace, where he served a shrine of Apollo. The god had forbidden him to eat meat or drink strong wine; he took cheese and greenstuff, and even that sparingly, because he was going to sing. His robe glittered with gold, and looked like some rich king's gift; but it lay folded on the bench beside him, while he ate in clean white linen. A quiet man, who talked of his art like a craftsman, and had a strain of the Shore People in his blood, as many bards have.

While we ate, we talked about making lyres: how to choose one's tortoise, stretch the sounding-skin, and set in the horns. The lyre I made afterwards was so good that I use it still. Then the tables were cleared; the servants wiped our hands with towels wrung out of hot mint-water; my mother entered, and took her chair by the column. From her greeting to the harper, it seemed he had already given her a song upstairs.

The servants went down the Hall to eat and listen; my grandfather had the bard's harp brought him, and invited him to begin.

He put on his singing-robe, which was blue, and spangled with small gold suns, so that by torchlight he seemed all sprinkled with fire. Then he withdrew into himself, and I stopped the young men from speaking to him again. I guessed he was a master, from his not sitting to eat in his robe. Sure enough, from the first chord onward, nothing else stirred but a dog scratching for fleas.

The song he gave us was the Lay of Mycenae; how Agamemnon the first High King took the land from the Shore Folk, and married their Queen. But while he was at war she brought back the old religion, and chose another king; and when her lord came home she sacrificed him, though he had not consented. Their son, who had been hidden by Hellenes, came back when he was a man, to restore the Sky Gods' worship and avenge the dead. But in his blood was the old religion, to which nothing is holier than a mother. So, when he had done justice, horror sent him mad, and Night's Daughters chased him half over the world. At last, all but dead, he fell on the threshold of Apollo, Slayer of Darkness. And the god strode forward, and lifted up his hand. They bayed awhile, like hounds robbed of their game; then earth drank them back again, and the young King was free. It is a terrible tale, and one could not bear it, but for the end.

When he had done, the cups beating the board could have been heard down in the village. Presently my mother signed that she wished to speak.

"Dear Father, this evening will be boasted of to those who were not there. Now, while the bard is taking a drink to cool his throat, won't you ask him to sit with us, and tell us about his travels? I have heard he knows the world to its furthest ends."

Of course my grandfather invited him, and his chair was moved. I went over too, and they put a stool for me by my mother's knees. After the drink and the compliments, she asked him what was his longest journey.

"Without doubt, Lady," he said, "the voyage I made two years back, to the land of the Hyperboreans. It lies north and west of the Pillars of Herakles, in that green shoreless sea which drowned Atlantis. But Apollo is the guardian god of the Hyperboreans. That year they built the second circle round his great sanctuary. I sang the work-song, when they raised the standing stones."

"What kind of land is it," I asked him, "at the back of the north wind?"

"A land dark with forests," he said, "and green with rain. They build on the bare hilltops and high moors, for safety against beasts and enemies. But it is a great land for bards, and for Apollo's priests to learn his mysteries. I was glad to go, being a priest myself. Thrace is my native land, but the god keeps me roaming. It was his oracle at Delos sent me on this journey. I was there to sing for him, when the envoys came with their offerings south down the Amber Road. The High King of the Hyperboreans sent to say he had this great work in hand, and asked for a priest from Delos, that being the center of Paian's worship, as well as of the Cyclades and of all the world. It was put to the oracle in the hill cave, who answered that they should send the Thracian singer. That was how I came to go."

He told us of the voyage, which had been cold, stormy, and perilous. A gale had driven them north of the island, where, he said, they had passed between two floating rocks as white as crystal, which almost closed on the ship; and on one sat a black monster with seven snaky necks, and barking dog-heads.

I glanced at my grandfather; he winked at me, when the bard was not looking. "After all," said his eye, "the fellow is not on oath."

My mother said, "And how had they built Apollo's sanctuary?"

"After the fashion of the place: a circle of standing stones, with lintels lying on them. The inner circle had been there time out of mind. It is an emblem of Apollo's mystery. While I was there, the priests admitted me to the Lesser Mysteries, and I learned such things as a man is better for all his life."

"Since those things are secret," my mother said, "tell us about the building."

"It was like Titans' work. Great blocks of rough-hewn stone, each as big as a poor man's house. Yet they had brought them many leagues, from a sacred mountain, rolling them round hills and floating them over rivers. Some had been years upon the way. But now when it came to lifting them, the High King had sent to Crete for masons. If the strongest men on earth had all been there together, without engines they could not have been stirred."

Then he told how this king, and six others who used the sanctuary, had brought all their people to the work; so many it needed, though the Cretans had halved it with their hoists and levers. And even that multitude looked poor and frail about the huge stones, like ants tugging at pebbles.

"Then I saw why Apollo had sent a bard. Cretans do not know everything, though they think so. They know how to raise stones, but not men's hearts. The people were afraid. So I understood why I was there, and called upon the god; and he put the power on me, to feel the work and make it music. I sang his praises, and gave the time. After a while, the seven kings with their sons and barons came forward and pulled for Apollo's honor, standing among the people. Then the stones rose up slowly, and slid into the beds the Cretans had made for them. And they stood fast."

Now he was rested, I asked if he would give us a verse or two of his work-song. He smiled, and said it would be like a dance without dancers; but when he sang it, I saw old barons whose hands had never known the feel of a common task sway in their seats as if they were pulling a galley. He was famous for these songs; all over the Achaian lands, kings planning some great work in stone sent for him to time the haulers, and put luck into the walls. Since he died there is no one to touch him at it; simple folk say, believing it, that the stones rose up for him of themselves.

It was now time to give him his presents. My grandfather gave him a good brooch; but my mother brought out a heavy girdle worked with gold, which would not have been mean to give a king. Since he had taught me so much, I felt I too should give him something uncommon; so I parted with my black ring, one of my best things. It was made of a precious metal from a distant land, very heavy, and so hard that you could turn even a bronze sword-edge on it. I was glad to find him pleased with its rarity; he already had gold enough.

My mother first, and then my grandfather, gathered their people and went up to bed. The slaves took down the trestles, and brought in the beds for the unmarried men. I saw the bard made comfortable, and asked if he fancied any of the Palace women; but he said he would sleep. Then I went out in the courtyard. The night was clear. The toothed roof-edge, the watchman with his spear and horn, stood black against the stars. Behind me in Hall, the House Barons were bedded with their girls, those who had captured or bought their own; and young men in want of company were seeking it in the usual way. A girl passed whom I knew; she belonged to my mother, and had sat that evening near her chair. I ran out and caught her round the middle. She only fought with the soft of her hands; we were not quite strangers to one another. We struggled and laughed in whispers, and she said, Well, what must be must, but I should be the ruin of her; and we went into Hall as they snuffed the last of the torches.

Later I asked her softly, so that no one else could hear, what my mother had said to the bard apart, when she rewarded him. But she was sleepy, and cross at being waked again, and said she could not remember.

4.

IN THE dark before daybreak, the girl woke me going away. I had been dreaming; and, being wakened, remembered my dream. I had seen the Hyperborean sanctuary, great hoists and engines standing against a gray sky, great stones rising, and kings leaning on the levers. And a thought came to me, sent straight from the god.

I got up, and went out to the yard of the Palace woodman. Dawn scarcely glimmered; not even the slaves were astir, it was only in the fields that men were waking. It was almost too dark to find what I needed; but I should have to take it with me, for no man puts a tool to the oaks of Zeus. I found a short thick log and two longer ones, whose ends I trimmed to wedges. I bound them up, and getting them unhandily on my shoulders—for I was not used to carrying burdens—set out for the oak wood.

Sunrise glowed red as I climbed along the gorge; when I reached the grove, I saw the altar-slab all scattered with brightness, like the harper's robe. I put down my load, and prayed to Apollo.

"Paian Apollo," I said to him, "Apollo Longsight! If I am offending any god by this, send me an omen."

I looked up. Blue had come into the sky; and wheeling high above I saw an eagle. He tilted his wing and swept away to the left, and the boughs hid him. "Well," I thought, "no god could say better than that," and then, "I should have come before to him." For I had felt too much and reasoned too little, hearing what I was ready to hear, not what had been said. There had been nothing at all about raising the stone with my bare hands; only that I must do it alone.

I worked the lever well under, and stretched my back; the end of the stone rose up, and I kicked the fulcrum under. Then, when I was going to bear down, I remembered there was something to get out from below; when I let go of the lever, the stone would fall again. I sat down to think, on the root of the oak tree; and, seeing it stand above the ground, I saw my way. It was lucky I had brought a longer lever. It would just reach to wedge under the oak root.

Bearing it down so far would have been easy for a heavy man, but was a hard fight for me. But this time I meant to do it if it killed me, because I knew it could be done. Twice I got it nearly there, and twice the weight bore it up again; but when I flung myself on it the third time, I heard in my ears the sea-sound of Poseidon. Then I knew this time I would do it; and so I did.

I stood away, getting my breath. The stone was tilted on its thick end, the thin end propped by the lever; its bed gaped like a mouth of darkness. And for a moment I wanted no more of it. I was like a grave-robber, when he pauses for fear of the angry dead. Perhaps I had hoped that what was there would come to meet me; a foal with wings, or a spring of salt water. But nothing came. So I lay down, and slid my hand under, and felt about.

I touched earth, and stones, and a slimy worm that made me start. Then I came upon moldy cloth, and a hard shape within. I pulled back my hand; it had a feel of bones. None of this was like my picture. The slither of the worm had sickened me. I talked sense to myself, and felt again. It was too straight for a bone. I grasped it, and pulled it out. The sunshine showed a long bundle, a few gold threads shining among the mold. Grubs had made houses there, and a yellow centipede wriggled out. I thought, "A mortal token. Surely I always knew it. Must I know more?" The bundle distasted me; I wished my work undone, and the hidden fate left sleeping in the earth. Then I shook myself like a dog, and snatched at the cloth and jerked it. Gold tumbled and flashed in the light. Some knowledge came to me, that I must not let the thing fall to the ground, that it would be a bad omen. I am a man who can move quickly on a thought, and I caught it in mid-air. Then I knew why it must not fall. It was a sword.

The cloth had kept clean the hilt from earth. I saw it was richer than my grandfather's. The grip was a cunning knot of twisted serpents; their outthrust heads made the guard, and their tails overlapped the blade, which, though green with time, was perfect still, the work of a master sword-smith. I thought, "A Hellene longsword. He was a gentleman, at least."

So my worst fears were done with. But so were my best hopes. I suppose all this while, in some deep cave of my heart, I had waited for Poseidon to relent and own me. And then I thought, "That old man in the Palace has known since I was in the womb. If he had let me alone, instead of cramming me with children's tales, today would have come well to me. It is he who has put this taste of ashes into my mouth."

I looked at the cloth again. There was something more in it. I found a pair of sandals, spoiled with mildew. The studs were set with amethyst, and the buckles were little serpents of wrought gold. I took off one of my own, and measured the soles together. There was very little in it. "So!" I thought. "All Troizen to a moldy fig, I got this the way he hid it." At that I laughed. But it was angry laughter.

I drew out my lever, and let the stone fall back. Before I went, I remembered Apollo, and vowed him a buck for answering my prayer. He is a gentleman, and one cannot be churlish with him, angry or not.

Down in the Palace, they were still at the tasks of early morning. I was hungry, and ate a whole bannock with half a honeycomb. Then with the sword at my belt I went to my mother's room, and scratched the door.

She was just dressed, and her maid was doing her hair. She looked first at my face and then at my belt, and sent the maid away. Beside her chair was a little table with the combs and mirror. She smiled and said, "Well, Theseus. Did the god send you a dream?"

I looked at her startled. But one does not ask a priestess how she knows things. "Yes, Mother," I said. "I have the sandals too. Who was he?"

She raised her brows, which were like a kestrel's feathers, fine and clear, but downy at the inner ends. "Was? What makes you think he is dead?"

It gave me pause; I had hoped so, rather than thought. My anger twisted, like a caught beast in a cage. "Well," I said, "I have his gift, then. The first in seventeen years; but he made me work for it."

"There was a reason," she said. She picked up the comb, and pulled her hair forward. "He said to me, 'If he has not brawn, he will need wit. If he has neither, he may still be a good son to you in Troizen. So keep him there. Why send him to die in Athens?'"

"In Athens?" I said staring. It was only a name to me.

She said a little impatiently, as if I ought to know, "His grandfather had too many sons, and he had none. He has never held his throne a year in quiet, nor his father before him." She looked at my face, and then down at the hair she was combing. "Come, Theseus. Do you think chiefs or barons carry swords like that?"

There was a roughness in her voice, like a young girl's, as if she were shy, and trying to hide it. Then I thought, "Why not? She is three and thirty, and it is near eighteen years since a man was with her." And I was angrier for her than I had been for myself before. "What is his name?" I said. "I must have heard it, but I don't remember."

"Aigeus," she said, as if she were listening to herself. "Aigeus, son of Pandion, son of Kekrops. They are of the seed of Hephaistos, Lord of the Earth Fire, who married the Mother."

I said, "Since when was Hephaistos' seed better than the seed of Zeus?" I was thinking of all the toil I had put myself to for this man's pleasure, thinking it was for a god. "It should have been enough for him, and more, that I was your son. Why did he leave you here?"

"There was a reason," she said again. "We must find a ship, to send you to Athens."

I said, "To Athens? Oh, no, Mother, that's too far to go. Eighteen years since his night's pastime, and he never looked back to see what came of it."

"That is enough!" she cried, princess and priestess all through; yet there was that shy roughness still. I was ashamed of myself; coming up to her chair, I kissed her head. "Forgive me, Mother. Don't be angry; I know how it is. I've laid a girl or two myself who never meant to do it; and if anyone thought the worse of them, it wasn't I. But if King Aigeus wants a spearman more for his house, let him get one at home. Though he didn't stand by you, he did the next best thing; he gave you a son who will."

She drew a sharp breath; then she let it out on half a laugh. "Poor boy, it's not your fault you know nothing. Talk to your grandfather. It is better from him than me."

I picked up a lock of her fresh-combed hair, and turned the end round my finger. I wanted to say I could have forgiven a man she had taken for her pleasure, but not one who had taken her for his, and gone away. But I only said, "Yes, I will see him. It is late enough."

I stayed, however, to change my clothes. I was angry enough to prize my dignity. My best suit was of dark red buckskin, the jerkin trimmed with gold studs and the drawers with kidskin tassels, to match the boots. I was buckling the sword on, when I remembered no one brings arms into the presence of the King.

At the top of the narrow stairs his voice bade me enter. He had had a chill lately, and still kept his room. There was a shawl round his shoulders, and on the stand by his chair a posset cup with the dregs still in it. His face looked sallow, and one began to see age there. But I would not be cheated of my anger, and stood before him silent. He met my eyes with his old pale ones; I could see he knew. Then he nodded to me briskly, and pointed to the footstool. "You can sit down, my boy."

From habit I pulled it out and sat. He had been a long time at his trade, and his fingers had command in them as a harper's have music. It was only when I found myself back in my childhood seat, my feet on the old worn bearskin, my arms round my knees, that I saw how he had made a fool of me. Near my face was the posset cup, with its smell of barley and honey, eggs and wine; a smell of old age, and of childhood. I felt my man's anger dashed down into a boy's. From above me, now, his watery eyes blinked down, with the touch of malice in them that old men feel to young men when their own strength is done.

"Well, Theseus. Has your mother told you who you are?" Crouched at his feet like a fettered captive, my heart full of bitterness, I answered "Yes."

"And you have things to ask me?" I was silent. "Or ask your father, if you prefer." I did not trust myself to speak; he was the King. "He will acknowledge you as his heir now, if you show him the sword."

I was startled into speech. "Why should he, sir? He has sons of his own house, I suppose."

"None in marriage. As for the rest, bear in mind that though he is an Erechthid, which is well enough, we are the house of Pelops, and Olympian Zeus begot us."

It was in my mouth to say, "As Poseidon did me, sir?" I did not say it; not, if you want the truth, because he was my grandfather, but because I did not dare.

He looked at my face; then drew the shawl about him and said testily, "Do you never shut a door behind you? This room is like a barn." I got up and saw to it. "Before you speak of your father with disrespect, let me tell you that but for him you might be a fisherman's or a peasant's son; or a slave's, for that matter."

I was glad to be standing. Presently I said, "Her father can tell me that, and go safe away."

"Your mouth is robbing your ears," he said. "Be quiet, boy, and attend to what I am saying." He looked at me, and waited. I held out for a little; then I came back, and sat at his feet.

"In the year before your birth, Theseus, when your mother was fifteen, we had a summer without rain. The grain was small in the ear, and the grapes were like hedgerow berries; the dust lay deep, so that men's feet sank in it, and nothing prospered but the flies. And with the drought came a sickness, which, sparing the old, took children and maidens and young men. First a hand would fail them, or they would limp; then later they fell down, and the strength went out of their very ribs, so that they could not draw in the breath of life. Those who lived are cripples to this day, like Thyestes the stillman, with his short leg. But mostly they died.

"I inquired what deity we had offended, going first to Apollo, Lord of the Bow. He said through the entrails of the victim that he had not shot at us; but he said no more. Zeus too was silent, and Poseidon sent no omens. It was about the time of year when the people drive out the scape-goat. They chose a squinting man they said had the evil eye, and beat him with such rage that by the time they came to burn him, there was no life left in him. But still no rain fell, and the children died.

"I lost three sons here in the Palace: my wife's two boys, and one who I must own was even dearer. He lay dying like one already dead, only for his living eyes that begged me to give him breath. When he was in his grave, I said to myself, 'Surely the time of my moira• is coming. Soon the god will send me the sign.' I put my affairs in order, and at supper would look at my sons about the table, weighing them to choose my heir. Yet no sign came to me.

"On the next day after, your father came to Troizen, journeying from Delphi to take ship for Athens. He was taking the two sea trips which avoid the Isthmus Road. I was in no mood for company; but the guest of the land is sacred, so I made what show I could. Soon I was glad of it. He was younger than I, but adversity had seasoned him; he had understanding of men. Over supper we began to share our troubles; what I had just lost, he had never known. His first wife had been barren; the second died in childbed with a stillborn girl. He had gone to the oracle; but its answer was dark and riddling, and even the priestess could not interpret it. Now he was going back to a harassed kingdom, with no heir to stand beside him. So there we were, two men in sorrow who understood each other. I sent away the harper, and had a chair brought up here for him; by this hearthstone, where you and I are now, we sat quietly and talked of grief.

"When we were alone, he told me how his brothers, in their greed to get the kingdom, had sunk to scandalling their own mother, a most honorable lady, and proclaiming him a bastard. Here, it seemed to me, were troubles equal to mine. Then, as we talked, there was a great commotion in the Hall below, wailing and outcry. I went out to see.

"It was the Priestess of the Goddess, my father's sister. Round her were the women, crying, beating their breasts, and making their cheeks bleed with their nails. I stood on the steps, and asked what it was. She answered, 'Grief upon grief, King Pittheus, you have laid on the people, setting

gifts before the Sky Gods who were full-fed already, and
starving the altar nearest your hearth. Now the second night
I have brought meat and milk to the Navel Stone, and the
second time the House Snake has refused it. Will you wait
till every womb in Troizen has lost the fruit of its labor?
Sacrifice, sacrifice. It is the Mother who is angry.'

"At once I had a holocaust of swine brought in, reproach-
ing myself for having left all this to the women. I should
have guessed from Apollo's silence that our troubles were
not from the sky. Next morning we killed the pigs about
the Navel Stone. The house echoed with their squealing,
and the smell of entrails hung in the air all day. When the
blood had sunk into the earth, we saw clouds coming from
the westward. They hung gray above us, but the rain in
them did not fall.

"The Priestess came, and led me to the Navel Court, and
showed me the House Snake's wriggling track, by which she
read the omens. 'He has told me now,' she said, 'what has
angered the Mother. It is twenty years, not less, since a girl
of this house hung up her girdle for the Goddess. Aithra,
your daughter, has been two years a woman; but has she
dedicated her maidenhead? Send her to the Myrtle House,
and let her not refuse the first comer, whoever he may be,
sailor or slave, or wet-handed from his own father's blood.
Or Mother Dia will not relent till this is a childless land.' "

My grandfather looked down at me. "Well, young thick-
head? Do you begin to understand?" I nodded, too full to
speak.

"I went off thankful, like any man in such a case, that it
was no worse. Yet I was sorry for the child. Not that she
would lose any honor with the people; the peasants who
have mixed their blood with the Shore People's have sucked
in such customs with their mothers' milk. Well, I had never
forbidden it; but nor had I enforced it; and certainly your
mother had not been brought up to expect such a thing. It
made me angry to see the Priestess glad of it. She had been
widowed young, and no one else had offered for her; she
did not like well-favored girls. The child was shy and proud;

I feared her falling to some low fellow, who from brutishness, or malice to those above him, would take her as roughly as a whore. But most of all I misliked the base blood it might bring into our house. If a child was born, it could not be let live. But that I would keep from her now; the day's concern was enough.

"I sought her in the women's rooms. She listened silently, and did not complain; it was a little thing, she said, to do for the children; but when I took her hands, I felt them cold. I went back to my guest too long neglected. He said, 'My friend, here is some new trouble.'

" 'Less than the last,' I said, and told him. I did not make much of it, not wishing to seem soft; but, as I say, your father understood men. He said, 'I have seen the maiden. She should bear kings. And she is modest. This is hard for you and her.' That table there was standing between us. Suddenly he struck it with his fist. 'Surely, Pittheus, some god had my good in mind when he led me here. Tell me, what time of day do the girls go to the grove?' I said, 'About sundown, or a little before.' 'By custom only? Or is there any sacred law?' 'None that I know of,' I answered, beginning to see his drift. 'Tell the Priestess, then, that the maid will go tomorrow; and if she is there before daybreak, who will know but you and I? So we shall all three gain: I an heir, if heaven relents to me; you a grandson of decent blood both sides; and your daughter—well, two brides have come to me virgins, and I know a little of women. What do you say, my friend?' "

" 'In the gods' name,' I said. 'They have remembered my house today.' "

" 'Then,' he said, 'nothing remains but to tell the maiden; and if it is a man she has seen already and knows no harm of, she will be less afraid.'

"I nodded; but a thought stayed me. 'No,' I said. 'She is of the Kindred; she must go consenting to the sacrifice, or it will lose its virtue. Let it rest between you and me.'

"When the first quarter of the night was gone, I went to wake your mother. But she was watching in her bed, with her lamp beside her. 'My child,' I said, 'I have had a dream, sent I don't doubt by some god or other, that you went to the grove before cocklight, to do your duty to the Goddess with the first of the day. So get up and make ready.' She looked at me in the lamplight with wide still eyes and answered, 'Why, then, Father, it will be sooner done.' Then she said, 'It is a good omen for the children.'

"Presently she came down wrapped in a foxskin cloak, for the night was chilly. Her old nurse, whom I had told nothing to, walked down with us as far as the shore, holding her hand, and chirping out like a cricket old wives' tales of girls in this case whom gods had visited. We put your mother in the boat, and I myself rowed her over.

"I beached where the glade runs down grassy to the shore. Great clouds were banking in the sky; the moon shone blinking on the shining myrtle leaves, and the house of cedarwood on the rocks by the water. As we reached it the moon went in. She said, 'A storm is coming. But no matter; I have my lamp with me, and the tinder.' She had brought them all the way, hidden in her cloak. 'That must not be,' I said, taking them from her. 'I remember my dream forbade it.' It went to my heart; but I feared some night-walking thief would see the light. I kissed her and said, 'To such things as this people of our kin are born; it is our moira. But if we are faithful, the gods are not far away.' So I left her, and she neither wept nor clung to keep me. And as she went from me, thus consenting, into the dark house, Zeus thundered in heaven, and the first of the rain began to fall.

"The storm came on quickly. I had not handled an oar since boyhood, and had ado to make the landing place. When I got there, wet through, I looked about for your father, to give the boat to him. Then I heard from the boathouse an old woman's cackling laughter, and saw by the lightning the nurse sheltering from the rain. 'Don't seek for the bridegroom, King Pittheus; he grew impatient. Tehee, young blood. I have got his clothes here, keeping dry; he won't need *them* for this night's work.' 'What do you mean, you old fool?' I said; the crossing had not sweetened me. 'Where is he?' 'Why, almost there by now, the Good Goddess give him joy of it. He said sea water was warmer than rain, and the maiden would need company, alone on such a night. A lovely man he is too; strips like a god; haven't I waited on his bath since first he came here? Ah, folk don't lie when they call you Pittheus the Wise.'

"Well, Theseus, that is how your father came to your mother. As she told me later, she stood at first in the doorway of the Myrtle House, for fear of the dark within. When the levin-light lit heaven, she saw Troizen over the water, and the boat already far away; when it ceased her eyes were dulled with it and she saw nothing. Presently came a great clap close at hand, the sound and the flash together; and there before her, on the rocky slab outside the porch, all gleaming and glittering in a clear blue light, stood a kingly naked man, with dripping hair and beard and a ribbon of seaweed on his shoulder. What with her awe of the place, and her being overwrought, and the old woman's tales upon the way, she did not doubt the Lord Poseidon himself had come to claim her. The next flash showed her to your father sunk on her knees, her arms crossed on her bosom, waiting the pleasure of the god. So he lifted her up, and kissed her, and told her who he was. Presently in the house she covered him with her foxskin cloak; and that was your beginning."

He ceased. I said at last, "She has the cloak still. It is all worn and the fur is falling. Once I asked her why she kept it." Then I said, "How was this hidden from me?"

"I bound the nurse with an oath that scared even her to silence. After the storm, your father went back the way he came; and I brought the Priestess to witness the proofs of what had been accomplished. But neither she nor anyone knew who was the man. Your father asked that of me; he said your life would be in danger even in Troizen, if the claimants in Attica knew what seed you came of. Your mother's fancy prompted me. I gave it out for the truth. When my wish was made known, folk who had other notions kept it to themselves."

He paused; a fly lighted on the gold rim of the posset

cup, crawled down to sip the dregs, and drowned. He muttered something about bone-idle servants, and pushed the cup away. Then he sank into thought, gazing through the window at the summer sea. Presently he said, "But I have thought to myself since then, What put it into your father's head, a sensible man past thirty, to swim the strait like a wild boy? Why was he so sure he had made a son, he who had married twice and never got one? Who can follow the way of the Immortal Ones, when their feet tread earth? And I have asked myself if after all it was I or your mother whose eyes saw clear. It is when we stretch out our hands to our moira that we receive the sign of the god."

5.

ABOUT seven days later, a ship touched at Troizen bound for Athens.

The Palace steward had taken my passage and seen to everything. But never having been on the open sea, I could not wait till sailing-time to see her, and walked down to the harbor. There she was, moored to the spit they call the Beard of Troizen: a dark-sailed ship, her sides painted with long serpents, her prow ornament an eagle with back-swept wings and a bull's head; a ship of Crete.

Cretan ships seldom came to us, except at tribute-time. The Beard was in a stir, and the people had set a market up. The potter and the smith, the weaving-woman and the carver, the farm people with cheeses and chicken and fruit and honeypots, sat on the cobbles with their wares about them; even the jeweller, who as a rule only brought his cheap stuff to the harbor, was showing gold. The Beard was full of Cretans, doing business and seeing the sights.

The small dark seamen were working naked, except for the leather codpiece Cretans wear. They keep it on under their kilts, making a show which a Hellene finds somewhat laughable; much cry and little wool, as the saying goes.

Some of those strolling round the market you might have
taken for girls. At first sight, the company seemed all youths
and graybeards. It was a custom in Troizen, as in most
Hellene towns, if a man had done something very disgrace-
ful, to shave half his face, lest he forget too quickly. The
sight of men who on purpose had taken their beards off was
something I could scarcely credit, even when I saw it. I
was always feeling after mine; but it was too fair to show.

They picked their way daintily about, their waists nipped
in like wasps', their kilts embroidered; some had found fresh
flowers to stick in their long hair. From their wrists hung
carved seals on bracelets of gold or beads; and the scents
they wore were strange and heady.

I went through the market, greeting the craftsmen and the
farmers. Though the Cretans could not well have taken me
for a son of the village, they heeded me no more than a
passing dog, except for a few who stared. I saw, as I looked
round, that they were treating the place as if tumblers and
mimes were putting on a show for them, pointing at people
or at the goods, calling out to each other or giggling with
heads together. One man had filled his cloak with radishes
and onions; going up to the potter, he said in his mincing
Cretan Greek, "I want a crock to keep these in. That one
will do." When the potter said it was his best piece, meant
for the table, he only said, "Oh, it will do, it will do," and
paid the price without question, and tossed his vegetables in.

Just then I heard a woman call out in anger. It was the
oilman's young wife, who sold in the market while her husband worked the press. A Cretan was thrusting money on
her, and clearly not for her oil jars, for he was grabbing
at her breast. Some village men were coming up, and there
were the makings of a brawl; so I tapped the Cretan's shoulder. "Listen, stranger; I don't know what your customs are
at home, but these are decent wives here. If you want a
woman, the house is over there, with the painted doorway."

He turned and looked at me; a sallow creature, wearing a
necklace of fake gold, which was peeling from the glass

below. Then he winked. "And what do you get out of it, eh, my lad?"

I could not speak at first. Something seemed to give him pause, and he jumped back. But he was beneath a lesson, so I only said, "Thank your gods you are a guest of the land; and get out of my sight."

As he went, an older man with a beard came up and said, "Sir, I ask your pardon for that low fellow. A nobody who can't tell a gentleman when he sees one." I said, "It seems he can't even tell a whore," and walked away. I could see, behind his civility, that he was pleased at having been gracious to someone below him. None of us was of consequence to these people. I remembered my grandfather's words; he had understood it.

I was going, but paused as a loud voice began to speak. It was the shipmaster, standing up on a stone bollard. "Anyone for Athens?" he was saying. "Now's your chance, good people; now's the time while the weather holds. If you've never crossed the sea, don't be afraid, *Sea Eagle* will get you there smooth as milk and safe as houses. No need to risk your necks on the Isthmus Road and get your throats slit by robbers. You'll meet no pirates on this run; that's what you pay taxes to King Minos for, so come and get the worth of it. Sail in *Sea Eagle*, for speed and ease. And if you can't judge of a ship for yourselves, let me tell you this: your King's own grandson is booked with us this trip."

So far I listened, standing behind the crowd. Then I said, "Oh, no."

It was the people of Troizen, all turning round, that brought him up short. He said, "And who may you be?" and looked again and said, "Sir?"

"I'm King Pittheus' grandson," I said, "and I've changed my mind. Your ship won't do; I'm used to better." At this all the Troizenians cheered. You might have supposed that they believed it.

The master looked at me, put out. "Well, my lord, that's for you to say. But you won't do better for a ship than this, any nearer than Corinth. They don't call at these small ports." I was getting angry, but would not make a show of myself before the people. I was at pains to keep my voice down, but somewhat surprised to find it saying, "I shan't need one. I am going overland, by the Isthmus Road."

I turned on my heel, hearing behind me the people clucking and the chattering of the Cretans. As I went, I had a glimpse of the fellow with the necklace, who had taken me for a pimp. I was sorry to leave him with a whole skin; and then for many years forgot him. Yet I see, when I look back, that he let flow the blood of as many men as if he had been some great War Leader; the blood of chiefs and princes, and the blood of a king. It may be that if all were known, palaces and kingdoms have fallen by such men. But they go to their unmarked graves, and never know it.

6.

THUS I set out by land for Athens. My grandfather, though he thought I had acted like a fool and was concerned for me, could not ask me to go back on my word before the people, and disgrace the house. My mother went to the House Snake, to get me an oracle. Though she saw dangers in my way, she did not see death. But she said weeping that the dangers were very great, and she had no surety for me. She made me vow to her that I would not tell my father's name till I had reached him; she was afraid of my falling into the hands of his enemies, and to comfort her I promised this. I asked her if she had any message for him; but she shook her head, saying I was her message, and for the rest, it was long ago.

So two days later my pair was harnessed, and I mounted beside my charioteer. I had meant to drive myself, but Dexios had begged to come. He had been suckled by a mare, as the saying is; for a driver or a friend, one could not do better.

We drove echoing under the great gate of Troizen, which

giants built, and where my great-grandfather set up the device of our house, a thunderstone on a pillar, with an eagle either side. My grandfather, and my uncles, and the young men set me on my way as far as the shore, where the road turns northward. Then they rode back, and our journey had begun. The first night we slept at Epidauros, at the sanctuary of Healing Apollo; the second at Kenchreai. When we saw at evening the round mount of Corinth stand above the plain, we knew that next day we should cross the Isthmus.

The crossing took a day. That is the truth, behind all the harpers' nonsense. Nowadays I am content to deny such fables as no grown man in his senses would believe, and let go the rest. They are dear to the people, and hurt neither them nor me.

I met no monsters, nor did I kill a giant with a cudgel; a fool's weapon for a man with spear and sword. I kept my arms, though more than one tried to have them off me; I had no need of monsters, with the men I met. It is rocky country, where the road tacks about, and you can never see far ahead. Among the rocks by the road, the robbers lie up.

Dexios saw to the chariot, while I took on whatever came. He had to be ready to get us sharply away. That was his work, and he did it well. Having no change of horses, we could not risk them. Now, after the years, these scrimmages get confused together in my mind, except for the last.

Deep blue, and black, the Isthmus is in my memory; blue sky above, with seldom a cloud to break it; and always on the right, black plunging rocks with their feet in a blue sea. The pink dusty road before us, the scrub and the dark pines, lay always between these depths of blue. The sea was calm; as one looked down, it drowned the eye like a second zenith, but bluer still; bluer than lapis, or sapphire, or whatever flower is bluest; and then again, in the dark clear shadows round the deep roots of the rocks, green and grape-purple, like the ring-dove's sheen. It must have been seldom I stood in quiet to gaze at it. My eye was sharpened for other matters. Yet it is the blue that I remember.

I remember that, and the feel of a land without law. On the Isthmus Road, a wounded man by the wayside, his blood black with flies and his mouth cracking for water, is the sign for wayfarers to flog on their donkeys and get out of sight. There was not much to be done, by the time one found him. I remember one I could only dispatch like a dog gored by the boar. I did it quickly, while he was drinking; he got the taste of the water first.

We found noonday shelter in a river-bed, with a summer trickle for the horses. It hid but did not trap us. When we had unyoked and eaten, Dexios went off among the rocks; and presently it seemed to me that he had been rather long gone. I called, but got no answer, and went to look. The rocks were steep, and to climb faster I left my spear at the bottom. It is hard to believe one was once so green.

From the top of the gully I saw him soon enough. He was lying at the feet of a thick-shouldered fellow who was stripping off his arm-rings. He must have been stunned from behind, never to have cried; I saw the club the robber had put down while he worked. Dexios moved a little; he was still alive. I remembered how I had saved him from the bull. Now again it was I who had endangered him. I was going to climb back for my spear when I saw the man, who had now got all he had, start rolling him toward the cliff. Just there the road skirts it near.

I shouted over the rock-edge, "Stop! Let him alone!" The man looked up. He was broad and red, with a thick neck and forked beard. When he saw me he laughed, and shoved Dexios with his foot.

I scrambled over the rocks; but they were rough, hard going. "Let him alone!" I called again, and heard my voice crack, as it had when it was breaking. The fellow put his hands on his hips and bawled, "What are *you*, Goldilocks? His girl, or his fancy-boy?" This he followed with some dirt he liked well enough to laugh at; and in the midst of his laughter, kicked Dexios over the cliff. I heard his cry, broken off in the middle.

Anger entered into me. It filled me body and limbs, so

that I seemed without weight; as I sprang out from the rock, anger bore me like wings, and carried me where I could not have leaped before. My very hair seemed to rise, as the mane of the King Horse does in battle. I landed on my feet, straightened up, and began to run. I hardly felt the ground beneath me. There he stood waiting, his mouth open and the laugh half out of it. As I got nearer, the sound ceased.

Afterwards I found on me the marks of his teeth and nails. At the time I felt nothing, but noted he was no wrestler, having trusted in his club. So I got an arm-grip as he tried to throttle me, and let him throw himself over my back. He lay, as Dexios had before him, dazed, with his head over the edge, all ready. I don't think he knew where he was going, till he was by himself in the air. Then I saw his mouth open again, but not for laughter. There was a great round-topped rock at the water's edge, shaped like a tortoise; he struck it head-on. The cliffs are high, just about there.

I went to see where Dexios had fallen. He lay dead across a sharp rock lapped by the sea, which rippled his white tunic and brown hair. I climbed down as far as I could above him, and sprinkled the earth to free him for his journey, promising him the offerings later. At least I had given him the one murdered men need most.

Feeding the horses and yoking them up, I was reminded by my clumsiness of his long-learned skill, consumed like a thorn-twig in the fire. I mounted and gathered in the reins, and felt what it is to be alone.

A little way on, a fellow met me with obeisance, and told me people were looting the house of Skiron, whom I had killed, offering to lead me there that I might claim my due. I told him to help himself to it, if he could get it, and drove on leaving him downcast. The jackal does not like to do his own hunting.

That was my last fight in the Isthmus. Either I was lucky, or people were avoiding me. By evening I was clear of it, and driving through the Megarian foothills beside the sea. Dusk was falling, and ahead to the east the mountains of

Attica looked thunder-black against the heavy sky. The road was desolate, the only sound wolves howling, or the scream of a rabbit nipped by the fox. Soon the track grew dangerous for horses in the bad light, and I had to lead them.

Other things go to make a grown man, besides proving himself with his hands. Now when no one threatened me, I was as lonely as a child. This dark rough road seemed forgotten by the Sky Gods, and given to earth-daimons not friendly to man. I ached from fighting, felt my wounds, and grieved for my friend. For comfort I called to mind that the King of Megara was Hellene, and my father's kinsman. But round me was only the friendless night, and I remembered rather that my father had sent no word to me since my birth. I thought of Troizen, the round hearth in the Great Hall, the fire of sweet-burning wood in its great warm bed of ash, my mother sitting among her women, and the lyre going from hand to hand.

Suddenly there was a great clamor of dogs, and whistling; and from the next bend I saw a fire. There was a fold of rough stones and thorn bushes, and round the fire six or eight little goatherds, the eldest not past thirteen and the youngest eight or nine. They had been piping, to keep their courage up with music against the ghosts of night. At sight of me, they scampered off to hide among the goats; but when I called to them, presently they came out, and I sat among them to get warm.

They helped me unyoke the horses—one could see them in their mind's eye charioteers already—and showed me where to find water and feed. I shared with them my figs and barley bread, and they with me their goat-milk cheese, while they called me "My lord," and asked where I had come from. Not all the tale of my day was fit for lads so young in a place so lonely, who had enough to fear from leopards and wolves. But I showed them Skiron's club, which I had brought away, and told them there had been an end of him, since he seemed a bugbear that haunted their dreams. They sat or lay around me, their rough hair falling over their bright eyes, their mouths opening in shrill sounds of wonder, asking what this or that place was like not ten miles off, as you or I might ask of Babylon.

It was full night. I could see no more the darkling sea nor the black mountains; only the rough walls of the fold, the dim shapes of goats within it, and the ring of faces flushed by the fire, which caught the polish of a reed pipe smooth with handling, a herd dog's yellow eyes, a bone knife hilt, or a tangle of fair hair. They brought me brush for a bed, and we lay down beside the embers. When they had crept together under two threadbare blankets like puppies scuffing for a place near the dam, there was one small one left outside, the runt of the litter. I saw him drawing his knees up to his chin, and offered him some of my cloak; he smelled of goats' dung, and had more fleas than an old dog, but after all he was my host.

Presently he said to me, "I wish we always had a man to stay with us. Sometimes it thunders, or one hears the lion." Soon he fell asleep, but I lay waking by the husk of the fire, watching the bright stars turn through the heaven. "To be a king," I thought, "what is it? To do justice, go to war for one's people, make their peace with the gods? Surely, it is this."

BOOK TWO

ELEUSIS

1.

I ROSE at daybreak, waked by the herd's bleating, and washed in the stream; a thing my hosts beheld with wonder, having had their last bath at the midwife's hands. From there on, the road grew easier, and dropped seaward. Soon across a narrow water I saw the island of Salamis, and all about me a fertile plain, with fruit and cornlands. The road led down to a city on the shore, a seaport full of shipping. Some merchants I met on the road told me it was Eleusis.

It was good to see a town again, and be in a land of law; and better still that this was the last stop before Athens. I would have my horses fed and groomed, I thought, while I ate and saw the sights. Then, as I came to the edge of the town, I saw the road all lined with staring people, and the rooftops thick with them.

Young men like to think themselves somebody; but even to me this seemed surprising. Besides, I found it strange that out of so many come to see me, no one called out or asked for news.

Before me was the market place. I pulled my pair to a walk, to save the traders' pitches. Then I drew rein; before me the people stood in a solid wall. No one spoke; and mothers hushed the babes they carried, to make them still.

In the midst, straight before me, stood a stately woman, with a slave holding a sunshade over her head. She was about seven and twenty; her hair, which was crowned with a diadem of purple stitched with gold, was as red as firelit copper. A score of women stood about her, like courtiers about a king; but there was no man near her, except the servant with the parasol. She must be both priestess and reigning queen. A Minyan kingdom, sure enough. That is what the Shore People call themselves, in their own places. Everyone knows that among them news travels faster than one can tell how.

Out of respect, I got down from my chariot and led the horses forward. Not only was she looking at me; I saw it was for me she waited. As I drew near, and saluted her, all the crowd fell into a deeper silence, like people who hear the harper tune his strings.

I said, "Greeting, Lady, in the name of whatever god or goddess is honored here above the rest. For I think you serve a powerful deity, to whom the traveller ought to pay some homage or other, before he passes by. A man should respect the gods of his journey, if he wants it to end as he would wish."

She said to me, in a slow Greek with the accent of the Minyans, "Truly your journey has been blessed, and here it ends."

I stared at her surprised. She seemed to be speaking words prepared for her; behind all this another woman peeped out in secret. I said, "Lady, I am a stranger in the land, travelling to Athens. The guest you look for is someone of more mark; a chief, or maybe a king."

At this she smiled. All the people drew closer, murmuring; not in anger, but like the goatherds by the fire, all ears.

"There is only one journey," she said, "that all men make. They go forth from the Mother, and do what men are born to do, till she stretches forth her hand, and calls them home."

Plainly this land was of the old religion. Touching my brow in respect, I said, "We are all her children." What could she want of me, which the city knew already?

"But some," she said, "are called to a higher destiny. As you are, stranger, who come here fulfilling the omens, on the day when the King must die."

Now I understood. But I would not show it. My wits were stunned and I needed time.

"High Lady," I said, "if your lord's sign calls him, what has that to do with me? What god or goddess is angry? No one is in mourning; no one looks hungry; no smoke is in

the sky. Well, it is for him to say. But if he needs me to
serve his death, he will send for me himself."

She drew herself up frowning. "What is a man to choose?
Woman bears him; he grows up and seeds like grass, and
falls into the furrow. Only the Mother, who brings forth
men and gods and gathers them again, sits at the hearthstone
of the universe and lives for ever." She lifted her hand; the
attendant women fell back around her; a man came forward
to lead my horses. "Come," she said. "You must be made
ready for the wrestling."

I found myself walking at her side. All round us followed
the people, whispering like waves upon a shoal. Clothed in
their expectation, I felt not myself but what they called me
to be. One does not guess the power of these mysteries, till
one is given part in them.

As I walked in silence beside the Queen, I recalled what
a man had told me, about a land where the custom is the
same. He said that in all those parts there is no rite in
the year that moves and holds the people like the death of
the King. "They see him," this man said, "at the height of
fortune, sitting in glory, wearing gold; and coming on him,
sometimes unknown and secret, sometimes marked by the
omens before all the people, is the one who brings his fate.
Sometimes the people know it before the King himself has
word." So solemn is the day, he said, that if anyone who
watches has grief or fear or trouble of his own, it is all
purged out of him by pity and terror; he comes away calmed,
and falls into a sleep. "Even the children feel it," he said.
"The herdboys up country, who cannot leave their flocks to
see the sight, will play out for one another on the hillsides,
with songs and miming, the death day of the King."

This thought awakened me. "What am I doing?" I thought.
"I have offered my forelock to Apollo; I have served Poseidon, the Mother's husband and lord, who is immortal.
Where is this woman leading me? To kill the man who killed
someone last year, and lie with her four seasons to bless
the corn, till she gets up from my bed to fetch my killer
to me? Is that my moira? *She* may have omens; but none

have come to me. No, an Earthling dream is leading me, like the King Horse drunk with poppy. How shall I get free?"

All the same, I was looking aside at her, as a man will at a woman he knows is his for the taking. Her face was too broad, and the mouth not fine enough; but her waist was like a palm tree, and to be unmoved by her breasts a man would need to be dead. The Minyans of Eleusis have mixed their blood with the Hellene kingdoms either side; her color and form were Hellene, but not her face. She felt me look, and walked straight on with her head held high. The fringe of the crimson sunshade tickled my hair.

I thought, "If I refuse, the people will tear me to pieces. I am the sower of their harvest. And this lady, who is the harvest field, will be very angry." One can tell some things from a woman's walking, even though she will not look. "She is a priestess and knows earth magic, and her curse will stick. Mother Dia must have her eye on me already. I was begotten to appease her anger. And she is not a goddess to treat lightly."

We had come to the sea road. I looked eastward and saw the hills of Attica, dry with summer and pale with noon, a morning's journey. I thought, "How could I go to my father, whose sword I carry, and say, 'A woman called me to fight, but I ran away?' No. Fate has set in my path this battle of the stallions, as it set Skiron the robber. Let me do the thing at hand, and trust in the gods."

"Lady," I said, "I was never this side of the Isthmus until now. What are you called?" She gazed before her and said softly, "Persephone. But it is forbidden for men to speak it." Coming nearer, I said, "A whispering name. A name for the dark." But she did not answer; so I asked, "And what is the King's name, whom I am to kill?"

She looked at me surprised, and answered carelessly, "His name is Kerkyon," as if I had asked it of some masterless dog. For a very little, it seemed, she would have said that he had no name.

Just inshore, the road sloped upwards to a flat open place at the foot of a rocky bluff. Stairs led up it to the terrace where the Palace stood: red columns with black bases, and yellow walls. The cliff below it was undercut; the hollow looked dark and gloomy, and had a deep cleft in its floor that plunged into the earth. The breeze bore from it a faint stench of rotten flesh.

She pointed to the level place before it, and said, "There is the wrestling ground." I saw the Palace roof and the terrace thick with people. Those who had come with us spread themselves on the slopes. I looked at the cleft and said, "What happens to the loser?"

She said, "He goes to the Mother. At the autumn sowing his flesh is brought forth and plowed into the fields, and turns to corn. A man is happy who in the flower of youth wins fortune and glory, and whose thread runs out before bitter old age can fall on him." I answered, "He has been happy indeed," and looked straight at her. She did not blush, but her chin went up.

"This Kerkyon," I said; "we meet in combat, not as the priest offers the victim?" That would have been against my stomach, seeing the man had not chosen his own time. I was glad when she nodded her head. "And the weapons?" I asked. "Only those," she said, "that men are born with." I looked about and said, "Will a man of your people tell me the rules?" She looked at me puzzled; I thought it was my Hellene speech, and said again, "The laws of battle?" She raised her brows and answered, "The law is that the King must die."

Then, on the broad steps that climbed up to the Citadel, I saw him coming down to meet me. I knew him at once, because he was alone.

The steps were crowded with people from the Palace; but they all hung back from him and stood wide, as if his death were a catching sickness. He was older than I. His black beard was enough to hide his jaw; I don't think he was less than twenty. As he looked down at me, I could tell I seemed a boy to him. He was not much above my height, being tall only for a Minyan; but he was lean and sinewy as mountain lions are. His strong black hair, too short and thick to hang in lovelocks, covered his neck like a curling mane. As we met each other's eyes, I thought, "He has stood where I stand now, and the man he fought with is bones under the rock." And then I thought, "He has not consented to his death."

All about us was a great silence full of eyes. And it moved me as a strange and powerful thing, that these watching people did not feel even themselves as they felt us. I wondered if for him it was the same.

As we stood thus, I saw that after all he was not quite alone. A woman had come up behind him, and stood there weeping. He did not turn to look. If he heard, he had other things to think of.

He came a few steps lower, looking not at the Queen but only at me. "Who are you, and where do you come from?" He spoke Greek very foreignly, but I understood him. It seemed to me we would have understood each other if he had had none at all.

"I am Theseus, from Troizen in the Isle of Pelops. I came in peace, passing through to Athens. But our life-threads are crossed, it seems."

"Whose son are you?" he asked. Looking at his face, I saw he had no purpose in his questions, except to know he was still King, and a man walking in sunlight above the earth. I answered, "My mother hung up her girdle for the Goddess. I am a son of the myrtle grove."

The listeners made their soft murmur, like rustling reeds. But I felt the Queen move beside me. She was staring at me; and Kerkyon, now, at her. Then he burst out laughing. His teeth were strong and white above his young black beard. The people stirred, surprised; I was no wiser than they. All I knew, as the King laughing turned my way, was that his jest was bitter. He stood on the stairs and laughed; and the woman behind him covered her face in her two hands, and crouched down and rocked herself to and fro.

He came down. Face to face, I saw he was as strong as I had thought. "Well, Son of the Grove, let us do the appointed thing. This time the odds will be even; the Lady won't know whom to beat the gong for." I did not understand him; but I saw he was speaking for her ears, not for mine.

A sanctuary-house near by had been opened while we spoke, and a tall throne brought out, painted red, with devices of serpents and sheaves. They stood it near the floor, and by it a great bronze gong upon a stand. The Queen sat down with her women round her, holding the gong stick like a scepter.

"No," I thought, "the odds will not be even. He is fighting for his kingdom, which I do not want, and his life, which I don't want either. I cannot hate him, as a warrior should his enemy; nor even be angry, except with his people, who are turning from him like rats from an empty barn. If I were an Earthling, I should feel their wishes fighting for me. But I cannot dance to their piping; I am a Hellene."

A priestess led me to a corner of the ground, where two men stripped and oiled me and gave me a wrestler's linen apron. They plaited back my hair and bound it in a club, and led me forth to be seen. The people cheered me, but I was not warmed by it; I knew they would cheer whoever came to kill the King. Even now when he was stripped and I could see his strength, I could not hate him. I looked at the Queen, but could not tell if I was angry with her or not, because I desired her. "Well," I thought, "is that not quarrel enough?"

The elder of the men, who looked to have been a warrior, said, "How old are you, boy?" People were listening, so I said, "Nineteen." It made me feel stronger. He looked at my chin, which had less down than a gosling, but said no more.

We were led to the throne, where she sat under her fringed sunshade. Her gold-sewn flounces caught the light, and her jewelled shoes. Her deep breasts looked gold and rosy, bloomed like the cheeks of peaches, and her red hair glowed. She had a gold cup in her hands, and held it out to me. The warm sun brought out the scents of spiced wine, honey, and cheese. As I took it I smiled at her, "For," I thought, "she is a woman, or what are we about?" She did not toss her head as she had before, but looked into my eyes as if to read an omen; and in hers I saw fear.

A girl will scream as you chase her through the wood, who when caught is quiet enough. I saw no more than that in it; it stirred my blood, and I was glad to have said I was nineteen. I drank of the mixed drink, and the priestess gave it to the King.

He drank deep. The people gazed at him; but no one cheered. Yet he stripped well, and bore himself bravely; and for a year he had been their king. I remembered what I had heard of the old religion. "They care nothing for him," I thought, "though he is going to die for them, or so they hope, and put his life into the corn. He is the scapegoat. Looking at him, they see only the year's troubles, the crop that failed, the barren cows, the sickness. They want to kill their troubles with him, and start again." I was angry to see his death not in his own hand, but the sport of rabble who did not share the sacrifice, who offered nothing of their own; I felt that out of all these people, he was the only one I could love. But I saw from his face that none of this came strange to him; he was bitter at it, but did not question it, being Earthling as they were. "He too," I thought, "would think me mad if he knew my mind. I am a Hellene; it is I, not he, who am alone."

We faced each other on the wrestling ground; the Queen stood up, with the gong stick in her hand. After that I only looked at his eyes. Something told me he was not like the wrestlers of Troizen.

Wood tapped sharply on the gong. I waited on my toes, to see if he would come straight in, like a Hellene, and grab for a body-hold. No; I had guessed right. He was edging round, trying to get the sun in my eyes. He did not fidget on his feet, but moved quite slowly and softly, like a cat before it springs. Not for nothing I had felt, while he spoke bad Greek, that we yet had a common language. Now we spoke it. He, too, was a wrestler who thought.

His eyes were golden brown, light like a wolf's. "Yes," I thought, "and he will be as fast. Let him come in first; if he

is going to take a risk, he will do it then. Afterwards he
may know better."

He aimed a great buffet at my head. It was meant to sway
me left; so I jumped right. That was well, for where my guts
should have been he landed a kick like a horse's. Even glancing, it hurt, but not too much, and I grabbed his leg. As I
tipped him over I jumped at him, throwing him sideways
and trying to land on him with a head-lock. But he was fast,
fast as a cat. He got me by the foot and turned my fall, and
almost before I had touched ground was slipping round to
get a scissors on me. I jabbed my fist at his chin, and saved
myself by a lizard's tail-flick. Then the mill on the ground
began in earnest. I soon forgot I had been slow to anger;
you cease to ask what wrong a man has done you when his
hands are feeling for your life.

He had the look of a gentleman. But the Queen's stare had
warned me, when I asked the rules. All-in is all-in among the
Shore People, and nothing barred. This slit in my ear, like a
fighting dog's, I got in that fight as a dog gets it. Once he
nearly gouged out my eye, and only gave over to keep his
thumb unbroken. Soon I got too angry rather than too cold;
but I could not afford to take a risk, just for the pleasure
of hurting him. He was like tanned oxhide with a core of
bronze.

As we twisted and kicked and struck, I could make believe
no longer I was nineteen. I was fighting a man in his flower
of strength, before I had come to mine. My blood and bones
began to whisper he would outstay me. Then the gong
began.

The starting stroke had come from the butt of the stick.
This was the blow of the padded hammer. It gave a great
singing roar; I swear one could even feel the sound in the
ground underfoot. And as it quivered and hummed, the
women chanted.

The voices sank and rose, sank and rose higher. It was
like the north wind when it blows screaming through mountain gorges; like the keening of a thousand widows in a
burning town; like the cry of she-wolves to the moon. And

under it, over it, through our blood and skulls and entrails, the bellow of the gong.

The din maddened me. As it washed over me again and again, I began to be filled with the madman's single purpose. I must kill my man, and stop the noise.

As this frenzied strength built up in me, my hands and back felt him flagging. With each gong throb his strength was trickling from him. It was his death that was singing to him; wrapping him round like smoke, drawing him down into the ground. Everything was against him: the people, the Mystery, and I. But he fought bravely.

He was trying to strangle me, when I got both feet up and hurled him backward. While he was still winded, I leaped on him and snatched his arm from under him and threw him over. So he lay face down, and I was on his back, and he could not rise. The singing rose to a long shriek, then sank into silence. The last gong stroke shuddered and died.

His face was in the dust; but I could tell his mind, as he felt this way and that to see if anything was left to do, and understood that it was finished. In that moment my anger died. I forgot the pain, remembering only his courage and his despair. "Why should I take his blood upon me?" I thought. "He never harmed me, except to fulfill his moira." I shifted my weight a very little, taking good care because he was full of tricks, till he could just turn his head out of the dirt. But he did not look at me; only at the dark cleft below the rock. These were his people, and his life-thread was twined with theirs. One could not save him.

I put my knee in his backbone. Keeping him pinned, for he was not a man to give an inch to, I hooked my arm round his head, and pulled it back till I felt the neckbone straining. Then I said softly in his ear—for it did not concern the people about us, who had given nothing to the sacrifice— "Shall it be now?" He whispered, "Yes." I said, "Discharge me of it, then, to the gods below." He said, "Be free of it," with some invocation after. It was in his own tongue, but I trusted him. I jerked his head back hard and fast, and heard the snap of the neckbone. When I looked, it seemed his eyes still had a spark of life; but when I turned his head sideways it was gone.

I got to my feet, and heard from the people a deep sighing, as if they had all just finished the act of love. "So it begins," I said to myself; "and only a god can see the ending."

They had brought a bier, and laid the King on it. There was a high scream from the throne. The Queen rushed down and threw herself on the corpse, rending her hair and clawing her face and bosom. She looked just like a woman who has lost her dear lord, the man who led her a maiden from her father's house; as if there were young children and no kin to help them. That was how she wept, so that I stared amazed. But now all the other women were crying and howling too, and I understood it was the custom.

They went off wailing, appeasing the new-made ghost. Left alone among staring strangers, I wanted to ask, "What now?" But the only man I knew was dead.

Presently came an old priestess and led me toward the sanctuary-house. She told me they would mourn the King till sundown; then I should be blood-cleansed, and wed the Queen.

In a room with a bath of painted clay, the priestesses bathed me and dressed my wounds. They all spoke Greek, with the lilt of the Shore People, lisping and twittering. But even in their own speech they have Greek words. There is so much sea traffic at Eleusis, the tongues have got mixed here, as well as the blood. They put a long white linen robe on me, and combed my hair, and gave me meat and wine. Then there was nothing to do but listen to the wailing, and wait, and think.

Toward sunset I heard the funeral coming down the long stairs, with dirges and weeping and the aulos' skirl, and disks of bronze clanging together. From a window I saw the winding train of women, robed in crimson with black veils. When the dirge ended, there was a great cry, between a scream and a shout of triumph. I guessed the King was going home.

Soon after, at fall of dusk, the priestesses came back to fetch me for the cleansing. A red glow shone in at the window; and when they opened the door, I saw everywhere a leaping torchlight. There were torches as far as one could see, filling the precinct and streaming up to the Citadel, and flowing on into the town. Yet all was quiet, though all the people were there, from about twelve years old. The priestess led me between them, in a deep silence, till the shore with its beached ships lay before us. When the water lapped our feet, the priestess cried out, "To the sea!"

At this, everyone began to walk into the water. Those who wore white robes kept them on; many stripped naked, both women and men, but all was done with deep solemnity, and they kept their lit torches in their hands. The night was calm; the sea seemed sown with a thousand points of fire every flame with its rippling image.

She led me forward till the water lapped my breast, and held her torch high for them all to see me. I was there to be cleansed of blood; they, I suppose, washed off ill-luck, and death. I was young, and had killed a man whose beard had grown; though it was the earth magic had put him in my hand, I felt my victory. Also I was going to the Queen; and with darkness came desire.

In Salamis, across the strait, lamps burned in the houses I thought of home, of my kindred, and of Kalauria across the water. Everything here was strange except the sea, which had carried my father to my mother. I loosed my girdle, and pulled off my robe, and gave it to the priestess. She stared surprised; but I plunged in and swam beyond all the people far into the strait. Behind me the torches were a fiery sun along the shore, and above were the stars.

For a while I was quiet, floating on the sea. Then I said "Blue-Haired Poseidon, Earth-Shaker, Horse Father! You are the lord of the Goddess. If I served your altar well in Troizen if you were there at my begetting, lead me on toward my moira; be my friend in this land of women."

I turned to swim back, head over heels in the water. As it rushed in my ears, I heard the pulse of the sea-surge, and thought, "Yes, he remembers me." So I swam back to the torches, and there was the chief priestess, waving her light about and crying, "Where is the King?" for all the world like some old nurse when the children get too big for her. That, I suppose, was what made me swim up under water, and bob out laughing right under her nose, so that she jumped and nearly doused her torch. I half expected a box on the ear. But she only eyed me muttering in the Minyan speech, and shook her head.

Walking back in my wet robe, it was strange to feel my wounds fresh-smarting from the salt, for it seemed a year since the wrestling. As for all the people, you might have supposed King Kerkyon had never been. But as I looked beyond the wrestling ground, where the precinct was lit with cressets, I saw beside the rock-cleft the woman who had wept for him, face down on the bare stone, her torn hair flung about her, still as the dead. Some women on the steps were calling out, upbraiding her. Presently they ran down clucking, and pulled her to her feet and led her up to the Palace.

At the sanctuary-house I was dried and oiled and combed again; then they brought me a tunic of embroidered work, a necklace of gold sunflowers, and the King's ring. The Goddess was carved upon the gold, with women worshipping her, and a youth done small. I had a cut on my cheekbone, where Kerkyon's fist had driven it into my face.

When I was ready, I asked for my sword. They said staring that I should have no need of that. "So I should hope," I said. "But since I am going to my wife's house and not she to mine, it is proper to bring it with me." This they made no sense of. I could not say it was my father's; but when I said "My mother gave it me," they fetched it at once. Earthlings inherit everything from their mothers, even their names.

Outside was a guard of young men singing, and musicians. They led me not to the Palace, but to the precinct below. The song was in Minyan, but the bawdy clowning told the story. One expects some fooling when they bring the bridegroom, but there is measure in everything. Besides, I thought, I knew what I was about, and had no need of teachers.

The song changed to a hymn. I got to know it after. It is the Corn Song of those parts, about how a whole ear springs where a grain was sown, through Mother Dia, from whose womb comes everything. Then they sang the Queen's praises, hailing her as Kore, which is her unforbidden name. Presently we came to steps going into the ground. At once the song ceased, and all was silence. The priestess put out her torch, and took my hand.

She led me down into darkness, and on through a winding way, and up a little. Then the walls opened to a space, and there was the scent of a woman. I remembered it on the Queen when I walked with her, heavy like asphodel. The priestess let go of me; I heard her fading footfalls and her hand brushing the walls. I stripped and dropped my clothes behind me, keeping only my sword in my left hand. Then I went forward, and felt a bed. I propped the sword against it, and reached out and found her. She slid her hands up my arms, then downward from my shoulders; and what I had learned with the Troizen girls seemed nothing, like the games of children before they understand.

Suddenly she cried out like a virgin. There was a clash of cymbals and blare of horns. Torchlight blinded me; I heard a thousand voices laughing and cheering. Then I saw we were in a cavern whose mouth had been closed with doors; the people had been waiting outside, to see them opened.

For a moment I was too stunned to move. Then anger lit in me like a mountain fire in summer. I snatched my sword, and shouted, and ran forward. But amid shrieks and squeals I·found myself entangled in women, who, if you please, had been standing foremost to see the sight. Everyone was calling out and exclaiming, as if I were the first man they had ever known to resent such a thing. I shall never, till I die, understand Earthlings.

I flung the women off, and crashed the doors together. Then I strode back to the bed and stood over it. "You

barefaced bitch!" I said. "You deserve to die. Have you no
shame for yourself, no respect for my honor? Could you
not have lent me some man of your house to keep the door
for me, seeing I brought no friend? Or have you no kinsmen
to see decency? Where I come from, the meanest peasant
on the folk-land would have blood for this. Am I a dog?"

I heard her quick breathing in the dark, which seemed
blacker after the torchlight. "What is it?" she said. "Have
you gone mad? There is always the Showing."

I was struck dumb. Not only with Kerkyon, but with the
gods knew how many men before, she had shown herself
to the people. There was music outside, a wild air on flutes
and lyres, with drums beating like blood in the ears. She
said, "It is over now. Come here." I heard her move on the
bed. "No," I said; "I have drunk poison; you have shamed
my manhood." The scent of her hair came close, and I felt
her hand on my neck. "What has the Mother done to me,"
she whispered, "sending me a wild horse-tamer of the Sky
Folk, a blue-eyed charioteer without law or custom or respect
for anything? Don't you understand even seedtime and reap-
ing? How can the people trust the harvest, unless they see
it sown? We have done what is needful now; they will
ask no more of us. Now comes the time when we can please
ourselves."

Her hand moved down my arm; she laced her fingers in
mine, and loosened them from the sword hilt. When she
had drawn me near, I forgot that what she knew, dead men
had taught her whose bones lay near us under the rock.
The drums were quickening their beat, and the flutes shrilled
higher at each clash of the cymbals. I learned more in
that one night than I had in three whole years from the
girls of Troizen.

2.

WHEN they led us up to the Palace in the fresh morning, and I saw from the upper terrace the glittering sun-path on the sea, I thought to myself, "Only four days out from home, and here I am a King."

Nothing is good enough at Eleusis for a new-made King. They drown his days in honey. Gold necklaces, inlaid daggers, tunics of silk from Babylon, rose-oil from Rhodes; the dancers throwing flowers; the bard, lest you should miss the compliment, singing it again in Greek. Young girls sighing; the King is everyone's beloved. Old women cooing; he is everybody's son. And among the Companions, the guard of high-born youths who are in the running themselves for King, it seemed too that I was everybody's brother. I did not notice at first that I was not the eldest brother, but the youngest spoiled by all the rest. I had other things to think of.

The great bedchamber faced southward. When one waked at morning, one saw in the wide window only the rose-flushed sky; then sitting up, the hills of Attica purpled with daybreak, and the gray landlocked bay. The walls were painted with white spirals and pink flowers, the floor had red and black checkers. The bed was of Egyptian ebony studded with gold barley-ears, and had a cover of civetskins bordered with dark purple. In a withy cage at the window lived a bird with smooth white feathers color-shot like pearl shell, which whistled at sunrise, and when one looked least for it sometimes spoke. It made me start, and she used to laugh. The earliest sunlight glowed deeply in her hair; strong hair, and springing; when one gathered it up, it filled both hands full.

I lived all day for the night. Sometimes I fell asleep at noon, and did not wake till evening; then I would not sleep again till dawn. I hardly noticed at the marriage sacrifice how, though I killed the victims, it was the Queen who offered them, as if she were the King. At the Games I won the spear-throwing and the jumping, and a silly horse race with little Minyan ponies. Also I won the archery, though I had thought my eye would be out from going short of sleep.

There was no wrestling; it seemed that had been settled already. But if you are supposing these were the funeral games of the dead King, you will be wrong; they were held in my honor. He was gone from sight and mind; I have grieved longer for a dog than they did for him. What is more, I was Kerkyon now. It is the style of Kings of Eleusis, like Pharaoh in Egypt and Minos in Crete. So the man had not even left a name behind him.

Days passed, and the Palace business began again. Down on the plain the army turned out to exercise, throwing spears at the stuffed hog, or shooting at the mark. But this, I found, was not supposed to concern me. It would not answer, for war leaders to come and go, one every year. The troops were led by Xanthos, the Queen's brother. He was a big man as Minyans go, on whom his sister's red hair was not beautiful. He had the russet eyes of a fox. There are hot red men and cold red men, and he was one of the cold. He used to speak to me man to boy, which made me angry. Though he could give me a dozen years, I was the King; and I was still new enough in Eleusis to suppose this meant something.

Every day the Queen held audience. Seeing the Hall filled with women, I did not understand at first that she was doing all the kingdom's business without me. But the women were heads of families; they came about land disputes, or taxes, or marriage portions. Fathers were nobody in Eleusis, and could not choose wives for their own sons, or leave them a name, let alone property. The men stood at

the back till the women had been heard; and if she wanted
a man's advice, she sent for Xanthos.

One night at bedtime, I asked her if there was nothing
in Eleusis for the King to do. She smiled and said, "Oh, yes.
Undo this necklace; it is caught in my hair." I did not move
at once, but looked at her. She said, "Why should the King
sit at clerk's business with ugly old men?" Then she let fall
her belt and petticoat and said, coming nearer, "See, it is
pulling here. It hurts me." And there was no more talk that
night.

Just afterwards, I learned by chance that she had seen
an embassy from Rhodes, and never even told me. I over-
heard it on the Lower Terrace; the stewards had heard it
first. I stood there in my tracks. No one had so insulted me
since my childhood. "What does she take me for?" I thought.
"Because I have less beard than her fox-eyed brother, does
she think I need a nurse? Thunder of Zeus! I killed her husband." Anger blurred my eyes.

There were voices about me. The young Companions were
escorting me, as they did everywhere. I hardly knew one yet
from another; there had been no time. "What is it, Kerkyon?
Does something trouble you?" "You look sick." "No, he looks
angry." "Kerkyon, is there something I can do?"

I said it was nothing. I had too much pride to say I had
been made light of. But when her women had gone that
night, I asked her what she meant by it.

She looked at me amazed. It seemed she really could not
see why I was angry. She said she had done nothing against
custom; and I saw it was true. As for making light of me
. . . she shook out her hair, and laughed at me through it
sidelong.

Next morning dawned green and gold. A tress of red hair
lay tickling on my breast. I lifted it off and slid away, and
went to the window. The Attic hills swam in gold mist,
across a shimmering sea, looking near enough to hit with an
arrow. I thought how strange are the ways of Earthlings,
and hard for a Hellene to understand. For she had chosen
me, and set me to the wrestling, and hallowed me King.

Yet neither she nor anyone else had asked if I consented to my moira.

The white bird woke and whistled. Her voice from the bed said wide awake, "You are thinking. What are you thinking of?" I made her the answer she liked best. I was the first Hellene she had ever married.

From this day on, I awoke from dreaming. I had spent the long days of Eleusis in sleep, in dancing or wrestling with the young men, playing the lyre, or looking out to sea. Now I began to seek for occupation. It is not in my nature to do nothing.

The Companions were nearest to my hand. If there was war, at least I should have command of my own Guard, though Xanthos led the rest. It was time I paid them some attention.

These youths, as I was saying, never left me, except when I was with the Queen in bed. They were all well set up, well bred and personable, or they would not have been where they were; they were chosen for such things, rather than for feats of arms. I had no need of their protection, for in Eleusis nothing was so dreadful as to kill the King out of his time. After suffering many pains, the killer would be sealed in a tomb alive, for Night's Daughters to do their will on him. It was long since it had happened, and then by misadventure. But the Companions were an adornment for the King, which the people liked to see about him.

They all had more or less Greek, which was the mark there of a gentleman. When I began to talk with them, they seemed to me very vain, full of petty jealousies and rivalries, feeling slights as a cat does water, and always trying to put each other down. They were curious about me, because I was a Hellene, and, as I learned after a while, because of some oracle concerning me which had been kept secret from the people. I remembered the dead King's laughter; but it told one nothing.

From all I could see, they had done little till now but play at war training. They did not lack spirit, so I suppose most of the kings had not looked beyond their own term.

But wherever I am, I must put my hand to what I find there.

Men soon get stale with courtyard exercise; so I got them into the hills. At first they went unwillingly; Eleusinians are plainsmen, and despise the mountains as poor barren land, fit for wolves and robbers. I asked them whatever they did when raiders came for their cattle, if they did not know the borderland. They took this quite well, and owned the Megarians often made away with stock, trying to make good their losses by the Isthmus bandits the other side. "Well," I said, "there's only one answer to that. They must be made to fear us more." So I took them scrambling; we got a buck, and roasted our kill by a mountain stream, and they were pleased with the day. But on the way home one of them said to me, "Don't tell anyone, Kerkyon. You would be stopped next time for sure."

"Oh?" I said, raising my brows. "Who would stop me, do you think?" There was some whispering; I heard, "Well, you fool, he's a Hellene." Then someone said civilly, "You see, it is very unlucky if the King dies out of season."

This is quite true. There is a Minyan song about some young King long ago, who got himself killed by a boar after the Queen had forbidden him to go hunting. Anemones are said to be dyed with his blood. The olives failed that year, and no one has ever heard the last of it.

All the same, we were in the hills again next day, and the day after. Eleusis lies between two Hellene kingdoms; when the youths found their mothers' rule bear heavy, they would cast an eye sidelong at the lands of men. So they came, and kept the secret, and were pleased with themselves. My trophies of the chase, which I could not show in the Palace, I gave away as prizes; but I had to be careful, or they would quarrel over them, being much given to rivalry. Time passed like this; as we got used to each other's speech, we had a language of our own, Greek-Minyan laced with our own jokes and catchwords. No one else could understand it.

One day, when we were straggled out on the mountain, I heard them calling to each other, "We have lost Boy!"

"Where is Boy, have you seen him?" I climbed into view and someone said, "There he is."

I had put up with a good deal in Eleusis; but I did not mean to swallow insolence. I came forward, reminding myself that I passed for nineteen, and the eldest of them was not one and twenty. "The next one who calls me Boy," I said, "I am going to kill."

They all stood gaping. "Well?" I said. "Here we are on the border. Anyone who kills me can run away; or you can throw my body off a rock, if you like, and say I fell. I shan't hide behind the Goddess' skirts; but let's see first who can kill me. Who thinks I am a boy? Come out and say it."

There was a pause; then the eldest, a young man called Bias who had a proper beard, said, "But, Kerkyon, no one here would insult you. It is the other way." More of them joined in, calling, "It is our name for you." "Kerkyon is nothing; it is cold." "All the good kings have nicknames." And one who was always bold and reckless said, laughing, "It's all in love, Kerkyon. You know you could have any one of us for a wink." At this two or three shouted out agreeing, between joke and earnest, letting me see it was an offer; and next moment two had started a fight.

I got them parted, and let it go as foolery. Everyone knows there is a good deal of this among the Minyans; and one cannot wonder. It comes of being tied to their mothers' petticoats after they are men. Their mothers even choose their wives for them. Then they go to the wife's house, and change one petticoat for another. When a man lives like this, a youth he can choose for himself, who looks up to him and copies him and boasts of his friendship, will give him more pride in himself than the womenfolk at home. I see no sense in looking down on this; most customs have a reason; even among Hellenes, in a long war where girls are scarce and the leaders are first served, the young men's friendships grow tenderer than they were.

One can be, as I am, a man for women, yet not dislike having friends in a strange land, or a loyal Guard. If they had been tiresome or importunate I might have wondered,

being young, how I was going to deal with it; but this time,
for once, there was something in being King. "Well," I said
to them, "even kings have names where I come from. Mine
is Theseus." So they took to using it, though it was clear
against the custom.

If I had fancied one of them, there would have been no
end to bloodshed and intrigue; one heard stories of former
years. As it was, it was only a matter of taking care. A few
meant what they said; with others it was a fashion; they had
friends of their own or were in love with girls, usually with
girls their mothers would not let them marry. Troubles like
this they brought to me, and when I could I urged their
causes with the Queen. But it hurts a man's pride, to coax a
woman when he has no power to do more. Just as when I
was a boy, I began to find wild ways of proving myself to
myself. I would have wished for war; but westward were
the Megarians, my father's hearth-friends and kindred; and
eastward was my father.

I heard a good deal about the cattle wars with Megara;
some of my young men were old enough to have been in
the last themselves. King Nisos, they said, was too old to
fight, but his son Pylas could fight for two. I learned, from
hints here and there, that the Queen's brother was not much
loved by his men. No one questioned his courage; but he
was thought overbearing, and greedy with the spoil. There
was a proverb among them, "Xanthos' share."

My grandfather had said to me, "Take care as you pass
through Megara not to give offense, or get into a brawl. King
Nisos is the only sure ally your father has, your grandmother's brother. King Pandion fled there from Athens once
during the wars for the kingdom; your father himself was
born there." As autumn drew on, these words stuck in my
mind. It is a time for raids, before winter closes the ways.
Once in the field, I thought, it would be a poor thing if I
did not single this Pylas out for combat; people might well,
then, call me Boy. Yet whether I killed him or he killed me,
my father stood to lose by it. I began to dread this war as
much as a man might who was scared of fighting.

Lying at dawn in the painted bedchamber, thinking my own thoughts before the white bird whistled at the sun, I saw it was time I slipped off to Athens. But how to do it? It would have been easier for a slave than for the King. I was always among people: dancing at festivals, parading at the sacrifice (though I never offered it); everywhere I went the Guard went with me; and at night I had only to move as far as the edge of the bed, for the Queen to wake. There were the hunting trips in the hills; but I knew the Companions, thinking I was lying hurt somewhere, would set the dogs to find me. Besides, they would be punished for losing me; killed, for all I knew; and I had begun to feel answerable for them. Being with them so much, I could not help it.

Then, supposing I did get away, I should still get to my father's court a beggarly fugitive, perhaps with the Queen theatening war. A fine fool I should look, in flight from a woman. I had wanted to go to him a man who has been heard of. I had wanted him to say, before he knew me, "I wish I had such a son."

"No!" I thought. "By Ever-Living Zeus! I have time before me: autumn, winter, and spring. If I can't get openly to Athens with my name running before me, I deserve to stay in Eleusis, and accept the moira of her kings."

I looked about me, and listened, and thought. I considered the Megarians, and Pylas, Nisos' son, who had the name of a warrior. There was only one way to avoid fighting him and keep my standing: somehow, and soon, we must make friends. I thought of this and that; but still I could not see my way to it.

Meantime, the night still had its sweetness; the harper's song at supper-time seemed always a verse too long. But I no longer asked myself how I could ever leave her.

I never spoke to her of business when anyone was listening, lest she should shame me with slight answers; but if I tried it at night, she would pet me like a child. At home, when I was only ten, my grandfather used to make me sit quiet while he gave judgment, and question me after to see what I had taken in. Here, I had even litigants coming to me with bribes to get them her ear, as if I were some concubine. Of course they were women, so I could not hit them in the teeth.

I often saw her children about the Palace. There were only five, though she had married ten kings. By the last she had had none; and I hoped, as any man will, that she would take by me. But sometimes I heard the nurses talking, as if these children were some favor she had shown their fathers; as if she chose which kings she would bear to. So I never asked her. I knew, if I ever learned that she thought me not worth breeding from, I should be too angry to answer for myself.

Then came a day when she heard I had been climbing after leopard. You might have thought, from the way she rated me, I had been caught up an apple tree in my first pair of breeches. I was shocked dumb. My own mother, who remembered me a babe as naked as a worm, would not have said such things. Afterwards I thought of answers, but too late. That night in bed I turned away from her, thinking that here was something she was not master of. But here too, in the end, she had the better of me, for she understood these matters. Next morning my eyes opened before cocklight, and I lay awake ashamed. I saw I should have to do something to get my standing back. I did not mean to be a man all night and a child all day, for any woman's pleasure.

I would hunt again, I thought; and this time it should be something big. Among the mountain herdboys I made it known that news of game would find me grateful. Before long, one came asking for me, all on tiptoe. "Kerkyon," he said, "the great she-boar, Phaia, is in the border hills. She has come over from Megara, and has a den on Broken Mountain. They say she has a litter there."

He went on to tell me of her; I had heard something already. She was said by the Megarians to have a javelin-head lodged in her side, which made her hate men; she would rush out from covert when no one hunted her, and kill the peasants for sport. There were five men to her count already.

This was just the kind of quarry I had been looking for. I gave the lad a reward that made him jump for joy. "The

Good Goddess do as much for you, Kerkyon. King Nisos has
put a price upon the beast; a tripod and an ox."

This gave me a new thought. I called him back as he was
going. "Does Pylas, King Nisos' son, hunt about the border?"
The boy said, "He will, sir, for sure, now she is there; he is
always after her." "Tell me," I said, "if he is seen."

He brought word a few days later. I beckoned the Guard
about me, and said to them, "I have news of a brave beast
in the hills."

At this the wildest of them, a dark youth called Amyntor,
gave a whoop and swallowed it. I heard someone's voice
claiming a bet. Of course they knew I had had my orders.
There is nowhere for gossip like a palace of women, where
it is common knowledge by noonday how many times you
embraced your wife last night. They had all been waiting
to see what I would do. All Eleusinians love strong happen-
ings more than wine.

"Pylas of Megara and his friends," I said, "think they can
bay the she-boar of Krommyon. I don't think we should let
that pass, when she's on our border."

Their eyes grew wide. I saw them nudging and whispering, and was rather surprised; I had not found them easily
frightened. Then one said aloud, "A she-pig!"

At this I remembered; these beasts are sacred in Eleusis.
It did not please me; from the moment I had heard of Phaia,
my heart had been set on her. But when I thought again,
I saw it might work out for the best. "Be easy," I said. "She
will not die in Eleusis. Those hills are No Man's Land. Nor
will her blood be on you; boar are lawful killing for Hellenes,
and I shall kill her."

They stared at me. I could see they thought I was mad;
and indeed I hardly knew myself why I was so resolved.

"Come," I said, "we must be off before the sun is high.
Pylas has the start of us." I was afraid one of them might get
faint-hearted and tell. If I kept them together, they would
egg each other on. It had become a fashion with them to be
Hellene.

We started out when the Queen was giving audience. No

one noticed. I knew better by now than to keep our spears and tackle in Eleusis. They were in a cave on a mountain farm. Up there we rested from our long climb, and the herdboy's brother, who had been watching the quarry, gave us his news. Pylas' party had bayed Phaia already; but she had broken through them, after killing two dogs and laying a man's leg open. Rain had laid the scent; and the boy, to keep her for us, had sent the Megarians on a fool's chase round the hill. She was still where she had gone to ground.

Rain hung about the hills; under dark-blue clouds the mountainside looked black and lowering. Down beyond it, far below and away, lay the plain and shore of Eleusis washed with pale sun. It was as if the dark came with us. One of the Guard, who was small and swarthy and Minyan all through, said, "Perhaps the Goddess is angry."

I looked at the dark scrub and tumbled rocks, under the brooding clouds, and shivered. The Mother at Eleusis is not like the Mother at Troizen. But I was a Hellene; I had pledged myself before all my men; if I turned back now I would be better dead. "The Lady shall have her share," I said, "along with Apollo." As I named the god, a patch of sun swept across the hillside.

In a tumble of great rocks from an old slide, leaning together with young trees growing in them, was the she-boar's lair.

We put up the nets as best we could. They were not very well staked, because there was rock under the earth. When they were in place, we slipped the dogs; they were mad to go, but not so eager to stay. They began to tumble out from the rocks, baying and belling. More came; and in their midst what seemed a great black boulder spewed out of the mountain. Then I saw it was alive.

I had thought, "Well, a boar-sow can only be so big." I was well paid for being cocksure. The males we had hunted at home were piglings to her. She was like something left from the world of Titans and earthborn giants, living on in a lonely cleft of the hills. Only she was not old. The great curved tusks in her long black mask looked white and fresh,

where they were not bloody. I had thought too slightly of
the Megarians; they had not been afraid for nothing.

"What have I got myself into?" I thought. "Death in front
of me, and shame behind. Death that way too, if my own
men despise me." I heard their voices as they saw her better.
They were scared; they took her size for a portent.

She was in the nets now, wallowing and heaving. I started
forward to take my one good chance. Next instant the stakes
pulled out of the ground, and she came on dragging the
whole tangle, full of dogs, behind her. If I did not stop her
now, she would be in among the Companions. But I could
never stop her. I had not got the weight.

There was a tall rock near by, with a flat side facing toward her. It showed me my last hope. She was at pause,
confused by the nets about her. They would slow her charge,
with luck. I vaulted over on my spear, and set my back
against the rock, and levelled the spear point. The movement drew her eye; she came straight at me.

She stumbled once on the way. Even so, it took all my
strength to check her rush just enough, and keep my spear
from breaking. It entered her breast just below the shoulder.
I had set its butt to the stone behind me. It was her own
might, not mine, that drove it into her. But it was I who
had to hold on.

She hated men. As she thrust and jerked and squealed, I
knew it was not her own life she fought for; it was mine.
Fixed by my slender shaft to this huge force of earth, I felt
as light as grass; I was beaten and bruised upon the rock
behind me, as if the very mountain were trying to kill me on
her breast like a pricking gnat. All the time I was waiting for
the spear to crack. Then when I was braced to the thrust
she pulled instead, so that my arm nearly sprang from its
socket. I knew I was nearly done; and then she thrust again.
It must have changed the line of the spear head. One more
great writhe and wallow she gave, that ground the spear butt
upon the rock; but it was her death-throe.

I stood and panted, too spent at first to feel or know anything. When I leaned on the rock, my blood stuck to it like

birdlime. Then, it seemed from far away, I heard the cheers of the Companions; and, though my feet would hardly hold me up, my life quickened within me. I felt like a man who has done what a god willed for him; free and shining, and full of luck.

The Companions rushed forward. Forgetting themselves, they shouted, "Boy! Boy!" and tossed me in the air. "Boy" I minded no longer; but my grazes hurt. Soon seeing the blood, they put me down, and shouted to each other for oil, which no one had brought, and blamed each other and bickered. I said, "Sow's fat will do," but a man on the hill-side just above said, "I have some oil. You are welcome."

I saw a Hellene warrior, about twenty-eight years old. His yellow hair was plaited and clubbed for hunting; his beard was trimmed and his upper lip shaved clean, and he had light-gray eyes, bright and quick. Behind him followed a youth with boar-spears, and a troop of hunters. I thanked him, and asked him for form's sake if he was Pylas son of Nisos, though I knew he was. It was all over him.

"Yes," he said. "You have robbed me of my quarry, lad, but the sight was cheap at the price. I think you are this year's Kerkyon, who came by way of the Isthmus."

I told him yes, and he looked half sorry to hear it, which already seemed strange after Eleusis. As for his calling me lad, one cannot in reason expect the heir of a Hellene king-dom to treat a year-king like royalty.

"Yes," I said. "I am Kerkyon, but my name is Theseus. I am a Hellene."

"So it seems," he said, looking at the she-boar; and called his spear-bearer to oil my back. I was glad to find him a gentleman, seeing he was my cousin.

Meantime there was a crowd round the quarry, and I could hear some of my boys taunting the Megarians. This could make trouble in no time, between men lately at war. I signed to them to stop, but they were too pleased with themselves. Just as I was going over, Pylas said, "You have a prize to claim from my father; a tripod and an ox."

In all the to-do I had even forgotten this, though it was

what I had been after. Nothing could have been better.
"Listen!" I called. "Here's a man who doesn't know what
meanness is. Though he missed the kill, he is reminding us
to claim the prize." They sobered down then, ashamed to
keep it up. I said, "The ox shall be our victory feast, for the
quarry belongs to the Lady and to Apollo. We will roast it
here, and ask these warriors to eat it with us." Pylas looked
like a man who could take a joke, so I said to him apart,
"Pig-meat is forbidden them; but an ox from Megara always
eats sweet." He laughed and clapped me on the shoulder.
Somewhere in the rocks there were piglings squeaking. "By
Zeus!" I said, "I forgot her litter. If your father cares for
sucking pig, take him these with my greetings." He sent a
man in among the rocks. The litter was four sows and seven
boars; so we had saved the people of those parts some
trouble.

They set about skinning the sow. Afterwards I had a good
war helm made of her skin and teeth; the leather worked
well, pliant and strong. Before the skinning was done, Pylas'
men came back with the prize. They brought wood too for
the roasting, and to burn the sacrifice. I saw him stare when
my Minyans offered to Apollo; but that was a custom of the
Guard these days. They thought well of a god who protects
men from the wrath of goddesses, and can hold off the
Daughters of Night. I had never brought them to think much
of Poseidon. In Eleusis the Mother's husbands, like the
Queen's, are of small account.

All this had brought us on to the time when shadows
lengthen. The clouds had cleared, and a sunlight like golden
wine lay on the mountains. I said to Pylas, "One can't travel
these hills in darkness; yet what a pity to throw down such
a feast as this like men upon the march. Why not find a
hollow out of the wind, and some brush to sleep on? Then
we can sing and tell tales till midnight."

His bright gray eyes opened wide. Then he looked as if he
was going to laugh. But he wiped it from his face, and said
courteously that nothing could be better. I turned to my
troop; and saw them all in a huddle. Bias came up and

muttered in my ear. "Theseus. Isn't that going too far?"
"How so?" I said. He whispered, "Surely you know the King
never sleeps out."

I had not given it a thought, I had been so pleased to be
living again like a man among men. For nothing on earth
would I excuse myself now to Pylas, and be the mock of his
Hellenes. "There is a first time," I said, "for everything." He
took a deep breath. "Don't you see? As it is you have put
your life in hazard, after Madam said not. And you have
killed a she-pig. And now, if you sleep out, she will think
you're with a woman."

He meant well, but it had gone far enough. "Those are
things for man and wife to settle between them. You have
spoken, Bias, and I have listened. Now go and help the
others."

The spits were fixed, the tinder kindled. Evening fell, and
the hollow was filled with firelight as an offering bowl with
wine. Wine indeed was all we lacked; when lo, men came
up from a village below, with a whole skin of it, to thank us
for killing Phaia. They stared at the trophy, and I thought,
"By dark the news will be in Eleusis. Well, in for a calf, in
for a cow."

The meat was done, and our teeth were sharp for it. Pylas
shared with me his cup of horn rimmed with gold; the rest
tipped the wineskin. Everyone sang, Hellenes and Minyans
picking up each other's refrains. My lads were first con-
strained, then wild; Hellenes for tonight, but in awe of the
morrow. I had thoughts of it myself.

As the noise grew loud, Pylas and I moved up together.
It was a time for talk. For this I had killed Phaia. Yet I felt
my youth more now than when she was on my spear. Often
at Troizen I had helped my grandfather entertain such men.
I had made myself civil in Hall; told the harper what to
compliment them on, or sung to them myself; taken them
hunting, to see they got good sport without being killed;
and seen them off with their guest gifts, after they came
down from the upper room with their business over. I had
been a lad on the fringe of men's affairs. While I was think-

ing this, I heard a Megarian mutter, "As the Queen gets older, the kings get younger. Now here is one with no beard."

This did me a good turn. For Pylas, being a gentleman and fearing I had heard, asked me to relate how I killed Skiron. It was half my work done for me.

After the songs had begun again, we were still speaking of the Isthmus. I said, "I fought my way through alive, and that's one man's work there. But by now someone else is working Skiron's bit of road. So it will be, till the place is swept clean end to end. Not one man's work, nor one kingdom's either." The singing was loud; the wine had just been round again. I said, "Two might do it."

I saw his eyes shine. But he was shrewd, and had lived ten good years longer in the world than I. "That would be a war! But would it tempt the Eleusinians? What about their sea trade, if the road were open?" I shook my head; I had given this thought. "The road runs through Eleusis too. It would bring them trade when winter closes the seaways. Besides," I said smiling, "their cattle might fatten in peace, if the Megarians kept theirs."

He laughed. I saw he was listening man to man. But I would soon lose him, if I sounded too simple or too rash. I said, "Your father would need to treat with Xanthos, the Queen's brother, not with me. But everyone knows in Eleusis that he fights for what he can carry away. Tell him the robbers' holds are stuffed with booty. That will make him listen."

Pylas passed me his drinking horn. Presently he said, "You have thought this out well, Theseus. Tell me, how old are you?" I said, "Nineteen." I almost believed it myself by now. He looked at me, and began laughing into his beard. "What have they done in Eleusis? They set traps for deer and got a leopard. Don't they know it yet? Tell me, lad, why are you doing this? What will it be to you, this time next year?"

"When you die, Pylas," I said, "they will make a tomb for you, lined with dressed stone. They will put your ring on your finger and your sword in your hands; your best spear they will give you, and your offering cup, and the cup you drink from in Hall. After a hundred years, when the ring lies loose on bone, old men will say to their grandsons, 'That is the tomb of Pylas son of Nisos, and these were his deeds.' And the child will tell his grandson, who will tell his. But in Eleusis dead kings are dug into the fields like horse dung, and have no names. If I don't write my epitaph, who will?"

He nodded, and said, "That is a good reason." But still he looked at me, and I knew what he was going to say.

"Theseus, I have lived near thirty years hard by Eleusis. I know how a man looks who foreknows his end. It is in the blood of the Earthlings; they go to it like birds before whose eyes the snake is dancing. But if she dances for the leopard, the leopard jumps first."

He was shrewd; I should have been a fool to lie to him. I said, "Where I come from, it is the consent that binds a man." Then I said, "But I might meet it in battle. Who wants to live on without a name?"

"Not you, that is clear. But with leaven like you working in the lump, the custom might alter in Eleusis. There are tales of such things, in our fathers' days."

His words waked thoughts that had lain sleeping in my heart. Now after my victory new things seemed possible, and I was too young to hide it. As I looked into the core of the fire he said, "Yes, and we might find you a restless neighbor."

I liked his frankness. We understood each other. "This is your father's ox we are eating," I said, "and my prize. I don't know which is host or guest, but we are hearth-friends either way." He scanned my face with one of his sharp bright looks; then he took my hand and gripped it.

The fire crumbled; the ashes grew red and gray with a few sparks of gold; the dogs mumbled their bones full-bellied. As it grew quiet, we leaned and fell to whispering; I could see more than one of my Minyans lying awake to watch if he would make love to me. We agreed together to press for war that autumn rather than wait for spring; like me, he was one to decide on a thing and do it. "Ask your father," I said, "to say he has heard that Kerkyon knows his way across the Isthmus. My young men won't like to be a rear guard." He laughed and promised. Then we slept; I on my face, because my back was sore. Next morning when we all set off home, he gave me his gold-rimmed cup as a guest gift. The Companions stared, and wondered if they had stayed awake long enough.

It was a little after noon when we got back to Eleusis. I saw the people looking out for us; they cheered the boar-mask, which two men carried on spears. I had had enough of hiding my doings like a naughty boy.

The Palace day room was empty of her, but only just. The chief nurse was still there with the children, and the shuttle swung from the loom. When I went upstairs, the chamber door was bolted.

I walked off with my face on fire. I was too young to take it easily. I thought it would be all over the kingdom that my wife could put me out like a slave. When I had knocked the second time, I had heard a maid giggle within; and two servants passed as I turned away, wiping smiles off their faces. She did not treat me so lightly when we were in bed.

Before me were the stairs that went up to the roof. I ran up them, and looked down to the royal terrace. It was not very far; and there was no one about but a woman far off drying clothes. I slid between the teeth of the battlements, hung, and let go. From a boy I had known how to fall lightly.

I landed on my feet, and wrenched my ankle a little; not enough to lame me, but it hurt, and sharpened my anger. I ran to the window of the bedchamber, threw wide the curtains, and found her in her bath.

For a moment, it put me in mind of my mother's room ten years back; the girl with hairpins and comb, the dress spread on the bed, the scented steam rising from the glazed red clay. My mother was whiter, and her scent more fresh and springlike; she had been younger, but I did not think of that. I heard the Queen's breath hiss, and I saw her face.

Once in my boyhood, when my tutor had a beating stored for me, I came in by chance before he looked for it, and caught him getting his face slapped by a Palace girl. The beating was a hard one. Now too I came before my time; there was a diadem put out for her higher than the one she wore every day. She stared at me, knees up in the bath, her face unpainted and wet with steam, one foot stuck out while the nails were pared. I saw she would make me pay for it.

She snatched her foot back, making the maid drop the knife. "Go out," she said, "and wait. We are not ready." I might have been a servant. It was all I needed. "It is no matter, Madam," I said, "that you were not there to welcome me. Something prevented you. We will say no more of it." And I sat down on the bed. There was a stir and flutter among the women. But I saw from their quiet they were afraid of her. In my mother's room, it would have been like a pigeon loft when the cat gets in.

She sat bolt upright in the bath. I picked up her purple bodice, and looked at the embroidery. "Fine work, Madam," I said. "Is it your own?" She signed to one of the women, who wrapped her in white linen as she stood up. "What is this insolence? Have your senses left you? Get up, and go." I glanced at the maids and answered, "We will talk, Madam, when we are alone. Let us remember who we are."

Suddenly she rushed toward me, the linen clutched about her, her red hair streaming. I can't remember all she called me: barbarian horsebreaker, son of cattle thieves, northern lout, a savage not fit to live indoors. The women shrank together like scared sheep, near to the door. I jumped up, shouted "Out!" and while their mouths were still gaping pushed them through it. Then I shot the bolt.

I went quickly back to her and grasped her elbows, holding her hands well back from my eyes. "Lady," I said, "I never yet beat a woman; but I never saw one so forget herself. It is not for my honor to let my wife abuse me like a thief. Be quiet, and don't force me to correct you. That would be no pleasure to either of us."

For a moment she stood all stiff between my hands. Then her mouth opened. I had known there must be guards in call. But it was that or let her be my master.

When her eyes looked past me, I set my hand across her mouth. She tried to bite me, but I kept it there. She was strong for a woman. As we swayed struggling, we tripped on the bath, and overturned it as we fell. There we lay in a wet welter on the checkered floor, among scents of spilled oils and unguents and broken jars from the bath stool. The linen sheet, which had not been girdled onto her, grew heavy with warm water and dragged away. "For once in this room," I thought, "it shall be a man who says when." In that same moment, I felt a pain in my shoulder like a bee-sting. She had caught up the dropped paring knife. It was not very long, but long enough, I think, to have touched the heart, only I moved and spoilt her aim.

Blood spread on the wet linen in great blots of scarlet. But I kept my hand over her mouth. "Think before you call," I said. "Your guards are beyond the door; my dagger is here. If you send me below before my time, by Zeus you shall come with me."

I gave her a moment more to think, and then let go. She drew a great breath—I suppose I had nearly choked her— then she turned her face against the bloody linen, and shook all over with weeping.

I was too young to have expected it. For a while I lay beside her staring like a fool, and could think of nothing better to do than pull out a broken crock from under her back, lest it should cut her, while my blood splashed down upon her breast. I wiped it off with the linen, and managed to stop the flow a little. Then I picked her up out of the mess and water, and carried her to bed.

After a while, one of the women scratched on the door, and asked if the Queen wanted anything. "Yes," I said, "bring us some wine." When it came I took it in; and after that we did not get up till lamp-lighting. It might have been longer, but she said the place must be cleared up before night. I must own it looked as if conquering troops had sacked it.

After this there was a time of quiet in Eleusis. I set myself to please her; once I had shown I was no one's dog, I had no wish for strife. I slept no more away, and indeed had no call to wander. There were one or two of her girls who looked aslant in corners, now they thought they knew I had a roving eye; but I looked away. Sometimes I saw the woman who had wept for Kerkyon. She was a bath-pourer; but when she came to wait on me I used to call someone else. A look of hate strikes cold when one is naked.

We had had the first touch of morning frost, when heralds came from the King of Megara, calling for the Eleusinians to help him purge the Isthmus. The terms were those I had agreed on with Pylas: no more cattle raids, a fair share of the spoils, and free passage through either kingdom for the other's traffic, when the road was open.

Xanthos called a war council, on the plain by the shore. This was the only men's assembly the law of the land allowed. I came with my Guard, and led them to the accustomed place. I had told them to make a good entry, bold without swagger, which, as I see it, is the mark of a man who conceives his courage could be doubted. The warriors seemed to approve their style.

The Megarian herald spoke, putting in those arguments which are not graceful for kings to write in letters. The council was quite orderly. They had picked up from the Hellenes the use of the scepter, and I saw no one speak without it. Before long they had agreed on war; but the older men were for waiting until spring.

This was all very well, for people with the rest of their lives before them. I stood up, and held out my hand for the gold-bossed staff. "In winter," I said, "men eat up the summer's wealth. Why should these misbegotten thieves feast through a season on fat livestock that might be ours? With captive girls warming their beds who would be glad enough to change masters?" The young men liked this, and cheered. "Besides," I said, "over so long, they will get wind of our coming. It will give them time to make their towers strong, and dig their gold into the ground. We should lose the richest of the booty, that at the best." They all saw sense in this; Xanthos too had listened. He reminded the men we should be in two days' march from home with no sea crossing, and gave his casting vote for war in autumn.

The Megarian herald then proposed that Kerkyon, who had done things in the Isthmus, should lead the vanguard. I kept my eye on Xanthos, from whom I looked for some hindrance or other; I thought he might not like the noise. But when he could be heard, he said very civilly that there could be nothing against it.

I felt well pleased with myself. I had thought I should have my work cut out with him. Once or twice, since the tussle in the marriage chamber, I had caught his eye on me. I thought my eloquence had won him over. A boy is youngest when he thinks himself a man.

3.

WHICH of youth's pleasures can compare with the making ready for one's first big war? One's spear shaft oiled and tried, one's sword and dagger and spear blade ground sharp enough to cut hairs with, one's chariot polished till one can see one's face in it, one's leather sweet with beeswax; thinking, as one goes about, of tricky thrusts and guards, or trying them out with a friend; visiting the stable three times a day to look at one's horses. I had wondered what I should do for a charioteer, but Xanthos had found me one. Before I came, his pair had been the only Hellene horses in Eleusis. I was pleased to find him so helpful.

The evening before we marched, I walked upon the Lower Terrace, and looked out across the wrestling ground to the mountains of Attica, fading into the dim eastern sky. Standing there in the dusk, with the Companions not far away, I thought of those who claimed to love me, and whether there was one to whom I dared say, "If I fall in battle, take my sword to Athens and give it to the King." But there was none I dared trust so far. "Better so," I thought. "Hope never hurt men yet, so why should I send him grief?" So I went back to the others, and joined in the laughing and horseplay. Their keenness was good to see.

The Queen rose early that night from supper. When I followed her up, not many words were spoken; but we did not forget there were lonely nights ahead. After our last embrace, it touched me to feel her eyelids wet. I told her to keep that for my death day, and not to go before the gods.

The trumpet woke me too soon, and the shouts of men assembling. I got up to arm myself, while she lay watching with half-shut eyes. The civetskin cover with its purple lining lay heaped on the painted floor. Her hair looked as dark as red porphyry in the glimmer of daybreak.

I strapped on my loin-guard and clipped my greaves, and put on a white quilted tunic, for the air was frosty. I wore my armbands too and my royal necklace; I have never cared to go into battle looking like a man who would rather not be singled out. When I had put up my hair, I fitted on my new helmet made of Phaia's hide, and looked at her smiling, to remind her how we had made up our quarrel. But she only lay still and heavy, her mouth smiling without her eyes. The window lightened; the white bird whistled softly, and said, "Kiss me again."

From the Great Court out of sight I heard my chariot clattering from the stables. As I turned to pick up my shield, I thought within myself, "Why be angry? I am a wolf in a dog-pack here. A Minyan would not be angry. Among the Earthlings, no man would hope to be higher than I am lifted. Men come and go, they say, but the belly carries the child. I should know no good to strive for beyond this, to be chosen for the Mother, to quicken a woman and to die; I should not ask to outlive the height of my fortune. Why am I angry, then? Is it because I am a Hellene that the blood about my heart says to me, 'There is something more'? Yet what it is I do not know, nor whether there is a name for it. It may be there is some harper, the son and the son's son of bards, who knows the word. I only feel it about my heart; it is a brightness, and it is a pain."

But as everyone knows, it is neither good nor wise for a

man to go off to war bad friends with his wife, and least of all for a king. So I did not ask why she lay there, when she should have been dressed to see me off. I bent to kiss her; she lifted her head like a wave drawn up by the spring moon, and her mouth as if of itself took hold of mine; then she sank down again without a word. I paused; it was in my heart to ask her if she had conceived by me; but I did not know if her silence was sacred, and unlucky to break. So I said nothing, and went away.

Across the border we joined with the Megarians, and marched to the end of the guarded road. After that it passed on into the Isthmus, where no one mended it, and the weeds grew over; and instead of the guard-towers that stand where a king's law runs, there were only the holds of the robbers, squatting in the rocks above. Some were nameless, some had both name and fame. The first of these was the castle of Sinis.

It stood on a pine-grown hillside, a square tower built by Titans, no man knows when, of gray-black limestone. Sinis had made his den in it, as the hyena does in an old burned city. Its walls were steep; we needed ladders and ramps to take it. When we came to hew the pines, we found that the tales were true. Tied into them were pieces of men's bodies, sometimes a limb, sometimes a trunk. It had been his custom to bend down two strong saplings, bind the man between them, and let them fly asunder. The ropes were still on the trunks, some of them great trees now, forty feet high; he had been at the game for years. And, in case you wonder whether some god he served demanded such a sacrifice, I may say he did it for pleasure, and had never pretended anything else.

We took the tower on the third day. He had not enclosed the spring within the walls, so sure of himself he had grown, offering victims to himself in his accursed grove. He fought in his courtyard like a cornered rat, after we had stove the gate in; and it was thanks to me we took him alive, for I remembered his face in the ambush, when I passed through before.

What we could get down from the trees, we gave a decent funeral; but there were things we could not reach, besides what the ravens must have carried off. The wood was alive at evening, like a cave of bats, with souls of unburied men keeking and flittering. We gave them what they were thirsty for. When he saw the saplings bent for him, he did not even face the reckoning like a man; he knew something of pain, who had made it so long his study. He should have been left to hang, as those others had, till life bled out of him. But when he did not die, and the greater part of him hung aloft crying, it made me feel sick, not having a stomach as strong as his had been. I was ashamed to let anyone see me give an enemy the best of the bargain, so I put my young men to shoot at him for sport. Before long a bad shot finished him. We had dispatched his men already. When we had taken his stuff and the women from the castle, we set fire to the grove. The beard of the flame hid the hilltop from us; and the smoke was seen at Eleusis.

We camped to windward of it, and then it was time to divide the spoil. Xanthos and Pylas split it fairly, as they were bound to; but when Xanthos came to give out our half, the share my young men got was more than mean; it was a slight to my standing. I should have liked to tell him what I thought of him; but though his troops did not love him much, at least they knew him, and I was a stranger. So I said to the Guard, for everyone to hear, "This is what Xanthos thinks of the way you fought today. Well, a War Leader, who has everything to see to, can't be everywhere at once. Perhaps he was not watching you as I was. But I will show you what I think myself." And I divided all my own share among them, not keeping as much as a girl to lie that night with, only the arms of the men I had killed with my own hand. They were much pleased, and Xanthos not at all; so both sides got what they deserved.

In three or four more days of war all the big holds were cleaned out and burned; but there were many small bands left, whose lairs were in caves and rock-clefts. I remembered, and showed the others, their marks beside the road, a cairn, or a rag tied to a thorn-bush, marking off their run for the next troop to see. And now the peasants, who had lived in dread of them and had to feed them when travellers failed, began to trust in our strength and tell us where they were. Then we would beat the coverts, or smoke them out.

Between two such hunts, the army was moving on along the road, up where it skirts the cliffs. I was leading in my chariot, going at a walk with my Guard behind me. Suddenly there was a great rattling and thudding on the hillside above, and down came two or three great stones, as big as your head. They were coming straight for me, but glanced off a ridge and struck the road in front, leaving deep dents in it and bounding on over the cliffs. My horses reared, and laid back their ears. I could feel them getting away from the charioteer, who ought to have held them since he was bigger than I, and grabbed the reins from his hands. Two of my lads risked hard knocks to run up and hold their heads, and among us we got them quiet. As for the driver, though we had had to carry him, there was no use in getting too angry, seeing there was no one else. Shore People are not much good with horses. Besides, he had had his lesson when he saw over the cliff ahead; it turned him white, and his teeth were rattling. Dexios and Skiron had died thereabouts.

Some of my young men ran up the hill, to see if there were robbers lying up there. Xanthos, who was not far behind, sent a party too. They all returned having met no one but each other. I said, "There are angry ghosts about here. Dexios did not have his offerings; and Skiron was not buried at all. We had better see to him, rather than have him killing wayfarers." His bones were still on the tortoise rock, picked raw by birds; with some trouble we got them up and buried them, and performed the rites for Dexios. I had more cause today than most days to wish him alive.

Even without its robbers, the Isthmus Road is steep and dangerous. Its army of dead men needed to be appeased, and Earth-Shaker entreated too to touch it lightly. That was why I put up his great altar afterwards on the neck of the

Isthmus, and founded his Games. As to why I chose that spot, I had good reason.

We came to it next day. Already we could see the stronghold of Corinth topping its blunt mountain, with smoke rising from the Mother's sanctuary upon the crown. And, just when we were thinking our work as good as over, we found a pitched battle lay before us.

The Isthmus is wild country, a gift to those who know it. More of our quarry than we guessed had slipped through our nets. Here they all were, their old feuds forgotten, their backs to the wall. For behind them were the lands of law, the kingdoms of the Isle of Pelops, where they had committed incest or parricide, murdered their hosts or guests, forced sacred virgins, robbed the gods' treasuries or the graves of kings. For such things as that, not some mere killing that a blood-price can settle and Apollo make one free of, a man would go to the Isthmus. Here, driven from their hillsides, in that same plain where now men hold the foot race before the god, and box and wrestle and cheer the chariots at the turn, their force awaited us, dark and bristling like the boar started from the covert who gathers his feet to charge.

We drew up our battle in a sickle shape, to hem them in. The Megarians took the center, because they had many chariots; I led the left flank of the Eleusinians, and Xanthos the right. It meant I was leading some of the men's army, as well as my own Guard, and I was pleased no one seemed unwilling. Though I had had my share of war, this was my first set battlefield. I daresay I could not have made more of it in my heart if we had been meeting the host of some great city, Hazor or Troy.

The day was clear, the air still fresh with morning. Birds sang in the stone pines on the heights above. As I stood in my chariot I saw stretching before me the shadow of my helmet plume and my ash-wood spear. Behind me the talk of my young men sounded as it ought before the battle, light, fierce, and gay. The smell of dust and horses was in my nostrils, the smell of oiled wood and leather and new-scoured bronze.

"When I give the word," I said to my driver, "drive well into them. Don't wait for the footmen; it's for us to clear the way. Is your knife ready, to cut the traces if a horse should fall?" He showed it me; but I wished again for Dexios. He did not look like a man whose heart was in it.

At Pylas' signal, we paced forward at a walk, as the he-cat does first before he springs. When we could see their teeth and eyes, we paused to make ready, and I gave my men the speech I had prepared. I had got it, to tell the truth, mostly from old battle songs, thinking I could not do better than the bards and heroes. "When the trumpet sounds, and we raise the war cry, charge like the hawk plunging on the heron, whom nothing can turn once he is launched in flight. We know each other; neither sword, nor spear, nor arrow can hurt us half so much as dishonor in each other's eyes. Blue-Haired Poseidon! Breaker of ships and cities! Bear us to victory! Before fall of sunset, put their necks under our feet and fill their mouths with dust!"

The warriors cheered; the trumpet split the shining air. I gave them the pitch of the paean, and the charioteer leaned forward. Two of my boldest lads, who were sworn lovers, took hold of the chariot either side, unwilling I should clear a path before them. My ears were full of good sounds, the clatter of chariots, the high yell of war cries, arms and shields rattling, the drumming of feet and hooves, shouts of challenge as men picked out an enemy. I marked out for myself a tall fellow giving orders, whose fall seemed likely to discomfort the rest. As the chariot bounced over stones and tussocks, I fixed my eyes on him and called to him to wait for me.

The line of faces rushed upon me, grinning or scowling or stiff-set; the chariot cut the press like a sharp-prowed ship thrust down the slipway into a dark sea. Then, all at once, it was as if earth hurled me from its breast. I felt myself pitched sidelong from the chariot, clean over the rail, upon some man who grunted and was hurled with me to the ground. My spear flew from my hand; my shield arm caught in the shield was nearly wrenched from the socket; the chin strap of my helmet burst, and my head was bare. I and the man below me writhed together, half stunned upon the ground. It was his foul smell that warned me he was none of mine. I came to myself just in time, and groped for my dagger and drove it into him. He sank back; I got my shield again and struggled to rise. Before I reached my knees, a dying man fell on me. This time I knew him. He was one of the boys who had charged beside my wheels. A spear blade had driven between his teeth and pierced his skull; as I got out from under him he gave his death-gasp. He had stopped a thrust on its way to me.

I found my feet, and my sword. In the press ahead the frightened horses thrashed and reared, dragging the chariot splintering on its side. One wheel was gone; the tilted axle-tree plowed the earth. Flat on the ground the charioteer lay with his white robe grimed and torn. There was no time to look again. I threw up my shield to ward a down-cut from my head.

For a moment, I seemed all alone among enemies. Then my head cleared and I knew the shouting voices round me. The Companions were all about and still coming up, yelling to each other like a pack of hounds after wild pig. I heard my name. A hand was waving my helmet; another snatched it and set it on my head. I gave the paean to let all the rest know I was alive, and we pressed forward.

I have never loved better any warriors serving under me then these, my first command. They were men of another country, of different blood; at first we had barely known each other's language, and now we no longer needed it; we knew each other's mind as brothers do for whom a look or a laugh is enough. In the year of the Games, when I make the sacrifice, I remember always that my life from that day forward has been their gift.

By noon the battle was over. We took no prisoners. They had fed the dogs and kites on many better men; it was their turn to be host. The day's surprise was the booty we took

after. Some had their own, others must have found the
hoards of their fallen masters. We set a guard on it, of
trustworthy men from all three forces, with barons of each
kingdom to count it over.

The warriors drew together, as men do after battle, to
dress each other's hurts, and rest, and talk. My men and
I were sitting round a spring which rose among some rocks;
some were drinking the good water, others had stripped to
wash in the stream where it flowed away. One man was
badly wounded, his leg broken with a spear; I had been
setting it, for want of anyone better, between two javelin
shafts, and praising his deeds to take his mind off the pain.
Someone called out to me. I saw Pallans, who had run
beside my chariot; he was the one left alive. I had missed
him, and thought he would be watching by the death-pyre.
But it was a living man he dragged toward us, dressed in
dirty white. I jumped to my feet; it was my charioteer.

"Why, greeting, Rizon," I said. "I thought you were dead
when I saw you fallen. Where are you hurt?"

Pallans thrust his flat hand into his back, so that he fell
forward. "Hurt! Look him over, Theseus. I will give him
a sheep for any hurt he has. I've looked for this man since
the battle ended; I watched what happened when your
wheel came off. *You* fell headlong; it took you by surprise.
But this fellow knew which side to hold. I swear his head
never touched the ground; he was shamming stunned till
the fight passed by him."

I looked at him as he grovelled, and saw his face. In
the glow of victory, and the pride of my men's courage, I
had been in love with all the world; now my heart felt a
chill of darkness. I thought, "This is a coward. Yet he chose
to drive a battle chariot leading the vanguard. Why?" Presently I said, "Let us go and see."

My men went back with me to the field. Already the car-
rion birds were settling, tearing the dried-up wounds, and
there was a buzzing of flies, mixed with the murmur and
groaning of men half gone. Here and there our men were
stripping the bodies of anything they had left. In the midst,

like a wrecked ship driven aground, lay the chariot with a dead horse beside it. The bronze wheel was lying a few yards off. I said to the men beside me, "Lift up the axle-tree."

They raised the end from the ground, and I looked at the hole for the linchpin. It was clogged with earth; but when I picked down with my dagger, I found what I sought. I rolled it between my fingers, and showed it to the others. It was wax. The linchpin had been made of it.

They exclaimed, and felt at it, and asked me how I had guessed. "There's an old song about it at home," I said. "They shouldn't have tried it on a man from Pelops' country. Well, Rizon?" But he stared at the ground trembling, and said no word.

"Tell me," I said, "why you did this. You have nothing now to lose." But he looked sick and said nothing. "Come, Rizon. Have I ever raised my hand to you, or hurt your standing? Did you go short when the booty was shared? Have I killed any kin of yours, lain with your wife or your handmaid? What harm have I done you, to make you wish me dead?"

When he did not answer, Pallans said, "Why lose time, Theseus? We have seen enough." Then when they began to lay hands on him, he fell down crying, "Have mercy, Kerkyon! I did not choose to do it. I never hated you. It was Xanthos threatened me. I did it for my life's sake. He put me in fear."

At this they all sucked in their breath through their teeth. They felt more awe than anger, because I belonged to the Goddess, and had not reigned a fourth part of my time.

"But," I said, "why not have brought this to me, if you did not hate me? Have I got such a name for forgetting my friends?" But he only said, "He put me in fear." Then he fell down again, and begged for his life.

My men were watching me. I had been well content beside the spring, in our proved fellowship, thinking I had found the only secret of kingship. But one cannot be a boy for ever.

"You are asking too much," I said. "Just now you tried to kill me, because you feared Xanthos more than me. You have been my teacher. If anyone here has used his spear through the battle, and kept his sword-edge sharp, bring me the sword." When they brought one, I said, "Put his neck across the yoke-pole, and hold him by the knees and by the hair." They did so, and I no longer had to see his face. I swung the sword high, and it struck through his neckbone and half his neck; so he died more easily than most men do, but for his fear.

After this we sacrificed to the gods, to give thanks for victory. The Eleusinians offered to their war god Enyalios, and I too gave him victims; it is never wise to neglect the gods of the place, wherever one may be. But I made my own altar to Poseidon; and that is where I built his precinct later.

We burned the dead. Pallans had put the corpse of Rizon under the feet of his dead friend; I saw why he had hunted the man down instead of mourning. Across the smoke of the pyre, I met the russet eyes of Xanthos watching me. But this was not the time.

They told me Pylas had been wounded in the battle, and I went to see him. He had his arm in a sling—the wound was in his shoulder—but was still giving orders. After we had talked, I took my leave of him, saying I was glad it was no worse. He looked at me with his bright gray eyes, and said, "I feel the touch of fate. You have a strong life-thread, Theseus. Where it crosses other men's it frays them. But that's as the Spinners spin it."

I was surprised at the time; but he must have had fore-knowledge, for his wound turned mortal, and he died of it in Megara. I was sad when I heard, to lose a sworn friend so soon. Yet if he had lived, the boundary-stone of Attica could not have stood where it does today, between the Isle of Pelops and the Isthmus.

Now dusk was falling. The smoldering altars were quenched with wine, and we gathered for the victory feasts. We had taken many fat cattle, and sheep, and goats. Already

the carcasses were turning on great spits above the pine-
wood fires, and the air was rich with the smell. But men's
eyes turned first to the open space in the middle, where the
booty was stacked up, ready to be shared. The cook-fires
lit it: cups and bowls and helmets and daggers, ingots of
copper and of tin, caldrons and tripods and good hide
shields. Beside them sat the women, muttering together, or
weeping, or hiding their faces in their hands, or looking
boldly about them to guess which man would be their lot
this time. A clear green dusk was falling, and Helios plumed
with rose-red and burning gold rode down into the wine-dark
sea. The evening star appeared, white as a maiden, trembling in the air that danced above the fires. A red glow shone
on the heaped treasure, on the eyes and teeth of the warriors, their worked sword-belts and polished arms.

I came down the slope, with my Companions behind me.
We were all cleaned and combed, with our weapons burnished. They had not asked me what I was going to do.
They followed me silent; only their footfalls told me when
they turned to look at one another.

Pylas was there already; he was too sick for the feast, but
would sit to watch the share-out, as anyone would who still
had breath in him, if he had Xanthos to deal with. I greeted
him, and looked about for my man. He was where I expected, standing over the spoil. He saw me coming, and
our eyes met.

"Greetings, Xanthos," I said. "You did me a good turn
in Eleusis; you found me a charioteer."

He said, "The man came to me. I did not know him."
Then I knew Rizon had not lied.

"Well," I said, "everyone knows you are a judge of men.
You found me a skilled fellow. Now he is dead, I don't know
where I shall find such another. He could turn his hand to
anything. He could make linchpins without bronze."

With the tail of my eye I could see a thousand faces
leaning nearer. The voices hushed, till you could hear the
hiss of the roasting meat. "It is folly," he said, "to listen
when a babbling coward is begging his life."

I said, "Yet if you did not listen, Xanthos, how did you know him so well?" He looked angry, and glancing at the lads behind me, said, "Young men are all talk."

If he had had any faith in his own good name, he would not have given them up so easily to a foreign man. But he knew he had lost their love; it was not hard for them to think him guilty. At his words they were angry, and shouted aloud.

I put up my hand for quiet. Then Bias, the eldest, came forward, and called out to the warriors, bearing witness to the waxen pin. "And," he said to them, "who loosened the rocks above the road, to scare the King's' horses over the cliff? One of you knows." There was muttering, as if some rumor had got about. I saw Xanthos' face go bright crimson with anger, in the way of red-haired men. He was cold, as a rule. Now he strode forward shouting.

"Can't you see, Eleusinians, what this man is at? He should know the ways of robbers, this thieving Hellene. So well he knows the Isthmus, perhaps he has lived there. Who can say what he did before he came to Eleusis? Now he thinks he can move you against the man who led you to victory, just when the spoil is to be shared."

I was on my toes to fly at him, but I held my hand. He had lost his head, and it helped me to keep mine. Raising my brows I said, "The mouth is near the heart," and even his own men laughed. Then I said, "This is my answer and the Eleusinians are witnesses. You have struck at me with other men's hands. Come out now, and use your own. Take up your spear and your shield, or, if you like, your sword. But first choose out your share of plunder, and put it aside. If you fall, I swear by Ever-Living Zeus I will not touch one piece of it, gold or bronze or girl. It shall be given out among your men by lot. And with my share the same, so that if I die my men will not be losers. Do you agree?"

He stared. It had come on him quicker than he looked for. Some of the Hellene barons cheered. Pylas moved his hand to quiet them, but it had set off the Companions, and they shouted, "Theseus!" At this all the rest stared; for it was against custom to give the King a name.

Xanthos hearing it cried out, "You young upstart! Attend to your own business that the Goddess chose you for, if you are fit to do it." To that I answered, "If she chose me, then why have you tried to cut me off out of my term? I call her to uphold my right." I had not heard the Minyan songs for nothing. I knew what the King must do if he is wronged. "Mother! Goddess! You raised me up, if only for a little while; you promised me glory in return for my length of days. Do not let scorn be put on me, but treat me like your son."

He saw then that he had no choice. A man does not call on these powers to witness a lie, and all the people knew it.

"Horsetamer," he said, "we have suffered you long enough. You have set yourself above your fate, and become an offense to the gods. They will punish us, if we do not stop your insolence. I accept your challenge, and the terms. Choose your prize, and if you fall your men shall share it. As for the weapons, let them be spears."

We chose our shares. I saw my boys laughing at his unwonted modesty. He did not want his men's wishes fighting for me. I took what I thought fair, not more or less. But it is the custom for Kerkyon to choose a woman first of all. His time is short, and the pleasure a man has had cannot be taken from him.

I went over to the captives, who had been stood up to be seen. There was a girl of about fifteen, tall and slender, with long pale hair falling about her face. I took her by the hand, and led her out. I had seen her eyes shining through her hair in the firelight; but now she looked down, and her hand was cold. Though there was no chance of her being a maiden, I thought of my mother setting out for the grove. I said to Xanthos, "If I die, see she is given to one man, and not made common sport of; we have got whores enough. She is a king's handmaid now; so treat her so."

We took our oaths before Pylas and the host, calling to witness the River, and the Daughters of Night. Then all men drew back, leaving a great space between the fires; and we took up our spears and shields. Pylas stood up, and said, "Begin."

I knew I should be slow; I was tired from the battle, and my wounds were stiffening; but it was the same for him. We circled once or twice, feinting with our spears. Beyond us I saw a great wall of faces red with firelight, floating on darkness and swaying with the fight. They were always in the tail of my eye, though I never looked at them; I remember nothing else so clearly.

I lunged at him, but he turned it aside; and I caught a thrust of his on my shield, but could not hold it long enough to get through his guard. We circled again, and gave each other glancing wounds, I on his shoulder, he on my knee. I had borrowed a long shield with a waist, because it was light; his was straight-sided, the kind they call man-covering. I wondered if he was fresh enough for the weight.

We circled and lunged, and the faces swung like a curtain in the wind. All this while, I was making up my mind to part with my spear. A throw is a gamble with one's life; it is suddener than a thrust and harder to parry; but if it fails, you are left with a three-foot sword against a seven-foot spear. Then you will be lucky to come well out of it.

I watched his eyes, which were like carnelians in the firelight, and let him see my side. He was quick, and nearly had me. I sprang back as if to save myself, and threw up my shield to mask my arm, and in the same moment threw. He must have known the trick; up went his shield and the spear blade pierced it. I had thrown so hard that half the blade went through the double bullhide, and stuck fast. He could not free the shield, and had to throw it away. But he had his spear still, against my sword.

He came for me, stabbing quickly here and there, and I turned the point with my shield or with my sword, which harmed the edge; but I could not hurt him, because he was out of sword-reach, and he was driving me backward. Something struck the earth close behind me, with a thud like a stone's. It happened again and I thought, "They are turning

from me at the last. I was always a stranger here." Then
as I fell back further, I saw what it was: a spear point-
downward, with the shaft ready to my hand. There were
three of them, here and there around me.

I stuck my sword into the ground, for want of time to
sheathe it, and snatched one up. Xanthos looked at me in
bitter anger; no one had tossed a shield to him. He was getting ready to throw, so I threw first. It sank between his
ribs, and he dropped his spear, and fell. As his helmet rolled
away, his long red hair tumbled unbound about him; and
I knew where I had seen such hair before.

His captains came round him, and one asked whether to
draw the spear out, for he was in pain. He said, "My soul
will go with it. Bring Kerkyon here."

I went over and stood before him. My anger had left me;
I saw his hurt was mortal. He said, "The oracle spoke true.
You are the chick of the cuckoo, sure enough." Now at the
last he looked puzzled, like a boy. He fingered the spear
that stood in his side, with the captain holding the shaft, and
said, "Why did they do it? What did they gain?" He meant
that they would have got my booty, if I had died. I said
to him, "Our ends are written from the beginning, and my
time too will come." He answered bitterly, "But mine is
now." Then I was silent, for it is a thing there is no answer to.

He looked long in my face. Presently I said, "How do you
want to be buried, and what shall we put in the tomb with
you?" He stared and said, "Do you mean to bury me, then?"
"Yes," I said, "why not? I have taken my due; the gods hate
a man who exceeds. Say what you want done." I thought he
had paused to think; but when he spoke he only said, "Men
cannot fight the Immortals. Pull out the spear." So the captain
drew it forth, and his soul went with it.

I had his body washed by the women, and laid on a bier,
with a guard against the beasts of prey. Of what he had on
I kept only his two swords; he had fought well, and was of
the royal kin. His share was portioned as we had agreed,
and his men saluted mé, when their lots were given them.
After that we feasted. Pylas left early, because of his wound,

and I did not stay drinking late; I wanted to take my chosen girl to bed, before my bruises stiffened again.

I found her good, and gently bred. A pirate had caught her on the shores of Kos, when she was gathering agate stones for a necklace and sold her in Corinth. Philona was her name. My wounds had stopped bleeding, but she would not lie down till she had dressed them. This was the first girl I had had of my own, and I thought I ought to show her from the beginning who was master; but in the end I let her have her way. Because of a promise I made her that night, I have still got her about my household, and have never lent her to a guest without her consent. Both her two eldest sons are mine, Itheus the shipmaster, and Engenes, who commands the Palace Guard.

BOOK THREE

ATHENS

1.

So I RODE a second time down the Isthmus Road to Eleusis, and the people stood on the roofs to see; but this time, not in silence.

I put the Companions to lead the march, and rode myself at the head of the men's army. The King of Megara had given me a riding horse, as a gift of honor. The Guard showed their trophies, and stepped out to the flutes, and sang. Behind us came the wagons of the spoil, the women and the herded cattle. Our tread was muffled in green boughs and flowers, flung down to us from the rooftops. At the hour when a man's shadow is twice as long as a man, we came to the ramp of the Citadel; and the Guard divided, to let me ride in first.

As I rode under the gate-tower black with people, the gates groaned open, and the watchman blew his horn. The flags of the Great Court stretched before me, and between the high walls my horse-hoofs echoed. Upon the roof, the Palace people were thick as winter bees; but they were quiet; no bright cloths hung from the windows. There was only a deep slanting sunlight; the toothed shadow of the roof-edge, clogged with shadows of heads; and on the broad steps between the painted columns, a woman in a wide stiff skirt and purple diadem, tall and unmoving, throwing like a column a long stiff shadow in the sun.

I dismounted at the stair foot, and they led my horse away. She stood waiting, putting no foot down the steps toward me. I went up till I stood before her, and saw her face like painted ivory, set with eyes of dark carnelian. On her shoulders, combed and plaited with threads of silver and

gold, hung the red hair I had seen mixed with blood and
dust upon the earth of the Isthmus.

I took her cold hand, and leaned toward her with the kiss
of greeting, for the people to see. But I did not touch her
with my lips; I would not add affront to the blood between
us. My mouth brushed the hair of her forehead, and she
uttered a set phrase of welcome, and we walked into the
Palace side by side.

When we were in the Hall, I said, "We must speak together alone. Let us go up; we can be quiet there." She
looked at me and I said, "Don't be afraid. I know what
is fitting."

The bedchamber was in shadow, except for a sunset shaft
against one wall. Some embroidery in white and purple was
laced upon a stand, and a lyre with gold bands lay in the
window. Against the wall stood the great bed, with its spread
of civet and purple.

"Madam," I said, "you know I have killed your brother.
Do you know why?"

She answered in a voice as empty as the shore, "Who can
give the lie to you, now he is dead?"

"What is the punishment," I said, "for killing the King out
of season?" I saw her lip whiten under her teeth. "Yet I killed
him in battle, and have brought him back for burial, because
I would not dishonor your kin. His men do not think I
wronged him. As you see, they let me lead them home."

She said, "What am I, then? The captive of your spear?"
Now anger warmed the paint upon her cheeks; I saw her
gilt-tipped breasts rise and fall. Yet at her words, my mind
turned from her to the girl Philona, the leavings of a pirate
and a thief, who had never lain with a man much better
than a beast, and was ignorant of all gentleness but what I
taught her. She had waked me from my first sleep with weeping, begging me not to sell her or pass her on.

"As always, Madam," I said, "you are the Queen."

"But now you are King, Hellene? Is that it?" I thought
that for a woman in mourning, more gravity and less sharp-
ness would have been seemly; but it was not for me to say

it. The last sunlight on the wall had turned rose-red; and in the wicker cage the white bird was making its feathers warm for sleep.

"There will be time later," I said, "to speak of that. Now I have blood on my hands you cannot cleanse me of, nor would it become me to ask it of you. When I am free of it, I will come back, and give the blood-price to his children."

In the falling dark she stared at me and said, "Back? From where?"

"From Athens," I said, hardly believing I could name it at last. "People say there is a temple of the Mother on the Citadel, and a shrine of Apollo with a holy spring. So I can be blood-cleansed both by the Sky Gods and the gods below. I shall ask the King to cleanse me."

There was a bracelet on her wrist, of a coiled gold snake. She tugged at it and said, "Athens now! Have you not done enough at Megara? Now you want to be hearth-friend of an Erechthid. A fine house to wash you clean! You had best take your water with you."

I had expected a different kind of anger from her. You would have thought I had put some slight on her, rather than killed her kinsman. "Don't you know," she said, "that his grandfather sacked Eleusis, killed the King untimely, and forced the Queen? Ever since then the Erechthids have lain under the Mother's curse. Why do you think Aigeus had to build her a shrine on his Acropolis, and send here for a priestess? And it will be a long while yet before he washes the curse away. That is the man you want to cleanse you! Wait till your young men, who think so much of you, hear where you are taking them!"

"A suppliant does not come with warriors. I shall go to Athens alone." She tugged again at the bracelet. She looked like a woman pulled two ways at once. "She is angry," I thought, "that I am going. Yet she wants to have me gone." She said, "I know nothing of this Apollo. When do you go?"

"When my courier brings his answer. Perhaps in two days, perhaps tomorrow." "Tomorrow!" she cried. "You came here at sunset, and the sun is not yet down." I answered, "The sooner away, the sooner returning."

She paced to the window, then back to me. I smelt the scent of her hair, and remembered how it had been to desire her. Then she turned to me like the cat who shows her sharp teeth and curled tongue. "You are a bold boy, Hellene. Aren't you afraid to put yourself into the hand of Aigeus, now he has seen what kind of neighbor you mean to be? He has fought for his slab of rock and his few fields between the mountains, like a wolf for its den; he has grown lean in war with his own kindred. Will you trust such a man, whom you never saw?"

"Yes," I said. "Why not? The suppliant is sacred."

The last dull stain of light was quenched upon the wall; hills were gray, only the highest peak was flushed like the breast of a maiden. The bird's feathers were as soft as wool, and its head was all hidden. As I looked to where already over Athens the night was falling, one of the Palace women came in softly, and turned back the great bed.

I was shocked at such unseemly folly; but it was not my place to rebuke it. I turned to the Queen. She looked at me with eyes I could not read, and said to the woman, "You may go." As she left, I said to her, "Make me a bed in the east room. I shall sleep there till I am blood-cleansed." The girl's eyes opened, as if I had said something unheard-of; then she covered her mouth with her hand, and ran out of the room. I said, "That is a fool, and impudent too. You would do better to sell her."

I shall never understand the Shore Folk. I had meant no slight to her household; I spoke quite civilly. I was amazed to see what offense she had taken at my words. She clenched her hands, and her teeth showed between her lips. "Go, then! Go to Aigeus the Accursed! Like to like." She laughed; but my mind was in Athens already. "Yes, go to him, you who want to be greater than your fate. And when the reckoning comes, remember that you chose it."

"Let Zeus judge me," I said, "who can see everything." Then I went out.

First thing next day I called for a pen and Egyptian paper.
It was a year or two since I had written anything; so I practiced first on wax, in case I had lost the skill, or forgotten
some of the characters. Not that there were secrets in my
letter; but I wanted my first words to my father to be my
own and not a scribe's. I found the knack came back, and
I could still write the fair hand my tutor had beaten into
me. I signed it Kerkyon, and sealed it with the King's ring;
and sat listening to the courier's hoofbeats fading on the
Athens road.

It is only a two-hour ride, and all that day I looked for
him. Though I had given my father no cause for making
haste, yet, being young, I ate my heart out with impatience,
and no reason for delay was too far-fetched for me to think
of. But next day's noon had passed before the man returned.

On the Lower Terrace was a black basalt seat, between
pillars hung with yellow jasmine. Here I went apart, and
opened the letter. It was shorter than mine, written in a
good clerkly script. He welcomed me to Athens as his guest,
touched on my victories, and agreed to undertake my puri-
fication.

After a while, I called someone to fetch the courier. I think
it was in my mind, as it had been many times with this man
or that since I came to Eleusis, to ask him what kind of man
the King of Athens was. Yet now as always, there seemed
something unworthy in it. So I only asked, as one asks any
courier, for the news.

He recited to me various matters, which I forget, and then
said, "Everyone is saying the Priestess will soon be Queen."

I sat up, and said, "How is that?"

"Well, my lord, the curse has lain hard on him. Kinfolk
claiming his kingdom, no son by either wife, and the Cretans
won't forgo the tribute for all his asking." I asked what
tribute. "Fourteen bull-dancers, due again next year, my
lord. And they only take the cream. The ladies of the shrine
say it's a sign for him." He paused, as if something stuck in
his throat.

"This Priestess," I said. "She came from Eleusis?"

"She served here, my lord, in the sanctuary. But she came first from some shrine up north, right beyond the Hellespont. They say she has the long sight, and can call the wind; the common folk in Athens call her the Cunning One, or the Scythian Witch. He lay with her before the Goddess a long while back, because of an oracle she had when the kingdom had some misfortune. They say the next thing will be that he must raise her up beside him, and bring the old customs back." I saw why he had looked askance at me. He went on quickly. "Well, my lord, but you know what Athenians are for talk. More like it's because of the two sons she's had by him, he having no heir."

I stood up from the basalt seat, and said, "You have leave to go."

He scampered off into cover. I paced up and down the terrace in the yellow autumn sunlight, and saw people who had come to speak with me go away silent. But presently my mind grew cooler. I thought, "I sent the man off too shortly. I ought to reward him rather; a timely warning is divine. As for my father, what right have I to be angry? These eighteen years he has taken no wife, for my mother's sake and mine. I should have been here sooner, if I had lifted the stone." The sun was still high, the shadow short before me. I thought, "The man who sleeps on a warning does not deserve one. Why wait till tomorrow? I will go today."

I went back to the Palace, and called the women to dress me. The red leather suit I had brought from Troizen was Hellene, and nearly new. I slung on the serpent sword of the Erechthids; and, to cover it till the proper time, a short blue cloak pinned on the shoulder, such as one can wear indoors.

I chose two body-servants to wait on me. A guard I thought unfitting to a suppliant; besides, I wanted to make it clear I came in friendship and in trust. Those two would have been all my company; but just as I was going, my captive girl Philona pulled at my cloak in tears, and whispered me that all the women were saying the Queen would kill her as soon as my back was turned. I kissed her, and said

Palace gossip was the same everywhere. But she looked at me as the coursed-down hare looks at the spear; and when I thought, I did not trust the Queen entirely. So though it was an inconvenience, I made one of the servants take her up on his mule.

When my horse was brought, I sent the Queen word that I was ready to take leave of her. She sent back that she was sick, and could speak to no one. I had seen her walking on her terrace; however, I had fulfilled the forms.

So I mounted, and in the court the Companions cheered me, but not quite as before; now I was War Leader, I was not so much their own. It would have made me sad at another time; but now I saluted them cheerfully, and soon forgot them, for in my face blew the breeze from the Attic hills.

The road followed the shore, and then swung inward. The autumn grass was parched and pale, the dark oleanders were dusty. At the border guard-tower I had to tell the Athenians who I was; they had not looked for me till morning. I felt my haste had been boyish and raw, and they would take me lightly. But they were very civil. As I rode on, one of their couriers posted past me to Athens.

Suddenly, at a turn of the road between the low green hills, I saw standing huge before me a great flat rock, like a platform raised by Titans to assail the gods from. Upon its top, glowing bright in the westering sunlight, stood a royal palace, the columns russet red, the pink-washed walls picked out with white and blue squares. So high it stood against the sky, the guards on the ramparts looked as small as goldsmith's work, and their spears as fine as wire. I caught my breath. I had guessed at nothing like this.

Before me, down on the plain, the road led to the city wall and the gate-tower. Its roof was manned with javelin-men and archers; on the teeth of the battlements their bull-hide shields hung like a frieze. Here no one asked my name. A massive bar dragged through its wards; the tall horse-gate swung open, turning on its stone trackway; within were a guard saluting, the market place, and little houses huddled under the rock, or climbing its foot slopes. The captain of

the Guard sent two men at my horse's head to guide me
to the Palace.

Everywhere the cliffs stood sheer, except to westward.
Here the road tacked back and forth up the steep slope,
flanked for defense with a great curtain-wall. The way was
ridged for foothold, but soon grew too steep to ride, and
they led my horse. A guardhouse topped the curtain-wall;
the men touched their spear shafts to their brows, and passed
me through. Far below me I saw streets and walls, the Attic
plain stretching to the sea and hills; and on the hilltops the
violet hues of evening, like a crown of purple and gold.
Before me was the upper gate of the Citadel; the lintel-stone
was painted with bands of blue and crimson, and with the
royal device, a serpent twined round an olive tree. The late
sunlight was like yellow crystal, brilliant and clear.

The place overawed me. Though I had heard tell of it, I
had pictured only a hill such as any king or chief will build
on. I had not dreamed my father the master of this mighty
stronghold. Now I saw why he had held out so long against
all his enemies; it might be kept, I thought, against all the
world in arms. I understood what I had heard in tales: that
since King Zeus made men, there was never a time when
a king did not live on the Acropolis of Athens; that even
before men were made it had been a fortress of earthborn
giants who had four hands, and could run upon them. You
can see the great stones they set together, time out of mind.

I passed through the inner gate upon the table of the
Citadel. There were the pacing sentries, men now not toys;
and before me the Palace, with its terrace looking to the
north. If my father had been on it, I thought, he might
have seen me on my way. My breath came faster than if I
had scaled a mountain, and I wet my dry lips with my
tongue.

I passed between the houses of the Palace people, and a
few hardy trees, pines and cypresses, planted as windbreaks
and for shade. Before the king-column of the great door, a
chamberlain stood with the cup of welcome in his hands.
After the long ride and the climb, the wine seemed the cool-

est and best I had ever tasted. As I drained it, I thought
at last I had reached the end of my journey; with this
draught I became my father's guest.

My horse was led away, and they brought me through the
courtyard to the guest rooms. The women had filled the
bath already, and the room was soft with scented steam.
While they brushed my clothes, I lay in the water and looked
about me. Coming up, I had been dazzled by the splendor
of the Citadel. But once inside, you could tell this was a
war-pressed kingdom. Things were quite well kept up, the
wall paintings retouched and fresh, the bath things polished,
the oils well blended. But the women were few, plain mostly
and past their youth, and on the furniture were empty rivet-
holes, where gold had been taken out. I said to myself, "He
has carried his burden too long alone. Now he shall want
for nothing."

I was dried and oiled and dressed and combed. At the
door a baron waited to bring me to the Hall. I walked along
a colonnade, over a floor of tiles painted with dog-teeth and
waves; on my left were columns of carved cedar, on my
right a frieze of gryphons hunting deer. Servants whispered
and peeped in doorways as I passed. My boots threw an
echo, and the rattle of my sword hilt against the studs of
my belt seemed loud. Now I began to hear the din of the
Hall ahead of me, voices talking, cups and plates rattling,
stools and benches scraped on stone, a lyre being tuned,
and someone scolding a slave.

At the far end of the Hall was a step up between two
columns. Beyond on this low dais sat the King. They had
just brought up his own table and were putting it before
his chair. All I could see from the doorway was that he
was dark-haired. This I had guessed, from my mother taking
him for Poseidon. Approaching, I saw that the brown was
streaked with gray, and that he was indeed a man whom
trouble had set its mark on. The skin about his eyes was
dark and drawn, and the folds beside his mouth were as
deep as sword cuts. His beard hid his chin, but his shaven
mouth had a settled weariness; it was wary too, a thing I

might well have looked for. I had thought to see in his face
the mold that had stamped my own; but his was longer,
the eyes not blue but brown, set deeper and not so widely;
his nose was a little beaked where mine is straight, and
whereas my hair flows backward from the temples, his hung
down beside them, narrowing his forehead. Wherever he
had sat in Hall, you would have known he was the King;
but the man who had felt Poseidon's breath and swum rough
water to the Myrtle House, I could not see. Yet he it was,
and I had known he could not but seem strange to me.

I walked forward between the staring benches, with eyes
for him alone. At his right hand was an empty chair crowned
with two hawks; and on his left sat a woman. As I came
near, he rose to greet me, and came forward. This made me
glad; I had not been sure if he would receive me as a king.
He was a little taller than I, about two fingers.

He said what custom ordains for such occasions, making
me welcome, and bidding me eat and drink before I troubled
myself with talking. I spoke my thanks, and smiled. He
smiled back, but only a little; not sourly, but stiffly as if his
smile had fallen out of use.

I sat, and they brought my table, and he showed the
carver the best bits to give me. My trencher was loaded,
almost more than I could eat, though I was hungry. He only
picked at some sweetbreads himself, and most of those he
slipped to the white boarhound by his chair. On the way I
had had some harebrained thought of discovering myself to
him in Hall before the people; now, seeing him in his state,
a king and still a stranger, I had more sense of seemliness.
Besides, I wanted to know him first.

As we ate, I saw out of the side of my eye the woman
peeping across him. Before I sat, I had saluted her and seen
her face. She was neither of the Hellenes nor of the Shore
Folk; her face was broad, the nose a little flat, the eyes narrow and slanted outward. She had a subtle mouth, curving
and closed on a secret smile. Her brow, which was low and
white, was crowned with a diadem a hand's breadth deep
of gold flowers and leaves; gold flower buds on golden

chains fell down each side among the streams of her strong black hair.

The chamberlain with the wine came round again. I was not ready, but the King had emptied his deep gold cup and motioned to have it filled. As he raised his hand, I saw my own beside it. The shape, the fingers, the turn of the thumbs, the very nails were the same. My breath caught; I looked, sure he would see it and stare amazed. But the woman was speaking to him softly, and he had not seen.

My dish was empty. When I had shown I was full and would take no more, he said to me, "Royal guest, by your looks you are a Hellene. And it seems to me that before ever you came to the Palace of Eleusis, there was some king's house where you were not a stranger."

I answered smiling, "Sir, that is true. What blood I came of, there is no man I will tell so gladly as you. But excuse me from it now, and I will tell you the reason later. The favor I came to ask, you know already. As for the man I killed, I fought him fair, though he had tried to have me murdered." And I told him how it was, saying, "I should not like you to think I am a man who works in the dark."

He looked down at the cup in his hand, and said, "First you must make an offering to the Daughters of Night. This is the Lady Medea, who will perform the sacrifice." The woman looked across at me with her slanting eyes. I said, "One must always appease the Mother, who takes slain men into her lap. But, sir, like you I am a Hellene. I ought to go first to Apollo, Slayer of Darkness."

I saw her look at him, but he did not catch her eye. "That shall be as you wish. The night is cold; let us go up, and drink our wine by my chamber fire. We can be easier there."

We went up the stairs behind the dais, with the white hound padding after. The room stood over the northern terrace. It was almost night, and a low autumn moon had risen. One could not see the town so far below, only the circling mountains. A fire of sweet-scented wood burned clear on the round hearth; there were two chairs before it, and near by another before an embroidery-stand. A lamp of green malachite stood on a carved pedestal; there was a deer hunt, with many horsemen, painted round the walls. The bed was of cedar-wood draped with red.

We sat; a servant set a wine-stand between us, but brought no wine. The King leaned forward, and held his hands to the fire. I saw them shaking, and thought, "He has drunk enough in Hall, and would rather wait."

Now my time had come. But my tongue stuck fast; I did not know how to begin. "He will say something," I thought, "which will start me going." So I only praised the Citadel and its strength. He said it had never fallen to an enemy, and I answered, "It never will while it is held by men who know it." For I had seen one or two places where troops used to mountains could scale the sides. He looked at me swiftly; and I thought I had been ill-bred to scan his walls so closely while he only knew me as a guest. So, when he spoke of the Isthmus war, I was glad to talk of that. Indeed, I had rehearsed on the way the story of my victories, as young men will. I wanted him to think me nothing he need be ashamed of.

He said, "And now you are King in Eleusis; the thing as well as the name. All this in one season."

"Yet," I said, "it was not to do those things that I crossed the Isthmus. That was a chance on the way, if such matters are ever chance." He looked at me searchingly under his dark brows. "Is not Eleusis the place of your moira, then? Do you look beyond?" I smiled and said, "Yes."

I thought, "Now I will speak." But as I drew breath, he rose from his chair and paced to the window. The tall dog heaved itself to its feet and strolled after. Not to sit while he stood, I got up too and joined him on the unlit terrace. Moonlight streamed over the land; across the pale fields far below the rock cast its huge shadow. I said, "The hills are dry. I should like to see them in springtime, and white with snow. How clear it is! One can see the ghost of the old moon. Is it always so clear in Athens?" "Yes," he said; "the air is bright here." I said, "As one climbs up, it meets one; as if her stones breathed light. Strong house of Erechtheus, the harpers call her. Truly they might call her Stronghold of the Gods."

He turned, and went indoors. As I followed, I found him standing with his back to the lamp, which shone into my eyes. He said, "How old are you?"

"Nineteen," I said. The lie came pat to me, after so much use. Then when I remembered whom I spoke to, the drollness caught me and made me laugh. "What is it?" he asked. His voice sounded weary, almost old. "I have good cause," I said. But before I could go on, the door swung open. Medea came in, and a servant with a tray of inlay-work. Two gold winecups stood on it, ready filled. The wine was spiced and mulled, and the rich scent of it filled the room.

She came in gently, with downcast eyes, and stood beside him. He said, "We will drink presently. Put it on the table." The servant put it down, but she said, "It will spoil with cooling," and offered it him again. Then he took his cup in his hands, and she brought me the other. It had beaded handles with doves perched over them, and was tooled with lions stalking through long leaves.

The wine smelt good, but my manners bade me wait until he pledged me. He stood with his serpent-handled cup between his hands; Medea waited silent. Suddenly he turned to her and said, "Where is the letter that Kerkyon sent me?"

She looked at him surprised, and went to an ivory coffer on a stand. I saw my letter in her hands. He said to me, "Will you tell me what it says?" I put down my cup, and took it from her. His eyes looked keen; I had not thought that his sight was thick. I read the letter to him, and he said, "Thank you. Most I could read, but a few words I was not sure of." I looked at it puzzled, and said, "I thought it was written fair." He said, in the harassed way of a man with half his mind elsewhere, "Yes, yes, a good fair hand. Your scribe can write Greek; but he spells like a barbarian."

I put down the letter as if it had bitten me. Not my face only, but even my midriff felt hot, so that I tossed my cloak back from my shoulders. Unthinking, rather than stand there like a fool, I picked up the winecup and lifted it to drink.

As my mouth touched it, I felt it plucked from my hands. Hot wine spilled on my face and splashed my clothing. The gold cup struck the painted floor tiles ringing, and made a spreading pool. A thick lees trickled from it, darker than the wine.

I stared at the King astonished, wiping my face. His eyes were on me, as if they saw death itself. No dying man could have been paler. The sight brought back my wits to me, and I saw the sword uncovered at my side. "I should have spoken," I thought. "How ill I have done all this! The shock has stunned him." I took his arm and said, "Sit down, sir. I am sorry. In one more moment I would have told you everything."

I drew him toward his chair. He grasped the chair back, and stood there out of breath. As I leaned over him, thinking what more to say, the white boarhound came padding in from the balcony, and licked at the spilled wine. He started forward, and dragged it back by the collar. I heard the rustle and chinking of a woman's ornaments; the priestess Medea, whom in her stillness I had forgotten, was shaking her head at him. It was then that I understood.

Hemlock is not so cold, nor verjuice so stinging, as the touch of that knowledge was upon my heart. I stood like stone; when the woman led the dog to the door, and slipped away with it, I let her go without raising a hand. The King leaned on his chair head, as if only that kept him from falling. At last I heard his voice, harsh and low as a death-rattle. "You said nineteen. You said you were nineteen."

The sound awakened me. I picked up the cup from the floor, and sniffed the dregs, and stood it before him. "No matter," I said. "It might have been enough that I was your guest. As for the other, that need no longer concern us."

He groped round the chair, and sat, and covered his face with his hands. I undid my sword sling, and laid the sword beside the cup. "Keep it," I said, "if you know it, and have some use for it. It is not mine. I found it under a stone."

I saw his nails dig into his forehead, pitting the flesh. A sound came from him, such as a man makes as the spear is pulled from his death-wound, when he has set his teeth trying to be silent. He wept as if his soul were being torn out of his body, while I stood leaden, wishing I might sink into the earth or melt in air.

Not till he wept had I felt he was my father; and now I felt it, it was only to be cold with shame at seeing him brought so low. I was ashamed as if it were I who had done the wrong. The floor was puddled with trodden wine stains; the dregs in the cup smelled sickly-sweet and sour. A movement drew my eye; across the room stood the servant gaping. At my glance he tried to creep into the wall. I said, "The King gives you leave," and he scurried away.

The fire fell in on a glowing core; its heat oppressed me, and my own dumbness, and the King's fingers tangling his gray hair. I turned my back on it all, and went out between the painted columns to the balcony. Now of a sudden there was stillness, and a great space of moonlight. Shadowy mountains closed it round, the color of dusky amber. Below on the ramparts two sentries passed each other and crossed their spears. Some singer, faint in the distance, chanted a tale and softly plucked a lyre. The Citadel stood between earth and sky in a still radiance that seemed to come out of itself; and dark below it the titan rocks plunged to the plain.

I set my hands on the balustrade, and looked along the walls whose roots were mortised in living rock. And as I stood, it was as if all this flowed into me, with a singing sea-surge, and filled full my heart, and lay there like still waters. And I thought, "This is my moira."

My soul leaned out to grasp her. All else, in this moment, was as passing dust-clouds or a summer shower. I thought, "What was all that clamor within me? She has known a thousand kings. Who can tell how many have hated their fathers or their sons, or loved false women, or wept for this and that? Such things were their mortality, which lies in the grave with them and withers. Only this lives, that they were kings of Athens, who made her laws, or widened her boundaries, or strengthened her walls. High city of the purple diadem, whose stones breathe light, your daimon led me here, when I thought it was my will. Feel my hand, then, know my step, receive me; I will come when your gods summon me, and at their sign I will go. A child I came to you, stronghold of Erechtheus; but you shall make me a king."

After a while, I felt a new quiet about me. Yet the drone of singing still stirred the air. The sound that had ceased was the sound of my father's weeping. I saw him, in my mind, standing where I stood now, looking out over the Citadel, when enemies beset her, or the fields were gray with drought; or when word came that there was a new king on the border, for whom Eleusis was not big enough. Only because he had kept her well, I stood here tonight. I thought of his hard struggle and his endless shifts, and of the long-held hope turned now to poison in his belly. The bitter anger left my heart, and I felt compassion, understanding his grief.

I went in. He was sitting in his chair, his elbows on the table, his face between his hands, staring dully at the sword. I knelt down before him and said, "Father."

He creased his eyelids, as if he were sure neither of sight nor of hearing. "Father," I said. "See how true it is, that fate never comes in the shape men look for. The gods have done this to show us we are mortal. Let us leave off grieving, and start again."

He wiped his eyes with his hand, and looked me over a long time in silence. At last he said, "Who can say what they have done, or why? There is that in you which never came out of me."

He brushed his hair from his face, and moved forward a little, and then drew back. I saw that after what had happened, it was for me first to embrace him. So I did, though I felt shy of it, and was afraid besides it might start him weeping again. He commanded himself, however, and we both felt, I suppose, that next time would be easier. Then he went to the door, and clapped his hands, and said to the man who answered, "Take a guard of four, and bring the Lady Medea, whether she consents or not."

As the man went, I said, "You will not find her." He answered, "The gate is closed for the night, and the postern too. She is here unless she can fly." Then he said, "What is your name?" I stared at this, and we almost smiled. He said, when I told him, "It is the name your mother and I chose together. Why did you not sign your letter with it?" I told him what I had promised her, and he asked me about her, and about my grandfather. But he had one ear for the sound of the guard returning. Presently we heard their feet. He broke off and sat thinking, chin on fist, and said to me, "Do not look surprised at what I say, but agree."

When they brought her in, she stepped out before them like a woman who wants to know why she is wronged. But her eyes were wary.

My father said, "Medea, I have had a sign from heaven, to take the King of Eleusis for my hearth-friend. His enemies are mine. Do you understand?"

She lifted her black brows. "You are the King. If that is what you have decided, so it will be. Did you have me dragged here like a thief to tell me that?"

"No," he said. "The King my friend, before he came to Eleusis, sailed north beyond the Hellespont, to Colchis, where you were born. He says you are blood-cursed; that you killed your brother. What have you to say?"

Now her surprise was true. She turned to me in anger, and I began to see my father's mind. "Everyone knew," I said. "You fled south to escape vengeance." She cried out, "What lie is this?" but I was watching her eyes; they were confused, not innocent; she had done some evil there. My father said, "He has told me all, and taken his oath upon it." At that she cried out in anger, "He is forsworn then. He never set foot outside the Isle of Pelops in all his life, until this year's spring."

My father looked in her eyes, and said, "How do you know?" Her face set like a mask of clay. He said, "You are a wise woman, Medea; they named you well. You can read pebble-cast, and water, and men's hands; you know the stars;

you can make the smoke that brings true dreams. Perhaps you know who his father is?"

She said, "I did not see that. The mist hid it." But her voice had lost truth and caught fear. I saw my father was a prudent judge, who knew his business, and had much to teach me.

He turned to me. "I was not sure. She might have done it ignorantly, from misreading the omens." He turned to the captain of the guard. "Where did you find her?" The man said, "On the South Wall. She had her two sons there, and was trying to make them climb down with her. But the rock is steep and they were afraid."

He said, "Now I am satisfied. Theseus, I give her into your hands. Do what you think fit with her."

I thought it over. Clearly, while she lived, men somewhere on earth would be the worse for it. I said to my father, "What kind of death do you give here?"

Suddenly like a snake she slipped through the guards (I could see they were afraid of her) and stepped up close to him. I saw in their faces, despite themselves, the nearness of man and woman who have shared a bed. She said quietly, "Is it worth it to you, what you are doing?" He said only, "Yes." "Think, Aigeus. These fifty years you have lived with the curse of Eleusis, and felt the weight of it. Have you chosen well?" He answered, "I have chosen with the gods." She sucked in her breath to say something; but he cried loudly, "Take her away."

The guards closed round her. But she turned to the one who looked most in fear of her, and spat on his arm; his spear dropped clattering, and he stood dead white, clutching his wrist. While the rest shifted about, making to take her but afraid to touch her, she cried out, "You were always close-fisted, Aigeus. What kind of bargain did you think you had made with us? To be free of the curse, and nothing to pay but the life of some foot-loose stranger? Gold for horse dung! Is that what you thought?"

My father looked at me, as one compelled to it unwillingly. Now I knew what words he had tried to silence. I felt a coldness in my belly; a kind of shock that was not amazement. I saw in mind the pearl-white bird that whistled at sunrise, the painted walls. I wondered how often I had lain with her, since first she conceived my death.

Seeing my father's hand move to an order, I said, "Not yet." Then there was quiet, except for the chattering teeth of the guard who had dropped his spear. "Medea," I said. "Did the Queen of Eleusis know too whose son I am?"

I saw her eyes search my face to see what answer I wanted. But I had grown older this last hour, and kept my thoughts to myself. Her voice grew spiteful. "In the beginning, she only wanted you put down, like a dog that bites. But when her brother failed, she sent me something of yours, and I looked in the inkbowl."

My father said to me, "Your wife sent warning me that you had vowed to rule in Athens. I would have told you, but not so soon. You are young, and perhaps you loved her." I did not answer, for I was thinking. He said, "She would have freed me of my grandfather's guilt, to make me my son's murderer. You serve a gentle mistress, lady."

I had finished my thought now, and looked up. "Never mind it, sir. This comes as a good to me. It makes my way straight."

On that she whipped round at me. Her slant eyes narrowed and shone, her mouth thinned and widened; and I found I had given back a pace before her, for I saw it was true she had the Power. "Oh, yes!" she said. "Your way is straight now, Hellene thief. Follow that long shadow you throw before you. Your father will feel it soon. Ten years he cut off his life-thread, when he took the posset from your hand."

Beyond her the guard stood with dropped jaws and stretched eyes. My father was pale, yet had not forgotten to watch how they took the news. But it was me she fixed her eyes on, swaying a little, as the snake does to freeze his prey. The guards had edged up all together; but I was alone.

"Theseuss," she said softly, as if her hissing tongue were

forked. "Theseuss of Athens. You will cross water to dance in blood. You will be King of the victims. You will tread the maze through fire, and you will tread it through darkness. Three bulls are waiting for you, son of Aigeus. The Earth Bull, and the Man Bull, and the Bull from the Sea."

Cold on my life I felt the touch of her evil wish, and ghosts with covered faces answering. I had never been ill-wished before. It was like the dark chill when the Earth Snake bites the sun. As the guards backed, my father stepped between her and me. "Do you want a good death, you bitch? If so you have said enough." She answered coldly, "Don't raise your hand to me, Aigeus," and it was as if she were taking the secrets of their bed to make witch-power, instead of his nails or hair. "Do you think you can cheat the Daughters of Night, you and your bastard? He will pay your debt; yes, and the interest too. You saved the son of a night, who came to you a stranger. But the son he kills shall be the fruit of his dearest love, the child of his heart."

I was young. I had got children here and there, but not yet begun thinking about a son of my house, or what I wished him to be. Yet, as a man may stand by night upon a cliff, and feel below him great depths which he cannot see, so I felt breathe upon me from far off the anguish which cannot be conceived before it comes, and, after, must not be remembered.

I stood a stranger to myself. The guard were muttering. Before my face my father's hand was held up in the sign against evil. She had made her moment well. Doubling like a hare, she was through them all and running to the balcony. I heard the rustle of her spangled flounces and swift feet; then only the scramble of the guard, making haste slowly.

I felt for my sword; remembered where it lay, and snatched it up. A sentry ran in from along the balcony, alarmed by the noise, and crashed into the guard within. "Where did she go?" I called. He pointed, and I ran outside. A breeze had got up, blowing in from the sea. Wet mist chilled my face and clung to the flagstones. The moon was like a handful of wool. I remembered what they said of her, that she could call the wind.

The balcony was empty. I ran in at a doorway, and fell over an old man asleep in bed. While he stuttered I picked myself up and found my sword. There was an opening covered with a curtain, which swung as if just moved. Beyond was a little stairhead, with light coming up from a lamp below. I started to run down it; then I saw against the turn of the wall the shadow of a woman, lifting her arm.

Without doubt it was the witch, for she put a charm on me. This was the nature of it. My hands grew cold and sweated. My knees lost their strength, and I felt them tremble. My heart leaped to and fro so that it shook my breast, and my breath came thickly panting; I almost choked with it. My skin crawled upon my flesh, and my scalp upon my skull, and the roots of my hair stood upright. And my two feet were fixed to the floor; they would not take me forward.

I stood rooted by this charm, my entrails working as if with sickness. The shadow moved, and left the wall. This loosed the cord of the spell, and it began to leave me. I ran down the stairs, but their steepness made me slow. They led me to a passage, and that to a court. It was dark, and full of a clammy mist. Nothing else moved there.

I turned back, and heard clamor above me. The old man I had tripped on was rousing everyone, shouting that a huge warrior had run out of the King's chamber with a drawn sword in his hand. The Palace was in uproar. A crowd of House Barons came running, naked behind their shields, and would have speared me, but my father came out in time. New-lit torches, damp with the mist, made stinking smoke; old men coughed in it, women ran about screaming, children cried, men yelled rumors across the courts. At last they found the herald, to quiet the din with his horn. My father led me out on the balcony, not to tell them who I was but to make sure that no one killed me. He calmed their fears and promised them good news tomorrow; then he said that Medea had done what is abominable to gods and men, and till she was taken the gates must not be opened.

When things were quieter, he asked if I had seen the
witch when I ran after her. I said no, which was true; for
I had not seen her, but her shadow only. And this I did not
wish to speak of; for the charm she put on me was very evil,
and if you talk of such things you give them power. Paian
Apollo, Slayer of Darkness, send that I never feel the like
again.

2.

THE witch and her sons were never found, though we
searched the Palace from roof to pillar-crypt, and right down
into the House Snake's sacred cave. Every crack in the rock,
and even the well, was sounded. People said the Dark
Mother had sent a winged serpent to fly away with her. To
that I said nothing. It was in my mind that she might have
put on the gate guard the spell that she put on me.

Next day my father summoned the people. From the
Palace window we watched them climb the long ramps back
and forth, and spread out over the rock. He said, "Today
they walk lightly, without their bundles and their children
stooping their shoulders. Yes, they know their way to the
Citadel. We shall see smoke again upon Hymettos, when
the Pallantids get this news. You have just come from a
war; are you ready for another?"

"Father," I said, "that is what I came for." He looked like
a man who has forgotten how to rest. "You are the only
one," I said, "who did not lie to me. From the rest I got
children's tales; but you left me a sword."

"What did they tell you?" he asked. I told him, trying to
make him laugh; but he looked long at me, and I feared he
was still grieving over last night. I said, "You did well by
me, to put me in Poseidon's keeping. He has never forsaken
me. When I have called on him, he has always spoken."

He looked at me quickly, and said, "How?" I had never

talked of it, and the words came slowly, but I said at last, "He speaks like the sea."

"Yes," he said. "That is the Erechthid token. It came when I was begetting you." I waited, but he did not tell me of the other times; so I said, "How are we called, then, at the end?"

"He calls us to a high place," my father said, "and we leap down to him. We go of ourselves."

When he said it, it seemed I had always known it. "That is better," I said, "than the Earthlings' way. One should go like a man, not like an ox."

The people were now packed tight below us; their voices hummed like bees when you fell their tree, and the smell of their bodies rose to meet us. My father said, "We had better go out to them."

Now it was time, my hands stuck to my chair-arms. I thought of all those eyes, while my father spoke. I like to do, not to be done to. "Father," I said, "what if they don't believe I am your son? We might have made a bargain for all they know; my sword against the Pallantids, to be heir of Athens. What if they think that?"

He came up with his spare smile, and put his arm on my shoulders. "Three out of five will think so. Shall I tell you what they will say? 'That old serpent Aigeus, he never wastes a chance. Here is this young King of Eleusis, a Hellene, who doesn't want to go the way of the rest. Just the lad for him; one who will be his debtor for the life-breath sure enough whoever his father was. Well, he looks like a fighter. Who's to say a god didn't send him? Good luck to him, and no questions asked.'"

I felt simple and young beside him. He went on, "My brother Pallas has ten sons in marriage, all of grown years, and about the same number by women of the house. And most of them have sons themselves. Once they were in, they would rend Attica among them like wolves on a dead horse. You have a great virtue, my son, which will carry all before you. You are one, and not fifty."

He grasped my arm, and led me out. I found he was right;

whatever they thought, they made me welcome. When we had gone in, he smiled and said, "A good beginning. Only give them time; they will see Erechthid written all over you."

We were getting to feel a little acquainted. I daresay if he had brought me up as a boy, we should mostly have been at odds; yet we felt liking now, and a kind of gentleness. It was as if the poisoned cup had drawn us together.

He gave orders for a feast that night, and a great sacrifice to Poseidon. When the priests had gone, I said, "Don't forget Apollo, sir. I've not been blood-cleansed yet."

"That will wait," he said. "Tomorrow will do."

"Well, sir," I answered, "there's not much time, if you are expecting war. I should ride to Eleusis tomorrow, and put things in order."

"To Eleusis!" He looked dumfounded. "The Pallantids must be settled first. They will be on us. How can I spare the men?" I could not follow this at all. "Men?" I asked. "Why, the two I brought can do all I need. I don't care to be much waited on."

"But," he said, "can you not see? The news will be there before you."

"This girl, Father," I said, "that I brought along; can you get your women to look after her? I would have left her in Eleusis; I'm not so tied to her skirts that I must have her everywhere; but the Queen had taken against her, and might have done her some harm. She's a good girl, useful and well-spoken; you won't find her troublesome, and I shan't be long gone."

He raked his hand through his hair, a way of his when harassed. "Are you out of your mind? From today on, your life's not worth a pressed grapeskin in Eleusis. When we have quieted the Pallantids, you can have the army to claim your rights."

I looked at him surprised. But I saw he was anxious for me, in the way of fathers. It touched me, never having come my way before.

"They would cut you down," he said, "at the frontier gatehouse. Has the witch cursed you with madness?" He struck his thigh like a man distracted. Because he was wise and forward-looking, it put him in a taking not to see his way. I was sorry to be a trouble to him so soon.

"But, Father," I said, "the young men saved me in battle. They shed their blood, and one of them died. How could I come on them like a robber, with spears behind me? Their Goddess chose me, I don't know why. They are my people."

He paced the room, and began to speak, and paced again. He was wise, and could see ten things where I could see only one. "But," I thought, "I must needs keep hold of the thing I know, and do what I can with that. I shall do worse with the others; wisdom is only from the gods."

"I shall have to go, Father," I said. "Send me with your blessing."

"In the name of the god," he said, "may your life-thread be stronger than the curse."

I was cleansed that day in the Cave of Apollo, in the cliff-side below the Citadel. In its low shadow, where the sacred spring runs down the rocks, they filled the pitcher to wash me from Xanthos' blood. Then in the bright sunlight we sacrificed a goat on the altar before the cave. At night there was a splendid feast, with harpers and jugglers. My father had everything tasted before we ate it. He did not keep a slave for this; the man who had cooked it brought it in, and my father himself pointed to his portion; a custom I thought both prudent and just.

Next morning I was up early. My father and I stood on the terrace cool with dew, while the rock cast its long blue shadow over the morning fields. He looked as if he had slept badly, and begged me to change my mind.

"If I could for anyone, sir," I said, "I would for you. But I have taken these Minyans into my hand. It would hurt my standing to run away from them." I felt sorry for him; I could see he would have liked to forbid me. It was hard on him, I thought, to have his only son come to him already a king. But that was a thing past remedy.

"One thing more, Father," I said, "before I go. If ever we can join these kingdoms, I won't have their children's children say of me that I led them into bondage. They must come as kindred, or not at all. Give me your word on it."

He looked at me hard; then he said, "Are you bargaining with me?"

I said, "No, sir," out of civility. Then I said, "Yes; it seems that I am. But my honor is in it."

He was silent so long that I asked if he was vexed with me. "No," he said. "You have done as you ought." And he took his oath then and there before me. Then he said, "I see your grandfather in you. Yes, you are more Pittheus' child than mine. I daresay you are the better for it."

My horse was waiting. I told my servants to follow later in the day. I had a feeling there was luck in going alone.

At the border watchtower, they returned my salutation and let me through at once. This seemed too smooth, till I heard one of them say behind me, "So much for that tale. All Athenians are liars."

Presently, rounding a bend, I saw the next hilltop crested with spears.

I was in bowshot already, so I rode on at leisure. Soon a man showed forth against the sky. Then I knew them, and waved my hand. He beckoned those behind him, and began climbing down. I drew rein, and waited, and said, "Greeting, Bias."

"Welcome home, Theseus." Then he shouted over his shoulder, "I told you so. Now what have you to say?"

The Companions scrambled down, quarrelling and cursing one another as they came. "I never believed it; it was Skopas' story." "What? We all heard you." "Take that lie in your teeth." Then daggers were out. It was just like old times. I had to dismount, and pull them apart like fighting dogs.

"An up-country welcome," I said. "Have you all turned plowboys in three days? Or what? Sit down, and let me look at you."

I sat on a bit of rock, and ran my eye over them. "A man is missing. It is Hypsenor. Where is he? Has someone killed him?" A voice said, "No, Theseus. He has gone to tell the army." There was a pause. Bias said, "To say you are alone."

I raised my brows. "When I want the army turned out to meet me, I will say so myself. Who does Hypsenor think he is?" Bias coughed and shifted. "Well, but they were out already; they are just over the hill there. We are the vanguard."

"Vanguard?" I said. "Yes, I should hope so. But whom were you expecting to fight?"

They all looked at Bias, who looked back at them in anger. "Come," I said, "spit it out." He swallowed, and said at last, "Well, Theseus, a tale came last night from Athens. None of *us* believed it. But the Queen thought it was true." He stopped again; then, "They were saying you had offered Eleusis to King Aigeus, in exchange for making you his heir."

My heart chilled and sickened. Now I saw why my father had called me mad. The last thing I had thought of, which should have been the first.

I looked from one to another, and they found their tongues. "They said you had been proclaimed on the Citadel." "We all gave them the lie." "We were angry." "We all swore that if it were true, we would kill you on the border or die ourselves." "Because we had trusted you." "Not that we believed it, Theseus. But if it were true."

All this gave me time. As they talked, I had felt my spirit lighten a little. It was nothing one can put a name to. The truth is, I have seldom needed a soothsayer to tell me my lucky day. I can feel it; I felt it then.

"This much is true," I said. "I have struck a bargain with King Aigeus." There was a silence as if they had all died. "I have got his oath that he will never wrong the men of Eleusis, but treat them as hearth-friends and kindred. What kind of bargain do you think a father makes with his son?"

They all stared in a deep hush. I did not wait till they began to look at each other instead of at me.

"I told you all," I said, "on the day the King died, that I was journeying to Athens. I did not tell my father's name, because I had sworn an oath to my mother, who is a priestess, not to tell it on the way. Which of you would have broken that? She gave me my father's sword to show him;

does it look like a common man's? Look at it. Look at the
device." They passed it round among them. It left me weap-
onless; but in any case, I was one among thirty.

I said, "I am the son of the myrtle grove, who the oracle
foretold would change the custom. Don't you think the Goddess saw me on the way? While my father passed through
Troizen to take ship for Athens, my mother hung her girdle
up for Mother Dia, and so I was conceived. Do you think
the Gift-Bringer forgot? She has a thousand thousand children, but she knows each one of us. She knew I come from a
king and from a king's daughter of the Hellenes, who are
ruled by men. She knew I am one to put my hand to what I
find about me. Yet she called me to Eleusis, and gave the
King into my hand. She knows best, who made us and calls
us home. The mother changes to her sons as they grow to
manhood. Everything has its term, except the gods who live
for ever."

They were all quiet, as if they heard the harper. I could
not have done it by myself. Something hung in the air between us, and out of that I spoke. A bard will tell you it is
the presence of the god.

I said, "I came to you a stranger. There are many men
who wander the world for spoil, burning towns and driving
off the cattle, throwing the men from the walls and taking
the women. So they live; and if one of them had bargained
as you thought, it would be good dealing for him. But I was
bred in a house of kings, where the heir is called Shepherd
of the People, because he stands between wolf and flock.
We come when the god calls us; and when he is angry, we
are the sacrifice. We go consenting, because the gods are
moved by a willing gift. So I will go for you, if I am called
to it. But I will only take my summons from the god; I will
only answer for you to him, and not to any mortal man. Even
my own father knows that, and consents to it. That was the
bargain I made in Athens. Take me as I am. I cannot be
other. You have heard me; if I am not a king to you, I am
alone, and you have my sword. Do what you think good,
and answer to heaven."

I waited. There was a long silence. Then Bias got up, and went over to the man who had the sword, and took it from his hands and put it in mine. On this the wild lad Amyntor shouted out, "Theseus is King!" and then they all shouted.

But Bias had grown quiet. When they had done, he jumped up beside me, and said to the rest, "Yes, you can shout now, but which of you will face the curse? Think now; don't bring him back to Eleusis and then leave him to die alone."

There was muttering, and I said, "What curse is this?"

Bias said, "The Queen put the cold curse on any man who let you pass."

"I don't know the cold curse," I said to them. "Tell it me." I thought I should feel better knowing what it was, than not knowing. They took it for boldness.

Bias said, "Cold loins and a cold hearth, cold in battle, and a cold death."

For a moment a chill ran down my neck. Then I thought, and remembered this and that. Then I started to laugh.

"While I was in Athens," I said, "the Queen tried to have me poisoned. It was then I learned that Xanthos too worked with her warrant. Once, for that matter, she tried with her own hand; you can see the wound. Why go to all that trouble, if her cold curse would stick? Or perhaps it did? Perhaps you have seen it working?"

They had listened solemnly; but now someone at the back yelled out a bawdy joke. I had heard it before, but not to my face. They all shouted with laughter; and then they cheered.

Presently a dark youth, he who had not liked the killing of Phaia, said, "All the same, she cursed a man two years back. He cried aloud, and fell down as stiff as a board; then when he got up, he turned his face to the wall, and did not eat or drink until he died."

"Why not?" I said. "Perhaps he deserved it, and no god protected him. But I am a servant of Poseidon. This time, maybe, the Mother listened to her husband first. In goddess or woman, no bad thing."

This pleased them more than anything; especially those who were courting girls their mothers did not care for. They all began to cheer again; this time they were won. And in due course, I may say here, they made these marriages their hearts were set on. The outcome was that about half got good wives and half bad, just as under the old custom. However, they could manage the bad ones better.

It must have been a god's favor that set the Companions first in my way. They were men I knew; I could feel my way with them, and see what answered best. That was my prentice piece. When I rode on to meet the army, I learned a thing one never forgets after: how much easier it is to move the many than the few.

They were drawn up at the seaside, where the foothills dip to the shore. That is the neck of the Athens road, where it had been held time out of mind. They had made a rough wall there, with stakes and boulders, and all who could scramble up it were standing on the top. I had no trouble to get a hearing; they were men of Eleusis, and eaten up with curiosity to hear what I would say.

So I called an Assembly, standing on the sands by the calm water of the strait, while gulls flashed silver in the blue air, and the breeze from Salamis fluttered the plumes of the warriors. I called to mind all I had learned of these people, and spoke. Since the times of their forefathers, they had had Hellene kingdoms hard by them. They had seen the customs of lands that are ruled by men; and I knew well enough that most of them felt a hankering.

When I had done, I saw which side they wanted to choose. But they were still afraid. "What is it?" I said to them. "Do you think it is heaven's will that women rule you for ever? Listen to me, and I will tell you how it began." Then they hushed and waited; for they loved a tale.

"Long ago," I said, "in the time of the first earth men who made swords of stone, all men were ignorant, and lived like beasts upon wild berries. They were so stupid that they thought women conceived by their own magic, without help of men. No wonder a woman seemed so full of power to

them! If she told a man no, who but he would be the loser?
She by her art could conceive from the winds and streams,
she owed him nothing. So all men came to her crawling on
their faces, till a certain day." And I told them the tale of
the man who first learned the truth. Every Hellene knows it;
but it was new to the Eleusinians, and made them laugh.

"Well," I said, "that was long ago; we all know better now.
But no one would think so, to look at some of you. You
cling to your fear as if it were ordained by heaven." Again
I began to feel that something joined us, like a birth-cord
filled with common blood. But the minstrels say it is Apollo;
that if you invoke him rightly, he will bind the hearers with
a golden thread, and put the end in your hand.

I said, "There is a measure in all things. I didn't come
here to slight the Goddess; we are all her children. Just as
it takes man and woman to make a child, so it needed gods
and goddesses to make the world. The Mother brings forth
the corn. But it is the seed of the undying god that quickens
her, not a mortal man doomed to perish. Wouldn't that be
the greatest of all shows, to make them a wedding? Why
not? The god to come from Athens to her home with the
bridal torches—for she is great, and it is the custom here—
and to be brought to her in the sacred cave, while both the
cities feast and sing together?"

I had not planned this. It came to me while I was speaking. I knew they loved a portent, and to see moira working
among mortal men. Perhaps that put it in my mind. But a
god goes with one on one's lucky day, and I think he sent
it. The time had come for a change, and I was there to his
hand. For, afterwards, I really made this rite for them. Or,
rather, I sent for the bard who had come to Troizen, because he seemed fitter than anyone else I knew. He talked
with the oldest priestesses, and prayed to the Mother, and
took counsel with Apollo; and he made it so beautiful that
no one has ever wanted it changed. He said himself that it
was the best work he had done in all his life, and he would
not complain if it should be the last.

He was a priest of Paian Apollo, and perhaps he had foreknowledge. The old religion is dear to the Daughters of Night; and whoever else is glad, they do not like to see it changed. Their hand fell on him, as it fell on me.

In Thrace, where he was killed, they keep the old custom for all his trying. Even in Eleusis, it dies very hard and its shadows linger. At any summer's end there, you will see the people of town and village gathered on the hill-slopes, sitting to watch the herdboys mime their old tales of the deaths of kings.

But that was after. Meanwhile, the men of the army tossed up their helmets and waved their spears, and begged me to lead them to the city. So I mounted my horse again, with the Guard about me; the Eleusinians followed after, singing paeans, and shouting, "Theseus is King!"

I did not ride straight up to the Palace. I took the lower road, that leads to the cave and to the wrestling ground.

All the women had run out chattering, and questioning the men; the slopes began to be full of people, just as on the day when first I came. I called two of the chief men and said to them, "Command the Queen to come down to me. Let her come of herself if she will do it; if not, bring her by force."

They went up. At the top of the steps, some of the priestesses stopped them; I should have known, if I had been older, that two men were not enough. I sent four more, to keep up each other's courage. They shouldered through, and went in. Then I waited. And I knew why I had chosen this place of meeting; to see her come down the steps as Kerkyon had come down to me, and the King before to him: every year for years uncounted a man in his flower of youth, charmed from his strength like the bird by the dancing serpent, to wrestle and to die.

Soon I saw the men returning; but they were alone. I was angry at this; if I had to go up myself, the people would lose their show. But when the men came near, I saw them pale. And the chief of them said to me, "Theseus, she is dying. Are we to bring her as she is, or not?"

I heard all about me voices passing the word along; it was

like the sound of benches being dragged about in an empty hall. "Dying?" I said. "Is she sick? Or has someone harmed her? Or did she lay hands upon herself?"

They all shook their heads; but they did not all speak at once. Eleusinians love strong events, and know how to display them. They turned to the eldest, who had a good carrying voice. He said, "None of these, Theseus. When the word came to her that we were bringing you home as High King from the border, she tore her hair and clothes, and went down to the Goddess, and cried to her for a sign. What sign she wanted they did not know, but she cried three times, beating her hands upon the earth. Then rising up at last, she had milk brought and set it down for the House Snake; but he would not come for it. So she called a flute-player to make the music snakes dance to, and at last he came. When he was listening to the music, and had begun to dance, she cried out again to the Goddess, and took him into her hand. And he struck his teeth into her arm, and ran back into his hole as quick as water poured into a jar. In a little she fell down, and now she is dying."

There was quiet all around. You could have heard a whisper.

I said, "Bring her here. If I go to her within walls, it will be put about that I killed her. The people must be witnesses." I felt in their deep silence that they approved. "Put her on a litter, and do not hurt her. Let two of her women come, in case she needs anything; but keep the others back."

So I and the people waited again; but Eleusinians are patient, when there is a sight to see. At last I saw the litter coming on the terrace above; four men bearing it, two women walking beside; and behind, kept back by warriors with crossed spears, the priestesses all in black, with bleeding faces and dishevelled hair, wailing aloud. The steps of the stair were not too steep for the litter. Every year, since time out of mind, a dead king had been carried down them, lying on his bier.

They came down, and brought her before me, and stood

the feet of the litter on the ground. It was made of gilded cornelwood, with lapis set in.

She was tossing, and breathing fast; her hair fell down over the gilded litter and swept the ground. Her face was white as new ivory, with a smudge of green under the eyes, and her mouth looked blue. There was a cold sweat upon her, and the woman beside her wiped her brow with a cloth stained with the paint from her lips and eyes. I would not have known her, but for her hair. She looked old enough to be my mother.

She had meant me greater harm than men I had given to kites upon the field, and gladly stripped of their spoil. Yet her ruin smote me, more than when the torch is set to some great hall of kings, with pictured walls and painted columns and hangings woven on the loom, and the flames rise up to the colored rafters, and the roof falls in with a roar. I remembered the morning sky in the high window, her laughter by the midnight lamp, and her proud walking under the fringed sunshade.

I said to her, "We are in the hand of moira, from the day we are born. You did as you must, and so did I."

She tossed upon the litter, and felt her throat. Then she said hoarsely, but loud enough to be heard (for she was an Eleusinian), "My curse failed. You came with the omens. Yet I am guardian of the Mystery. What could I do?"

I said, "A hard choice was laid on you."

She said, "I chose wrong. She has turned her face away."

"Truly," I said, "her ways are dark. But it was ill done to set my father's hand to my death."

She half rose on one arm, and cried, "A father is nothing! A man is nothing! It was to punish your pride." Then she fell back, and one of the women held a wine-flask to her mouth.

She drank, and closed her eyes, and rested; I set my hand on hers, and found it damp and cold. She said, "I felt a new thing at the gates. Kerkyon before you presumed too much. Even my brother . . . Then a Hellene came. *The myrtle grove shall hatch the cuckoo's chick.* . . . Are you even nineteen, as you said you were?"

I answered, "No. But I was bred in a house of kings."

She said, "I crossed her will, and she treads me in the dust."

"It is time and change," I said. "Only the happy gods are free of them."

She turned upon the litter, for because of the poison she could not be quiet. The eldest of her children, a dark girl of eight or nine years, slipped through the guard and ran to her weeping, and taking hold of her asked if it was true she was going to die. She made herself still and stroked the child and said she would soon be better, and made the women take her away. Then she said, "Put me on a fast ship with my children, and let me go to Corinth. I have kindred there to care for them. I want to die on the Sacred Mountain, if I can get so far."

I gave her leave. Then I said to her, "Though I shall change the sacrifice, I will never root out the Mother's worship here. We are all her children."

She had closed her eyes, but now she opened them. "Children and men want everything for nothing. Life will have death, and you will not change it."

They picked the litter up, and began to bear it away, but I put my hand out to stay them. Bending down, I said, "Tell me before you go: are you with child to me?" She turned her head and answered, "I took the medicine. He was only a finger long, but you could see he was a man. So I did right. There is a curse upon your son."

I signed to the bearers, and they carried her toward the ships. To the women behind I said, "Take her her jewels, and anything else she asks for." They began to run about all in confusion, in their black robes, their solemn mourning forgotten; it was like an ants' nest when the spade cuts it through, for there was no precedent. On the slopes around, the women of the city were talking like starlings. It is the custom of the Shore People for all the girls and women to be in love with the King, who is forever young since when one goes there is another. So now they did not know what to think.

I was looking after the litter, when a tall gray-haired
woman with a big gold necklace walked up to me, freely as
Minyan women do to men, and said, "She has fooled you,
boy. She will not die. If you want her life, you had better
go after her." I did not ask why she hated the Queen, but
only said, "Death was in her face, if I ever saw it." The
woman said, "Oh, I daresay she is sick. But she took broth
of snakeshead in her youth, and was bitten by young serpents, to make her venom-proof. It is the custom of the
sanctuary. She will be in pain a few hours more; then she
will sit up and laugh at you." I shook my head. "We had
best leave that to the Goddess; it's ill-meddling between
mistress and handmaid."

She shrugged her shoulders. "You will need a new Priestess. My daughter is of the Kin, and a girl to please any
man. Look, there she is."

I raised my brows at her. I could have laughed aloud,
seeing the pale, biddable girl, and the mother all ready to
rule Eleusis. I turned from her toward the Queen's women,
still running and scolding up and down the stairs. But one,
less busy, stood by the rock-cleft, taking a last look at it.
It was she who had lain there on the wedding night, weeping
the dead King.

I went up and took her wrist and led her out, while she
hung back in fear, remembering, I suppose, how she had
hated me, and had let me see it. "Here is your Priestess,"
I said to the people. "One who does not rejoice in slain
men's blood. I shall not lie with her; only a god's seed can
quicken the corn. But she shall offer sacrifice, and take
omens, and be nearest to the Goddess." And I said to her,
"Do you agree?" She stared at me confused; then said like
a child, because surprise had made her simple, "Yes. But
I will never curse anyone; even you." It made me smile.
Yet, ever since it has been the custom.

Later that day I appointed my chief men, from those who
had been resolute in defying the women. Some of these
would have had me put down women from every office in the
land. Though I tended myself to extremes as young men do,

yet I did not like this; it would bring them all together to work women's magic in the dark. One or two, who had pleased my eye, I should have been glad to see about me. Only I had not forgotten Medea, who had fooled a man as wise as my father was. And there were the old grandmothers, who had run a household for fifty years, and had more sense than many a warrior with his mind only on his standing; but besides their magic, they had too many kindred, and would have managed the men. So I thought again about what I had seen in Eleusis of women's rule, and chose from those sour ones who took their pleasure in putting the others down. And these did more than the men to keep their sisters from rising up again. A few years later, the women of Eleusis came begging me to appoint men in their stead. Thus I was able to make a favor of it.

On the second night after I took the kingdom, I gave a great feast to the chief men of Eleusis, in the royal Hall. The meat I provided from my booty of the war; and there was plenty too to drink. The men rejoiced at having snatched their freedom, and toasted the good days ahead. As for me, victory is sweet on the tongue, and to lead men, and be no one's dog. And yet, the feast lacked something; without the women it seemed a rough, up-country thing. Men drank themselves stupid, and threw bones about, and made fools of themselves boasting of what they could do in bed, as they would never have dared if the women had been there to laugh at them. It was more like being on campaign than feasting in a king's hall, which is why I have never made a custom of it. But that night it served my turn.

I called for the harper; and he sang, of course, of the Isthmus war. He had had time to work it up, and made a rousing thing of it. They were full already of themselves and of good wine; by the time they were full of the song too, they were spoiling for battle. So then I told them of the Pallantids.

"I have news," I said, "that they are planning war. Once let them hold the Citadel of Athens, and no one will be safe between there and the Isthmus. They will rend the Attic plain like wolves on a dead horse; and those who are left hungry will look to us. That horde, if it gets through to Eleusis, will not leave an ear standing, a sheep running, a jar unbroken, or a girl unravished. Lucky for us if we can fight them across the Attic fields, and not our own. They have great spoil in their house on Sounion Head, and I will go surety you get fair shares. Then, after the victory, you will hear men say in Athens, 'These Eleusinians are warriors. We were fools if we ever thought of them lightly. If we can get men like that for hearth-friends and kindred, it will be the best piece of work we ever did.' "

Next morning, at the Assembly, I spoke better. But no one will ever be found to say so. They were so drunk, and so big-headed with having mastered the women, that they could not have been more pleased with this speech if Apollo and Ares Enyalios had made it up between them.

So, when two days later my father sent word that there was smoke upon Hymettos, I sent for the Palace scribe, and made him write, and sealed it with the royal ring. The letter said, "Aigeus son of Pandion, from Theseus at Eleusis. Honored Father, the gods all bless you with long life. I am coming to the war, and bringing my people. We shall be a thousand men."

3.

THE war in Attica lasted nearly a month. It was the longest war since the time of Pandion my father's father. As all men know, we scoured the Pallantids off the land. We took South Attica, pulled down their stronghold on Sounion Head, and raised the high altar to Poseidon there, which is seen from ships at sea. And we took the Silver Hill hard by it, with the slaves who worked the mine, and fifty great ingots of smelted silver. So the kingdom was doubled, and the plunder very rich. The men of Eleusis went home as well-found as the men of Athens, with cattle and women and weapons and everything we took. I had cause for pride in my father's bounty. It was true, as Medea had said, that he had a name for being close-fisted; but he had always had the next war to think of. I can testify before anyone that he opened wide his hand to me.

We lived well that winter, for we had got in our crops before the war, and taken Pallas' too. All the feasts were richly kept. When there was a festival in Athens, the Eleusinians came to see, and turn about; there were many hearth-friendships made, and many marriages. Because I had brought the kingdom safety and wealth, they thought in Eleusis that the Goddess favored me; and with my father's counsel to help, I began to get things in order. Sometimes I went my own way, because I knew the people better. But I never told him so.

I spent a good deal of time with him in Athens, and listened when he gave judgment. It made me feel for him; for the Athenians were very quarrelsome. Time out of mind, the Citadel had never fallen; but the plain had been overrun in old days by all sorts of people, Shore Folk at one time and Hellenes at another, so that Attica was as mixed as Eleusis, yet had never blended. You got patches of people under chiefs like petty kings, who had not only their own customs, which was natural, but their own laws, so that neighbors could never agree on what was just. As you may suppose, blood-feuds were nearly as common as marriages, and no feast ever went by without someone being killed, that being a time when enemies waited for their man to show himself. When they had got themselves to the edge of a clan war, they might come at last to my father to judge between them, with a tale twenty years long. No wonder, I thought, his face was lined and his hand unsteady.

It seemed to me he would wear himself out before his time. I don't know why, seeing he was a wise man and had kept the kingdom all those years; but I felt dangers threatened him everywhere, and that if any ill befell his life, the blame would be mine for not taking better care of him.

One evening, when he had come from the judgment hall

dead tired, I said to him, "Father, all these people came to the land of their own will; they all own you as High King. Can't they learn they are more Athenians than Phlyans and Acharnians and so on? I reckon the war lasted near twice as long as it should, because of their bickering."

He said, "But they are fond of their customs. If I take any away, they will think their rivals are being favored, and then they will help my enemies. Attica is not Eleusis."

"I know it, sir," I said, and fell to thinking. I had gone up to his room to drink a posset by the fire. The white boarhound nudged my hand; he always begged for the lees to lick.

Presently I said, "Have you ever thought, sir, of calling all the men of good blood together? Some things they must all want: to hold their lands, keep order, get in their tithes. In council, they might agree on a few laws for their common good. The craftsmen too, they all want a fair price for their labor, not to be beaten down to what the hungriest man will take; the farmers must need some working rule about boundaries and straying stock, and the use of the high pastures. If these three estates would each agree on some laws for their own sort, it would draw them together and break the pull of the clans. Then, if chief disputed with chief, or craftsman with craftsman, they would come to Athens. And in time there would be one law."

He shook his head. "No, no, there would be two causes of strife where there was one before," and sighed, for he was weary. "It is well thought of, my son; but it is too much against custom."

"Well, sir," I said, "just now they are well shaken up, with all these new southlands joined to the kingdom. They might take it better now than ten years hence. In summer, there is the feast of the Goddess, whom they all worship under one name or another. We could have some victory games, and make a new custom of it, and they would come together for that. Thus you would have them ready."

"No!" he said. "Let us have rejoicing for once instead of blood." His voice had sharpened, and I reproached myself for troubling him when he was tired. Yet all the while there was a beating in my head, like a caged bird's, which said to me, "A lucky time is being wasted, a great chance let go by; when my day comes, I shall have to pay for it." But I said nothing of this to my father; for he had been good to me, and rewarded my men, and done me honor.

There was a girl in his household, a prize he got in the war, dark-haired and high-colored, with bright blue eyes. She had belonged to one of the sons of Pallas, in the house at Sounion. Seeing her among the captives, I had had half a mind to her, and had meant to pick her out when the spoil was shared. I had never thought of my father choosing a woman. He saw this girl and chose her before anything else. Now Medea had gone, there was no one about him fit for a king's bed; but when it happened, being young and foolish I was surprised, and even somewhat shocked, as if I could have expected him to choose a woman of fifty. Of course I put such thoughts aside. I had my Isthmus girl Philona, a good enough girl and indeed worth ten of the other, who proved a baggage, always with one eye for a man. I did not care to warn my father. One day, I remember, on the terrace, she came hurrying out of a side door and ran right into me. She begged my pardon; and leaned so hard on me that she might as well have been naked. Her shamelessness filled me with anger. I threw her off (she would have fallen, if she had not struck the wall) then dragged her to the parapet, and held her half over. "Look well, Bitch-Eyes," I said. "That's where you'll go, if I ever catch you playing my father false, or doing him harm." She crept away frightened, and was more modest after. So I had no need to trouble my father with it.

Between Athens and Eleusis, and riding about Attica to bring order after the war, winter passed and the snow-streams ran down the mountains. In the wet banks you could smell violets hidden. Young deer came after the green crops; when I went hunting them, I urged my father to come too, and get the good air; he never went out enough. We were on the foot slopes of Lykabettos, and had ridden up through the pines to where it gets stony, when his horse stumbled, and threw him on a rock. A clod of a huntsman had set up a net there, and gone away and left it. Up he ran excusing himself, as if he had cracked a kitchen pot, instead of nearly killing the King. I got up from helping my father, who was badly bruised, and knocked three or four teeth down the fool's throat, to make him remember. I told him he had got off lightly.

One day my father said to me. "Soon ships will be taking the sea again, and women can make journeys. What if I send for your mother? She will like to see you; and it would be good to look on her face again."

I saw him watch how I took it; and guessed he was not speaking all his thought, because he was a careful man. He had it in mind to make her Queen of Athens; and for my sake, too; for she had been younger than I when last he saw her. "For sure," I thought, "when he sets eyes on her, he will want to take her to bed again. Except when she is sick or tired, her skin is like a girl's still, and she has not one gray hair. And this is what I have so long wished for, to see her honored in my father's house." I remembered how when I was a child I had looked at her in her bath, or wearing her jewels, and thought that only a god was worthy to embrace her.

I said, "She could not leave till the House Snake wakes with his new skin, and she has made the spring sacrifice and received the offerings. She has a great deal of business then. After that she will come." So he put off sending, because it was too early.

I remember a fright my father gave me about this time. There is a corner of the upper terrace straight over the rock-face. When you look down, the houses below are as small as if children had pinched them out of clay, and the dogs sunning on the roofs no bigger than beetles. There is a prospect over half the kingdom, right out to the mountains. One day I saw my father leaning there, and right beside him a great crack in the stone balustrade. It shocked me so much that I stopped breathing. Then I ran and pulled him back.

He looked at me startled, for he had not seen me coming; when I showed him his danger, he made light of it, and said the crack had been always there. So I sent for the mason myself to mend it, in case he forgot. Even afterwards, to see him stand there made me uneasy.

My father liked to have me often in Athens, to sit with him in Hall or go among the people. I had nothing against it, except that it took me from Eleusis, where I could do things my own way. In Athens I looked on, and sometimes saw people I doubted put too high, or people put too low who were able for more, or things done with trouble that might have been made easy. My father had had too many cares to see to it, and now had grown used to things as they were. If I said anything he would smile, and say that young men would always build the walls of Babylon in a day.

There was a woman in the Palace, who had belonged to his father before he was born. She was more than eighty years old, and did not work much, but used to blend the bath-scent and the oil, and dry the sweet herbs. Once, when I was in the bath, she came by and pulled a lock of my hair, and said, "Come back, lad. Where have you flown off to?" She was allowed her liberties because she was so old; I smiled and said, "To Eleusis." "And what does Athens lack, then?" "Athens?" I said. "Why, nothing." My father had given me two fine rooms, and had the walls new painted with mounted warriors, and with some very good lions, which I liked so well I have kept them to this day. "Athens lacks nothing," I said. "But there is work in Eleusis I ought to be at now."

She picked up my hand from the side of the bath, and turned it palm upward. "A meddling hand. Always doing, never letting be. Wait, Shepherd of the People, wait on the gods; they will send it work enough. Have patience with your father. He has waited long to say, 'Here is my son'; now he wants to live thirty years in one. Bear with him, lad; you are the one with time before you."

I snatched back my hand into the bath. "What do you mean, old scritch-owl? He has thirty years to go, before he is as old as you are; and you look good for another ten. Why, before the god sends for him, I myself may be as old as he is now. Are you ill-wishing him, or what?" Then I was sorry, and said, "No, but you should not talk carelessly, even though you mean no harm."

She peered at me under her gray wrinkled lids. "Be at peace, Shepherd of Athens. You are dear to the gods. The gods will save you."

"*Me?*" I said staring. But she had shuffled off. She was the oldest woman in the Palace, and her wits were failing.

Spring came on; there were pale green buds on the black vinestocks, and the cuckoo called. And my father said to me, "My son, about this time of year you must have been born."

I said, "Yes, in the fourth month's second quarter. My mother said so."

He struck his fist into his hand. "Why, what have we been about? I must make a feast for you. Your mother should be here! Now we can't wait for her; all Athens knows when I passed through Troizen, and if this is not your birth-month, you are not my son. Well, well, it is not strange I forgot. You grew into a man ahead of your years, and I have missed your boyhood. It will be your victory feast as well."

I thought of my mother, and what was due to her. Presently I said, "We could sacrifice on the day, and send for her to Troizen, and make the feast later." But he shook his head, saying, "It will not do. No, it would be coming on tribute-time, and the people would not like rejoicing then." What with the war, and all that had happened since I came to Athens, it did not come to my mind what tax he meant, and thinking about my mother I forgot to ask him.

When the day came, I was early up, but he had risen earlier. The priest of Apollo trimmed my hair, and shaved the down from my cheeks and chin. I had more to dedicate than I thought; it had not showed much, being fine and fair.

My father smiled, and said he had something to show me, and led me to the stables. The grooms flung wide the doors. Within was a new chariot, of dark polished cypress-wood, with ivory inlays and silver-bound wheels, a craftsman's masterpiece. Laughing, he bade me look well at the axle-pin; I should not find wax this time.

It was a gift beyond my dearest wish. I thanked him on one knee, putting his hand to my brow; but he said, "Why this haste, before you have seen the horses?"

They were matched blacks, with white-blazed foreheads; strong and glossy, sons of the north wind. My father said, "Aha, we slipped them up here, as neat as Hermes the Trickster lifting Apollo's steers. The chariot while you were in Eleusis; and the horses this very morning, while you still slept."

He rubbed his hands together. I was touched at his taking all this care to surprise me, as if I had been a child. "We must take them out," I said. "Father, finish your business early, and I will be your charioteer." We agreed that after the rites, we would drive to Paionia below Hymettos.

There was a big crowd waiting on the slopes around the shrine of Apollo. As well as the chief people of Athens, those of Eleusis had been bidden to the festival, and all the Companions. While the priest was studying the victim's entrails, and taking a long time about it, I heard a buzz among the Athenians, as if some news were being passed along; and it was like a dark cloud crossing the sun. I am a man who likes to know what goes on around me; but I could not leave my place to question anyone, and we went on to the sacrifice of Poseidon and the Mother, at the household shrine. Afterwards I looked for my father, but he had gone off somewhere; to finish his business, I supposed, as we had planned.

I changed my clothes for a driver's tunic and tooled leather greaves, and tied back my hair; then I went out to my horses, and gave them some salt, and made much of them, to let them know their master. I heard some bustle and stir in the Palace beyond, but it was to be looked for on a feast day. There was a young groom, a graceful lad, polishing harness; someone called him to come, and he put down his rag and beeswax, and went off with a face of fear. I wondered what he had done that had found him out, and thought no more of it.

From the horses I went to the chariot, and looked at the inlay-work of dolphins and doves, and felt the balance; till even these pleasures I had had my fill of, and could not help thinking, "How slow old men are! By now I could have done it all three times over." I called a groom, and told him to take the chariot down the ramp; as for the horses, I could not bear to let them out of my sight. It seemed to me he looked at me strangely as he went; I shrugged it off, yet began to feel uneasy.

I waited and waited, till the horses grew restive, and resolved to go and see what kept my father. Just then he came up, alone. He had not even changed his clothes; I could have sworn he had forgotten why I was waiting. He blinked and said, "I am sorry, my son; that must be for tomorrow."

I answered that I was sorry to lose his company, which was true, though I thought too that now I could race the horses. Then I looked at his face again. "What is it, Father? You have had news, and bad news too."

"It is nothing," he said. "But business keeps me. Take out your horses, boy. But have them brought round below the postern, and go down yourself by the stair. I don't wish you to cross the market place."

I stared at him frowning, and said, "Why not?" It was in my mind that I had just fought a war for him; and this was my feast of manhood.

He straightened his neck, and answered sharply, "Sometimes you must obey without asking reasons."

I tried not to be angry. He was King, and his counsel was his own to keep. But something of moment was going on; it drove me mad to be in ignorance; besides, being young and cocksure I thought he would bungle it without me. "And I shall pay for it," I thought, "when my day comes, if I live so long."

I felt anger take hold of me, and put myself in mind of my duty and his goodness, and closed my teeth and hands

I found I was shaking all over, and even sweating, like a horse that is both reined and spurred.

"You should trust me," he said fretfully, "to have your good in mind."

I swallowed, and said slowly, "It seems we have counted wrong, sir. I am not a man today, but still a child."

"Do not be angry, Theseus." There was even pleading in his voice. I thought, "I must do as he says; he has loaded me down with kindness; he is my father, he is King and priest; thrice sacred to Ever-Living Zeus." And then I thought, "He has not strength to face out even me; what work does he mean to put that shaking hand to?" But I felt myself shaking worse than he. I was afraid of myself, and of I knew not what, as if some dark shape hovered between me and the sun.

While I stood silent, a man came out from the Palace; one of the House Barons, a dull slow fellow. "King Aigeus," he said, "I have looked for you everywhere. The boys and girls are all ready in the market place; and the Cretan captain is saying that if you do not come, he won't wait for the lottery, but will choose fourteen for himself."

My father drew in a harsh breath and said softly, "Get out, you fool." He stared and went. We were left looking at one another.

Presently I said, "Father, I'm sorry I was hasty, when you've trouble enough. But why in the world did you not tell me this?" He did not answer, but passed his hand across his brows. I said, "To run off down the postern, and slip away; what kind of fool would that make of me? Thunder of Zeus! I am Lord of Eleusis. Even Cretan insolence won't reach to carrying off a king. Why should I hide myself? I ought to be down there now, in my old clothes, showing the people I don't feast while they are mourning. And, besides, I must send my Companions home. It is not seemly to have them walking about while Athenian boys are taken; such things make ill-feeling. Where is the herald? I want them called in."

Still he stood silent. My skin crept, like a dog's before a storm. "Yes?" I said. "What is it?"

He answered at last, "You cannot call them now. The Cretans came early: they were rounded up with the rest."

I took a step forward and said, *"What?"*

I had spoken louder than I meant. The horses were startled; I motioned the groom to take them away. "Father," I said at last, "was this well done? I am answerable for them to my people." Trying not to shout, I was almost whispering; I could not trust myself. I said, "How dared you keep this from me?"

"You are too hot," he said, "to meet the Cretans in anger." I saw he was close to tears; it put me nearly beside myself. "There was a brawl here once before, and one of their princes was killed. This tribute is the fine for it. Next time, they would send a hundred ships and lay waste the land. What could I do? What could I do?"

This sobered me. I felt he had judged me justly. "Very well, Father, I will take care not to make trouble. But I must go at once and get my men away. What are they thinking of me, all this while?"

He shook his head. "King Minos hears everything. He knows the kingdoms are joined now. I don't think he will forgo his claim."

"But," I said, grasping my dagger hilt and trying to be steady, "I swore to them they should not join Athens to their loss."

He stood in thought, rubbing his chin. "If the lot should happen to fall on a man of yours, you would have a good case for having your own tribute remitted. Sometimes, Theseus, it is expedient one man should perish for the sake of the people."

I lifted my hand to my head. My ears were ringing. He went on, "They are only Minyans, not Hellenes, when all is said."

The ringing dinned in my ears, rising and falling. I shouted, "Minyan, Hellene, what does it matter? I have vowed to stand for them to the god. What does this make me? What am I?"

He said something; that I was his son, and Shepherd of Athens. I could just hear him, like a voice beyond a wall. I pressed my clenched fist against my brow. "Father!" I said. "What shall I do?" But once the words were out of my mouth, I knew it was not to him that I had spoken. Presently my head quieted a little, and then I could hear him, asking if I was sick.

"No, sir," I said. "I am better; I see what I must do, to save my honor. If they will not free my people, I must take the luck of the draw myself, just like the others."

"*You?*" he said, opening his mouth and eyes. "Are you mad, boy?" Then his face closed up again, and he stroked his beard. "Well, well," he said at last, "you were right when you went back to Eleusis. You have a feeling for such things. It will make the people patient, if you stand among them. Yes, after all, it is a good thought."

I was glad to see him calm again. I put my hand on his arm. "Don't be anxious, Father. The god won't take me if it is not my fate. I'll change these clothes and come back." I went off running, and flung on the first thing that came to hand, a hunting-suit of undyed doeskin with green tassels down the sides of the thighs. I hardly looked at it then; but I got to know it later. My father was where I had left him; a chamberlain he had been giving orders to was hurrying off.

From the North Terrace one could see down to the market place. It had been cleared of its stock pens and stalls for the festival. The boys and girls were standing on the north side, where the altar is to All the Gods. As we went down, we heard the wailing.

By the time we got there, the Cretans had been over them. The tall ones and the fat ones, the sick and halt and ackwit, had been let go; the little quick ones, the strong and slim, remained; youths on the right and maidens on the left. Or so it had begun; but some had run together in the middle, and you could tell, from the way they stood, which had been openly betrothed and which had kept their secret till today. Many of the girls were almost children. Only virgins could be bull-dancers; there was a rush of weddings before tribute-time. The Cretans always brought a priestess with them, to settle arguments.

A good third of my Companions were there among the boys. As I came nearer, they waved their hands. I saw they looked to be free at once, now I was here. I waved back, as if I thought so too. Then I felt eyes in my back, and saw the Athenians looking at me. I knew what they were thinking, as they saw me walking free at my father's side. Penned up for the lottery I could see boys not sixteen years old, the same height as I. I remembered my grandfather telling me I was just the build for it. My heart felt sick with it all, sick and angry. I turned to the Cretans.

At the first sight of them I started; for they were black. I had forgotten Minos' foreign levies. They had on leopardskin kilts and helmets made of horses' scalps, with the manes and ears. Their shields were black and white, from some striped beast unknown to me. Their glossy shoulders gleamed in the sun, and they rolled up their eyes to look at the Citadel, showing the whites. Otherwise they were quite still, as I had never seen troops still before, shields and javelins all in line, one body with a hundred heads. In front was the Captain, the only Cretan there.

My notion of Cretans I had got from those who came to Troizen. I should have guessed that those were merchants, aping the airs of Knossos Palace where no one knew the difference. Here stood the pattern; and I saw the copies had been poor.

This one too looked girlish at first glance. He was dressed for parade, bareheaded; a pretty black boy held his helmet and shield. His dark hair, rippling and sleek like a woman's fell to his waist behind, and his face was shaved so smooth it took time to see he was near thirty. His only garments were a thick rolled belt round his slim middle, and a loin-guard of gilded bronze. Round his neck was a deep collar of gold and crystal beads. All this I saw before he deigned to

ook at me; this and the way he stood; like a painting done
n a wall of a princely victor, whom words do not touch, nor
me and change, nor tears, nor anger; but he will stand so
a his ease and pride, uncaring, till war or earthquake shakes
own the wall.

I went over, and he looked up at me under his long black
ashes. He was about two thumbs shorter, and let me see
early that this was the proper height for a gentleman. Before
had opened my mouth, he said, "I am sorry, but unless you
ave exemption in writing, I can do nothing at all."

Feeling myself get angry, I kept my father's words in mind,
nd said quietly, "It is no such matter. I am Theseus, King
f Eleusis." He said, "I must beg your pardon," with cool
vility and no pretense of shame. "You have over there," I
aid to him, "a dozen young men of my bodyguard, all those
ho are still beardless. They are guests in Athens. You will
ave to wait, while I fetch them out."

He raised his brows. "I am instructed that Eleusis is in
assalage to Athens now; a feoff of the King's heir, whom, I
ke it, I have the honor to speak with." It was like talking
o a man of polished bronze.

"I am no one's vassal," I said. "Eleusis is my kingdom. I
lled the last King according to custom." He lifted his brows
ato his curled hair. "And," I said, "our tribute, paid two-
early, is corn, so much, and so much wine." I have a good
emory for such things.

"Well," he said in his light hard voice, "if you had applied
writing to the Treasury, it might have been looked into.
am not an assessor; I collect where I am told. Kings, after
l, are a good many in these parts. In Crete we have only
ne."

My hands itched to pick him up and break him across my
ee. But I remembered the people. He saw I was angry, and
id without any heat, "Believe me, Prince, this lottery is no
oice of mine. It is an inconvenience I put up with. I con-
der the customs of the place, wherever I can. In Corinth,
hen I come into port I find the boys and girls ready on the
ayside. It saves me time and trouble, as you may suppose."

"No doubt," I said. "Whereas in Athens you must wa:
while justice is done, and the people witness it."

"Yes, yes; that is understood. Clearly, then, I cannot cor
sider what you ask. See for yourself how it will look, if yo
go about picking out this lad and that. The people will sup
pose that at your age you will hardly act without you
father's knowledge; that the sons of his friends are bein
begged off, or perhaps some youth dear to yourself. Then w
shall have trouble. I am putting up with all this delay; bu
a riot I cannot do with. Believe me, I know something (
these things."

I kept my hands off him, and even my voice down. I onl
said, "You have not been half a day here. Are you telling *n*
what the people think?"

"No offense," he said lightly. "I am telling you what
know. You, or your father rather, chose this custom. Well,
consent to it, cumbrous as it is; but I will see it carried ou
That is my last word, I am afraid. Where are you going!

His voice had changed; a ripple went through the line (
black warriors behind him, like the ripple on a leopard's bac
before it springs.

I turned back, and said so that I could be heard, "I a:
going to join my people, and share the lot of the god."

I heard a deep sound of voices, and saw my father lookir
here and there. As I walked on, a touch on my shoulder mac
me start. I turned; there was the Cretan Captain. He ha
left his men in line, and run after me on his small light fee

Speaking softly in my ear, he said, "Think again. Don't l
the glory and the glitter fool you. A good bull-dancer las
six months at best. Listen; if you want to see the world,
can get you employment in the Little Palace; you can s:
with us free."

I had nothing now to lose by pleasing myself, so I sai
"Send me your big brother, little lady, and let *him* ask me
serve Minos for pay." As I turned from him I saw his qui
dark eyes, not very angry but sharp and reckoning.

I crossed the market place, and stood with the Co:
panions. They reached out and drew me in, and clapped n

on the back, just as in the old days when I was only a year-king. A sound ran round the market place, dull at first, then loud. The Athenians were cheering; I was amazed at it, seeing their trouble. "Truly," I thought, "these are my people too; now I can stand for all of them."

They set a table before my father, and put on it two great round bowls with painted borders. He said to the people, "Here are the lots, Athenians, with your children's names. And here is the lot for my son." He dropped the potsherd clinking into the right-hand bowl, and the people cheered again. Then he called the Cretan Captain, as a stranger without kindred here, to stir the bowls. As he did it with his spear butt, looking as if he found it tedious, my father lifted his hands and invoked the god, asking him to choose the sacrifice himself, and hailing him as Earth-Shaker, Lover of Bulls. At these words, the witch's curse came to my mind, and my neck shivered. I looked at my father, but he kept his countenance well.

They drew first for the girls. The Priest of Poseidon, blindfold, put his hand into the bowl, and gave the sherd to my father, who gave it to the herald to read the name. Each time I saw the faces of the kindred, fixed on the sherd, so that the line of faces was like one long pale serpent filled with eyes. Then the name would be read and a family would cry and wail, or a man run out from somewhere and start fighting the guards till they knocked him down. And for a few moments all the rest would be glad, till the next sherd was drawn. Only the last girl was so fair and gentle-eyed and young that not only her own folk, but everybody, wept for her. The blacks formed round them in a hollow square, to keep off the people. Then it was time for the youths.

Two were drawn from Athens; and then I heard the name of one of my Guard, a lad called Menesthes, whose father was the master of seven ships. He went out firmly, only looking back once at his friend and once at me. Next came an Athenian, whose mother made an outcry as if she were being torn in pieces, so that the boy went white, and trembled all over. I thought, "Mine would never have disgraced me so.

But it is my father I should be thinking of. It is worse for him than for most of them, seeing he has no more sons." I looked over to the dais where he was standing. The Priest of Poseidon was just putting his hand in to draw again. At that same moment, there was some stir in the crowd, a woman fainting or some such matter. I saw my father look aside, to see what it was.

Stillness fell on me, as if Helios drew rein in the midst of heaven. If a man could prevent knowledge before he has it, I would not have known. But it was there, before I could forbid it. From ten years old, I had sat in the hall of judgment, looking at people. Before I could understand the cause, I knew already who was concerned and who was not. I looked at the line of eyes, fixed on the urn, all together like the soldiers' javelins. But my father was not afraid.

It came home to me slowly, creeping on the heart. My belly and loins grew cold; shame seemed to coat my very flesh, like a skin of dust. My mind ran to and fro, coursing a rank scent. "What was on the lot he dropped in for me? Not a blank; someone might see it. Some other youth has been given a second chance. Perhaps he is drawn already; I shall never know."

So I thought. Then anger leaped on me like a storm-wave, drumming in my head and shaking my body, so that I was almost mad. I stared out before me, and saw on a high dais a man wearing a kingly robe and necklace. And it seemed I looked upon my enemy, on a stranger who had spat in my face before the people; my fingers longed for his throat, as they had for Kerkyon's while we wrestled for the kingdom.

I stood half out of my wit, with Night's Daughters black about my head, clapping their wings of bronze. And then Apollo, Slayer of Darkness, came and freed me. He took the shape of the youth beside me, who touched my shoulder saying, "Theseus, steady."

The red cleared from my eyes. I could speak, and answered, "These Cretans make me angry." Then I could think.

I thought, "What was it? What has my father done? What every father here would do if he could. And he is King. He has to think for the kingdom. It is true enough that I am needed here. I ought not to think like a warrior only. Has someone else gone to Crete for me? I have led such lads to war, and never thought I wronged them, though some were sure to die. Why then do I hate my father, and myself still more, and feel I cannot bear my life?"

Meanwhile a lot had been called; it fell on Amyntor, a high-born Eleusinian, wild and proud. Unlike the last boy or because of him, he came out gaily, waving to friends and joking. The priest made ready to draw again.

"What hurts me?" I thought. "What is this anger?" I looked at my father; and remembered how he had invoked Poseidon, praying him to choose the victims. And I thought, "Yes! That is it! He has mocked the god, the guardian of the house, who brought him to beget me. Well may I be angry! This man has mocked my father."

Now I understood myself.

I could not speak the thing aloud to the god, for all the people to know it. So I kneeled on one knee, and set my hands on the earth, and whispered so that only he could hear. "Earth-Shaker! Father! If you have been robbed of any offering, tell me, and show me what to give."

I waited, to feel if the earth would tremble; but the dust under my palms was still. Yet I knew he had a message for me, and did not want me to go away. So I bowed my head lower, till my hair trailed in the dust; and then he spoke to me. I heard, as if it rose from the depths of earth, the sound of the sea-surge, waves that mounted and broke in hissing foam, and their sound said, "The-seus! The-seus!"

Then I knew what the god was asking.

It was like a spear in the heart. I had come here to take a chance of one in thirty. Now when I saw before me the certain thing, sorrow fell black upon my eyes and the sun grew cold. I thought of what I had planned to do in Athens: small things I had hoped to force my father's hand to, great ones when my own time came. I knelt where I was, with my hanging hair hiding my face and my name sounding in my ears, and thought of my life; of hunting with the Guard, of feasts and dances, of my room with the lion walls; of a woman I wanted, and had meant to speak to at the festival; of my beautiful horses, who had scarcely felt my hand; of the war paean, the bright rage of battle, and the triumph song. And I thought, "The god cannot mean it. He sent me here to be King."

"Father Poseidon," I whispered, "take something else from me. I will not ask to live long, if I can make a name and be remembered in Athens. Now it will be as if I had never been born. If you want my life, let me die here in battle, and leave some record, a bard's song and a tomb." I heard the name called of some Athenian. It was the last of the seven. "Lord Poseidon, I will give you my horses, the best I ever had. Take anything but this."

The sea-sound grew fainter in my ears. I thought, "He will accept the horses." Yet it was not fading as always before, dying in air, but with a long sound of withdrawal, ebbing and slow. And I thought, "The god is leaving me."

I listened. It had a note that said, "Do as you please, son of Aigeus. Look, there is your father. Forget my voice, which you will not hear again, and learn to reign as he does. Be free. You are not mine, unless you choose."

I looked back at my life, as far as my childhood. "It is too late," I thought, "to be Aigeus' son."

I got up, and threw the hair back from my face. The last-drawn boy was being fetched out. He had not come of himself, being afraid; now as they led him off, he kept looking about, as if he could believe in this happening to anyone but him. "He will be surprised," I thought, "when he finds he is right." I almost laughed; for I had felt the god return to me.

My heart had lightened. It felt secure, as on a lucky day. I breathed bright air. The threat had lifted, the bronze wings and talons hovering to pounce. Fear fell back from me; all was well with me; I walked with the god. As I went forward, an old man's voice said in my memory, "The consenting sets one free."

I walked with a light step to the dais, and leaped upon it, and said to the herald, "Give me that last lot."

He gave it. There was a voice speaking my name, but I kept my face turned away. Drawing my dagger I crossed out the name scratched on the sherd, and wrote "Theseus." I gave it back to the herald, and said, "Call again."

He stared. A hand I knew reached over and snatched it away. So I shouted to the Cretan, "That call was wrong, Captain. The name on the lot is mine."

A noise began among the crowd. I thought they were going to cheer again. But instead I heard a great wail of mourning, lamenting to heaven, as when the herald cries that the King is dead. I did not know what to do with these sounds of grief. In my heart was a solemn music. As I stepped out toward them, a hand clutched at me, but I shook it off, and called aloud to them, "Don't grieve, Athenians. The god is sending me. He has called me to the bulls, and I must obey his sign. But don't weep for me. I will come again." I did not know these words till I had spoken them; they came to me from the god. "I will go with your children, and take them into my hand. They shall be my people."

They had left off weeping, and their voices sank to a hush; only here and there you could still hear some mother sobbing, whose child had gone. I turned, and faced my father.

I saw the face of a man who has got his death-wound. It was like the shape of a frightful dream, from which one has thought to waken. And yet, as if his eyes mirrored my own, he too looked like a haunted man who has shaken off the pursuer.

He suffered, that at least was sure, and it broke from him in anger. With no care who heard, he asked me why I should hate him, and abandon him in his last years to his enemies; how had he wronged me; what had he done? It must be witchcraft, he said; he would have me exorcised, and what I had done in madness should be annulled.

"Sir," I said, "do you think I would have done this of

myself? I know the voice of Poseidon. You must let me go, or he will be angry. It is bad dealing, to rob a god."

When he looked away, I was ashamed. He suffered enough already. "Father," I said, "the god means good to us. Everything is well. If the bulls kill me, he will accept the sacrifice, and take off the curse. And if I come home again, that will be good too. All is well; I feel it."

The Cretan Captain was edging up to listen. My father gave him a look that made him move off, humming and playing with his wrist-seal. Then he said quietly, "It seems no man can outrun his fate. How did you know your name was not in the bowl?" Our eyes met. Then he said, "I could not do it. I fancied men saying for ever after, 'He feared his son, who was a leader and a warrior. So at tribute-time, he sent him to the bulls of Crete.'"

His words amazed me, that such a thing should have crossed his mind. "Father," I said, "it must be the Goddess. She is angry with us; she hates all men who rule."

I heard a cough near by. It was the Cretan, getting impatient. It came to me that now by my own act this man was my master.

I unslung my sword, and put it into my father's hands. "Keep it for me," I said, "until I come again. What the god wants me for, I do not know. But if a man came back from the bulls of Minos, he would have offered his life many times for the god to take, and many times renewed his dedication. Then perhaps some power might come to him, to lead the people. So I was taught, while I was a child. I will be such a king as that, or else I will be nothing."

He came near and took my face between his hands, and looked in it long. It was seldom I thought of him as a priest. But now I felt it. He said at last, "Such a king will be King." Then he paused in thought, and said, "If that day comes, paint the sail of your ship with white. I shall post a lookout on Sounion Head. When his beacon burns, the god will have a message for me. A white sail. Remember."

"My lord," said the Cretan in his high cool voice, "it is all one to me whether your son comes or not, provided there is no disorder. But kindly settle the matter now. These women will be tearing each other's eyes out."

I looked round. The mothers of the chosen youths were disputing which of their sons should be released in place of me. Their menfolk were coming up; he was right in fearing trouble.

"There is nothing to dispute," I said. "The last lot carries my name. Herald, proclaim it."

The last-drawn boy came up and knelt and put my hand to his brow, and begged to do me some service. He seemed a poor creature. I looked past his shoulder, and saw Bias weeping. He had more sense than any of the Companions; but I saw in his face a tale he had never told me. There was nothing to do but take his hand.

"Father," I said, "let the Eleusinians have their own Assembly, unless the women try to seize power again. Everything is in order."

I had not finished; but the Cretan had had enough. He yapped at his troops, sharp as a dog-fox, and they formed a hollow column, all stepping in line, a wonder to see. My father embraced me; I felt from his touch that he never looked to see me more. The mothers of the victims were bringing little bundles of food, put up in haste for the voyage. The last boy's mother came up shyly, bobbing with hand on brow, and gave his bundle to me.

As I fell in line, I remember thinking I would have looked a better suit out, if I had known I was going to Crete.

BOOK FOUR

CRETE

1.

"I was a king and a king's heir," I thought as the ship cast her moorings. "Now I am a slave."

She was a big ship. The figurehead was a bull, with a flower on his brow and gilded horns. Amidships between the rowers were the black soldiers; there was a bridge for the rowing-master, and for the Captain's chair. We victims lived on the afterdeck, and had an awning to sleep under, just as if we had paid our passage. We belonged to the god, and had to be brought unspoiled. There was a guard all day on us, and a double guard all night, to see no one lay with the girls.

It was a time of pause with me. I had passed from my own keeping. I lay in the god's hand, as once in boyhood, cradled on the sea. Dolphins raced along with us, diving under the waves, and blowing "Phoo!" through their foreheads. I lay and watched them. My life was still.

South of Sounion a warship, a fast pentekonter, took us in convoy. Sometimes on island headlands we saw pirate camps; the beached ships and the lookout tower; but none put out after us. We were bigger game than they had teeth for.

These things passed by me while I took my ease as one who hears the harper. "I am going to sacrifice," I told myself. "But Poseidon claimed me, who once was no man's son; and that is mine for ever."

So I sprawled in the sun, and ate and slept and watched the sights, and heard unheeding the sounds of shipboard. Morning broke rose and gray as we threaded the Cyclades. About sunup I heard angry voices. There are many on a ship; we were passing between Kia and Kythnos, and there were things to see. Yet the sound drew tugging at me, and made me look. One of the Athenian boys was fighting an Eleusinian. They rolled grappling on the deck; the Captain was strolling up the bridge toward them, with weary eyelids, like a man who has done this a hundred times. A thin-lashed whip was looped in his hand.

It woke me like mountain water. I took a running leap on them, and pulled them apart. They sat gaping and rubbing bruises; the Captain shrugged and walked away.

"Remember yourselves," I said. "Do you want to be beaten by a Cretan, before those slaves? Where is your pride?" They both began speaking at once, with the onlookers taking sides. I shouted for silence, and saw thirteen pairs of eyes all fixed on me. There was a check in my mind, and I thought, "What now?" It was like reaching for your sword when your side is bare. "What am I doing?" I thought. "I am a slave myself. Can there be a king among victims?" The words echoed in my head.

Everyone was waiting. I pointed at the Eleusinian, whom I knew, and said, "You first, Amyntor. Well?"

He was a black-haired youth, with thick brows meeting over a falcon nose and eyes. "Theseus, this potter's son, with the clay still in his hair, sat in my place; when I told him to move up, he became insolent." The Athenian, who was pale and sharp, said, "I may be Minos' slave, but I am not yours. As for my father, Earthling, I can name him at any rate. We know what your women are." I looked from one to the other, and guessed Amyntor had done the first wrong; yet that at bottom he was the better man.

"Have you done insulting each other?" I said. "While you were about it, you insulted me. Phormion, I chose the customs in Eleusis; if you don't like them, I am the man to tell. It seems, Amyntor, you keep more state here than I do. Tell us what you expect of us, lest we should offend you."

They stammered something. All of them sat around, with trusting dog-eyes. Where there was anger, they hoped for strength. You find the same thing among warriors. But once you have roused this hope, woe to you if you fail it.

I sat on a bale of wool, some small town's tribute, and

looked at them. While we ate, I had picked up the names of
the four Athenian youths: Phormion; Telamon, a small-
holder's son, quiet and steady; a modest graceful lad called
Hippon, whom I had seen somewhere before, and Iros,
whose mother had screamed so at the lottery. She was some
baron's concubine; the boy was slight and high-voiced, with
girlish airs, but away from her petticoats seemed as steady
as anyone else.

The girls I knew still less of. One, Chryse, was a child like
a lily, flawless, white and gold; she was the one the people
had wept for. Melantho was Minyan, a firm bouncing girl,
busy and managing. Of the rest, Nephele was bashful and
snivelling; Helike slim and silent, with slanting eyes; Rhene
and Pylia seemed pretty fools; and Thebe was honest and
kind, but plain as a turnip. I studied their faces, trying to
guess what they would be good for; and they gazed at me,
like swimmers at a floating plank.

"Well," I said, "it is time to talk." They waited. They
had nothing else to do.

"I don't know why Poseidon called me to the bulls;
whether or not he wants me to die in Crete. If not, I shall
put my hand to what I find there. Meanwhile, we are all in
the power of Minos; I am the same as any of you, just a
slave of the god. What do you want me to do? Look out
for myself on my own, or be answerable for you too as I
would at home?"

Before my mouth was shut, they were crying to be led.
Only the slant-eyed Helike was silent; but she never spoke.
"Think first," I said. "If I lead you I shall give laws; will
you like that? There is the man with power to do it." And
I pointed to the Cretan, who had sat down again, and was
paring his nails.

"We will take an oath," said Amyntor, "if you ask us to."

"Yes, I shall. We must swear to stand together. If anyone
dissents, now is the time to say so. You too, girls; I am calling
you to Assembly. We must make our own customs, to suit
our state."

The Athenian girls, who were not used to public business,

hung back whispering; then the dark brisk Minyan, Melantho, said, "We are out of our own lands, so a man ought to lead us; that was always Minyan law. I vote for Theseus." I said, "That is one. What about the other six?" She turned to them scornfully and said, "You hear him. Put up your hands, if you can't talk." Five put them up, and Chryse, the gray-eyed child whose hair hung straight like a sheet of gold, said gravely, "I vote for Theseus."

I turned to the men. "Who is against it? In Crete we shall have to depend on one another. So speak now; and I will bear no grudge, by my father's head."

The young Athenian Iros, the mother's pet, said seriously without his usual mincing, "No one is against, Theseus. You gave yourself to the god; we were only taken. No one else can be King."

"Very well," I said. "In his name be it. We need a mace for the speaker." There was nothing about, except a distaff Thebe was twirling to pass the time. "Throw your wool away, little sister; you will need other skills in Crete." So she threw it overside, and we used the distaff.

"Here is our first law," I said. "We are all one kindred. Not Athenian nor Eleusinian, but both at once. If anyone is highborn, the bulls won't know it; so let him keep his honor only, and forget his rank. Not Hellene nor Minyan, high nor low; no, not even men and women. The girls have got to stay maidens, or lose their lives. Any man who forgets that forswears our oath. Soon we shall all be bull-dancers, men and girls alike. Since we can't be more than comrades, let us swear never to be less."

I drew them together in a ring, while the Cretan priestess squinnied between to see no petticoats got lifted. Then I swore them with a strong oath; for as it was, only misfortune bound us. They looked better after, like all frightened people when given something to do.

"Now we are children of one house," I said. "We ought to have a name."

As I spoke, Chryse looked upward with her wide-set eyes, and I heard a hollow cry. A line of cranes, with long

stretched necks and winnowing wings, was crossing between
the islands. "Look," I said, "Chryse has seen an omen. Cranes
are dancers too; everyone knows the crane-dance. We'll be
the Cranes. And now before we do anything else, we will
commend ourselves to Ever-Living Zeus, and to the Mother.
We must share our gods too, then none will be offended.
Melantho, you shall invoke the Goddess; but there must be
no women's mysteries. The Cranes share everything." To
tell the truth, I was not sorry to pay Mother Dia some
respect. She does not like men who rule; and in Crete I knew
she was supreme.

"Well," I said afterwards, "we are still in council. Does
anyone want to speak?"

The graceful boy, whose face I half remembered, put out
his hand. Now it came back to me where I had seen him:
polishing harness in the stable, while I waited for my father.
Without looking at the Eleusinians, who being from the
Guard were both divinely descended, I gave him the mace
and said, "Hippon is speaking."

"My lord," he said, "is it true we are sacrificed to the bull?
Or has he got to catch us for himself?"

"I should like to know too," I said. "Can anyone tell us?"
This was a mistake. Everyone talked at once, except the
silent Helike, and when I got them using the mace, it was
not much better. All the old wives' tales came out: that we
should be bound to the bull's horns, or thrown into a cave
where he lived on human flesh; even that he was a monster,
a man bull-headed. They were all scaring each other sick.
I shouted for silence, and held out my hand for the mace.

"Which of you," I said, "were frightened with these tales
as children, to keep you quiet?" Several looked sheepish.
"Anyone would think, from the way you go on, that all these
things could be true at once. If even one is, then all the
rest are lies. Hippon is the only one with sense; he doesn't
know, and knows it. We must find out, and stop guessing.
Perhaps I can get the Captain to talk."

The Athenians did not know why I should think so, and
looked amazed, especially the girls. To the Eleusinians I

said, in the slang of the Guard, "If anyone laughs, I will push his teeth in." They grinned, and said, "Good luck, Theseus."

I went over to the ship's side, and stood there pensive. When the Captain looked my way I greeted him. On this he beckoned, and the guards let me on the bridge. He packed off the black boy, who had been sitting at his feet, and offered me his footstool. As I had seen, he had only been held back by fear of a public insult. Our persons were sacred, so he could not have avenged it, beyond a flick of his whip.

As for getting him to talk, he would have been as hard to stop as some old warrior remembering the battles of his youth. He was what they call in Crete a man of fashion. There is no Hellene word for this; it means something more than a gentleman, and something less. Such people study the bull-dance as a harper does old songs. He was still running on when his supper was cooked, and would have kept me to share it. I said the others would kill me for sure if they saw me taking favors, and got away; evening drew on, and it was only the bull-dance I wanted to learn about.

I went back to the Cranes. Dipping in the common pot brought all our heads together.

"Well," I said, "you were right, Hippon; the bull has to catch us. But it is we, in the first place, who must catch him; cut him out of the herd, and bring him in. I can tell you as much about the bull-dance now as anyone can who hasn't seen it. To begin with, before we dance at all we have three months' training."

They had been resigned to death as soon as we touched land. Three months was like three years to them; you would have thought I had given it them myself.

"We live in Knossos Palace, the House of the Ax, and we never leave it. But from what he says, it is pretty big. It is old too—a thousand years, he says, as if anyone could count so many. He says Poseidon lives underneath it, deep in a cave, in the form of a great black bull. No one has ever seen him, he lives too far down; but when he shakes the earth he bellows. Lukos—that's the Captain—has heard it himself and says no sound on earth is half so dreadful. And his deeds in Crete have been like his voice. Two or three times, in former ages, he has had the house down to the very ground. So he is a god they have to pay heed to; and that is how the bull-dance began.

"Lukos says the sacrifice goes back to the very beginning, to the first earth men who made swords of stone. Then it was rude and simple; they just put a man into the bull pit for the bull to gore. But sometimes if he was quick-footed, he would dodge about for a while, which they took sport in, being barbarians. So time went on, and they learned civility from Egypt, and from the men of Atlantis who came flying eastward from Poseidon's anger. Now they are become the most skillful artificers anywhere; not only for pots and jewels and houses, but for music and rites and shows. Since time out of mind they have been working on the bull-dance. First they made the bull pit bigger, and put more victims in, so there was a longer chase before someone was killed. The rest were brought back next time; but the longer they lived, the cunninger they got at dodging, till sometimes the bull tired first, and then they said the god was content for the day. So the neat and the quick lived longest, and taught their craft to others. Thus it went on, each generation adding some flourish to the show; all men will seek honor, even victims doomed to death. It was thought nothing of, just to dodge the horns; you must make a graceful dance of it, and never look flurried or scared, but play the bull as if you loved him. And then, so Lukos says, came the golden age of the bull-dance. There was so much honor in it that the noblest and bravest of the Cretan youth did it for love, to win themselves a name and honor the god. That was the day of the first great bull-leapers; the day the songs are sung of. It is a good while back now, and the young lords and ladies have other pastimes. But sooner than lose the show, they brought in slaves to train. Even now, he says, a kind of glory sticks to a bull-dancer. They think the world of him, if he can keep alive."

"Alas! Alas!" cried moist Nephele, beating her breast as if it were a funeral, "Must we suffer all this before we die?"

I had not finished my tale; but, I thought, better not. "If you cry yourself all to water," I said, "it will not help you. So why cry? When I was a boy at home, we played the bull for sport, and I'm still alive. Don't forget they only drew the lot among the likely ones. If we learn this dance, we may live long enough to escape."

"Theseus," said Melantho, "how many—" "Oh, let him eat," Amyntor said. She asked him sharply if he had left his manners in Eleusis. She would have taken it from an Athenian; but the Minyan girls did not like to see their own men getting above themselves. I said, "Yes? I can eat and listen." She turned her shoulder to Amyntor, and asked, "How many dance at once?" "Fourteen," I answered. "Seven of each." She said, "Then are we a team? Or will they send us here and there, as people get killed?"

"That's the question," I said. It had been on my mind all the while; I had hoped that no one else would think of it. "I dared not ask the Captain; he might have thought we were planning something, and taken care we were split up. Let me think about it."

I never found hunger better my wit; so I ate, and thought. At the end, I said, "Whatever we do, the Cretans will please themselves; we know that. So we must do something or other that will make them think us a team worth keeping. Well, what shall we do, and when shall we do it? Once on shore we may not get the chance. Yet here on shipboard, no one of consequence will see us. This Lukos may be small fry in Knossos, for all his airs. So it will need chewing on."

Menesthes of Salamis, the wiry brown-faced boy whose father owned ships, spoke up for the first time. "Well, we could do it as we come into harbor. Like the Phoenicians, who always come in dancing and singing." I clapped him on the shoulder. "Both answers in one! Yes, we must dance for them, all together."

But at this a squeal went up from the Athenian girls, as from a farrow of piglets. They said that never, never had they stood up to dance with men; that the mere tidings of it would kill their parents dead with shame, and it was enough to lose their lives, without their honor. Nephele led in this. I was sick of her modesty, which she reminded us of too often.

"When you have done," I said, "look at the Captain there. See what he is wearing." He was sitting down, which hid his little loin-guard; he looked stark naked, but for his boots and jewels. "What he has on," I said, "is what you will dance the bull-dance in before ten thousand Cretans. And if you don't like it, ask him to put about and take you home."

She set up a wail. I looked at her, on which she swallowed it.

"And now," I said, "we will dance the Cranes." "But," said Rhene, stretching her eyes and gulping, "that is a dance for men." I stood up and said, "It is our dance from now on. In line!"

So on the little afterdeck, we danced the Cranes in the westering sunlight. The sea was dark blue, like the enamel-smiths' fire on bronze; the islands looked smoke-purple, or dusty gold. When I looked back along the line it was like a plaited garland, white arms and brown, and the mingled colors of the tossing hair. As we danced we sang. The blacks amidships flashed their teeth and eyes, and slapped the beat on their striped shields; the steersman watched with his hand upon the tiller lines, the pilot from the beak; and on the bridge, with the little Negro curled at his feet, the Captain played with his crystal necklace, and arched his brows.

At last we flung ourselves on the deck, panting and smiling. Looking at them all, I thought, "It is beginning. As a hunting pack is more than so many dogs, so too are we."

When I thought about it, it was a good while now since I had spent much time with people my own age. With some of them, such as Chryse and Hippon, I felt old enough to be their father. Not only was I the eldest of us; I was the tallest too, except for Amyntor.

"Good," I said. "That should make them look twice. I don't suppose many victims come in dancing. And people will be there to see, so Lukos says. It seems they bet on the new bull-dancers, which will last longest. I never heard of a sacrifice being treated so lightly. The better for us; even their own gods can't think much of them."

We were making for an island, to lie up for the night, a lovely spot, with high mountains inland, whose slopes were clothed with vines and flowering fruit trees. From one tall peak, that had a flattened tip, a thin smoke was rising. I asked Menesthes if he knew where we were. He said, "It is Kalliste, the fairest of the Cyclades. That mountain is sacred to Hephaistos. You can see the smoke of his smithy, coming out of the top."

The land came near, and my skin prickled. It seemed I saw a doomed and holy brightness, like the beauty of the King Horse groomed for the god. I said, "Is he angry?" "I don't think so," Menesthes said. "It always smokes; the pilots steer by it. It's the last port before Crete. From here it is open water."

"Then," I said, "we must polish our dance, while the light still holds."

In the sunset glow, and in the twilight with lamps appearing, we danced at our mooring on the water-front; and the people of the port stood gaping, knowing where we were bound. Being young and in health, we started to laugh at it; the boys threw cartwheels and somersaults; and suddenly silent Helike, still in silence, bent herself back into a hoop, and stood up on her hands.

"Why," I said laughing, "whoever taught you that? It's as good as a tumbler!"

"Why not?" she said coolly. "That is my trade." She dropped her skirt, making nothing of it; underneath was a little gold-sewn breech. All her bones were like gristle; she could run on her hands as easily as her feet. The black soldiers, who had been telling long tales in a circle, sprang up pointing, and crying "Hau!" She took no notice of them; but except when dancing she was very modest. Girl tumblers have to be chaste; they are no use when they are carrying.

When she stopped, I asked whyever she had not told us.

She looked down a moment, then met my eyes. "I thought everyone would hate me, for having the best chance to live. But we are all friends now. Shall I dance for the Cretans?"

"By the Mother, yes!" I said. "You shall do a turn to finish the show." She said, "But I shall need a man to catch me." "Here are seven; take your choice." She hesitated, and said at last, "I was watching the dance. You are the only one with the knack, Theseus, and that would not be fitting."

"Tell that to the bulls," I said. "It will be news to them. Come, show me what to do."

It was not hard work; she was light as a child, and one only needed to be steady. At the end she said, "If you were a common man, you could make this your living." I said smiling, "We shall all have to live by it, when we get to Crete."

When I had spoken, I looked and saw the eyes of all the others fixed on me in despair. I thought, as one does sooner or later when one has charge of people, "What is the good of it? Why do anything?"

"Believe in yourselves!" I said to them. "If I can learn it, so can you. Only believe, and we may all keep together. Lukos said something about dancers being dedicated in the names of princes and nobles, as an offering to the god. Perhaps one might take us all. Let them all see, when we come in harbor, that we're the best team that ever came to Crete. We *are* the best team. We are the Cranes."

For a moment they stood silent, their eyes like leeches, draining my blood. Then Amyntor waved his hand and cheered, and everyone joined in. At that moment I loved Amyntor. He was haughty, wild, and rash; but he was in love with his honor. You could break every bone in him before he would break his oath.

Next morning, with our breakfast porridge, we finished the food we had brought from home. It was our last link with Athens broken. We had nothing now but one another.

2.

THE seas round Crete are dark blue almost to blackness, wild, bare, and empty. None of us had been before on water where one saw no land. There indeed man is a dust-grain in the palm of the god. But no one was awed except ourselves. The stout priestess stitched in the sun; the seamen trimmed up the ship; the soldiers polished their black limbs with oil; and the Captain sat combing his long dark lovelocks, stripped to his codpiece, while the boy polished his gilded loin-guard and his helmet chased with lily flowers.

Toward evening we got a head breeze; the sail was lowered, and the rowers strained at the oar. The ship, from rolling, started to pitch. At supper-time no one was hungry but Menesthes. A few forced something down; but before dark we threw it up again. Then we lay on the deck and wished to die.

"If tomorrow is the same," I thought, "we are finished." Helike lay moaning, green as a duck's egg. I felt my body sticky with cold sweat. My belly heaved, and I staggered back to the side.

When I was empty, I looked about me. Evening was falling. The sun girdled with purple was sinking in the burnished sea; eastward the first stars blinked in the cloud-rack. I stretched out my hand to Poseidon, but he sent no sign. He was away perhaps, shaking the earth somewhere. All about us I felt another power, dark, past man's thought, giver of desolation or of joy, she who can cherish or cast away but abides no question. Two gulls flew by me, one following the other with wild cries, the pursued screaming as if in scorn. I was cold and weak, and grasped the bulwark to keep from falling.

"Sea Mother," I said, "Foam-Born Peleia of the Doves, this is your kingdom. Do not forsake us while we are in Crete. I have no offering now for you; but I swear, if I get back to Athens, you and your doves shall have a shrine upon the Citadel."

I sank on the deck again, and pulled my blanket over my head. Lying down eased the sickness and I slept. When I woke, the stars were paling, and the wind had changed; we had tacked and it was behind us. The ship flew smoothly; stretched out like spent dogs the rowers lay sleeping. The Cranes woke up, and reached hungrily for last night's uneaten food.

When day was bright, we saw before us the high shores of Crete: huge wrinkled yellow cliffs, sheer-standing, the land hidden above them. It looked a cruel coast.

The great sail was hauled down, and another hoisted. All the royal ships of Crete had their dress sails, kept fresh for making port. This was dark blue, with a device in red. It showed a naked warrior, with a bull's head on his shoulders.

The Athenians gazed with eyes of stone. Nephele, always the first to weep unless the grief was another's, sobbed, "Oh, you deceived us, Theseus! There is a monster after all!"

"Shut your noise," I said. She put me out of patience. But she liked roughness in men, and dried her eyes. "You fool," I said, "it is the emblem of a god. So they draw the Earth Snake manheaded; did you ever meet him?" They cheered up, and I felt better myself. "At the harbor bar," I said, "be ready."

Where the cliffs opened to a river-mouth, we saw the port of Amnisos. Since it was bigger than Athens, we took it for Knossos itself. The soldiers formed up forward; the Captain, curled and oiled and burnished, stood on the bridge gilt-helmed and spear in hand; we could smell his scent from the afterdeck. They had taken down our awning, to let us be seen. Ahead was the mole, with people on it.

I knew nothing yet; but they gave me pause. There was an air in their looking and strolling, before one could see a face. They seemed people broke to wonders, as the chariot horse is broke to noise. They had not come to stare, but to glance idly and pass on. Women with parasols leaned together heads crimped and bound with gems; slim men half bare, with gilded belts and jewelled necklaces and flowers behind their ears, led spotted hounds as languid and proud as they. Even the laborers seemed to look at us over their shoulders, as if in passing at a common thing. I felt the pride drain out of me, like blood from a mortal wound. These were the people I had thought to amaze. My toes curled on the deck, as I pictured their laughter.

I looked round. The Cranes too had seen. They were waiting, as a tired slave waits for bedtime, to hear me own we were beaten. "They are right," I thought. "We have got to die; let us come to it decently at least." And then I thought, "This is Crete. We have come to the end, but for this one thing. I have made myself answerable for these people; now I must go on if the whole world mocks me. I undertook it."

I clapped my hands, and shouted, "Sing!"

They formed their circle, and now in the first comers I knew the bravest and the best: Amyntor, Chryse, Melantho, Iros and Hippon and Menesthes, and good ugly Thebe. As for Helike, she was there already, the only one who had not faltered. Poised as proudly as the Cretans on her slender feet, she seemed to say she had no awe of such people, she who had danced for kings. It was she who saved us. Till now she had been playing, saving her best for the show. The rest looked at her, not at the Cretans, when we passed the mole. I tossed her up as she had taught me, and felt her little hands, clever and strong as an ape's, grasp my shoulders as she stood upside down. "Fate is our master," I thought. "Yesterday a king, and today a tumbler's man. I hope my father never hears of it."

I heard the twitter of voices, calling out to each other, but could not move to look. Picturing all those scornful eyes, I wished myself at the bottom of the sea. Then Helike signed to me to catch her; and as her face passed mine she winked at me. The dance ended. I looked, and saw Lukos on his bridge waving gaily to the people. He looked so pleased with himself that I could have kicked him, even when I saw what it meant.

We tied up at a high stone wharf. Beyond were houses like rows of towers, four or five floors high. The dockside swarmed with faces, brown and quick-eyed. In the midst were some priests, who I thought had come to receive us. But they stood there, pointing and tittering. They wore petticoats, to show they served the Goddess; and I saw from their smooth plump faces and shrill speech that they had offered her their manhood. They were only here to stare.

We stood for a long while in the hot Cretan sun, with the troops drawn up beside us and the Captain idling on his spear. No one kept the crowd away from us. Women clucked and giggled; men disputed; in front was a crowd of flashy fellows with gimcrack jewels, like the man at Troizen. But I could not tell them this time to get out of my sight. They were the gamblers and the bookmakers, come to reckon the odds on our length of days.

They walked round us, chaffering together in Cretan stuck with Greek words misused, the speech of such men in Knossos. Then they came up and kneaded our muscles, or, nudging each other, pinched the girls on their breasts and thighs. So long as no one damaged us, we were anybody's meat. Amyntor would have struck one, but I held his arm. It was beneath us to notice them. Death I had been ready for, but not this, to go to the god with less honor than an ox or a horse. Better I had leaped in the sea, I thought, before I made myself a mountebank for scum like these.

Suddenly a great trumpet blast sounded behind us. I jumped round to face it, as anyone would who had been a warrior. But there were only the gamblers, pointing and shouting odds. It was a trick they used on the new bull-dancers, to see who moved quickest, and who was afraid. Chryse's eyes were wet with tears; I don't think she had known a rough word before she left her home. I took her hand, till I heard the lewd talk, and then I dropped it.

A stinking fellow wearing stale scent poked my ribs and asked my name. When I took no notice, he shouted as if

I were a deaf idiot, in barbarous Greek, "How old are you?
When were you last sick? How did you get those scars?"
Turning from his foul breath, I caught the eye of Lukos,
who shrugged, as if to say, "I cannot be answerable for
these low fellows. When you had a gentleman, you were
not thankful."

But the heads of the crowd were turning. I followed their
gaze, up the steep street of tall houses. Three or four litters
were coming down it. Soon there were more, filling the
causeway between the middens. Lukos looked well pleased
with himself. I saw it was not to amuse the rabble he had
kept us here.

The litters approached: first a man in a carrying-chair,
nursing in his lap a cat with a turquoise collar; then two
women's litters, the curtains open, the servants running side
by side to let their mistresses gossip. They leaned together,
their hands in fluttering talk, and the shoulders of the inside
bearers nearly breaking, for they were all little men. The
people in the litters were much bigger than the Cretans
round them, and fairer too. This made me sure they were
from the Palace; for I knew the house of Minos had Hellene
blood and that the court spoke Greek.

Litter after litter was set down; lords and ladies were
lifted out like precious jewels, and handed their lap dogs,
their fans, or their parasols. Each seemed to have brought
some toy or other; one young man had a monkey with its
fur dyed blue. And yet, if you will believe it, out of all
those men, the King's daily companions fed at his board
with his meat and wine, not one carried a sword.

They all met and greeted, kissing cheeks or touching
hands, talking together in the high clear voice of the Palace
people. Their Greek was quite pure, but for the Cretan
accent which sounds so mincing to a mainland ear. They
have more words than we, for they talk continually of what
they think and feel. But mostly one could understand them.
The women called each other by such baby-names as we
would use to children; and the men called them "darling"
whether they were married to them or not; a thing which

from their behavior nobody could guess. I saw one woman alone kissed by three men.

They greeted Lukos gaily, but without much regard; one could see he looked rather too much a Cretan. However, he got some kisses. A woman with a pair of love-birds on her shoulder said, "You see, dear man, how we trust you; all this way in the noon heat, just at the whisper that you have something new to show." The man with the cat said, "I hope your swans are not geese." Just then a woman came up richly dressed, with an old face and young hair; I had never seen a wig before. She was leaning on a young man's arm, her son or husband, one could not say. "Show! Show!" she cried. "We are here the first and must be rewarded. Is t the girl?" She peered at Chryse, who had drawn close to my side. "But she is a child. In three years, yes, oh yes, a face to burn cities. What a thousand pities she will not live!" I felt Chryse's arm tremble against mine, and touched her hand softly. The young man bent and murmured in the woman's ear, "They understand you." She moved away raising her brows, as if she found us presumptuous. "Tut, my dear, they are barbarians after all. They don't feel as we should."

Meantime Lukos had been talking to the man with the cat, whom I now heard saying, "Yes, yes, no doubt; but does it signify much? These mainland kings breed like conies; I daresay he has fifty." Lukos said, "But this one is legitimate. More than that, the heir . . . Certainly I am sure; you should have heard the scene. And what is more, he came of his own desire. An offering to Poseidon, so I understand."

A young woman, with large doe's eyes painted to look larger, said, "Is it really true, then, that the mainland kings still immolate themselves? Just like the old songs? What it must be, to be a man and travel, and see these wild savage places! Tell me, which is the prince?" A friend lifted to her mouth her peacock fan, and whispered, "You can see."

They both slanted their blue-lashed eyes, and then looked down. I began to notice that whereas these ladies looked at the girls, and spoke of them, as if they were already dead, toward us men they were not quite the same. I believe, on that first day, I wondered why.

Two of the men had just walked round us to stare their fill, not lewdly like the gamblers, but coolly, as if we were horses. I heard one say, "It passes me why Lukos put on this show. If he had kept quiet till the bidding, he might have had a chance himself." The other said, "Never; he's not the only one who knows form. It must be something to him to be talked about; or he would have sold the news, we all know where." The first man looked round, and said, dropping his voice, "No one from the Little Palace. If he is the last to hear, Lukos will be sorry." The other, without speaking, raised his brows and moved his eyes. I followed their glance.

Another chair was coming; or, rather, a kind of car. Two great oxen drew it, whose horns were painted crimson and tipped with gold. A tooled leather canopy on four poles shaded a thronelike chair, in which sat a man.

He was very dark; not russet like the native Cretans, but greenish-dark like the ripe olive; and as thick as a bullock. His neck was no narrower than his head, and only a line of blue-black beard marked off one from the other. Coarse oiled black curls hung on his low brow; his nose was broad, with wide black nostrils. One would have said a beastlike face, only the thick mouth was a mouth that thought. And the eyes told nothing. They only stared, while behind them the man seemed making ready to do what he would do. They put me in mind of something seen long ago, which I could not recall.

The chair came up and the servant who led the oxen stopped them. The court people made graceful salutations, touching their finger-tips to their brows; the man's answer was rough and careless, hardly more than wagging a finger. He did not get down, but beckoned, and Lukos came up bowing. I could just catch their words.

"Well, Lukos, I hope you have pleased yourself today. I

you thought to please me, you are a greater fool than you look."

From a chief among warriors, it would have been nothing much. But after all the fine manners and courtly speech, it came like a savage beast breaking in among people who were afraid of it. They had all drawn back, lest they should seem to listen.

Lukos was saying, "My lord, no one here knows anything. This show in the harbor, the boys and girls put up themselves, for sport. People thought I trained them, so I said nothing, and kept the truth for you. There is more here than they think."

He nodded as if saying openly, "Well, you may be lying, or perhaps not." Then he ran his eye along us, while Lukos whispered in his ear. Amyntor, who was near me, said, "Is this Minos himself, do you think?" I looked again, and raised my brows. "He? Never. The house is Hellene. Besides, that is not a king."

As these words left me, I heard all the twittering voices sink, like bird song before a storm. We had stood there so long, being talked of like cattle without understanding, I had forgotten we could be understood ourselves. The man had heard.

The courtiers looked as scared as if I had thrown a thunderbolt among them, which they must pretend not to see. I thought, "What is all this to-do? Either the man is King, or he is not." Then I saw his eyes on me, large staring eyes that bulged a little. And I remembered where I had seen them; they were like the eyes of the Palace bull at Troizen, just before he put down his head to charge.

"What have I done?" I thought. "That old woman at home was right to call me a meddler. I was resolved to get us talked of here, and what has come of it? This brute, who can clearly have what he wants, now wants to own us; the worst master in Knossos, without a doubt. This is what comes of presuming; I should have left everything to the god." And I began to wonder how I could get us out of it.

Just then he stepped down from his chair. From his bulk

I had expected him to stand six feet or more; but he was hardly the common height of a Hellene, so short were his thick legs for his trunk. As he got nearer, I felt something about him that gave me gooseflesh. It was more than his ugliness, or his wicked look; as it might have been something against nature.

He began to walk round us, and to look us over. He handled the boys like a steward buying meat; but with the girls he was shameless, in spite of the people watching; I saw he thought himself above their opinion. Melantho was angry, which pleased him; Helike, who I suppose had had things to put up with in her calling, stood in silent scorn; Nephele winced, which made him laugh and slap her bottom. Watching him draw near Chryse, who was my darling of all the girls, I said to her quietly, "Don't be frightened. You belong to the god." His eye slewed round at me; and I saw he was leaving me to the last.

To seem careless, I looked away; and my eye fell on a litter that had not been there before. It had been set down on its feet not far away; but the curtains of thick rich stuff were still close-drawn. One of the bearers was fetching Lukos over. He went at once, bowing low before it, and setting his clenched hand to his brow in the salutation we use for gods. The curtains parted, a little crack that showed nothing; though I could hear no voice, someone within was speaking, for, to hear better, he sank down and knelt with one knee in the dust.

At this I expected the rest to do some homage. But after one glance they went on as if nothing were there. It made a deep mark upon my mind. I had thought I knew a little about command, and what is due to a man of standing. "But this is something," I thought, "to summon invisibility, like a god." I had no time to think more; for the man had come to me.

He looked me in the eye; then he put his black hairy hands on Chryse and ran them all over her. Anger almost burst me; but I guessed that if I struck him she would be first to pay. So I commanded myself, and said to her, "Take no notice. The people here are ignorant."

He turned, moving faster than I had thought he could, and took hold of my face by the chin. His body was scented with musk, heavy and sickening. He held my face with one hand and slapped it across with the other, so hard that my eyes watered. Something weighed down my right arm; afterwards I found the marks of Chryse's nails. I should have forgotten everything, but for her; there was strength under her sweetness. Beyond, among the courtiers, I heard a murmur, as if custom had been offended; they sounded indeed more shocked than I was, for no one expects a slave to have any rights, and I should have been ready for such things, but for the care taken of us on the ship. At the sound he turned round swiftly, to find their faces blank; they were expert at this. For my part, I hated them only because they had seen it. I was afraid they might think I was weeping.

With my face still in his hand, he said, "Don't cry, little cockerel; the bulls will hurt you more. What do they call you, where you come from?"

I answered aloud, so that no one should think I was crying, "In Athens they call me Shepherd of the People; and they call me Kerkyon in Eleusis. But in Troizen, they call me Kouros of Poseidon."

"What is it to me," he said, breathing in my face, "what titles your tribesmen give you, you mainland savage? Tell me your name."

"My name is Theseus," I said. "I would have told you before if you had asked me."

He struck my face again, but this time I was ready and stood still. There was a pause, while some thought was born behind his staring eyes.

The closed litter still stood there. Lukos had gone away, but the crack still gaped a little, though I could see no hand. The man had not looked that way since it had come, being busy with us. I wondered if whoever was inside would be angry to see him slighted. "Surely," I thought, "the odds are on anyone hating him, from a god down to a dog. And he was not called to speak. But nothing in Crete is simple."

"Kouros of Poseidon!" he said to me grinning. "And how are you Poseidon's? Your mother went bathing, did she, and met an eel?" He turned round to the courtiers, who offered thin laughter, like people paying a tax.

I said, "I am his servant and his sacrifice. It is a thing between him and me."

He nodded, with a scornful mouth and blank stare hiding his mind, looking all round, to see he had the people's eyes. There was a gold ring on his forefinger, heavy and big; he drew it off, and tossed it in his palm. Then he flipped it in the air, so that it drew a bright line in the sun, and fell beyond the wharf into the sea. I saw it gleam and sink. And from the crowd of Cretans came a strange murmuring, as if they had seen impiety, or some ill omen.

"Well, Kouros of Poseidon," he said, "if you are so thick with your fish-daddy, he will give it back to you. Go down and ask him."

We were still a moment, looking at one another. Then I turned and ran to the wharfside and dived in. It was quiet and cool in the sea, after the hot wharf with its staring crowds. I went down and opened my eyes, and saw the shining sea-roof above me, and, below, the harbor floor patched with dark sponges, and strewn with the refuse of ships; broken pots and baskets, sodden skins of fruit and gourds, and old gnawed bones.

I thought, "He has made game of me. He knew I would not deny the god. Here I am diving for him like the slave-boy of some poor fisherman getting shellfish for his master. He did it to break my pride; no, to kill me, for he saw I would not come up with empty hands. If I die down here, it will be on my own head; no one can say he murdered a sacred victim. Yes, he is a beast that thinks. Someone should kill him."

All this while, I was searching about in the dirty water. I had breathed in before I dived, but not enough, having no practice in it, and already my chest felt tight. "My eyes will blacken soon," I thought; "then I am done." There was a stone before me, and under it a squid waving its arms as if it mocked me; out and in; it seemed to grow bigger and smaller, like something in a dream. And then I heard a roaring in my ears, like waves beating on shingle. "You boasted of me, Theseus," said the voice of the sea, "but did you pray to me?"

So I prayed with my heart to the god, since my mouth was sealed with water. "Help me, Father. Save my people. Let me avenge my honor." The blackness cleared from my eyes; and I saw in the mud under the squid a bright thing settling. I snatched at it; the slimy grip of the squid lashed my wrist, then he took fright and let go, filling the water round with his black ink. He must have seized it for food, and given it back at the command of the god.

I shot up to the light, and breathed like one coming back from the dead, and swam toward the wharf steps, with my hand clenched on the ring, for it was loose upon my finger. The Cranes waved and called my name. Then I looked at my enemy. I saw he had got ready, while I was down there, what he would say when I came up ashamed, or when I did not come. Now his mouth straightened and set. But his round stare did not alter. Presently he said in his coarse arrogant voice, "Well, well, it seems you have missed your calling. A fish-boy, sure enough." And he held his hand out for the ring.

I drew it off and looked at it. It had a goddess carved on it, with a high diadem and serpents in her hands. I held it out on my palm, so that it could be seen; I did not want him saying I had cheated with a pebble. "Here is your ring," I said. "Do you know it?"

"Yes," he said, his chin looking lower on his thick neck. "Give it here."

I took a step back. "You have seen it, then. But it was an offering to Poseidon. We must give it him back again." I threw it into the water, and said in the silence, "If you want it, it is between the god and you."

Everything was so still that the ring's splash sounded clearly. Then all the poor Cretans, the porters and sailors and rowers, started jabbering together as shrill as monkeys. Even from the Palace people came whispering and twittering, like birds hidden in leafy trees. I looked at the covered litter. The crack was a little wider, but still one could not see in. I felt that this unseen watcher had made me dare to throw the ring back in the sea, and wondered if it was sense or madness. The circles of its fall died on the water; and I turned to face its master.

I had looked to see him swollen with anger, and readied myself to be beaten if not worse. But he was quite still; hard, still, and staring. Then his head went up; his mouth opened; and the place was filled with his bellowing laughter. It startled the harbor gulls, and they flew up screeching.

"Well done, fish-boy!" he roared. "Your fish-father gets the prize! Commend me to him; tell him not to forget Asterion!" He rocked round laughing on his heel, toward his ox-car. It brought him round facing the litter; he saw it then for the first time. For a moment the laughter slipped from his face, like a mask when the string is broken. But he caught it back again, and the chair shook as he drove away.

3.

THE Knossos road climbs from the port between orchards and silver olives. It is a rich land, within its deathly cliffs. The black troops still escorted us; but Lukos avoided me, which I did not find strange, for I had angered a powerful lord, and that is a catching sickness. The houses of the rich merchants lining the road were like small palaces; I was always expecting one to be the house of the King, but ceased to ask when I saw the black men grinning.

We passed the houses, and Lukos came nearer, like a man pondering a doubtful horse. I said to him, "Who was that man in the ox-car?" He looked about him, hiding it, in the way of the Palace people; then he said, "You were foolish. That was the King's son, Asterion." I laughed and said, "A starry name for an earthy king." He answered, "It is not for you to use it. The style of the heir is Minotauros."

Something came back to me. A feather seemed to brush the short hairs on my neck. But I said nothing to the others; it concerned my own moira only.

The road was coming out on a fertile plain, with a range of mountains beyond. The shape of the ridge was for all the world like a great long bearded man, lying flat on a bier. I pointed it out and Iros said, "I've heard of that. They call it the Dead Zeus." "Dead!" cried the Cranes all together, shocked at the impiety. "Yes," he said. "These Earthlings think he dies each year." I was still staring at the mountain when Melantho called, "Look! Look!" And then, on a spur of the foothills that thrust into the plain, I saw for the first time the House of the Ax.

Picture to yourself all the kings' palaces you ever saw, set side by side and piled on one another. That will be a little house, beside the House of the Ax. It was a palace within whose bounds you could have set a town. It crowned the ridge and clung to its downward slopes, terrace after terrace, tier after tier of painted columns, deep glowing red, tapering in toward the base, and ringed at head and foot with that dark brilliant blue the Cretans love. Behind them in the noonday shadow were porticoes and balconies gay with pictured walls, which glowed in the shade like beds of flowers. The tops of tall cypresses hardly showed above the roofs of the courts they grew in. Over the highest roof-edge, sharp-cut against the deep-blue Cretan sky, a mighty pair of horns reared toward heaven.

The sight winded me like a blow in the belly. I had heard travellers' tales third-hand, but pictured them in the likeness of what I knew. I felt like a goatherd who comes in from the back hills and sees his first city. My mouth fell open in just such a peasant's gape, and I shut it quickly before Lukos could look. Now when no one was hurting me, I could have wept indeed. All about me the Cranes were chattering and gasping. Presently Amyntor said to me, "Where are the walls?"

I looked. The Palace stood on an easy slope; yet it had no more walls than a common dwelling-house might have, to keep thieves out and slaves in. The roofs were even without battlements, crowned only by their insolent horns, a pair facing each way. Such was the power of Minos. His walls were on the waters, which his ships commanded. I stared in silence, shutting my face on my despair. I felt like a child come among warriors with a wooden spear. Also I felt up-country, rude and ignorant, which hurts a young man more. "All very fine," I said. "But if war came to Crete, they could not hold it a day."

Lukos had heard me. But here on his home ground he was too easy for anger. He said with his careless smile, "The House of the Ax has stood here a thousand years, and never fell yet except when the Earth Bull shook it. It was old when you Hellenes were herdsmen still on the northern grasslands. I see you doubt me, but that is natural. We have learned from the Egyptians to reckon years and ages. You, I think, have a saying, 'Time out of mind.'" He strolled on, before I had an answer.

We entered the Palace precinct by the great West Gate. On either side there were staring people. Before us was the great red lintel-column, the painted shadows beyond. I walked ahead, looking straight before me. If someone spoke, or anything new confused me, I would pause, and turn slowly as if I had just deigned to notice it. When I look back, all this seems laughable, a boyish vanity, not to be caught like a bumpkin at a loss. And yet, the mark of those days has never left me. I have heard people say in Athens that my bearing is more kingly than my father's was. But I was quick-moving as a youth, pricking like a dog at every-thing around me. It was in the House of the Ax that I learned stillness, and to keep my speed till I had call for it.

The Palace people had swarmed to look; yet I thought these seemed of less consequence than those who had come all the way down to the port to see us. It puzzled me, but I could make nothing of it. We passed the guardhouse, and entered a great Throne Room of audience. It was full of guards and priestesses and priests and Palace people; and against the far wall was a tall white throne, but it was empty.

Once more we waited, but this time in deep decorum. The people peeped discreetly, and murmured together. To pass the time, I raised my eyes to the walls; and then I forgot my resolve to stare at nothing new. For pictured there was the bull-dance, from the taking of the bull to the very end: beauty and pain, skill and glory, fleetness and fear and grace and blood, all that fierce music. My eyes were glued to it, till I heard a woman whisper, "Look at that one. Already he wants to learn." But just then voices said, "Hush."

The guards' spears rattled. King Minos entered, and went up the side of the dais, and sat upon his carved white throne, resting hands on knees like the gods of Egypt. He wore a long red belted robe, and he looked tall; but that might have been his horns. The light from the portico gleamed dimly back from his gold face and crystal eyes.

In the quiet, I heard from the Cranes soft indrawn breaths. But that was all. Old Cretans say we were the first band of victims, seeing Minos in his bull-mask, of whom not one cried aloud for fear.

The mask was the work of some great artificer, solemn and noble. But before I had looked enough, the show was over. Lukos stepped out and spoke some words in Cretan; all the rite of the bull-dance is in the ancient tongue. For a moment we felt ourselves watched from behind the crystal; then a gold glove gestured; the spears rattled again; the King went out; and we were led onward from the presence chamber, through painted corridors, and colonnades barred with shadow, and up a great stair open to heaven, and through more passages and halls, till we knew north from south no longer, deeper and deeper into the House of the Ax, which Cretans call the Labyrinth.

At last we came out into a great chamber. Within the door stood either side on a pillar mount the Cretan double ax, the sacred Labrys. So I knew this huge place was a shrine. And at the far end, picked out in light that slanted from the roof, I saw the Goddess. She stood ten feet tall, crowned with a golden diadem; round her waist a gold apron lay over a skirt of many flounces, worked cunningly in enamel and precious gems. Her face was ivory; ivory were her round bare breasts, and her outstretched arms entwined with golden serpents. Her hands were held out low over the earth, as if they said, "Be still."

We went forward, between walls pictured with her worship. I saw before her feet a long offering table inlaid with gold, and round it faces I knew again. Here were the nobles who had come down to the harbor; and among them, as broad as any two, swarthy Asterion whose title was Minos' Bull.

Lukos halted us ten paces off. We waited. The people at the table whispered together. Then, from behind the painted goddess, came out a goddess of flesh.

Beside the great image she seemed little, and even for a woman she was not tall, in spite of her high diadem. She wore the whole costume of the Goddess, all but the snakes. Even her skin, pale golden, polished and clear, had a look of ivory. Her high round breasts had golden tips, like those above her. Their faces were painted just alike, the eyes drawn round with black, the brows arched and thickened, the small mouth red. It seemed the face below must be itself the same.

Since childhood I had seen my mother dressed for her priestly office; yet I was awed. She had never claimed to be more than a servant of the deity. This small stiff figure had a bearing that might claim anything.

She came forward to the offering table and set on it her outstretched hands. It was the very posture of the Goddess. Then she spoke, a few words only in the ancient tongue; a cool clear voice, like cold water on cold stones. Between the heavy painted eyelids, dark eyes moved, regarding us; for a moment they met mine. A shock went through me, such as Minos' bull-mask had not struck into my flesh. A woman-goddess; and young.

She stood at the table waiting, and the nobles came forward, each with a clay tablet in the hand. Each would point to one of us or the other and put the tablet down. I saw these must be offering-tokens, such as my mother received at home in the Goddess' name, so many jars of oil or honey, so many tripods; she would read them out, and the worshipper paid later. This seemed the same, though all in Cretan; only here they were buying their beasts of sacrifice. I saw the man with the blue monkey point to Iros, the man with the cat to Chryse, the old woman to me. Last stepped up Asterion, and tossed his token down so that it rattled. She read it out; the rest all stared and muttered, and fell back sullenly. She spoke a phrase, in which I heard his name, and he nodded, satisfied, looking scornfully at the rest. For a moment she stood still at the table with her hands upon it, in the ritual posture. Then, meeting his eyes, she lifted up his tablet in her palms, and showed him it was broken.

There was silence, and the air prickled. I saw him stare at her, his jowl settling in his neck, his color thickening. She met his gaze, but her face was still, keeping the likeness of the image. Then she turned and went out the way she had come, and everyone raised fist to brow in homage. I too saluted her. It is never wise to neglect the gods of the place, wherever one may be.

The courtiers left the shrine; as they passed the door one saw their heads coming together. Asterion came up to Lukos, jerking his head at us, and giving some order. Lukos bowed deeply; he seemed struck with new awe. As for me, I stood up straight, waiting to hear what was in store for me. But our new master turned on his heel, and did not even look at me.

Nor did the Cranes. Their eyes were downcast.

"How can I face them?" I thought. "They will all pay for my pride. Yet how could I have denied Poseidon? The god would leave me."

It was clear to me now why only the richest nobles had come down to the port. They were the ones who could afford to dedicate a bull-dancer; they wanted one who would do them credit. This rite at the shrine was a solemn business, going back, I suppose, to a time when they had more reverence for their gods. Down there they could look well, and appraise us.

"I must have been mad," I thought, "to fancy insolence would keep him from buying me. Of course he has bought me for revenge. But what about the others?"

Just as I was wondering whether if we ran for it any would get away, a young man came and said lightly to Lukos, "Am I late? I will take them off your hands." I saw he was doing some common office; so I went with him, and the Cranes followed.

Once more we threaded corridors and stairs and terraces, and crossed a great open court. Then there was a low entry, and another passage, which sloped downward. And I began to hear a sound. As I listened, I felt cold fingers touching my hand. They were Chryse's; but she kept silent, while the others caught their breath. A bull was bellowing in some hollow place, roaring and bawling between walls that flung back the sound; and we were walking toward it.

I looked at the man who led us. He walked carelessly, and seemed neither sorry nor glad, but to be thinking of his own concerns. I squeezed Chryse's hand, and said to the others, "Listen. That is not anger." For now we were nearer, I could judge the sound, and knew it.

We came out into a low crypt, lit with windows close to the roof, which were at ground level; the rest was all below. In the midst, sunk lower yet into the earth, was a big square pit of sacrifice. The bellowing of the bull filled it with a noise that nearly split one's head in two. He lay on the great stone altar, trussed up and hamstrung, waiting for the knife.

He roared, and heaved, and beat his head up and down upon the stone; but in the pit all else was quiet and orderly: the strong young priest, bare but for his apron, holding the double ax; the table with the jugs and the libation bowls; the three priestesses, and the lady of the sanctuary.

The young man who had brought us led us to the edge of the pit, which was about as deep as a man is high, with steps going down. He made the sign of homage, and stepped back. I raised my brows at him, and he said impatiently through the din, "You have to be purified." He would have gone then, but I caught his arm. "Who is that girl?" I asked, and pointed, to be clear, because of the noise.

He looked shocked past speech. Then he hissed in my ear, "Be quiet, barbarian. That is Ariadne the Holy One, the Goddess-on-Earth."

I looked. She had seen me pointing, and her back was stiff. I saw she was not one to be lightly affronted. I touched my brow and was silent.

She paused long, to reprove me. Then she beckoned us down the steps. We stood in the pit before her, while the bull-cries beat on our ears. Then she spoke in Cretan, words of a ritual, and made a sign. The priest swung up the ax, and struck, and the blood spurted like a fountain into the libation bowl. The roaring choked and fell silent, and the head lolled down.

A priestess brought a long rod with a tuft upon the end, and held it for her hand. But she put it away, and said in Greek, "You are to be made clean for the gods below. Is there any one of you who has shed the blood of a kinsman? Speak truly. There is a death-curse on him who lies."

While she spoke Cretan she had been all goddess; but on the Greek she stumbled once, and I heard a human voice. The priestesses had turned to look, as if the ritual were broken.

I stepped forward and said, "I have. Lately I killed some of my cousins, three with my own hand. My father's brother died too, though I did not kill him myself."

She nodded, and said something to the priestesses. Then she said to me, "Come out, then. You must be cleansed apart." She motioned me toward the altar where the bull's blood was draining down. Now I was quite near her, and saw within the painted brows a down of soft hair. The place was thick with the hot stink of blood; yet now I thought, "Goddess-on-Earth she may be; but she has the scent of a woman." A little shudder stabbed me through, and my heart quickened.

She said, speaking precisely as if each word were a grain of gold she was counting out, "For what cause did you kill these men? In a brawl? Or to pay a blood-debt?" I shook my head and said, "No, in war, defending my father's kingdom." She asked, "And is he the lawful King?" Her hair was fine and dark, with a soft burnish on it; a curling lock had fallen down over her breast; I could see tiny creases in the gilded nipple. I remembered where we were, and took a step back from her, and said "Yes." She nodded gravely; but I saw the lock rise and fall again, and my blood sang in my ears.

Presently she said coolly, word by word, "And you were born in his house, of one of his women?" I looked her in the face. She did not look down; but her eyelids quivered. "My mother is the Lady of Troizen," I said, "daughter of King Pittheus by Klymene his queen. I am Theseus son of Aigeus son of Pandion, Shepherd of Athens."

She stood as straight and stiff as the image in the sanctuary; but a little disk of gold in her diadem caught the light as it trembled. "Then," she said, "why are you here?" I answered, "I made the offering for the people's sake. I had the sign."

For a little there was silence, and I waited. Then she said in a light quick voice, "You may be cleansed of this blood, because you saved your father's."

The priestess offered her the rod again, but she turned away and dipped her finger in the steaming blood-bowl, and made on my breast the signs of the trident and the dove. I felt the blood warm and sticky, and with it her finger-tip, smooth and cool. The touch went right through me. I resolved not to look at her; it is dangerous to strip a goddess, even in thought. Then I looked. But she was looking at the water-bowl they held her to rinse her fingers.

Presently she made a gesture, as if impatient, and the priestesses led me aside. Then she took the rod of aspersion, and dipped the tuft in the blood and sprinkled the Cranes with it, and uttered an invocation. Then she went straight to the steps. When she picked up her skirt to climb them, I saw her little feet, arched and slender, and softly rouged on the toes and heel. All the great ladies of the Labyrinth go barefoot. They never go outside, unless they are carried.

Once more we threaded the House of the Ax. Sometimes we saw a painting we had passed before, then turned aside and were lost again. But at last we came to a passage that ended in a great door, all studded with bronze nails. The young man tapped with his dagger hilt; a guard opened it, and let us in, and made us wait. The passage went on beyond; and at the far end was the sound of voices echoing in a lofty hall. The voices were many, and all young.

Presently there came a man about forty years old, by his looks half Cretan and half Hellene; a wiry man with a short dark beard, who had something of a horse-master or charioteer. The young man said, "Here is the new batch, Aktor. To train as a team. That is the order."

The man looked us over with a narrow black eye. Here was another who sized us up like horses. But this was no buyer. This man would do the work. He snorted and said, "It's true, then? He took them all?" and looked again. "All one team?" he said. "What is he about? Am I not to give them a leader? And the Corinthian, what am I to do with *him*?" The young man shrugged (it is a gesture Cretans are fond of) and said, "That is my message. Ask the patron." He went away.

The door clanged shut behind us. The man looked us over again, frowning to himself, and whistling through his teeth. He made no difference between girls and boys. When he got to me he said, "You're old for this game. How did you get here? You've a beard coming." And then, before I could answer, "Well, you're built for it, we shall see, we shall see. We must make what we can of what we get, with patrons teaching us our business." He muttered on to himself, like a groom currying a horse; then said suddenly, "There is the Bull Court. Practice is over; you will be eating soon." He jerked his thumb and was gone.

I had thought we should get some account at last of what we were to do. But we were only raw colts being turned into

the horse field. I walked down the passage, the Cranes behind me. At the doorway, the noise came to meet us.

We were in a great hall, whose roof stood on cedar pillars;
it was lit from high windows under the eaves. The blank
walls were plastered white, and covered all over with chalked
scribbles and drawings. Boys and girls were everywhere;
calling and quarrelling and laughing, chasing each other,
playing leapfrog, throwing balls, gossiping in twos and
threes, a few moping alone; youths and maidens of every
color man was made in, white and black and brown and
golden, all naked but for their little loin-guards of colored
leather, and their beads or jewels. The high walls threw back
a dozen tongues, and as many kinds of broken Greek, which
seemed their common language. Right in the midst of the
hall was a great piebald bull. It stood stock-still, though two
boys sat on its back and a girl was swinging on one horn.
I was astonished, and went nearer.

A girl saw us first. She had a Phoenician face, hook-nosed
and olive-skinned; her mouth was painted, and her loin-
guard embroidered in blue and gold. She was slender, but
her muscles rippled like a young wrestler's. She stared a moment; then put two fingers in her mouth and whistled shrilly,
so that the hall echoed. The shouting stopped. Everyone
turned to look, and I saw a scuffle round the bull. It bellowed, and its head swung round toward us. Nephele
screamed.

"Be quiet," I said. I had seen the expectant looks, and
knew we were being somehow baited. The bull came no
nearer, only bawled and swung its horns. Going toward it, I
heard creaking within, and smothered laughter. A thin dark
lad tumbled out grinning through a hole in its belly. It was
carved in wood, with a bullhide stretched over, and horns of
gilded bronze. Its feet were fixed to a low slab of oak-wood,
with bronze wheels set in.

A crowd gathered round us, staring, and throwing questions, which we could not understand because they spoke
bad Greek and all at once. Some fingered the blood-sign on
my breast, and pointed and called to others. On the back of

the wooden bull there was one rider left, sitting at ease. Now balanced on his fingertips, he vaulted down and landed before me. He went beautifully through the air, as if he were flying.

He was slight, and smaller than I; a Minyan, with some Hellene blood. He stood poised on the balls of his feet, like a dancer, then took a step back and looked us over. I had never seen such a youth as this. At first sight he could have been a mountebank. But his heavy gold necklaces, his arm-rings of jeweller's work, the gems on his glittering belt and loin-guard, were not gilded shams; he was wearing a prince's ransom. His light-brown hair hung down in long curled tresses, groomed as sleek as a girl's, and his eyes were painted. But with all this frippery, he was like a young panther, lean and spare and hard. A thick red scar, like a long burn, curved round the ribs on his right side.

He cocked his head sideways, shaking his crystal earrings and showing his white teeth. "Well!" he said. "So here are the gay Athenians, who danced all the way to Crete. Come, dance for us now, we're all impatience."

There was malice in his laughter. Yet it did not anger me. To me he was as a priest, who would show me a mystery. I felt I had been in this place before, that my soul remembered it; that it had been woven into my moira before I was born.

I answered him simply, "None of us are dancers, except Helike here. But we danced to show we belonged together."

"So?" he said, arching his brows at me. "And whose was that notion; yours?" I answered, "We planned it together, when we were in council." He raised his brows again, and then walked round us, staring at each in turn. Many had stared at us that day; but this one saw us. I felt as if a fine sharp blade pricked me over, searching for flaws. When he got to Nephele, he peered at her with a quirking smile, then chucked her under the chin saying, "Think nothing of it, darling; you will do when you have to." Chryse he found staring wide-eyed at a tall girl with a turquoise necklace, who held her hands and whispered in her ear. "Calf stealer!"

he said, slapping the girl's buttock, "give her time to look about." Melantho snatched Chryse away, and stood with an arm around her. The youth laughed, and strolled back to me.

"Well," he said, "sure enough you are all together. Do you know you're the first team to be given a green leader?"

I said surprised, "How did you know? The trainer himself has only just heard it." He gave a light scornful laugh. "He! He never knows anything unless we tell him. All Palace news comes to us first; bull-dancers go everywhere." A boy near by said slyly, "You do, we know," but he took no notice. "When I heard you were to lead instead of me, I made sure the Minotaur wanted you dead. But now I wonder."

I said, "I daresay he does. There is a quarrel between us."

"A—!" He took a standing jump straight up in the air, flinging back his head in a great laugh, and slapping his thigh so that all his jewels tinkled. "Oh, I shall like you, Athenian; yes, I must after all. Is it true you threw his signet in the sea? What odds are they laying on you, do you know?"

I was beginning to get the air of this place. It stirred me like strong wine.

"Don't know your odds yet?" he said. "You must keep your wits about you here. What is your name?" I told him all our names, and asked his own. He said, "In the Bull Court, they call me the Corinthian."

"Why?" I asked. "Are you the only one from Corinth?" He answered lightly, "I am now."

I understood then his flourish and his load of jewels, and why when he talked no one broke in. Once, far away, I had wanted to be a warrior; to be a king. Now it was forgotten; only one ambition burned me. No one I have told this to at home has understood it, not even Pirithoos, my nearest friend. As the saying is, only those the snake has bitten can tell each other how it feels.

"The trainer thought," I said, "that you were going to lead us." It seemed to me my ignorant meddling had done the Cranes nothing but harm.

He looked in my face, cocking one eyebrow. He had an eye that stripped one's courage to the bone. Then he shrugged his shoulders in the Cretan way, making his earrings dance and catch the light. "Oh, he knows nothing. I told you so. He wants me laid off to train with a new team, because he's bet on me for three months more. The man's a fool. Your bull knows your name before he is calved; that's what we say in the Bull Court."

"It is moira," I answered, understanding him. "Does everyone here belong to Asterion?" He clicked his tongue. "Belong! One might take you for a peasant. He is a patron like any other. Only he is rich enough now, it seems, to dedicate a team, instead of this dancer or that. It has made talk. Only the King has done it before. My lord holds his head very high these days. But you did not get in here, you Athenians, without being purified? I suppose you are Sky God folk; still, you should have learned by that whom we all belong to."

I said, "To the Earth-Shaker?" Then I paused, and said as carelessly as I could, "Or to the Goddess-on-Earth?"

He said, "Oh, I suppose to both, by the custom here. But you'll not see her again, except at the bull-dance. She is Ariadne the Most Holy, the Mistress of the Labyrinth. You'll only see her in her shrine. Otherwise no one sees her, any more than they do the King."

Just then someone shouted in Greek that the food was ready. The trestle was set at the end of the hall, and the dancers were racing over. I saw our talk must end; it would be presumption in me to sit beside him. Whatever he was at home in Corinth, a shepherd or a sailor-boy for all I knew, here he was a great prince and I was nothing. Already I did not find this strange.

The food was simple, but plenty and very good. Indeed, after the house of Minos had been served, the pick of everything went to the Bull Court. Bull-dancers lived well in Knossos; as well as the King Horse in the year he goes to the god.

4.

WE LIVED in the Bull Court: a city sealed in a palace, and a life sealed in with death. Yet it is a proud city, and a strong fierce life. A man once in it is of it till he dies. So I, who have gray beginning in my beard, still say "it is," as if the Bull Court stood and I might yet go back to it.

Though the beginners trained apart, learning the first things of the dance, handsprings and somersaults and tumblers' skills, all bull-dancers lived and ate together in the Bull Court till after supper, when the guardian priestess fetched the girls away. For the men there were ways into the Palace precincts, all of them winked at. We had the run of the Palace after dark, if we kept clear of the gates and walls. No runaway had ever passed them. It was said too that there was a curse on the attempt, and that your next bull after always killed you. Apart from that, bull-dancers went everywhere, as the Corinthian had said; though it was such a warren that lovers and mistresses would always send a servant for a guide. But the girls were locked in at night and watched all day. Their maidenhood was closely kept.

At first I thought it would be enough to drive one mad, playing about all day with girls near naked, and never to have one. But soon I learned one need never be short of a woman in the Labyrinth. As for the girls, they made do with one another, so old a custom that no one questioned it. But there were some who were all virgin, right through to the heart. They had given themselves to the bull-dance, and lived for it awake or asleep.

From the time of lamplighting, our lives were secrets from one another. But in the Bull Court we were comrades, men and girls, and sharers in a mystery, and craftsmen bound by

224

our craft; often enough we were only hands to hold off death from one another, that and no more. Yet we were young, and made of the same stuff as other creatures Mother Dia brings forth into the light. Always drawn between us was a tight-wound lute-string that never snapped, yet never slackened; and, brushed or breathed upon, filled the air between with its secret sound. Many a time, when I have been with some Cretan lady, flounced and pinned and scented and crimp-haired, whose bed one could hardly get to for paint-pots and mirrors and toilet-stands all round it, I would fall asleep after on my pallet in the Bull Court, and embrace in dreams a waist like green willow, or wrestle a love-fall against strong slender limbs naked and cool and ringed with gold.

Never in the House of the Ax was this dream made flesh for me. Not till years after, when the Bull Court was far behind me and had ceased to be, did I meet such a girl again and have her for mine. After I had ceased to seek her, only then I found her, riding in her Scythian trousers bareback among the spears. Though she was taller than the girls of the Bull Court, yet she was fine-boned, and light to carry. Twice I have carried her off a battlefield in my two arms. Even the second time, though the dead weigh heavier than the living.

I have seen her hold a leopard alone upon her spear. But me she never harmed after that javelin wound when first I took her, which I am glad to carry since it is all of her I have. Then, and once more unknowing, when she gave me a son six feet and three fingers high. But the Maiden Goddess, whom she had served in arms, and the gods below were good to her; before she could see the end, they closed her eyes with darkness.

But all this was still unspun upon the distaff. If I had known, perhaps it would have pulled me by the foot, and one day the bull would have been faster. Or maybe not. For your own bull will always have you, he is born knowing your name. So we all said in the Bull Court.

When we had finished beginners' lessons, we could do a

handspring, and somersault forward or back, and some of us could run at the vaulting-horse and swing ourselves over straight-standing on our hands. Iros and I could do it every time, Chryse quite often, and sometimes even Nephele. The Corinthian had judged her shrewdly. Her finicking was a show put on for men; she had deceived even herself with it, but when in the Bull Court she found it not admired, no girl in the team was tougher. As for Helike, the trainer saw at once that she knew it all, and sent her off to practice with the bull-leapers on the wooden bull.

From anywhere in the Bull Court, you could see the Bull of Daidalos. It was called so after its first deviser, though since then every part of it had been renewed a dozen times, save for the fine bronze horns worn smooth with unnumbered hand-grips. Everyone said the horns were Daidalos' own handiwork. There was a perch in the hollow body, between the shoulders, where the trainer's boy would sit to work the levers which made the head swing or toss. We would dance and sway out of the way, while Aktor shouted, "No! No! Move as if he was your lover! You lead him on, you give him the slip, you make him sweat for you; but it's a love-affair and the whole world knows it." It was the youths he thus exhorted, rather than the girls; for this was Crete.

Every day, in those first weeks, I looked for Asterion to send for me, and give me my punishment. But he never came, and I was treated like all the others.

After the dancing came the bull-leaping. Here on the wooden bull it was a mime, a shadow of what only the living beast gives meaning to, and few of us would achieve. No team had many bull-leapers; some only one; but of such were the princes of the Bull Court. At our first lesson, Aktor sent for the Corinthian. He strolled up idly, sparkling and tinkling, and gave a loose seal-bracelet on his wrist to someone to hold. Then he ran to the lowered bull horns and, as they tossed up creaking, swung himself to a handstand. At the height he let go, his birdlike flight still curving on, till his toes touched the bull's back. Then he bounced off, light as a roebuck; and Aktor showed us how the catcher should steady him down. When the bull is alive, the leaper may fall less neatly; and if he wants to live too, he had better land on his feet.

That is the bull-leap. But every great bull-leaper had tricks of his own; these were what he was known by. The names of such men and girls (there had been girls among the greatest) were remembered for generations. Old men would make light of the present dancers, saying you had not lived if you had not seen So-and-So fifty years ago. Such a one was the Corinthian. They said he had learned how to make the bull toss high or low; on a high toss he could turn a half-somersault in the air, landing on the bull's back hands down and back-springing to the catcher.

The leaper is the glory of the team, but the catchers are life to him; each of the team is life to all the rest. There were no cowards in the Bull Court, or not for long. Once people guessed you would fail them at the pinch, they took care you should not live to do it. In the bull ring that is easy. Nor did it do to make many enemies. Even one could be enough.

We learned on the Bull of Daidalos how dancers can save each other and themselves: how to twine the bull's horns with your legs and arms so that he cannot gore you; how to grasp the horns from before and from behind and sideways, in leaping on and in getting away; how to confuse him by covering his eyes. You are not allowed to harm him, even to save your life; he is the dwelling place of the god.

At first I did not see how such things could be possible with an able-bodied bull. But in Crete they have been bred to the bull-dance for a thousand years. They are splendid to look at: huge, strong, and with great godlike heads; but they are slow, and the wits have been bred out of them. One that was brisk and busy, like the bulls at home, and would make his kill before there had been a show, was used for sacrifice. Still, Cretan bulls are bulls when all is said; you can never be sure of them. When they grow helpful, and seem to know the dance as well as you do, that is the time to beware.

In the second month of our training, we saw the bull-dance for the first time.

We had wanted to go before, but Aktor forbade it. He said if beginners saw it before they had learned some skill, they despaired of themselves, and it spoiled their nerve.

The bull ring stood on the plain east of the Palace. It was built of wood, for Crete is a land of timber. The bull-dancers had their own gallery, just over the dancers' door, and facing the bull gate. It faced the King's box too; but it was a long time, people said, since Minos had seen the bull-dance. The chief priest of Poseidon hallowed the bull. For the rest, the rite is ruled by the Goddess-on-Earth.

In the chief place of the ring stood a gilded shrine, upheld by crimson pillars and crowned with the sacred horns. On either side were seats for the priestesses, and all around sat the Palace ladies. As we sat down they were coming in from their litters, their slaves spreading cloths and cushions for them to sit on, and giving them their fans. Friends greeted friends, and kissed, and called for their seats to be moved together; soon it was like a spreading tree in which a flock of bright birds has settled, cooing and twittering and preening. Massed like dark leaves, the little russet Cretans filled the upper tiers.

Horns blew. A door opened behind the shrine. There she stood; I remembered the shape of her, like a field lily, upright and small, round breasts and thighs, a waist to snap in your fingers. But now she was stiff with gold; you could only see the red of her dress when the flounces stirred. Her foot-high diadem was crested with a golden leopard. If she had not moved, I should have taken her for jeweller's work.

The men all stood, laying fist on breast; the women touched their foreheads. She took her tall throne. There was a music of harps and flutes.

The bull-dancers came in from the door below us. They stepped slowly but lightly, two by two, a girl and a boy, in a solemn dance-step. Their lovelocks sleeked and combed bounced on their smooth shoulders, their arm-rings and neck-laces caught the light; the girls' young breasts, and the backs of their little loin-guards, jigged prettily in the dance. They all had their hands and wrists strapped round to strengthen their grip; boots of soft leather were laced up to their calves. In the first couple was the Corinthian, blithe as a bird.

They circled the ring, and fetched up in one row before the shrine, with the Corinthian in the middle. There they all stood, and made the signs of homage, and spoke a phrase in old Cretan. I tapped the shoulder of the dancer who sat in front of me, and asked, "What do they say?" She was a black girl from Libya, and had not very much Greek. She said slowly, thinking it out as she spoke, "Hail, Goddess! We salute you, we who are going to die. Receive the offering."

"Are you sure?" I said, for the words had shocked me. "Have you got it right?" She nodded her head, which had blue and gold beads plaited into the black wool, so close to the scalp that they looked to have been sewn there. Then she said it again.

I made no answer, but shook my head, thinking, "Truly and indeed, for all their great cunning works these Cretans are ignorant. That lady there may be the greatest priestess in the world, the highest born, the nearest to the Goddess. But she is a woman. I don't care if ten thousand Cretans deny it. She is a woman, as sure as I am a man. I *know*."

I looked up at the shrine. She had sat down again, and once more was still, as if made of gold and ivory. I thought, "What is coming to her? She has done what the ever-living gods don't permit to mankind. Nor will they forgive her youth, it is not their way. But who can save her? She is too high to reach."

The dancers had turned, and strung themselves in a circle round the ring. A trumpet sounded. In the wall facing us the great bull gate opened, and out came the bull.

He was a kingly beast, white spatchcocked with brown; thick-barrelled, short-legged, wide-browed, and, like all his breed, very long-horned. The horns curved upward and forward, then dipped and rose again at the tips. They were painted lengthwise with stripes of red and gold.

The Corinthian stood facing him across the ring, with his

back to us. I saw him lift his hand, saluting; a noble gesture, graceful and brave. Then the dancers began to move around the bull, turning in a circle as the stars do round the earth, far off at first, but getting nearer. At first he did not take much notice; but you could see his big staring eyes following them round. He switched his tail, and his feet fidgeted.

The music quickened; and the dancers closed in. They swooped round the bull like a flight of swallows, nearer and nearer. He put his head down, and his forefoot raked the ground. Then you saw what a fool he was. The bull at Troizen would have singled someone out and made a race of it. This one, as each dancer flew past his head, would look, and get ready with a lumbering scrape of his feet, and then say to himself "Too late," and look sheepish and start again. Now the dancers slowed their spinning, and started to play the bull. First one and then another would pause till they had drawn him, then skim or sway out of his path and leave him for the next. The more daring the dancers are, the more they work the bull, the better for them in the end. He is the stronger; but he is one to their fourteen. He may tire first, if they keep him at it.

So it went on, till the first edge was off him, and he seemed to say, "After all, who is paying me for this?" Then the Corinthian ran round to face him, and held out both arms; and the circling stopped.

He ran smoothly up to the sullen bull. It was the leap I had seen often in the Bull Court. But that was a shadow; now, he had a living thing to dance with. He grasped the horns, and swung up between them, going with the bull; then he soared free. The beast was too stupid to back and wait for him. It trotted on, when it felt him gone. He turned in air, a curve as lovely as a bent bow's, and on the broad back his slim feet touched down together; then they sprang up again. He seemed not to leap, but to hang above the bull, like a dragonfly over the reeds, while it ran out from under him. Then he came down to earth, feet still together, and lightly touched the catcher's hands with his, like a civility; he had no need of steadying. Then he danced away. There was a joyous screaming and cooing from the bird tree, and shouts from the men. As for me, I stretched in secret my right hand earthwards, and whispered under all the noise, "Father Poseidon! Make me a bull-leaper!"

The dancers circled again. A girl paused on tiptoe, arms lifted, palms outspread; an Arabian, the color of dark honey, with long black hair. She was straight as a spear, with the carriage of women used to carrying their burdens on their heads; big disks of gold hung from her ears and threw back the sunlight. Sometimes in the Bull Court I had seen her white teeth flashing. She was a haughty, mocking girl, but she looked grave now, and proud.

She grasped the horns, and pressed upward. Perhaps something had been going on in the bull's dull mind; or perhaps her balance was less true than the Corinthian's. Instead of tossing up his head, he shook it sideways.

The girl fell across his forehead. Yet she had somehow kept her hold upon the horns. She hung on them like a monkey, riding the bull's nose, her feet crossed on his dewlap. He started to run round and round, shaking his head. I heard a deep mutter from the men's seats, and from the women's a high breathless twittering. I looked up at the pillared shrine. But the golden goddess sat unmoving, and her painted face was still.

The dancers swooped about, clapping their hands and flipping their fingers to confuse the bull. Yet I thought it was mostly show and they could have done more. I hammered with my fist, muttering "Nearer! Nearer!" till the next youth said to me, "Keep your hands to yourself, Hellene"; I had been beating him on the knee. "He will have her!" I said. "He is going to the barrier to beat her off." The youth muttered, with his eyes upon the ring, "Yes, yes; they won't go in for her. She has been insolent and made enemies." The bull was trying to find the barrier, but the girl's long hair was in his eyes, and she kept twisting her shoulders to blind him. I said out of breath, "The Corinthian, can't he help?" He answered leaning forward in his seat, "It's work for the catcher, not the bull-leaper. Why should he? He never worked with this team before."

Just as he spoke, the Corinthian leaped forward. He ran at the bull from its left side, and caught the horn and hung on it swinging. The girl, whose strength was finished, dropped off and scrambled to her feet and ran.

Before he jumped, I had seen the Corinthian look swiftly round and beckon. The youth beside me had leaped to his feet and was shouting in his native tongue, which I think was Rhodian; I could tell he was cursing. I was shouting myself. No one can last long as the Corinthian was, unless someone comes up to pull on the other horn. He had counted on that; but no one had done it.

One of the youths came running at last, and made as if to leap and catch the horn. But I could tell it was from shame, and his heart was not in it. So he was too late. The bull swerved from him and put its head down sideways, and scraped off the Corinthian with its foot. Then I saw him rise in the air again; but he soared no longer. He was speared on the horn, which had pierced his midriff, just above the belt. I don't know if he cried out or not. The din was too great to hear. He was tossed and flung down with a great red hole in him. The bull trampled him, then trotted away. The music ceased. The dancers stood still. A deep sigh and murmur ran round the galleries.

They use a little double ax, of the sacred pattern, to dispatch the victims. When they lifted it over his neck, I saw his hand come up for a moment, as if to ward it off; then he changed the gesture to a salute, and turned his head to take the blow cleaner. He was a gentleman, and he died like one. I found myself weeping, as if I had been in love with him. So I was too, though not as it is understood in Crete. No one took notice. To weep once is thought lucky in the Bull Court. Besides, a lady had fallen down screaming, and there was a crowd about her, fanning her and holding essences to her nose and catching her marmoset.

The bull was roped and led away. You could see it was getting tired; it would have had enough before long. The dancers filed out. The Rhodian next me was saying, "Why did he do it? Why? He had no need." Then he said, "I suppose he was called. I suppose it was his time." I said nothing. My tears had dried; I had begun to think.

The priest of Poseidon had filled a shallow offering cup with the Corinthian's blood, and poured a libation on the earth. Then he came forward and stood before the shrine, and poured the rest till the cup was empty, and spoke in Cretan. The Mistress in the shrine stood up and raised her palms outward, in the gesture that means "It is accomplished." Then she went out through the little door behind the shrine. I remembered the small rouged feet upon the steps, the tender breast with the ringlet on it. My flesh shivered.

When we were back in the Bull Court, I said to Amyntor, "Fetch the Cranes."

I waited by the Bull of Daidalos. No one felt like playing with him just then, so we had that place to ourselves. The Cranes came up. I saw Phormion pale, while Amyntor still shook with anger. Of the girls, it was Chryse and Thebe who had been crying; Nephele's eyes were dry. Helike was shut up in one of her silences, and spoke to no one. "Well," I said, "now we have seen the bull-dance."

Amyntor burst out, cursing the team that had let the Corinthian die. He was a nobleman, and thought of them as a royal guard that had failed its master. I let him run on awhile; he meant it well.

"Yes," I said. "But think; he was not of their kin; they owed him nothing; they had sworn him no oath. Why should he have been dearer to them than their lives?"

They looked at me, wondering that I could be so cold.

"On the ship," I said, "when I swore us in, it was only to keep us together. I was all ignorance; but I suppose the god prompted me, because I am in his hand. Do you all know now why we must be like kindred?"

They nodded. They were soft metal now, ready for striking. I had been right not to delay.

"The Corinthian is dead," I said. "But so are all his team.

They gave themselves to death just when they thought to live a little longer. They know it, too. Look at them now. Shame would not weigh so heavy on them. They are afraid."

"Yes," said Amyntor. "That is true."

"When you love your life too much in the ring, that's when you lose it. Now they are goods no one will buy. They are not worth a graze or a scratch or a trickle of blood to anyone. And they have lost their pride in themselves. If any of them has had a guardian god, they must hear the music of his passing. Look at their faces."

But instead they all looked at mine, as if I had power to make things other than they were. They thought me hard.

"We are going to renew our oath," I said, "so that the gods of this place can witness it. But now we will swear it stronger. 'The life of every Crane shall be as dear to me as mine. What I would look for if I were in his danger, that I will do for him, the very same, not less by a single hair. So witness the River, and the Daughters of Night, and Bull-Faced Poseidon down below Crete. On the day I am forsworn, may they destroy me.'"

They looked at me with great eyes. Chryse and Amyntor both stepped forward, in a hurry to repeat the words while they had them right. They had not even looked behind them. I motioned them to wait; I could see the others. Not that I blamed those who hung back; it was a strong oath, and heavy.

"What is it?" I said to them. "Do you think you are doing it for me? Why should you, indeed? I am a king without a roof of his own, without food or clothes or gold or anything to give, except, like any one of us, whatever I am good for with the bulls. Do this for yourselves. We are only mortal. There will be quarrels among us, love rivalries, and such things. If you swore there would not, you would be forsworn within a week. But this we can swear: never to bring them into the ring. There we must be limbs of one body, as if we shared one life. We do. We must have no more doubt of each other than the spear arm has of the shield arm. Swear to that."

Then some came forward. I said to the rest, "Don't be afraid. You will walk lighter after, when there is no looking back. That is a mystery I am telling you. I learned it from a priest who is also a king."

When all had sworn, there was a silence. Then silly Pylia looked surprised, as if she had gulped strong wine. "Yes, it is true. I *do* feel better." We all laughed, more at her face than anything else. But all that day, we found that we were merry.

That night, after the girls had gone, a boy came up to me; a Minyan from Melos, whom I only knew by sight. "The Corinthian told me," he said, "who was to have his things when he met his bull. This is for you."

He opened his hand. There was a little bull in his palm, of polished crystal. The ring to hang it by was a slender gold bull-leaper, bent in a somersault on its back.

"Me?" I said. "He hardly knew me." I did not want the Corinthian to lose his last wish, because of this boy's stupidity. He shrugged his shoulders. "Oh, it is not a love-gift. Don't flatter yourself. He said he liked to put something on his fancy. Would it be to settle a bet?"

I took it away, and hung it round my neck by a strong thread. I did not reproach myself for having laughed and clowned with the Cranes before his blood was dry. He would have understood that better than anyone.

After dark I went round behind the cookhouse. The wicket gate was ajar as usual. Aktor the trainer, seeing me there, said, "Which girl tonight? Make the most of her. When you get to the bulls, you'll have less to spare."

I said something he could laugh at. I was not after a girl that evening. He was right already; the bull-dance is a jealous mistress. But in the daytime one was never alone.

The Great Court was empty under the moon. Tier upon tier rose the pillared balconies, dimly glowing. Lamps flickered behind curtains of Eastern stuff. The pots of lilies and of flowering lemon trees shed a sweet heavy scent. A cat slipped from shadow to shadow, and a Cretan who looked as if his errand were the same. Then all was silent. The great horns upon the roof-coping reared up as if they would gore the stars.

I stretched out my hands palm downward, and held them over the earth. "Father Poseidon, Horse Father, Lord of Bulls, I am in your hand, whenever you call me. That is agreed between us. But as you have owned me, give me this one thing first. Make me a bull-leaper."

In our last month of training, we went to the pasture to take our bull.

The bull chooses the team, not the other way. You bring a cow, and tether her, and wait with nets. It will be the king bull who mounts her, the one the others give best to. While they are mating, you must hobble him to a tree, and net him.

We were in luck. They had just taken a rogue bull out of the herd. That means, in Crete, what you or I would call a proper bull with his wits about him. He had killed a rival, and one of the men who went to bring him in, and both too quickly. Now he bellowed in his pen, while he waited for sacrifice.

Aktor led us down to the water meadow. We saw the Palace roofs all furred with people watching. It is a time when odds are laid; also it is not unknown for a dancer to be killed at the bull-catching, and this, of course, they would be sorry to miss.

But Poseidon favored us. When the cow was tethered, two bulls came up and made a fight of it. The new king, who was black, was much the quicker, and his horns were splayed, which is always bad, for such bulls will gore sideways instead of tossing. But, by chance I am sure rather than by wit, the rival, who was red and white, broke one of them in a headlock. The black ran off bawling, scared as a warrior whose spear breaks in his hand. The other trundled to the cow.

I saw to the hobbling, having met bulls before. We got him netted with no worse than grazes when he dragged us to our knees. I made everyone wait for him to finish what he was at; there was no sense in making him hate us. Then we threw and pulled tight. After he had stumbled a few times, and fallen once, you could see him say to himself, "This needs more thought." So while he was thinking, we hitched him to the pole between the oxen, and brought him away.

I named him Herakles. This was a hero I had thought very well of, in the days when I had meant to be seven feet tall. Later, though no doubt he was a worthy son of Zeus while he walked the earth, I had taken somewhat against him. This bull looked like my notion of Herakles, handsome and hulking and rather simple. If you don't learn in the Bull Court to laugh at yourself, it's certain you never will.

To this day, I sacrifice to Herakles once a year, though I do not tell the hero for whose sake I do it. He was a huge bull, with a broad brow, and great thick horns springing out just as they should, well forward, which made him come at you straight. In his heart he was lazy; but he had a great conceit of himself, and did not care to be made light of. So he got the name of a busy bull. But though he was a long way from safe, he was safer than he looked, having half his mind on his stall and his feed of mash to follow. Best of all, he had a back like a barrel.

There are two ways of practicing with your bull once you have caught him. He is chained to a stake in the practice pit, so that you can learn to dodge the horns with grace. Or he is roped down so that he cannot run, but only toss his head. This is for the bull-leaping. You are not given long at either; if there were time to get him even half tame, there would be no sport as Cretans reckon it. However, there is no law that you must make him your enemy. We all brought Herakles a lick of salt or a handful of greenstuff when we came to dance with him. But he eyed us askance, blaming us for his captivity.

I was getting to know the other dancers now, both men and girls. It was no soft fellowship, the company of the Bull Court. One knew one's own odds and everyone else's; daily one ate and talked and scuffled with people doomed to die; those who were bull-shy, those who had given up, or had a bad oracle from their gods. Gods of all the earth are worshipped in the Bull Court; which is why the altar outside the dancers' door of the ring is sacred to them all. And there were nearly as many ways of divining: with sand or pebbles, with water-droppings or with bees or slivers of ivory, with birds, like the Hellenes, or, as the Sauromantians do, with lizards. Those marked for death died and were remembered little, as a dropped stone leaves ripples in a pool according to its weight. Yet there were a few who had looked for death since their first dance, and had faced it certainly, and yet death held off from them.

One never knew. It was that gave spice to the Bull Court. It was said that if a dancer lived three years, the Goddess set him free. No one could remember anyone lasting half as long. Yet one could not tell one's fate. One said to oneself that there might be war, or some tumult we could get away in; or that the Palace might burn down. Sometimes at night I would remember how the Labyrinth had no walls, and the seas round Crete are empty, with no neighbor islands to give warning of surprise.

It was a hard fellowship; but it was one without envy. Anything you were good for was good for all the rest. There was none of that jealousy one finds among warriors or bards or craftsmen. People would throw you to the bull if they did not trust you; but they would rather have you fit to trust, and would help you learn. Among the bull-leapers there was bound to be emulation, and they would not teach their show tricks; but I never knew them enemies, unless it was for love. As for the glory of our patrons, that was nothing to us. Our concern was first, like the victims in the ancient pit, to stay alive; and after that, to have honor among each other. Patrons and lovers and gamblers would send jewels to the dancers, who wore them all, for bull-dancers are showy and love finery. But no one could judge like us.

In the evening, after the girls had gone, we used to dance, and sing the songs of our homelands, and tell tales. Sometimes then, looking about me, I used to think, "These are men one could bind to a common cause, who would stand together. And most of the girls are as good as men." I was a learner still, and counted for nothing yet. But I cannot keep from putting my hand to what I find about me.

I had enough with the Cranes at present. Pirithoos my friend, who also came young to a kingdom, told me once how heavy he found his first year's reign. So did I too. I did not bear it in a citadel, with my barons about me and gold in my hand to give. Far off in Crete, in the Bull Court, I bore the weight of it.

I learned there, a thing that came hard to me, what one must leave alone. First there was young Hippon, who had been my father's groom; a modest, quiet, sensible lad, fresh-faced and graceful. He had been taken up by a young Palace noble, and within a week, it seemed, had more airs and graces than Iros; posed and shrugged, and made long Cretan eyes at any man who spoke to him. It made me angry; it was bringing down the Cranes to the common level of the Bull Court; I felt my own standing touched by it. I let him see what I thought, which wounded him, for his skin was thin. Then he would be clumsy, and fumble his jumps; whereas, when he was pleased with himself, or had had a gift from his lover, he was neater than even Helike with the living bull. In Athens he had been nobody; here he could win a place in the sun. I saw all this before it was too late; it was I, not he, who had been harming the team. He had found his nature for better or worse, and might yet be good of his kind. If he was worked against the grain, he would be good for nothing. I took the edge off my jokes, praised his new earrings, and watched his style improve.

Then, as the time drew on for our first bull-dance, came trouble where I had least looked for it. Helike grew pale and silent, and slipped away from us to sit alone. She had a look I knew, after a month or two in the Bull Court. It was the look of those who had had bad auguries; those who had been brought young from home, and were growing out of their strength and speed; those who had given up. But it made no sense in Helike. On the wooden bull she had a perfect style. The nakedness of the Bull Court suited her; though she was

thin and had hardly more breast than a boy, her dancer's
grace made her look like one of those gold and ivory bull-girls
the Cretan jewellers make.

I went up to her alone, and asked if she was having a sick
day. It was a thing the girls did not talk of much; but it was
a trouble to them, since all were virgins. Sometimes they
were killed then; and I felt answerable for the Cranes.

She swallowed, and looked about her, and said it was
nothing. Then she told me the truth. Helike was bull-shy.
She had been afraid since our first practice with the living
beast.

"I trained with my brother," she said. "He is my twin; we
danced before we could walk, and he thinks with me. Even
with you I was not afraid; you have a tumbler's hands. But
this is a brute, who would as soon kill me as not. How can
I tell what he will do?"

I thought within me, "This is the end of the Cranes." All
teams but ours were built round a seasoned bull-leaper.
Chryse had the makings of it, and Iros, and I myself; but I
did not know how soon. It was Helike I had trusted to please
the people at our first dance, while the rest of us found our
feet. If she would not leap, someone must; a team that gave
no show would be broken up before next day was out, even
if no one died.

It was no use to rebuke her. She was a mountebank, not
a warrior, and had not chosen to come to Crete. It had
needed courage to tell me. Moreover, it could not have happened in any other team. If they as much as guessed you
were bull-shy, they left you to the bull; by the law of the
Bull Court, it was only shameful to forsake the brave. But
she had trusted me, because of our vow. This was the first
test of it.

I talked to her awhile, and made her laugh, though only
to please me; then I went off to think. But I could only remember a colt I had had in Troizen, who shied at chariots.
I had cured her in the usual way, by walking up to one myself before her, then leading her up gently.

That is the true reason, which was never told in Crete,

why the Cranes let loose their bull in the practice pit. The Cretans thought we did it from wildness, and for sport, and tell it so to this very day. But it was my desperate remedy to start her out of her fear, or at the worst to see if I was good enough to leap instead.

When the bull was tethered, and we had worked him awhile, I made pretense to take a message at the gate, and sent Aktor back to the Bull Court. Then I shouted, to warn the team, "The shackle's loose!" and let it slip while I feigned to fix it.

It was a place never meant to loose a bull in; small like the old pit of sacrifice, with high walls to trap one. But there was just room for a run and a leap, if you were quick, and the bull was slow. Cretan bulls, when something unwonted happens, need time to think. I ran in and grasped the horns and flung myself upward. As my body thought, and I soared and hung in air, I knew the practices had been nothing; this was life and glory, like one's first battle, one's first girl. I made a fool's landing, my belly across his back, but I knew what I had done wrong, and got it right the second time. Then Helike came after me, and I caught her safely. We were doing our crane-dance round the bull, from pride in ourselves, when Aktor came back and found us at it.

He promised us all a beating from his own hand, and he kept his word. We soon saw why; it was hardly more than a tickling. By that we knew he meant to bet on us, and did not want to make us stiff.

There is madness in youth; but sometimes a god inspires it. We were captives and slaves, whose comings and goings were our own no longer. Where pride fails, there too sinks courage. But now we had gone to the bull in our own time, as if we were free, and it freed our hearts. Never again did we feel like helpless victims, after we had gone halfway to meet the god.

Next day Aktor called us to the wooden bull, and put us through our paces. With the dancers watching, we set our best foot foremost. Patrons and lords and ladies would bribe their way in to watch; but the praise of one bull-leaper was worth twenty of them. Presently he told Helike and me to leap again, and walked away. I jumped, listening to the levers' creak and the dancers' chatter. Then when I was down, I saw whom the trainer had gone to greet. It was Asterion. He had come at last.

While Aktor talked, he ran us over with his round staring eye, which never changed when it met mine, any more than the eye painted on the wooden bull. He nodded once or twice, and went away. I thought, "Now it is coming to me." But when I thought what he might do, my first thought was, "He will keep me from being a bull-leaper." I was so set on it that only death seemed worse.

The trainer came back, but he said nothing. At last my ignorance burst me. I said, "What did the patron want?" He raised his brows and shrugged. "What does any patron want? To know the form. My lord, when he offers a hundred oxen for a team to do him credit, likes to get value for it. Take care he does; that's the best advice I've given you yet."

He went away. The dancers and the bull-leapers closed round us, praising and finding fault and making the hard jokes of the Bull Court. One was never alone till dark, and then only with trouble.

A little later young Hippon came up to me. "What is it, Theseus? I hope you are not sick?"

He sounded like a bath-woman and I nearly said so. My anger wanted something to bite; but he had meant no harm. "How do *you* like it," I said, "that any good we do in the bull ring will be profit for that insolent swine? If we even live, we must live for him."

Iros was with him. They looked at one another, making long eyes, like a couple of Cretans. "Oh," said Hippon, "don't trouble yourself with him. He is nothing; is he, Iros?" They grew knowing, and leaned their heads together. They were getting, I thought, to look just like sisters. "Oh no," said Iros. "He is rich and does what he likes, but he is a very common fellow, not worth a thought. Surely, Theseus, you know the story?"

"No," I said. "I have not kept him in mind. But tell it me."

After each had invited the other, giggling, to begin, Iros said, "He passes as Minos' son. But everyone knows his father was a bull-leaper." He did not trouble to drop his voice. The Bull Court was the only place in the Labyrinth where speech was free.

Hippon said, "It is quite true, Theseus. Of course it is not talked about; but my friend, who told me, is so high-born that he knows everyone."

"So does mine," said Iros, tossing his hair. "My friend not only makes songs, he writes them down. It is a Cretan custom. He is very accomplished. He says this bull-leaper was an Assyrian—"

"Ugh!" said Hippon. "With their thick legs and great black beards." Iros said, "Oh, don't be foolish; he was only fifteen or so. It was Minos who fancied him first, Theseus, and kept him for months out of the ring, lest he should be killed."

"But," I said, "that would have been impiety. He must have been dedicated, just as we were."

"Oh, yes," said Hippon. "A great impiety! People said it would bring a curse. Well, so it did. The Queen was angry; and that made her notice the youth herself. They say the poor King was the very last to hear, after it was the talk of the Labyrinth and even of Knossos town. There is a bawdy song of how she used to follow him into the Bull Court, she was so besotted, and hide herself in the wooden bull. My friend said that is only vulgar talk. But she was mad for him, quite out of her head."

"And when the King found out," I said, "I suppose he put her to death."

"In Crete? How could he? She was Goddess-on-Earth! No, all he could do was to get the Assyrian sent back to the bulls. I suppose he was out of training, or the god was angry; at any rate his next bull killed him. But he left his tokens behind."

"But," I said, "surely at least Minos could have exposed the child?" Iros, who was never anything but civil, said patiently, "But, Theseus, the Cretans have the old religion. The child is the mother's. So the King kept quiet to save his face, and let it pass for his. I expect he would not like to give it out that he had not been with her. People would know why."

I nodded. One could see that, indeed.

"At first," said Hippon, "Asterion was kept in bounds. They say Minos was very hard on him; one can hardly wonder. Now it's another story. He is clever; and he has got his hand on so many threads he is almost ruling the kingdom." He looked at me, not following my thoughts, but concerned to see they moved me. I saw, under all his nonsense, the sensible stable-lad I had seen polishing harness, with a shrewd eye for a horse. "But you see, Theseus, how he is beneath your notice, an upstart like that."

"You are right," I said. "Old Herakles is more worth studying. But what does Minos have to say about it?" His voice grew hushed; from awe rather than fear. "Minos lives very retired, in his sacred precinct. Nobody sees him."

The day passed. When night had fallen, I slipped away to the courtyard. I sat on the black base of a great red column, hearing women tittering in some room above, and a boy singing to one of those curved harps of Egypt. Now I was like a man whom vermin have been biting under his clothes, able at last to strip and scrape. But the sting had gone deep, and burned me still.

I remembered the Corinthian's laughter, when I said I had a quarrel with Asterion. But I had seen no joke in it; we both came of kings' houses, and were such men as would seek out each other on a battlefield. My being a god's slave did not alter that. I had challenged his anger to keep him from bidding for the Cranes, but also from pride. When he bid for us, I thought it was to get an enemy in his hand. Today I knew at last how he rated me. He had bought me as a rich man will buy a chariot horse though it has kicked him, because it looks to be fast and a stayer, and he hopes to win a race with it. The kick does not bruise his honor; a beast kicked him, not a man.

When he had called me a mainland savage, I had thought it a studied insult. I had done myself too much honor; the man had spoken his thought. So he had bought me for his stable, and handed me to the trainer and thought no more of me; me the son of two kings' houses, both god-descended, Lord of Eleusis and Shepherd of Athens; me who had had the sign from Earth-Shaking Poseidon. So light he had held me. And he not even kingly got.

The Labyrinth had fallen silent. The lamps were out; the moon was rising, to quench the bright stars of Crete. I stood up, and said aloud for the gods of the place to hear me, "By my head, and by my father's head, one day he shall know me again!"

5.

It is a life out of life in the Bull Court.

One wakes often at night, in a hall where fifty-odd youths are sleeping, who come from everywhere, and have manners not all to a Hellene's taste. There was a scuffle once, and some trouble, when I broke a Tyrian's nose. People said I was uncivil. But as I told them, if he had a right to his customs so had I mine; and it was a custom where I came from, if a stranger came creeping to your bed at midnight, to take him for an enemy. His nose set somewhat askew; which reminded others I was one to let alone.

Once I asked Helike what it was like in the girls' place, after they were shut away. She said it was a world to itself, and I would not understand it; but she did let fall that sometimes the girls would fight like young warriors, if two were rivals for another. More than once I saw bruises on girls who had not been in the ring. I did not think hardly of them for it; it was the life they were trained to, and I like a woman to have spirit.

As I say, the nights were broken with such things as this, or with someone dreaming aloud, or crying out, sometimes, in fears he would not own by day. One did not ask people their dreams in the Bull Court; nor what they thought about when they were wakened and lay silent in the dark. I know I thought of many things: of death, and fate, and what the gods want of man; how far a man can move within his moira, or, if all is determined, what makes one strive; and whether one can be a king without a kingdom.

Then I would ask myself what would happen if Iros, or Helike, or Amyntor should turn out a better bull-leaper, and lead the team. The Bull Court is a world to itself, with laws which spring from its own nature and cannot be gainsaid.

Thus I would trouble myself, in the first weeks of training. But once we were in the bull ring, I forgot such cares. For the dance took hold of me, head and hand, heart, bones, and blood. To be a bull-leaper seemed enough for one man's life; I was so filled with it that my danger leaned the other way: only by striving could I remember I was a king. But I remembered I was team leader, and often that served instead.

For a bull-leaper to last three months, though it is not bad, is not remarkable. But the old men of Knossos said they had not known such a thing in all their days, a whole team to last three months and none to die.

We lived because we all knew what each was good for, and that it would be there at need. Even those who had been careful of themselves, like Phormion and Nephele, had kept their oath; first from fear of Night's Daughters, who visit perjurers, and even from fear of me; then because they saw it paid the best; and at last, like the others, from pride in being Cranes.

It is a saying of the Bull Court that the longer you live there, the longer you may. You know the dance, and the dancers; and you know your bull. Indeed, there is no woman I have shared a bed with, save one alone, whose moods I have known as I knew old Herakles'. Poor Helike; she never forgave him for being a beast and not a man. In spite of all her skill, she was never more than a middling bull-leaper. Thinking him mindless, she would not try to learn his mind. When she did leap, she was so polished that the people always cheered her. But I often had to cover for her, or go in instead, whereas Chryse never faltered. Everyone loved Chryse, even in the Bull Court; she had come, I think, to take love as in the nature of things, and half expected it from Herakles too.

Amyntor too had the courage of lions. I have never done a harder thing than tell him, as I had to, that he must let the bull-leaping alone. He was too big for it (he had grown even since we came) and too slow; it would have ended in someone's death. He took it like a gentleman, but very hard. Yet, after, he proved the best catcher I ever saw, the steadiest and most daring. I myself, and every Crane who did the bull-leap, owed him our lives over and over.

After four months, the last bull-leaper died who had been there before us. From then on, when a new batch of dancers came in, still wearing the clothes of their own land, huddled together or staring open-mouthed, it would be a Crane who would hide in Daidalos' bull to make them jump; and when I came to look them over, people would wait and watch, to see what I thought.

One never knew what would arrive. Egyptians we never got, for they are a strong people: Minos sent gifts to Pharaoh, jewels of gold and crystal, carved rhytons and rare flowers and precious dyes, rather than demands for tribute. But all others we had, from every shore the stream of ocean washes, and further yet: Persians pale as ivory, with blue eyelids, graceful and frail; Minyans from all the islands; wild barbarians, dark like polished cornel-wood, from the forests of Africa, who would be fierce and merry, or grieve to death, sinking into the earth without laying hands on themselves, only by a wish. And it was in the Bull Court that I first saw Amazon girls from Pontos, proud-faced and slim, free-striding, with slender fingers hard from the bow and spear, who looked you in the eye as cool and measuring as young princes at war. They were much prized in the bull ring, and the Cretans got as many as they could. Whenever I saw such a girl, my heart would stir and quicken, I could not tell why. Men would be as gods, if they had foreknowledge.

All kinds of outlanders we got, by ones and twos, from unheard-of places, caught on a journey perhaps and sold as slaves. One such, though he did not last long, I remember for his strangeness; a son of wandering cattle herders in the back hills beyond Jericho. He had a hatred of the Goddess; or, rather, he denied that she was anything, only a doll that men had made. When I asked if he was mad to mock her in her own precinct while he was in her hand, he answered that his people served no she-deities at all, but only the Sky Father, whose name he would not pronounce, that being forbidden them. He called him the Lord. They hold like the Hellenes that he lives for ever; but they say he has neither father nor mother, brother nor sister, wife nor child, but reigns all alone in the sky, and there was never a time when he was not. Stranger still, it is unlawful among them to make an image of him; when I asked what countenance he had, this youth said that his face was made of fire. I could not learn how they had offended him, to make him appear to them so dreadfully. But they have an oracle that he will someday beget one son to be their guardian hero. Finding the youth so ignorant, I told him Zeus had got many sons on earth, from one of whom I was descended myself. But he did not like it. He came of up-country people, frightened of towns, and so simple that they think Ever-Living Zeus is concerned with no one but them.

His team thought him unlucky, and I myself advised them to get rid of him; but after all he took it out of their hands. For the very first time he came into the bull ring, he pulled out a knife he had hidden in his loin-guard, and rushed at the bull like a madman, shouting out that he would smite the god of the Philistines (so he called the Cretans) in the name of the Lord. I don't know if he thought the bull would stand and wait for it. No bull is such a fool as that, even in Crete. But Zeus the Merciful did him a favor, in return for all his offerings; he was killed outright. If there had been any life left in him, he would not have got off quickly, that is sure. We were glad to see the last of him. The fingers of two hands would hardly count the gods he had offended; and in the Bull Court, the bulls are hazard enough.

By now most of us had a scar or two from Herakles; he had his brisker days, which one got to know from the switch of his tail as he came out of the bull gate. Then there was no foreseeing him as long as he was fresh. I used to go in first a time or two to take the edge off him; it seemed only right, as I did not really expect to die without a sign from Poseidon first. When I had got the feel of him he would steady a little, and I could put in some of the turns that people knew me by, such as throwing a second somersault off his back. Often those days turned out the best. I can still see his wicked eye saying to me, "I have been too soft with you, and let you get insolent. Don't think so well of yourself." There was a little dance I used to do with him before I went in, which I polished up because it amused the people. One had to be careful, because it gave him a better chance than the leap itself. Once he nearly plugged me straight through the breast. I just turned in time to get it glancing; it gave me the biggest scar ever seen in the Bull Court, clear across me from right to left. There was a wise woman I used to go to, the best of several who knew salves for wounds. She would put all kinds of filth upon them, spiders' webs, or green mold; but she knew earth magic, and they always healed.

After we had been five months in the ring, dancers were living longer even in other teams; they saw how we worked, and one or two swore vows of fellowship, which they mostly kept as far as was in them. But they did not know each other's minds as we did. By now we had forgotten we were ever Athenians or Eleusinians, or that the same womb had not borne us all.

Whenever before the dance we stood before the shrine, and dedicated ourselves to the Goddess-on-Earth in the ritual words, we would stretch our hands palm down toward Mother Dia herself, to purge us of impiety. But one had to look up, out of respect. Often I stared at her eyes to see if they would move. But she stood like a gilded image, stiff and still; even when she lifted her hands, she hardly seemed made of flesh. After a while, having my mind upon the dance, I almost forgot she was alive.

Such was our life in the Bull Court. But once one's name gets known there, it is little of the Labyrinth, outside the royal rooms, one does not see sooner or later. One no longer needed to go looking for a woman at night, but rather to fend off the importunate; a man cannot afford excess in this or anything, who has the bull-dance for a wife.

Even the women could write in Knossos Palace. This I say of my own knowledge, for some of them wrote to me. And I am not speaking just of messages scribbled on a leaf of wet clay, telling one where to meet them, or when the husband would be out. These were whole histories, filling as much as two sheets of Egyptian paper, long as the record of a war. I could not make out above half, and often not so much. They had a hundred ways of stringing things together and knotting them up; I will swear they knew more words than a harper does, though he has only the sound to learn.

But it was not only the bedchambers one went to. Lords and princes would invite one to their feasts, and ask no return beyond one's presence. As to the food and drink, to look at so much was only vexing, for weight is death in the bull ring. But I used to go, from curiosity, and from vanity, and for the sake of what I could learn. Since the gods had spared us so far, we did not yet despair of getting away from Crete.

Cretans are full of fine manners and fanciful customs; thinking, for example, that a man's own fingers are not good enough to serve his mouth with food, but he must use a tool. At first I went in fear of mockery; for they think anyone uncouth who is ignorant of these toys. But I had too much pride to show it. If I could not learn their customs by watching, I used my own as if I chose to. Soon I found this pleased them, especially the women. They love nothing so much as what is new.

All kinds of lords and nobles had houses in Knossos Palace, built right into it, or at least within the precinct. As I say, it was almost a town. But though it was so rambling, it was very well guarded all about, and no one passed the gates unchallenged. At first I thought this was only to keep us in.

Though the name of Minos is old Cretan, and the kings have borne it time out of mind, this house had only a strain of the ancient blood. Ever since the great raid from Mycenae, when the royal kin were put to the sword and the Lion King's brother married the Goddess-on-Earth, the kings had ruled in their own right as well as the Queen's, and were no longer sacrificed in the ninth year. Many of the victors had taken Cretan women, so that most of their customs were still of the old religion; but after that, their houses married among each other, and now they held the native Cretans, who came of the land both sides, in the greatest scorn. I could see no sense in this, for they were not barbarous, being as everyone knows the best craftsmen anywhere; it was they indeed who taught these half Hellenes to write. They are small-made, like most Earthlings, and reddish-dark, but not unpleasing to look at; and some of them came from very ancient lines, though now brought down and poor. As far as I could see, they were being humbled only to make their masters think better of themselves. It set my teeth on edge to hear them miscalled by scornful nicknames, Scabby or Bandy or Squint, and talked of in their presence as if they were dogs. At home, my grandfather would have thrashed me till his arm was tired, if he had heard me so insolent. They were harshly taxed too, though one heard little of such matters in the Bull Court and cared less. One feels another's grief most where it touches one's own.

When we had been about six months in the bull ring, and I had almost forgotten him, I had a summons from the patron, bidding me to a feast.

I stared at it frowning, at a loss what to do. If I offended him now, he had power to break up the team, and they would begin to die. Yet I felt it would choke me to sit at a man's board whom I meant to be revenged on if I could;

it was a question of my honor. After a while, I opened my mind to Amyntor, who understood such matters better than the rest. He was pleased at being asked for counsel, and sat considering. At last he said, "It seems to me, Theseus, that you can eat at his board without being his guest. It is the bread of captivity there, just as it is in the Bull Court; you are getting it served with sauce, that's all. I don't see how that can hurt your honor, even if you kill him. Look at his message. He orders you; he does not ask."

This satisfied me, for Amyntor had the feelings of a gentleman, and more sense than had first appeared. The Bull Court had steadied him.

The Little Palace stood southwest of the great courtyard, with its own gate and guards. I put on my best, since there is no sense in half doing things. When I went visiting in the House of the Ax, I used to wear the Cretan kilt, and had two or three of them; this one was made of a thick blue silk from east of Babylon, and had a bullion fringe. A general's wife had given it me, my chief mistress at that time, and a good one for a bull-leaper, easy and gay. One cannot afford to be worn out with tears and tantrums. But sometimes gifts would come without any name, and then one had to be careful. If one wore them, the giver would point it out to friends and rivals and claim to be one's lover; and the women had no more shame about it than the men.

Often one's richest presents came from lords and princes who had made a good win. All sorts of wagers were laid upon the bull-dance: how long it would last, whether blood would be drawn, how many leaps and how perfect, besides the betting on life and death. Bribes do not tempt a man whose life is the stake already; but a showy gift was the fashion. I had more necklaces than I could wear at once, wrist-seals, and rings for the arm and finger. But the only jewel I never took off was the crystal bull from the Corinthian. Always, in the Bull Court, our most precious trophies were the gifts of the dead.

That night I put on most of my things; I was enough a bull-leaper now not to think myself dressed unless I sounded with gold. Also I had myself freshly shaved. I had yielded, though grudgingly, to this Cretan custom. From fifteen years old, like any growing lad, I had waited for my beard, trying to nourish it with boar's grease and all the other nonsense boys pass on to each other; it seemed absurd just when it was growing to take it off. But here it was the mark of a barbarian; women would shrink at it, or wriggle and laugh. Sometimes I pictured my grandfather staring in disgust at my smooth chin, and asking if I had been gelded. However, he was far away; and it was allowed in the Labyrinth that I had not.

I thought I had seen some rich rooms by now; but they were nothing to the Little Palace, as I found when they led me through. I passed one whole room set out only for gaming, with ebony tables and checkerboards inlaid with gold. But I did not look much about me; Cretans think less of you, if you seem to wonder.

There was a splendid feast laid out in the great guest-hall, and a high-born company was gathering. Most of them knew me, and spoke to me as I went to salute the host. He greeted me with such loud jesting compliments as are meant for the party and mean nothing. I saw he had invited me to please the guests, as he might have hired a dancing-girl. Amyntor was right; I was not his debtor.

We ate off fine painted ware; Cretans cook fish food better than any other people. But I was in no danger of overeating. It killed one's hunger to see even great lords (some of whom I knew to hate him) fawning upon Asterion, changing their faces in time with his like soldiers drilling. While he cracked his coarse jokes, his eyes missed nothing; I saw him watch guests out of hearing as if he could read their lips, and his stewards lingered like spies. Beyond my hatred of him, there was something about him that sickened me. Any man will want power to get what he desires: glory, or lands, or a woman. But this man wanted it for itself, to put down other men, to fatten his pride with eating theirs like the great spider that feeds upon the less.

A brown juggler danced for us, a Sidonian; he had a

monkey that helped him with his turn, and understood all he said. At the end, Asterion threw down his gift for him to grovel after; but the monkey picked it up and handed it to his master, bowing with hand on brow. The guests laughed. After he had gone, Asterion spoke to a steward, who went out. I heard another servant ask him where he was going; he answered, "For the monkey. My lord will have it." Just so, I thought, it had been with me.

Sweetmeats came in, and Rhodian wine. I sat at the table's foot, talking to some guests who had moved down to speak with me; when of a sudden he leaned forward in his chair, and bawled, "Theseus! Here!"

I felt the blood rise in my face. It was in my mind to be deaf. But then I thought, "No. If I am not his captive, then I am his guest." So I left my place, and walked up without too much haste, and stood before him.

"Well, Theseus," he said grinning. "How is it to be cock of the ring? It's a different lad now from the one who came from the mainland in leather breeches, hah? Do you think better now of Crete?" I did not answer. He flipped my necklaces with his finger. "Look at these!" he said, speaking to the guests. Me he hardly looked at. "I'll wager not all these were won for leaping bulls. Hey, boy?" Still I was silent, and kept command of myself. I was studying him. It concerned me to know him. I looked at his heavy mask, wondering how one became such a man as this. Before long he looked away. "A jewel," he said, "from every lord in the Labyrinth. Of the ladies I say nothing. Their mysteries must not be profaned." And he winked at a lady not long married, whom I had had no dealings with, and who blushed right down to her breasts. "All this, yet nothing yet from the patron. I'll swear you wondered why."

He grinned, and waited. I said, "No, my lord."

He gave a great bellow of laughter. "You hear that? He thought I had a rod in pickle for him, because he was unruly in the harbor. You young fool, what do you think we look for in a bull-dancer? We have our divinations, we who follow the ring."

I stared at him. I who had faced him that day with his eyes a handspan from mine. This time he did not meet them. He looked at the guests. "Well! You agree Asterion can pick a winner?" There was a gust of acclamation. I was ashamed for them, more than for myself; they passed for free men.

He clapped his hands. A servant brought upon his palms what I took for some dish or other. For a moment I wondered if he meant to poison me; I pictured him staring about, daring the company to remark upon my death. Then I saw it was a little tray, lined with purple leather, on which was spread a great collar of gold and gems. The servant held it out to Asterion, who, without touching it, waved him to give it me.

I felt an itching in my fingers. They ached to pick it up and slash it across his face. I had sworn to hold every Crane's life as dear as mine; but no dearer than that, and my honor was dearer. It was not my oath that held me. I suppose it was the habit of being king, and answerable for people to the god.

I held my hand, and spoke quietly. "You are too liberal, Minotauros. But have me excused; I cannot take it."

The slave wavered the tray about, not knowing what to do with it. I heard a soft stir along the table, and women's dresses rustling. But Asterion, after one hard look from his round eye, said heartily as if he were presenting some show to them, "You cannot, eh? Why not?"

"I come of the royal Kindred," I said. "It would hurt my standing, to take a gift from a man who struck me."

Everyone was listening. But this seemed even to please him. He waved a hand, displaying me. "Hark to him! Still as mad as when he came. For that I backed him. They are all wild and mad, all the great bull-leapers. Born for the bulls, and good for nothing else. It is their daimon leads them to Crete." He clapped me on the shoulder; he was like a man who owns a dangerous dog and boasts of its fierceness. "Very well, have your way then." He snapped his fingers at the servant, who took the gift away.

You would have supposed that having faced out this

affront, he would have kept me out of his way. But not at all. Every so often he would command me to one of his feasts, and go through some like pantomime. I would even hear him, beforehand, saying to someone, "Only watch, and see how proudly he will answer me. He is wilder than a mountain hawk. Have you heard how he loosed the bull? I saw it when he came raw from the mainland." He had turned even my honor into a mountebank's act for his guests to laugh at. I never told even Amyntor what I put up with on these days. I was ashamed to speak of it. I only said, "I have paid for my supper." He knew what I meant.

The other noblemen I found civil enough; among the younger indeed I was a kind of fashion. Any bull-leaper may be taken up so; but they found me curious because of the blood I came of, not having had a king or a king's son in the ring before. Some of them asked me why, if the god was angry, I did not sacrifice someone else to him, rather than go myself; if I dressed him in my clothes, they said, he would stand for me. Being a guest, I did not ask if they took the gods for fools, but only said I had been called by name. They would stare at this, then catch each other's eyes. Nearly all their rites have grown frivolous and like play, just as with the bull-dance.

These young lords and ladies were full of nonsense, having almost their own language, like children's games. And they held their honor as light as they held their gods. The deadliest insults passed for jest among them; and if a husband would not speak to his wife's seducer, it was considered something great. Once, when alone with a woman, I asked her how long it was since any of them had washed out a slight with blood. But she only asked me how many men I had killed myself; as if, through two wars and a journey overland, I should have kept a tally. Even in bed, the women would keep one talking of such things.

Chiefly these people took to me as something new. New things were their passion, and hard for them to come by; Lukos, I found, had spoken the truth about their records going back a thousand years. They would stand on their heads for the sake of newness, if nothing else new was left. You could see this in their pots and vases. No one needs telling that Cretan potters lead the world, though you must go to Crete to see the best. There were many in the Palace, working for the King; the great nobles too maintained their own. I never tired of looking at the work; the colors are more and richer than ours at home, the patterns gay yet free, and full of harmony. They are fond of drawing sea-creatures, starfish and dolphins and squids and shells and twining weeds. It was a pleasure only to take their pots in your hands, to feel the shape and the glaze. But lately they had begun to spoil them with all kinds of gaudy stuck-on finery, flowers and dangles which might show their skill, yet gave the thing a look of being fit for no use and good for nothing, but to gather dust. The truth is that what had not been tried in a thousand years was not worth doing. But even beauty wearied them, if it was not new.

I remember one lord I dined with, taking us to see his potter's workshop and the latest work. There was a great deal of talking, which I could not follow, for they have many more words than we. So, finding a lump of raw clay, I amused myself for a moment by pinching out of it a little bull, such as children make at home when they play in mud, but not so good, since I had lost the knack of it. Just as I was about to roll it up again, there was crying and twittering, my host and his friends holding back my hand, and crying out that it must be fired. "How fresh!" they said. "How pure!" (or some such word). "How he has understood the clay!"

I felt affronted at being so made light of. Even though I might be from the mainland, still I was a guest. I answered, "Clay I do not understand; I was not born in a craftsman's house. But bulls I understand, and that is no bull. At home just as here, a gentleman knows the look of good work, though he cannot do it. We are not so backward as you suppose."

At this they begged me not to be offended; swearing they had spoken in earnest, and that I had done what their very newest craftsmen were winning praise for. To prove it they led me to a shelf, covered with such wretched botched things as you will see at home far up in the back hills, offered at a little shrine of no reputation, the work of some ham-fisted peasant who never saw inside a workshop, but can sell them for a handful of olives or of barley, because the place has no one better. "You see," they said, "how we learn strength from the early forms."

I said I saw they had not mocked me, and was sorry; then I could think of no more to say. Presently, seeing me stand in thought, a woman touched my arm. "What is it, Theseus? Are you angry still? Or is it thinking of the bulls that makes you look so grim?" I laughed, and said what such ladies wish to hear. But the thought in my mind had been, "If I had my Companions here, and a few thousand warriors, I could sweep Crete from end to end. These people are in second childhood; fruit for the plucking; finished, played out."

Meanwhile there was still the ring. We Cranes, being of one mind with trust in each other, polished our dance till the oldest men preferred it to their memories. We had had close calls; by now there was not one of us who did not owe his life to the team. Between Phormion and Amyntor, who had each drawn off the bull from one another, there was no more talk of insolence or of clay-streaked hair. In the Bull Court both were chiefs and both were craftsmen. One day, when Chryse lost her balance and was left clinging on the horns, I had to take that same leap which had been death to the Corinthian. But Hippon was there at once on the other side, and we all got off with a graze or two, though we had a shaking.

After this same dance, I was on my way to the bath when a waiting-woman stopped me in the courtyard. "Theseus, come at once, do come, and show yourself to my lady. She got word that you were dead, and is in such grief that she is sick with it. She has been crying and screaming quite beside herself; poor little Madam, she is more soul than body; a turn like this could kill her."

I was somewhat impatient, having already more women on

my hands than I could well do with. "Salute Madam for me,"
I said, "and thank her for her concern, and say I am very
well."

"It will not do," the woman said. "Last time she was in
love with a bull-dancer he died, and she found I had kept it
from her. Now nothing will do but she must see you herself." I raised my brows. "By now," I said, "you will find her
consoled again." But she tugged at my arm, crying, "Oh, do
not be cruel, do not kill my lamb. Look, it is hardly a step
out of your way." And she pointed to the royal stairway.

I stared at her. "What!" I said. "Don't you think the bulls
will kill me quick enough?" She bridled just as if I had insulted her. "You ignorant boy! Do you take me for a bawd?
What next, these mainlanders! She is not ten years old."

I went with her as I was, in my bull-dancer's dress and
jewels. She led me up the broad stairway, lit from above
through a hole in the roof, and upheld by crimson columns.
After much turning round and about, she brought me to a
big light room, with a child's bed in one corner, a bath of
alabaster, and dolls on the floor. The walls were very pretty,
painted with birds and butterflies and apes gathering fruit.
I was looking at them when I heard a squeal as high as a
bat's, and the child was running across the room to me,
mother-naked from her bed. She leaped straight into my
arms, as light as one of the painted monkeys, and clung
about my neck. The nurse who had brought me, and another
who was there, cackled with laughter and cracked their
jokes. But I was sorry for the child; I saw she had really
been in grief. Her face and even her hair were drenched
with tears, and there were stains like crushed purple under
her eyes. She was one of those thin-skinned girls you find in
very old houses; light-brown hair as fine as silk, little hands
carved from ivory, and eyes of a clear green. I kissed her,
and said this would teach her not to cry ahead of trouble.
Her body was as delicate to touch as a fresh lily flower, and
her breasts were just beginning. I carried her back to her
bed, and put her in.

She curled on her side, hugging my hand to make me sit

by her. "I love you, Theseus, I love you. I am almost dead with it."

"The omens say you'll live," I answered. "Now go to sleep."

She rubbed my hand with her wet cheek. "You are so beautiful! Would you marry me, if I were old enough?"

"Why, for sure. I would kill all your suitors, and carry you off in a golden ship."

She looked up at me; her lashes were all stuck together with weeping. "Aketa says that when I am a woman you will be dead."

"That's with the god. I shall be too old for the bulls, that's certain. Then you fine ladies will all forget me."

"Ah, no!" she cried. "I will love you for ever! When you are an old man, twenty, thirty years old, I will love you still."

"We shall see," I said laughing. "This I'll tell you; when you are grown, if I live I shall be a king. A gamble for you, Bright-eyes. Will you bet?"

"Yes, I will. So now we are promised, and you must give me a token." I offered her a ring, having plenty more; but she shook her head. "No, rings are only gold; I must have a piece of your hair. Nurse, come here and cut it off."

"My hair?" I said. "No, that I can't give you; I have offered it to Apollo. Besides, someone might get hold of it, and use it to do me harm." Her mouth drooped; and I heard one nurse whisper to the other, "You see? He is still a barbarian, under the skin." So out of pride, though I did not like it, I said lightly, "Oh, yes, take it if you want."

The nurse brought a woman's razor, and cut the lock for her. "Don't be afraid," she said. "I will take good care of it. No one shall have it but me." As I went, she had laid it in her palm, and was stroking it softly with the tips of her fingers.

I paused at the door to wave to her. "Good-by, Bright-eyes. You never told me your name."

She looked up from the hair, and smiled.

"Phaedra," she said.

6.

ONE day the Bull of Daidalos broke a lever, so that his head would not move. Craftsmen were fetched to mend it; the dancers crowded at first to watch, then wearied of the long careful job, and went away.

I lingered on, being always curious how things are made. I had picked up some Cretan now, from the words of the rituals, and from hearing servants talked to. So I could follow mostly what the men were saying as they worked, about a tower that was building on the south coast, for a lookout against the Egyptians in case of war. Another answered that he for one had nothing against Pharaoh; it was said he worshipped only the Sun God, and slighted other deities, but he was good to craftsmen. "Before it was nothing more than copying; they thought it impious in a man to look at things for himself; now they can get some joy of their own skill. They say there are even craftsmen's laws there, and they work for whom they choose. The Egyptians can come, for me."

I came nearer, saying, "We have craft laws in Attica. And for the farmers too. They meet in council of their craft, and the King sees justice." I was so far from home, I was seeing it not as it was, but as I had dreamed of making it. The dream had grown and spread unknown to me, as it were in sleep. They listened, at first, because I was Theseus of the Cranes; all Cretans follow the bull-dance; but suddenly the foreman said, "Well, if the King of your country ever lands here, Theseus, he'll find plenty of us to fight for him, in return for laws like that."

Others joined in agreeing. I walked away, with a dazzling in my mind, and could hardly break off my thought when people spoke to me. But soon the brightness died. The Hellene lands were far across the seas, and I had no messenger.

But I could not forget. Every night I prayed to Father Poseidon, stretching my hands over the earth. Nor did I cease when no answer came. I dinned at the god's ear till it must have grown weary. And at last he heard.

I was sitting at some feast, when a tumbler came in to dance for the guests, a small slender youth, too fair to be anything but Hellene. I too must have caught his eye, for I saw it fixed on me. He was a skillful dancer; you would have thought that like a snake he had joints all over. And all the while, I was thinking I had seen him somewhere before. When he was resting our eyes met again; I beckoned him over, and asked his city. His face quickened at my Hellene speech. "My trade takes me about," he said. "But I was born in Athens."

I said, "Speak to me after."

I excused myself early, which no one noticed, for bull-dancers need their sleep. In the courtyard he came up softly; and, before I could ask him anything, whispered in my ear, "They say you are chief of the bull-dancers?" I answered, "So they say." "Then, for Merciful Zeus' sake, tell me where the dead victims are buried, and how I can get there. I have come all this way to make the offerings for my sister, who was taken from Athens last tribute-time. I have had to work my way, or I would have seen these Cretans dead before I danced for them. She and I were born at one birth. She was my partner. We danced before we could walk."

My heart leaped so that it nearly choked me. "Take home your offerings. Helike your sister is still alive."

He blessed me and ran on a little, then besought me to tell him how he could get her away. I said, "Yourself you never could. Even we men never leave the Labyrinth; and the girls are shut in the Bull Court. You would die a hard death and leave her grieving. But you may still save her before she meets her bull, if you will take a message for me to the King of Athens."

I saw him start in the shadow. He caught at me, and drew me to a shaft of light from a doorway; then he dropped my arm, and whispered, "My lord! I did not know you."

All bull-leapers paint their eyes. It marks one's standing, like wearing gold. He was too civil to remark on it. "I never saw you so near in Athens. All the City mourned for you, and the King looks ten years older. How he will praise the gods for this news!"

"You too will find him grateful." His eye brightened, as was natural enough, and he begged for the message, to hide it well. I said, "No, it would be your death if it came to light. You must learn it off. Remember it's your sister's life, and say it after me."

I thought a little, and then said, "Greeting, Father. Crete is rotten-ripe, and five hundred ships can take it. The native Cretans hate their masters. Ask the High King of Mycenae for his ships; there will be great spoil to share. And gather the fleet at Troizen, for the Cretan warships do not call there. When your men come, I will arm the bull-dancers and seize the Labyrinth."

He learned it soon, being quick-minded; then he said, "Have you some token, sir, I can give the King? He is a careful man." This was true, but I could think of nothing to send. "If he wants a token, say, 'Theseus asks you whether the white boarhound still drinks wine.'"

So we parted. I told him when he could watch Helike dance, but said, "Send her no word of it. It would take her mind from the bull. I will tell her after."

When I had given her the news alone, I called the Cranes together, and swore them all to silence, and told them the plan. "It is the secret of the Cranes," I said. "It is too soon to tell the others. Someone will talk, out of so many. As for friends and lovers in the Labyrinth, we will spare them when we strike; but till then our oath must bind us. Meantime, we must find a place to hide arms in, when we can get them. We have the girls too to arm."

I looked about the Bull Court. It seemed barer than a field; we had only our little bundles. Then Melantho said, "In our rooms we could hide them easily. It is an old rambling warren, all holes and corners and loose boards. Only the outer doors are guarded." I said, "That will do for your own weapons, but not for ours. Ten to one we shall have to break out at night, and force your gate after." There was a silence. Then Hippon looked at me under his lashes. "Theseus. If we wanted the girls let out at night, I think I could get in there."

We all stared at him. He turned to Thebe, and whispered to her, and they went off together. He was gone some time and talking we forgot him. Then Thebe appeared, not in her bull dress but her Athenian clothes. "What has she done," I thought, "to look so pretty? That's not Thebe at all." The girl came up, looking under her eyelids, and hugging a shawl about her breast. It was Hippon. He had repaid our patience, after all. Everyone knew he had picked the post of danger. Then Iros said, "But wait, my dears, till you have seen *me!*"

This promised something. I knew by now that only men were kept from visiting the girls. There were many Palace ladies who came calling after dark, with a bribe for the guard and a gift for the priestess. Our spirits lifted.

I had one great fear, that hope might keep us too much at stretch, and we would dance the worse for it. I felt I could not bear to lose one of my people now, when it might be the last watch before dawn.

If one wore a loose necklace into the ring, one always made a weak line of thread in it, in case it caught on the horn. That was old custom; but now I made the Cranes do the same with their belts, under the clasp. This was after I had seen a Median tossed by his belt and killed. Many dancers copied this device; but, as it happened, I was the first to test it. I had slipped by Herakles very close, and felt him hook me. My belt held a moment, and I thought I was finished; then it gave way. Scrambling off without much grace, but none the worse beyond a nick in my side, I felt my loin-guard about my foot, kicked it away, and stood in the ring stark naked.

All round the stands, the people had been yelling and groaning and screaming, thinking to see me killed at last.

Now their tune changed; there came from the men a shout of laughter, from the women flutterings and little squeals. Menesthes and Pylia meanwhile had drawn the bull, and Chryse was leaping him. But the people had seen all that before, and I had all their eyes. If one Cretan was in the stands, there must have been fifteen thousand.

I had given no thought to this beforehand; but now I felt hot all over, trapped in the open till the end of the dance. I even missed the bull turning my way, till Nephele called my name. She drew him off, and Amyntor and I had to look after her, which made me forget myself; but when there was time again, I was angry with the Cretans. Anger is bad in the ring. It showed me my folly.

"What!" I thought. "A slave made my garment; but All-Knowing Zeus made me. Shall I be ashamed before these foolish Earthlings, who think he dies each year; I who am a Hellene?"

So I ran round to face the bull, and danced with him to keep him in doubt of me; when I had fooled him cross-eyed I did the leap with the half-somersault, and vaulted off my hands; the people stopped laughing, and cheered instead. Soon he started sulking, then turned and plodded off; the dance was over, and I went to face the ribald Bull Court. I suppose I only remember this foolish trifle, because of what happened just after.

Next evening a slave brought me a token scribbled on clay, bidding me to a feast with a young lord whom I knew. After dark I bathed and dressed. (There are running conduits everywhere about the Labyrinth; no water needs to be carried in. They even have some to carry night-soil away, so that one need not go out to the midden.) As I passed along a colonnade, a woman slipped out from behind a column, and touched my arm, and said, "Telephos has no feast tonight."

Her head was covered with a mantle; but I saw she was gray and bowed with age. "He has just bidden me," I said. "Is he sick, then, or in mourning?" She answered, "He did not send. Follow me; I will show you where to go."

I drew back from her hand. I had had enough already of such fooleries, which ended all the same way, with a woman one did not want. Sometimes all they wanted themselves was to be even with a rival. The place was sticky with such intrigues. I said, "If he did not send, I will go and sleep. But I will ask him first."

"Hush!" she said. I peered at her in the dimness. She had not the look nor sound of a bawd; not even of a servant. She had gray Hellene eyes, and the bones of breeding; and when I looked, I saw she was afraid.

It puzzled me. The bookmakers stood to win if the bull should kill me; but bets did not cover a death outside the ring. I could not think of any husbands I had cuckolded who would take it beyond hard looks; in the Labyrinth they were mostly used to it. And I kept clear of jealous women. Yet I had the feel of danger; danger and something more. There were secrets here; I was young; it would have tormented me to go away now unknowing. "What do you want of me?" I said. "Tell me the truth, and I will see."

"I can tell you nothing," she said. "But I will take an oath, for myself and for those who sent me, that no harm is meant you, and none will come if you do as you are told." "A pig in a poke. Is it something against my honor?" She answered with an edge, though quietly still, "No, indeed! More honor than you are worthy of." And then, turning her face away, "It is no choice of mine that brings me."

For sure, she was neither bawd nor chambermaid. She sounded more like the head of a great household. "Let us hear this oath," I said.

She pattered it off, in the old Cretan of the rituals; and then it came to me that she was a priestess. The oath was heavy, so I said, "Lead on." She took from her arm a cloak she had been carrying, and said, "Wear this. You are too gaudy; you catch the light."

I put it on, and she made me keep ten paces behind her. She scuttled along like an old rabbit in a warren; presently reaching a little lamp from a bracket, she led me into places I had never seen, through smithies and carpenters' shops and kitchens and stinking midden-yards. At last we entered a store piled up with firewood, and she let me overtake her. We sidled between the stacks; behind them was a cleared space, and a wooden trapdoor. She pointed to its ring in silence. Certainly, she had never been a servant.

It had been freshly oiled, and opened silently. There were wooden steps below, and a far dim lamplight shining through them. They went down deep. There were smells of grain and oil and wax, and a cold smell of earth.

I went down a few steps, and looked round below me, and saw great store jars standing, taller than men. The clay was worked in handles all about them, so that they could be moved; in the half dark these looked like ears and fingers. I waited for my guide; she leant down, and spoke in my ear. "Go to that column there, beyond the grain jars. A thread is tied about it. Take the thread in your hand, and follow where it leads you. Keep hold of it, and you will not come to harm. If you stray into the treasure vaults, the guards will kill you."

"Why are you leaving me?" I said, and took her wrist to keep her. I did not like it; it had a smell of treachery and ambush. She said proudly and angrily, "You have my oath. Neither I nor those who sent me are used to be forsworn. Let be; you hurt me: you had best be more civil, where you are going." Her anger rang true, and I set her free. She said, with a bitterness aimed beyond me, "Here my errand ends; to know the rest does not concern me. So I am commanded."

I went down the steps, and heard the trap close softly. Around me every way stretched the vaults of the Labyrinth; long pillared passages lined with bins, or shelves for jars and boxes; crooked nooks full of clay-sealed vases with painted sides; tunnels with bays set back for casks and chests; a maze of dim caves, stoppered with darkness. A great gray cat leaped past me, something fell clattering, and a rat gave its furious death-squeal.

I went round the grain jars, of which each could have held two men standing, and found the pillar. It had a ledge with a little lamp, a twist of wick in a scoop of clay. Joined to the dressed stone was an offering bowl, smelling of old blood. Black stains with feathers stuck in them ran down to the floor and a shallow drain. It was one of those master-pillars of the house, at which the Cretans offer sacrifice, to strengthen them when the Earth Bull shakes the ground.

The thin cord round it had been tied there lately, for it was clean of blood. When I picked up the slack from the pavement, a house snake went whipping into its pierced clay pot, not a yard from my hand. I started back with gooseflesh on my arms; but I had the cord, and followed it.

It led winding through dark narrow storerooms, smelling of wine and oil, of figs and spices. Every so often, at a turn, there would hang on the black dark a little seed of light, from such a lamp as the first, beckoning the way rather than showing it. As I groped round a pillar, a strange harsh cry, low down, made my hair rise. In the moist floor an old well smelled dankly; a great frog sat on its coping, pale as a corpse. Then the way narrowed, and either side I touched rough stone walls, where creeping things scurried from my fingers. And as I paused, I heard from within the wall a muffled beating, uneven like a heart in terror; when I laid my ear upon the stone, faint and deep a voice was cursing and shouting, calling for light, and upon the gods. But only a few feet on I could hear it no more; the prison must have been a good way off.

Next I found a great place full of crooked shadows, where old furniture was stored, lamp-stands and vases. A long arm of it stretched away into the dark; but peering down it, I could just see piles of dusty shields and spears. Then I was sorry I had not marked my way; and working out a flake from the nearest pillar, I scratched on it the trident sign of Poseidon. After that I marked each one I passed.

From there the thread led into a passage all in darkness, where I could only feel my way along the walls. My face tickled with cobwebs, and a rat ran over my foot. I thought of snakes, and trod delicately. This passage sloped upward, and the air felt warmer. At the end was another lamp, and

a great room of archives: shelves of scrolls rustling with
mice; moldy rolls of ancient leather; bundles of palm leaves
inked with faded signs; chests and baskets full of clay tokens
and tablets. The dust made me sneeze, and the mice went
scampering.

Then after a narrow place again there was a light. I came
into a long chamber that was a storehouse for sacred things.
There were tripods and bowls, anointing vases with wide
bases and narrow necks; libation cups with breasts sculpted
on their sides; sacred axes and masks and knives of sacrifice;
and a great stack of dolls with jointed limbs. The thread
wound about, round piles of incense-stands, and emblems on
long poles, and a gilded death-car such as princes are
wheeled on into their tombs. It passed a tall press, bulging
open with women's vestments, gold-crusted and smelling of
cassia. Then there were stone steps leading upward, and a
door ajar. The end of the thread was tied to its handle.

I pushed the door, which opened without a whisper. Now
there was tall space all about me, and a clean floor below. I
smelled scented oil, beeswax, incense, spiced wine, and burnished bronze. A great shape reared before me, dark against
glimmering lamplight; the back of a woman ten feet high,
standing on a plinth and crowned with a diadem. It was
the Goddess of the great sanctuary, where the nobles had
bid for our dedication when first we came. But now I stood
behind her, in the hidden place.

Then I saw that within her shadow another stood, smaller
and darker. It was a woman, wrapped head to heel in a long
black robe. Nothing showed but her eyes. They were Cretan
eyes, dark and long, with thick lashes and soft brows, and
the forehead above them was smooth as cream. More I
could not see, neither her shape nor her hair, for the robe
she was folded in covered everything; only that she seemed
slender-waisted, and was not very tall. I closed the door on
the thread behind me, and came in. My borrowed cloak was
filthy with dust and cobwebs. I dropped it, and stood
waiting.

She made a little gesture to call me nearer, just slipping

her finger-tips out of the robe. I approached to within two paces of her; then I could tell by her eyelids she was young. But she did not speak, only drew the robe about her so that it hid even her fingers. So I said, "I am here. Who sent for me?"

She spoke at last, but without dropping the robe from before her mouth, so that her voice came small and muffled; yet it had a clearness, as a blade has though it is sheathed. "Are you Theseus, the bull-dancer from Athens?"

I thought it strange she should not know me; all Knossos goes to the dance. "If you doubt that," I answered, "I cannot prove it." But her eyelids trembled, and were young; so I said, "Yes, I am Theseus. Who wants me, and why?"

"I am a priestess," she said. "I serve the Goddess-on-Earth. She sent me here to question you." Then she let the robe slip down from her face. I saw it was made delicately, unpainted, and very pale. Her nose was straight and fine, and her mouth seemed small because the eyes were so dark and wide. When she had unveiled her head, she paused, looking at me, and pressing herself back against the base of the statue. I waited, and then said, "Yes?"

I saw the tip of her tongue move across her lips. The old woman, too, had been afraid. Yet I could not believe that here in the holiest place anyone would murder me. Nothing seemed sensible. I saw the robe moving, where her fingers twisted within.

"It is a heavy matter," she said, "touching impiety. The Goddess says you must be questioned." There was a tight bunching in the robe, where she had clutched it up. "You must answer, on pain of cursing. We have heard that the High Priestess of Eleusis chose you King of the Year; that after you had married her, you roused the people against her, and put her to death; that you have maimed the Mother's worship and profaned the Mystery. Are these things true?"

"Only," I said, "that I am King of Eleusis. The Goddess chose me, or so I was told. And it was the last year's King I killed, according to the custom, not the Queen."

She wrapped the robe tighter, so that it showed her

crossed arms. "What is that custom? How did you kill him?"
I said, "With my hands, at wrestling." She gazed at me with
big eyes, then only nodded. I said, "I was away in the border land, when the House Snake stung the Queen. She took
it as a sign of the Mother's anger, and went away. I do not
even know if she is dead; I will swear, if you like, that I did
not kill her."

She looked down at her hidden hands. "Did you grieve?
Was she very dear to you?" I shook my head. "She had
tried three times to have me killed, once by my own father's
hand unknowing. She deserved to die. But I left her to the
Goddess." She paused, then said still looking down, "Why
was she angry? Had you been with someone else?"

"Only in war," I said, "as happens everywhere. No, it
was not for that; she thought I would change the custom.
And so I did; I come of a house of kings. But I never profaned the Mystery. The people were content, or they would
have killed me themselves."

She said after a pause, "And you will swear all this is
true?"

I answered, "What oath shall I take? I have told you, as
it is, on pain of cursing." Her lips parted, and shut quickly.
I thought, "She had forgotten that. She is a priestess, yes;
but what else?"

"That is true," she said. "You need not swear." Then she
was silent again. I saw the cloth stirring over her hands.

"What now?" I thought. "And if all this is so heavy, why
not an older priestess? It is not common, to trust such things
to girls."

She stood in thought, twisting and untwisting a fold of
the robe. I said, "I have been with the bulls three seasons.
If the god is angry, or the Goddess, they have not far to
reach for me."

She said again, "That is true." I saw her lick her lips and
swallow hard. "Perhaps the Mother has some other thing
in mind for you."

I thought, "Now for the truth," and waited. When no more
came, I said, "It may be so. Has she sent you some omen?"

She opened her mouth; but only breath came out of it. Her breast rose and fell within her arms. "What is it?" I asked, and came a little nearer.

Suddenly she spoke in a little high voice, swift and breathless. "I am here to question you. You must not question me. We must know these things in the sanctuary; that is all. That is why we sent for you."

"I have answered," I said, "as well as I can. Am I to go back the way I came? Or can I walk across the courtyard?" And I bent down for my cloak; but I was watching her.

"Wait," she said. "You have not leave to go." I dropped the cloak again; I had only wanted to get some sense from her. While I waited I saw that her hair was fine, waving of itself, with a silky burnish. There was a small waist in the close-drawn robe; and they must be tender breasts, which her arms cradled so softly. "Come, speak," I said to her. "I shall not eat you."

A lock of hair, which fell down within her robe, went suddenly straight as if the end were being pulled. "I was to ask you," she said, "to ask you for the Goddess, that is, for the records of the sanctuary . . ." She stopped, and I said, "Yes, what?" Her eyelids blinked, and she said faster than ever, "We have no account of the Mother's rite in Athens. What is the ceremony, how many priestesses take part, how many girls? What victims are offered? Tell me from the beginning, and leave nothing out."

I stared at her surprised. At last I said, "But, Lady, there are six girls in the Bull Court, all Athenian born, who know the ritual. Any one of them could tell you, better than a man."

She began to speak, then bit it off in the middle. Suddenly her face, which had been so pale, was as pink as the morning mountains. I strode toward her, and rested my hands on the plinth either side of her shoulders, to keep her where she was. "What game is this? Why ask me things to no purpose? You are keeping me here—for what? Is it an ambush? Are my people being harmed while I am gone? No more lies now; I will have the truth."

My face was close to hers. Her eyes were swimming like the eyes of a netted fawn; and then I saw she trembled all over. Even the thick robe shook with it. I was ashamed I had threatened her as if she were a warrior; yet it made me smile too. I took her between my hands to hold her still, and she gave a little gasp, like a swallowed sob. "No," I said, "do not say anything. I am here, and it is no matter why. See, I obey you, and do not ask a reason any longer. I have reason enough."

She turned up her face, flooded with changing color; and something hovered in my mind, that I could not name. Now I was near, I smelt the scent of her hair and of her body. "Who are you?" I asked. Then my breath caught in my throat; I knew.

She saw it in my eyes. Hers opened black and wide; with a quick cry she ducked under my arm, and ran. I saw her shadow slipping away round the great image, and ran after. All the huge hall stood empty and echoing, but the only footsteps were my own. The black robe she had been wrapped in lay trailed along the floor; even the whisper and clink of her skirt was still. I paced about, looking where she might have hidden; the further door she could not have reached in time, yet I had heard something closing. "Where are you?" I called. "Come out, for I will surely find you." But my voice rang too loud in the hollows of the sanctuary; I felt the Presence angry, and dared not call again. Then, as I stood still, my shadow leaped out black before me, from some new light behind. I sprang round, remembering I was unarmed. But when I saw whence the light came, then indeed my breath grew thick. The plinth had opened beneath the image. Within, a clear blue fire danced on a tripod. It shone upon the Earth Mother, living, crowned with her diadem; her arms stretched forth over the earth were wreathed with twisting serpents. Her hands grasped their middles; the light shone on their polished skins, and I heard their hissing.

My heart was a hammer shut in my breast; I made the sign of homage with a shaking hand. Rooted on my feet I looked at the Earth Mother; and the Earth Mother looked at me. And as she looked, I saw her eyelids tremble.

I stood still, and stared. The flames flickered, and the Earth Mother looked straight before her. I took a pace forward, softly, and then another, and one more. She had not had time to paint her face, and the diadem leaned a little. As I came, I saw her gasp from holding her breath. She held out her arms stiffly, and the serpents wriggled, disliking the light, and wishing for their house again. But I did not watch them as I drew near; I watched her face. When I stretched out my hand toward them, I knew well enough that their teeth were drawn.

In her dark eyes, two little mirrored flames stood flickering. At the mouth of the shrine, I reached inward, and slid my fingers over her hand. As I closed it in mine, the snake, released, twined for a moment round both our wrists, and bound our two hands together; then it fell slithering, and poured itself away. Out of the Earth Mother, mistress of all mysteries, looked a maiden flying; a girl who has gone one step forward and three back, and wants to punish what scared her. I took her other hand; its snake had escaped already.

"Come, little Goddess," I said. "Why are you afraid? I will not hurt you."

7.

IN THE corner of the temple, behind the image, was a curtained doorway and a little room. It was where she went to eat, when the rites were long; to be dressed, and painted. It was simple like a child's, only that the litter was sacred emblems and vessels, instead of toys. There was a bath in the corner, painted blue inside with swimming fish. Also a bed, for her to rest on if she was tired.

To this room I carried her. It was where she put off her gold-weighted diadem, and her heavy robes; where her women loosed her jewelled girdle, which no man had undone before. She was shy, and I only saw the place a moment before she blew out the lamp.

Later the moon came up, plunging down a steep court to spill light upon the floor. I lifted myself on my arm to look at her; my hair fell down on hers, and she twisted them both into one rope.

"Gold and bronze," she said. "My mother was fair, but I am all Cretan. She was ashamed of me."

I said, "Bronze is more precious. From bronze come honor and life. Make my enemy a golden spear, and a sword blade too." I did not like to speak of her mother, after all I had heard; so I kissed her instead. She hung all her weight upon my neck, and pulled me down to her. She was like a young salamander meeting flame; afraid at first, and only when flung in knowing its own element. There is an old saying that the house of Minos has sun-fire in the blood.

We slept, and woke, and slept. She would say, "Am I awake? Once I dreamed you were here, and could not bear to waken." I proved to her she was awake, and she slept again. We should have been there till morning; but in the hour before dawn the old woman came into the temple, and prayed aloud in her high cracked voice, and struck the cymbals, before she pattered away.

It was about this time that I learned to sleep by daylight. Even the shouts of the echoing Bull Court could not wake me.

The second night, the thread was stretched a new way for me. There was a trap in an old disused lamp room, very much nearer. It was the old woman who had led me so roundabout, to keep me from learning the way. She was a kinsman, on the distaff side, to Pasiphaë the dead Queen. The new way got me there much quicker; and it still passed the ancient armory.

This night there was wine set by the bed, and two gold cups to drink it from. "They look," I said, "like libation cups." She answered, "So they are," making nothing of it. My mother had taught me respect for sacred things. But my mother was only a priestess.

The lamp burned on unquenched tonight. As for me, my eyes had been blind to all women else, and that day's dusk had seemed unending.

Deep in the night, she said to me, "I do not live, unless you are here. A doll walks and talks and wears my clothes, while I lie here waiting."

"Little Goddess, tomorrow night I cannot come." It came hard to me, but I was still a Crane, bound by our oath. "Next day is the bull-dance. Love and the bulls don't go together. But we shall see each other, when I come into the ring."

She clung to me, crying, "I cannot bear it. It is a sword stuck in my heart, every time you leap. Now it will be worse a thousand times. I will have you taken from the Bull Court. They can think what they choose. I am Goddess-on-Earth."

She was all girl, saying this. It made me smile. I saw, now, that it had never crossed her mind to make herself like the gods. It was an old title, showing her rank and office. All the sacred rites here had become like play, or mere court trappings. She did not know why I smiled, and her eyes reproached me.

"Bird of my heart," I said, "you cannot take me from the Bull Court. I offered myself to the god, to answer for my people. While they dance, I dance with them."

"But that is a . . ." She checked herself and said, "only a mainland custom. Here in Crete no king has been sacrificed for two hundred years. We hang our dolls on the trees instead, and the Mother has not been angry."

I made over her the sign against evil. Her dark eyes, with little lamp-flames in them, followed the movement of my hand as a child's eyes do.

"You offered yourself," she said, "and the Mother gave you to me."

"We are all her children. But Poseidon gave me to my people. Himself he spoke to me; and I cannot leave them."

She reached out for the Corinthian's bull-charm, which

I wore even when I wore nothing else, and tossed it back over my shoulder. "Your people! Six boys and seven girls! You who are worthy to rule a kingdom."

"Not unless I am worthy to rule them. Few or many, it's all one, once one has put oneself in the god's hand."

She drew back to look in my face; but she kept a hank of my hair clutched in her fist, as if I might run away. "I am in a god's hand too," she said. "Peleia of the Doves has caught me. This is her madness, this love like a barbed arrow that cannot be pulled out. When you try, you drive it deeper. My mother called me a little Cretan; I hated Hellenes and their blue eyes; but Peleia is stronger than I. I know what she is doing well enough. She sent you here to be Minos."

I stared at her, feeling my mouth part with horror. Yet her eyes were innocent, it seemed, of everything but wonder at mine. At last I said, "But, Lady, it is your father who is King."

She looked quenched, like a child who does not know what it did wrong. "He is very sick," she said, "and he has no heir."

Now I understood her. But it was a great matter; my mind moved to it slowly.

"What is it?" she said. "Why did you look at me as if I were evil?"

She lay on her side; her waist had little folds full of soft shadow. I stroked them with my hand. "I am sorry, little Goddess. I am a stranger here. At Eleusis, when I went to the wrestling, it was the Queen who led me."

She looked at my hair still in her hand, then up at me, and said not angrily but as if in wonder, "You are a barbarian. My nurse said that they ate bad children. I love you more than I can bear."

We talked then without speech. But a man is not a woman, and cannot long be kept from thinking. Presently I said, "Your father may have no son; he should know best. But he has an heir."

Her face sharpened in the lamplight. "I hate him," she said.

I remembered her in the temple, looking at him over the broken tablet.

She said, "I have always hated him. When I was little, my mother would leave me when he came. They had their secrets. She laughed at me, and called me her little Cretan; but never at him, though he was twice as dark. When she died, and they buried her, I scratched my face and breast until they bled; but I had to throw my hair all over my eyes, to hide that I could not weep."

"Did you know then?"

"I knew without knowing, as children do. My father is a silent man; he rarely spoke to me. But I knew they mocked him when they whispered in corners. It made me love him." She dug her fingers into the bed. "I know who has killed him. I know; I know."

"But," I said, "you told me he was sick."

"He is dead," she said. "Dead alive. For a year and more his face has not been seen; now he never leaves his room. When he goes, it will be on the death-car." She paused and said, "Swear to keep this secret. You must bind yourself; I could never, never curse you."

I bound myself with the oath. Then she said, "He is a leper."

I felt, as one always does, the word like a cold finger on my flesh. "That is a heavy thing. But it comes from the gods."

"No. It comes from another leper, or from something of his. All the doctors say so. When they found it on my father, they stripped and searched everyone about him; but all were clean. I thought myself it was magic, or a curse. But then he remembered how more than a year before, he had lost an arm-ring, one he wore every day. It was gone nearly a month; then it was found, in a place that had been searched before. So he put it on again. It was under the ring that the marks began."

This seemed to me too fanciful. "If there were a traitor

among his household," I said, "why not poison, which is quick? Lepers live long, if they have a roof and people feed them." To myself I was wondering why Minos had not gone back to the god, on the first day. "Asterion might have years to wait; he would find something surer."

She said, "He has found the surest thing. If my father had died outright, and he had been proclaimed Minos, there would have been war. The Kindred would not have suffered it. Now little by little he has been getting power in his hands; buying some men, putting others in fear. At first, when my father sent out orders, they were obeyed. Now they do not reach the men he sends them to, and the Captain of the Guard has bought a new estate. No one knows now who belongs to Asterion. No one dares ask." And then she said, "He rules like a king already."

Then indeed I understood, not only this but all the rest.

"But," I said, "then Crete is being ruled by a man who does not belong to any god; who was never dedicated. He has all power; yet he has not consented to make the sacrifice. Has he consented?"

There was a shadow on her cheek, as if she would smile; but her face grew grave, and she shook her head.

"Then," I said, "the god will never speak to him. How can he lead the people? Who will see their danger coming? What will happen, if the god is angry, and there is no one to offer himself? He takes service, tribute, honor; and he gives nothing! Nothing! I knew that he was monstrous! He will be death to your people, if they let him live. Why do the chiefs obey him? Why do they bear it?"

She was silent awhile; then she reached over my shoulder, and pulled the crystal bull to hang upon my breast. "You said to me, 'Make my enemy a golden sword blade.' That is what we have done here; made our swords of gold. I did not see, till I knew you."

Her words surprised me. She said, "You think I am a child, because I was never with a man before. But some things I know. I knew you brought some fate or other, down at Amnisos, when you married the sea."

"It was you, then, peeping through the curtain!" Then there was some young lovers' talk. But I said later, "What did you mean, when you said I married the sea?"

She looked at me with deep bright eyes that were not childish. "Why do you think he threw the ring?"

"To drown me, of course. He could not put me to death."

"So you did it without knowing; that makes it sure." When I asked her what she meant, she said, "When a new Minos is proclaimed, he always marries the Sea Lady. He throws her a ring." I remembered the native Cretans, staring and muttering. He had given them an omen to remember, that would seem to come by chance as true omens do. He had used me; a dog would have done as well. He had made light of me even in this.

"So," she said, "it made a fool of him when you brought it up again. But then you threw it in the sea, and married her yourself! How I laughed, inside my curtain! And then I thought, 'Perhaps it is a true omen.' I could tell the Cretans thought so. He could tell it too, so he patched it up the cleverest way, by making himself your patron. He must always own the best of everything. He saw you would make a bull-leaper, and he thought it would keep the last laugh for him."

I thought awhile. Presently I said, "How does he get on with the native Cretans? According to their old customs, the Queen's blood should be good enough for them; they don't set much store by the father." I was afraid this might seem too blunt; but it was not what troubled her.

"Yes," she said. "He knows. Until lately he was very scornful of them; they were nothing to him, except for work. It was me they came to. That is my office, to hear suits and prayers; Cretans would always rather pray to a woman. And I tried to help them. I know how it feels to be made light of. I used to bring their prayers to my father; that was how I first came to talk with him. He used to say, 'You are only a goddess, little Ariadne. To be an envoy is a serious matter.' But often he did as I asked."

I wiped her lashes with my finger, saying, "And now?"

"Asterion courts them. Once if they were wronged he would not lift a hand. Now he will back them even in an unjust cause, unless it is against one of his creatures. Even among the Palace people he is gathering men with Cretan kindred, men like Lukos. You see why my father must die slowly?"

"That is bad," I said. "Has he won many?"

"Cretans have long memories. Those he has insulted don't forgive him. But if any have been injured by a Hellene, they turn to him."

We talked longer, but I remember no more of it. My head was spinning with sleep, and thinking, and the warm scents of her hair and breast.

At the next bull-dance, when I looked up to the shrine, it seemed to me that the world must know, and I guessed she felt the same. But no one noticed anything. I brought off a new trick, jumping off Herakles with a standing back-somersault, and landing on my feet. I had been practicing it all morning on the wooden bull, to show her what I could do.

Afterwards I told the Cranes all I could in honor; I had not wanted to disturb them before the dance. I said I had heard that the King was sick, that Asterion was plotting to set the Cretans against the Hellenes and seize the throne. "It means we have not long. If the Cretans back him, he can hold the coasts against a Hellene fleet as long as he keeps their love. And that will be till he is safe on the throne; a year, or two, or three; longer than we shall last here. We shall have to strike quickly."

Iros said, "We are doing what we can, Theseus; but we haven't got many weapons yet." He looked reproachful. He and Hippon had stolen more arms than anyone else; their chances were better. I said, "I know of a weapon-store; with luck there will soon be arms for everyone." I meant to bring them a few at a time and hide them where we could get them quickly. But I did not want too many questions.

That night in the little robing room, we flew together as the spark to the tinder. Two days and a night apart had been like a month. The night before, indeed, I had almost gone to her, bull-dance or no; only that when I sat up I saw Amyntor sleeping, and remembered my people.

Already in three nights our love had its memories and its past. We had our secret words to laugh or kiss at. Yet even while we laughed and played, or sank as deep in love as a diving dolphin, I felt a kind of awe; whether of the place, or because the love of kings and queens, even in secret, is a rite done for the people before the gods.

After I left her, I took the lamp from its bracket on the sacred column, and went to the store of arms. As I had foreseen, it was all old stuff; what was new and good was in the armory above. One could see the steps and guess where they led; but it would be well guarded. I trod softly, and greased the hinges of the chests with lamp oil. They were full of arrows; but the bows looked time-warped, and the strings had perished. It was the spears and javelins that drew me. They were an old pattern, a little heavy, but quite sound. Only they were too long to conceal about one, even under a cloak.

Nonetheless I set myself to move them, night by night, to the vault under the lamp room, where they could be quickly got. There was a pile of old oil jars by the pillar, mostly empty; the cobwebs showed they were never stirred, and there was room behind them. A few nights later I found a box of spearheads, and a whetstone. This was best of all. I began to grind them down for daggers, and to bring them into the Bull Court, a few at a time, for the girls to hide.

I had sworn the Cranes to silence, even with lovers and mistresses; so I felt bound to it myself. Besides, she was not a girl to give half your mind to. She had that vein of wildness which stirs a man because it lies deep, like Hephaistos' fire which only the earthquake loosens from the mountain. Afterwards she would look at me with still eyes of wonder; then sink into a milky calm like a full-fed baby's, and fall asleep.

Sometimes, when she talked of her father and the kingdom's troubles, I thought of speaking, and asking her help. Her heart I trusted. For her head, she was young, barely sixteen; she had told her secrets quickly; and most of all I feared her hatred of Asterion. He was no such green lad as I had been in Eleusis. If a woman's face said to him, "Something is coming to you, though you do not know it," he was not one to miss the message.

About this time, he bade me to another of his feasts; and I saw she had told me true.

I did not see one guest who looked even half Hellene. They were all Cretans, or near-Cretans; the small gentry, whose houses had been great in the days before the Hellenes came. And his manner to me had worsened. Not that he openly insulted me as such a man thinks of insult. That would have won him no praise, for every Cretan loves a bull-leaper. But he made it very clear that I was only there to entertain his honored friends; and I could feel, at the back of it, that he wanted to take a Hellene down before them. Presently he asked me to sing a song of my homeland. He spoke smoothly; but he spoke too as the conquerer does to the captive.

I bit on it awhile in silence. Then I thought, "Good. If I submit to this, no man alive could say I am his guest."

I asked for a lyre, and tuned it to the Hellene mode. Asterion sat back smiling. But I saw sly Lukos looking under his eyelids. He had travelled. He knew what the skills of a gentleman are among our people.

It does not become a captive to sing the triumphs of his forebears. Nor did I want to warn anyone my thoughts were upon war. Yet I wanted to make these Cretans remember me, and not as quite the fool Asterion hoped. So I sang one of those old laments I had learned at home in Troizen. It is the one they sing all over the Isle of Pelops; often when the bards tell of a sacked city they will work it in, but sometimes they sing it alone. It is about the King's heir, the Shepherd of the People, kissing his wife farewell at the gatehouse, as he leaves for battle foreknowing his death.

"Let me go," he says, "and do not try to keep me. If I hung back, I should be ashamed before the warriors, and the gold-belted ladies with their flowing skirts. Nor would my heart consent, for I was reared to valor, to fight in the vanguard for my father's honor and mine. In my deep heart I know the sacred citadel must fall, the King and his people perish; yet that is not what I grieve for most of all; no, not for my father, nor my mother, nor for my bold brothers tumbled in the dust. I grieve for you, when they carry you off in tears to the hollow ships, and end your days of freedom. Far away, in the house of some foreign woman, I see you working the loom, or driven with heavy water jars up the steep path from the spring. And someone who sees you weeping will tell another whose wife you were, bringing your sorrow freshly home, that your man is gone who would have kept you free. May I lie dead, and the earth heaped over me, before I see you led away, and hear you cry."

In the Labyrinth, they have servants to make their music for them. He had not expected a king's son to have been properly taught. When I saw the Cretans wipe their noses, I knew that now they would not mock me. At the end, they came crowding all about; by which I knew those who were not his lackeys yet, a good many it seemed. It was all I could do to keep a straight face. But there was nothing he could say; I had only done as he asked me.

That night I said to Ariadne, "I have been at the Little Palace. You were right. If he is to be stopped, it must be quickly."

"I know," she said. "I have thought of killing him myself, if I knew how."

She felt as soft in my hands as a nestling dove. Though he was her brother of the same belly, her words were too wild to shock me. She had been alone, with no one to turn to. I said, "Hush, and listen. If I could get word to my people at home, and they sent me ships, what then? You understand it would mean war. Whom would the Cretans fight for?"

She turned over in the darkness, and lay thinking, her chin propped in her hands.

"They would fight for themselves. They would rise against the Hellene houses, when the chiefs went to the war. There would be terrible things done, blood everywhere. But that is what Asterion will do himself; that's what he wants with the Cretans. When he has used them, he will take care that uprising is their last. Yes, they will have died to buy themselves a heavier chain." She folded her arms and laid her head upon them. Presently she said, "But if . . ."

"Yes?" I said, stroking her hair. But she shook her head, and said, "I must think. Look where Orion is; how quick night passes." So we began our good-bys, which took a long while, and no more was said about it.

I had now moved arms enough for every dancer in the Bull Court, men and girls, and had told Amyntor where they were, so that someone should have the knowledge if I died. The girls had about thirty daggers hidden in their sleeping place. Winter was come, and sometimes the bull-dance was not held because of the rain or snow; it was a long while since the people of the Labyrinth had put themselves out to honor a god. But if we missed a dance, we practiced on Daidalos' Bull, or sometimes held our own Games, boys against girls, or drawing for sides; or we danced, if we were feeling stale; anything to keep us limber. I had seen other teams get slack, and what always came of it.

This was our third season in the Bull Court. We had learned by now every chance that can happen to bulldancers, whom the Cretans call Poseidon's little calves. We knew what they live by, and how they die; what kills a dancer in the first week, and what kills him after half a year. And one day Amyntor touched my arm, while the girls were wrestling (the priestess would not let them wrestle with boys), and said to me softly, "Chryse is growing."

Our eyes met. There was no need to say more. She had been fourteen when she sailed from Athens; and she was all Helene, head to heel. If she lived, she would be like the Maiden Goddess, upright and tall. But tall girls did not live long in the bull ring.

I said to Amyntor, "After the winter, and before the great spring winds, that is when the ships will come." I measured him against me, when he was not looking. He had grown three fingers himself.

Amyntor had grown dear to me. We had worked together till we thought like one; he knew how I would leap before I knew myself. It was rumored in the Palace that we were lovers. We no longer put ourselves out to deny this. It saved us from the nonsense of the Knossos courtiers, with their flowers and seals and mincing verses and lurkings in the night, and gave us something to laugh at. Lately it had served me well; we could talk secrets unregarded, and, now my wanderings among the women were over, it saved me from too much guessing.

But the night before the bull-dance, I always lay alone; two nights even, if I felt my eye out at practice. It came hard, for I was young, and had not so much as kissed another woman since I came to her. But my people and I were far from home. To keep me a king I had neither laws nor warriors, only what I could find within me. It was a little kingdom; the finest crack could shiver it.

If I told her I could not come, she never reproached me, or not in words. But from her hands I knew her mind. She wanted to hear me say, "Let tomorrow go, let the bull have me and my people die; it is all well lost for one night in your arms." Then she would have answered, "No! Do not come; I swear you will not find me." She only wanted to hear me say it. But I was young, and took my calling gravely, as a holy trust, which it would be impious to play with, or toss to a girl like a string of beads. In those years, I had always one ear listening for the god.

Nowadays it would cost me nothing to please a woman so. He speaks no more to me, since my son died on the rocks beside the sea. I had felt the warning in the ground; "Beware the wrath of Poseidon," I said to him, and he could take it as he chose; I too was angry. He chose to take it for a curse, and I would not speak again. I watched him off, the tall lad and his big Troizenian horses, riding to the narrow way. I kept my silence. Now the god keeps his.

But I remember, though it is long ago, how the night after the bull-dance our meeting was like unmixed wine, all fire and spiced honey, making it worth while to have stayed away. I remember how she wept over some silly graze, my first since we were lovers. After a while I said, "Have you thought of any plan?"

"Yes," she said. "Tomorrow night I will tell you." I asked, "Why not now?" But she said it would take too long, there was no time tonight, and bit me softly, like a kitten. Often I had the marks of her teeth next day. But a bruise is nothing, in the Bull Court.

The next night I was going to her through the vaults, when in the shadows of the temple store I saw something move. I reached to my belt for my homemade dagger; then the figure stepped into the light, and it was she. We embraced between the gilded death-car and the stack of dolls. She was wrapped in the dark cloak she had worn before. "Come with me," she said. "There is someone you must speak with."

She gave me from a shelf a round clay lantern, such as one can darken by covering the hole. When I opened my mouth to question her she laid her hand on it, saying, "Don't make a sound. We must pass right under the Palace." After she had led me past the archive room, she turned aside. There was another thread tied to a different pillar. She whispered softly, "It is a hard way to find. Once I was almost lost myself." She took the thread in one hand, and my wrist in the other. The lamp was dim, and the place pitch-dark around.

The way went winding, through the Labyrinth's very bowels. We passed old uncouth masonry that looked like the work of Titans or the first earth men. For this was the core of the foundations, belonging to the earliest House of the Ax, the stronghold of Cretan Minos, two palaces ago. These mighty piers, made strong with the blood of a thousand victims, had withstood the rage of Poseidon when every wall had fallen that stood above the ground.

Sometimes she would squeeze my hand, warning me to shade the lamp; there would be a fine crack in the stone above, with light glinting through, and voices arguing or making love. Little by little our way slanted lower, which made me think we were going westward, with the slope of the hill.

Here were no stores, but now and then the rubbish of the ancient earthquakes, broken pots shaped without the wheel, or old crude tools. And once, where the earth had settled, there was a man's white skull sticking out of the ground from the eye-sockets upward, before one of the great pillars. He still wore shreds of an old hide helmet. He was the Watcher of the Threshold, the strong warrior they bury living under a sacred place, for his ghost to fight off demons from it. I started, and then saluted him as became his honor. Ariadne had passed that way before, and only drew her skirt aside.

At last we came to a few steps and a narrow door. She signed to me to take my sandals off, and not to speak. She took the lantern from me, and quenched it, and set it down.

The door opened softly. Two plates of my necklace chinked together; she stilled them with her hand and made me hold them. Then she led me through some small dark room, where my feet felt polished tiles. Beyond was another door; then air and space, and what seemed light after the blackness. It was starlight coming from three flights above, through the roof-hole over a great stairway.

Beyond the stair-foot was a hall, and going down from it a sunken shrine. There was a solemn, old, sacred smell. On the wall that faced the shrine were paintings it was too dark to see, and midway of the wall a tall white throne.

Through all this she led me, and out beyond. Then there was a door, under which a dim lamplight showed. She whispered, "Wait," and opened it; within was an embroidered curtain, which fell to behind her. I heard whispers, and a sound of metal. Then a voice spoke, which was not hers. It was the voice of a man, but strangely altered; muffled, and dimly booming. It made me shiver. Yet it was gentle and weary, even sad. It said, "You may come in."

I put aside the curtain, and smelled sweet gums burning.

The air was blue with the smoke. I peered through it and stopped dead, with my heart knocking my ribs.

The room was small and plain, with dying embers on the hearthstone. There were shelves for cups and plates and toilet vessels, a shelf of scrolls, and a table with writing things, on which burned a lamp of greenstone. In a chair beside it, hands laid on knees, sat a man with a golden bull-head, and crystal eyes.

The weary voice, hollow within the mask, said, "Come, son of Aigeus, and stand where I can see."

I came forward, and touched my fist to my brow.

He drew a long sigh, which rustled in the mask like wind in reeds. "Do not be affronted, Shepherd of Athens, that I cover my face from your father's son. It is a long while now since I sent away my mirror. This face which Daidalos made for the Cretan Minos is better for a guest to see." He lifted the lamp from the table, and held it up, moving his head because the mask blinkered his eyes. Then he said, "Go out, my child, and watch the stairway."

She went softly out, and I waited. It was so still that I could hear the sputter of the incense in its porphyry dish. Behind its precious scent hung the heavy smell of sickness. His right hand, bare on his knee, was long and fine; the left was covered with a glove. Presently he said, "I had heard King Aigeus was childless. Tell me something of your mother."

I told him about my birth, and, when he asked, about my rearing. He listened quietly. When I mentioned some sacred rite, he reached for his tablets, and made me tell it all, and wrote quickly, and nodded. Then he said, "But you changed the custom at Eleusis. How was that?"

"It came by chance," I said, "from putting my hand to what I found." And I told him how it was. Once I stopped, hearing him choke within the mask and thinking his breath had failed him. But he motioned me to go on; and I perceived he had been laughing.

When I had told him how I got to Athens, he said, "They say, Theseus, that you wrote your own name on the lot to come here. Is this true? Or is Lukos trying to excuse himself? I should like to know."

"Oh, it is true," I said. "He is a man who loves order. I was sent by the god. He gave me his sign, to sacrifice for the people."

He leaned forward in his chair, and lifted the lamp again. "Yes, so she told me. Then it is true." He pulled a fresh tablet toward him, and took up a new sharp pen, moving briskly, like a man who is pleased.

"Come," he said, "tell me of this. The god spoke to you, you say. You have heard the voice that calls the king. How does it speak? In words? In a sound of music, or the wind? How does it call?"

I thought, "He is right, seeing my birth is unattested, to prove if I have the Hearing." But I had scarcely spoken of it even to my father, and the words came hard.

He said, "I shall be beholden to you. My time hangs heavy here. I am making a book upon the ancient customs, and this is a matter where the archives give no help."

I stared at him. Amazement rooted my tongue. I thought I must have heard wrong, yet knew not how to ask. For courtesy's sake I began to stammer something; but the words died, and we were silent, looking at one another.

He was the first to speak. He leaned his head on his hand, and said in his sad muffled voice, "Boy, how old are you?"

I said, "If I live till spring, my lord, I shall be nineteen."

"And after dark, when the bats fly over, you hear their cry?"

"Why, yes," I said. "Often the night is full of it."

"They cry to the young. And when the old man passes, they are not silent; it is his ear that has hardened. So also with kings' houses; and it is time then to think of our going. When the god calls you, Theseus, what is in your heart?"

I paused, remembering. In spite of what I knew, I thought he would understand. Which is strange, for it had not always been so with my father. Finding what words I could, I opened my heart in this small close room to Star-Born Minos, Lord of the Isles.

When I had said my say, his heavy mask sank forward on his breast; and I paused, ashamed to have tired him. But he raised his crystal eyes again, and slowly nodded. "So," he said, "you made the offering. And yet, it is your father who is King."

His words went sounding through me, deeper even than my grandfather's long ago; deeper than my own thought could follow. "No matter," I said. "A good Shepherd will give his life for the sheep."

He sat in thought awhile; then he sat up and pushed the tablets from him. "Yes, yes; the child was right. I own, I doubted her. There is a daimon of perversity that haunts our house. But she chose soundly. Out of death, birth. You are what must come; I question it no longer." He made a sign with his hand in the air between us. Though his forebears had been long from the Achaian lands, I saw he was still priest as well as King.

He shifted in his chair, and made as if he would clear a space on the table; then he shook his head. "This sickness clings to what one touches. Or I would ask you to sit down, and offer you the cup of kinship, as a man should who gives his daughter's hand."

I almost knelt to him. Only I saw it was not reverence he wanted, but an arm to trust in. "Sir," I said, "with my heart I pledge you. I will not rest till I have made her a queen."

He nodded, and I felt he smiled. "Well, Theseus, so much for the courtesies. They are due to your blood and honor. But my daughter will have told you, they are all I have to give."

I said something or other, and he scratched among his papers, shaking his head, and sometimes muttering, as sick men do who are much alone; whether to himself or me I could not tell. "When he was a child, he followed me like a shadow, the black bull-calf branded with our shame; he never let me forget him. He would have dogged me to the hunt, on shipboard, to the Summer Palace; he wept when I sent him back where he belonged. He would call me Father, and stare when he was silenced. I should have known he would destroy me. Yes, yes, a man might laugh; it has been as pat as an old song. I withheld the sacrifice, and it bred my death. If there were really gods, they could not have done better."

He paused, and I heard mice rustling behind the bookshelf.

"Only slaves come here now. The higher stand at the door, and make the lowest enter. The man is dead, and overripe for the death-car. But the King must live a little longer, till the work is done. With the child, Theseus, there must be a new beginning." Then he said softly, "Look if she is out of hearing."

I stepped to the door, and saw her by starlight, sitting on the coping of the sunken shrine. I came back and said, "Yes."

He leaned forward in his chair, grasping the arms. His low voice rustled in the bull-mask; I had to lean near to hear. The close smell choked me, but I hid it from him, remembering what he had said about the slaves.

"I have not told her. She has seen already too much of evil. But I know what this beast of our house will do. He will promise these Cretans a Cretan kingdom; that has begun. But in a Cretan kingdom, he can only reign by right of the Mistress. In the ancient days of the Cretan Minos, they married as they do in Egypt."

My heart paused; there was a stillness within me as I understood. Now indeed I saw why great Minos had received a bull-boy from the mainland, a bastard son of a little kingdom, and offered him the Goddess. And I saw why she had spoken of killing her mother's son. She had guessed, having seen evil already.

It made up my mind. "Sir," I said, "I have sent word to my father I am alive, and asked him to send ships for me."

He straightened in his chair. "What? My daughter said nothing of it."

"It was too heavy," I said, "to lay upon a girl."

He nodded his gold head, and sat in thought. "Have you had an answer? Will they come?"

I drew breath to speak. Then I knew I had been going to speak like a boy. This meeting taught me to know myself.

"I do not know. My father has not ships enough. I told him to try the High King at Mycenae." His head moved, as if to stare. But I was thinking as I spoke. "I daresay the High King might say to him, 'Theseus is your son; but he is not mine. *He* says that Knossos can be taken; but he is a bull-dancer who wants to see his home again. What if we send ships and Minos sinks them? Then we shall all be slaves.' My father is a prudent man; if the High King says this, he will see sense in it."

He nodded heavily. "And now it is too late to send again, across the winter sea."

"Then," I said, "we must trust in ourselves. If the Hellenes come, so much the better."

He leaned back in his chair, and said, "What can you do?"

"There are still the bull-dancers. They will all fight, even the bull-shy ones, even the girls; they will fight for the hope of life. I am getting them arms as fast as I can. I can take the Labyrinth with them, if we can get help outside the Bull Court."

He reached out for some papers beside him. "There are a few men left who can be trusted." And he read me some names. "Not Dromeus, sir," I said. "He's trimming now; I've seen him at the Little Palace." He sighed, and pushed away the papers, saying, "I brought him up from a boy, when his father died."

"But there is Perimos," I said. "He has stood out, and he has sons. He will know who else is safe. We need two things: arms, and someone to win us the Cretans."

We talked of such things awhile. At the end he said, "However weary I grow of life, I will live till you are ready."

I remembered how I had thought worse of him for not returning to the god, and was ashamed. He said, "Let me know, if you get word from Athens."

I said I would. Then I pictured my father driving in at the Lion Gate, and up the steep road to the Great House of Mycenae. I saw him at table with the High King. But I could not see him in the upper room firing the King for war, making him impatient to launch his hollow ships. My father had had a bellyful of trouble, and it had made him old before his time. I saw the rough dark seas that tossed round Crete; and I saw them empty.

"Ships or no, sir," I said, "we shall know our time when it comes. I am in the hand of Poseidon. He sent me here, and he will not fail me. He will send me a sign."

So I said, to cheer his solitude, because I doubted there would be ships until I went myself to fetch them. But the gods never sleep. Truly and indeed, Dark-Haired Poseidon heard me.

8.

A FEW nights after, Ariadne said to me, "Tomorrow is the day when I give my oracles."

"You should be sleeping," I said. I drew her in and kissed her eyelids. She was too tender, I thought, to bear without bruising the madness of a god.

She said, "Not many Hellenes come. To those I shall say the usual things. But I shall tell the Cretans that a new Summer King is coming, to marry the Goddess and bless the land. Hyakinthos flowering in a field of blood. They will remember that."

I was amazed, and asked her, "But how can you tell what the Holy One will say through you, before you have drunk the cup or smelled the smoke?"

"Oh," she answered, "I don't take much of it. It makes one giddy; one talks nonsense, and one's head aches after as if it would split."

I was shocked in my heart, but I said nothing. If it was true the god spoke to them no longer, it was strange she could tell of it without weeping. But I remembered how Cretans play at such things like children. So I only kissed her again.

"I will make it stick in their minds," she said. "I shall paint my face white, and draw a line of red under my eyelids. I shall have a cloud of smoke (it is all the same to them what one makes it of) and roll my eyes and toss about. When I have spoken, I shall fall down."

I was slow to speak. At last I said, "It is a woman's mystery. But my mother told me once that when she is in the Snake Pit, whatever the question is, something any fool should know without troubling a deity, she always pauses before her answer, and listens, in case the Goddess forbids it."

"I always pause too," she said. "I have been properly taught as well as your mother. A pause makes people attend. But you can see, Theseus, Crete is not like the mainland. We have more people, more cities, more business to fit together. We have ninety clerks working in the Palace alone. It would be chaos every month, if no one knew what the oracles were going to be."

She stroked her fingers back from my temples through my hair; I felt them say, "I love you, my barbarian."

I said to myself it was no matter; that when we were married, I would be there to stand between the god and the people. Yet I was sorry she had not the Hearing; a king, like a craftsman, wants to breed his skill into his sons.

Soon there was less time to think; from then on we were busy.

In the old archive store under the Labyrinth, I met with Perimos and his two sons. The office of his family was to write down the King's judgments; only they and their chief clerks ever used the place, these records were so old. If Minos wanted to know the precedent before a judgment, he sent for the Recorder. It is an ancient mystery, inherited father to son from the founder of it, a prince called Rhadamanthos.

After the King was sick, and Asterion heard the causes, he had sent for Perimos, told him a judgment he meant to give, and asked for a precedent to uphold it. When Perimos brought him instead nine clear judgments the other way, he told him shortly to look again. The Recorder said nothing; he shut himself among the records, searching, till the time was up and Asterion had to do his own injustice. But everyone knew he would only bide his time; and Perimos did not want to wait.

He was about fifty, with stiff brows and beard streaked black and gray like wood-ash, and the fierce round eyes of an owl in a hollow tree. I was sorry for him; he would have got on well with my grandfather. It was against his grain to plot in cellars with painted bull-dancers. I had always to leave the Bull Court bedizened as if for a feast or tryst, else people would have wondered. However, I had not forgotten all I had learned in my grandfather's judgment hall, my father's, and my own; in time he forgot my bull-boy's finery. His sons seemed men of honor; the elder rather clerkish, the younger a lieutenant of the household, very Cretan-looking, lovelocked and willow-waisted, but with the nerve of a soldier. He said we could count on about one in three of the King's Guard, those who respected their oath of service, and those who hated Asterion. It was time, now, I thought, to push things forward in the Bull Court.

I had trusted the Cranes from the beginning. But soon it would have to go beyond them; and I looked for another team leader I could rely on. My choice fell on a girl called Thalestris, a Sauromantian. They have many customs of the Amazons, serving the Moon Maid in arms, and fighting in war beside the men. When first she came she looked very outlandish, dressed in a quilted coat and deerskin trousers, and smelling of goat-milk curd. Her country is at the back of the northeast wind, beyond the Caucasus, and they only undress there once a year. But stripped and cleaned she was a fine girl, a little too mannish for one's bed, but with all the beauties of a bull-leaper. The courage too; for on her very first day she was eying me with envy.

Liking her spirit, I taught her all I could; and when she was made leader of the Gryphons, she came again for counsel. I warned her of one bull-shy boy who would do them no good; when they had given him to the bull and got someone better, she bound them with a vow like ours, and in more than two months not one had died. So people were used to seeing us in talk. I told her everything, except that

I was the Mistress's lover. Thalestris was a girl for girls; but it is a thing I have found, that no woman likes to hear you hold forth about another.

When she had heard, she threw a back-somersault, for she was a wild thing still. But she was no fool. After she had run on awhile about her mountain home and friends, whom now she might hope to see again, she asked me to get her a bow, for that was her weapon. I said I would try; now we were in with the loyal Guard, good stuff was coming down into the weapon store from the armory above. She begged to tell her Gryphons, saying they had no secrets apart; and as I thought it spoke well for them, I gave her leave. Before long all the teams knew, who had vows of fellowship. As for the others, they would fight when the time came; but for their tongues one had no surety.

So the leaven worked silently in the dough; there was no folly. The secret was with people whose life-threads were closely bound; to fail the team was to meet your bull next time. You could only see it in their eyes if you knew already.

Now we began to bring up arms into the Bull Court. Amyntor and I showed the other boys of our team, and three or four team leaders, the way down through the lamp room; our friends of the Guard had stacked the arms below it. It was cold, so we had cloaks to hide things in, though we had to saw down the shafts of the spears and javelins. Cretan bows are short, and a good weight for women. The girls hid all these things, and many arrows, in nooks and holes under the floor.

Ariadne had given her oracles to the Cretans. She told me, full of pride, how she had talked in broken phrases, neither too clear nor yet too dark; how she had rolled up her eyes and sunk down among her fangless serpents, and waking dazed had asked what she had been saying. Now, she said, she had sent out an old woman she could trust, to whisper among the gossips and recall the ring in the harbor. Before long, it would be time to warn the chiefs and headmen.

Spring comes early to Crete. The painted vases in the Palace rooms held daffodils and sprays of almond flowers; the young men dressed their hair with violets, and the ladies decked their boy-dolls, which they would dandle till midsummer and then hang on the fruit trees, for they play at sacrifice as at everything else. The sun shone warmly, the snow shrank higher up the mountains, and in the lull before the south wind began blowing, the sea was calm and mild.

I went to the feasts of the Palace people, and sometimes there would be a juggler or a dancer or a girl with tame birds, or a bard from oversea. I would go near when I could, and let them hear my name and my Hellene speech. But no message came from Athens.

Days passed, and the almond blossom in the painted vases snowed down upon the painted tiles. A chieftain of the Kindred, who had land near Phaistos, which he would not sell when Asterion asked him, died suddenly of a strange sickness; his heir took fright and sold the land. The native Cretans whispered in corners, and told long tales of the ancient days. In the Bull Court, the dancers had their heads together, as bull-dancers often have, being full any time of gossip and intrigue. But you could hear, if you listened, that they were talking of their homes and kindred, as when the frozen stream melts in spring. Days passed. And one night I heard the sound of a rising gale, whistling over the horned roofs and through the courts of the Labyrinth. It was the south wind blowing, which closes Cretan waters to ships from the north.

I lay on my back with eyes wide open, listening. Presently a dark shape came near. There was always someone prowling about in the Bull Court after the lamps were out. But this was Amyntor. He leaned down to me and said, "It is early this year. Half a month early, the Cretans say. It is moira, Theseus, no one can help it. We can do with what we have." I said, "Yes, we shall do. Perhaps Helike's brother never got to Athens." The Cretans had been looking for the wind a week already. But he had fought under me in the Isthmus and in Attica, and wanted to save my face.

Next day in the Bull Court, Thalestris got me in a corner.

"What is it, Theseus? You look downhearted. No one thinks any worse of you because the wind is blowing. It was good warriors' talk, about the Hellene ships; it kept us in heart while we were getting ready. Now we don't need it." She clapped me on the shoulder like a boy, and strolled away. But I felt the shadow upon the Bull Court, as well as she.

I walked slowly to the next meeting in the archive vault. But old Perimos only nodded with a grim smile, as if we had won a bet. He was a man of the law, as they say in Crete; it is the nature of their calling to expect the worst. I had done myself good with him because I had promised nothing. Presently he said, "My son has a plan. Though it is foolhardy, it may do for want of better." His voice was dour; but I saw in his eye both pride and grief.

The warrior son, whose name was Alektryon, stepped forward, looking among the dusty shelves and withered parchments like a kingfisher in a dead tree. The dim lamplight glittered on his rose-crystal necklace and his arm-guards of inlaid bronze; his kilt was stitched with those shining green beetles they dry in Egypt and use for jewels, and he smelt of hyacinths. He said that if a chief man of Asterion's faction were to die, they would all attend his funeral, and we could seize the Labyrinth while they were out of it.

"Well thought of," I said. "Is someone sick?"

He laughed, showing his white teeth. There is a gum called mastic, which Cretan beauties chew to blanch them. "Yes, Phoitios is, though he doesn't know it."

This was the chief of Asterion's private guard; a big fellow with Hellene bones, and a nose broken from boxing. I raised my brows and asked, "How can it be done?"

"Oh, he takes good care of his health. The only way is openly. I shall make him fight me; I expect he will choose spears."

It was news to me that mortal insults were still known in Crete; but I was thinking that here was a man we could hardly spare. There was nothing I could say, seeing he was five years my elder, except, "When will it be?"

"I can't say yet; I must find a likely quarrel, or he will guess at something behind. So have your people ready."

I said I would, and we parted, he and his father going off to the stair they used, and I up to the sanctuary. We never watched each other go. Even their friends among the courtiers did not know of this meeting place; everything hung on keeping the secret of the vaults.

I went up to the robing room, and told my news. Ariadne said she was glad it was not I who was fighting Phoitios; he would be a hard man to kill; then she asked when the fight was to be, for she must see it. I told her I did not know, and we said no more; with all this business, we were always short of time for love. At parting we would tell each other how, when we were married, we would lie till the sun stood high over the mountain. Next night was the fast before the bull-dance.

But next night, after supper, I heard laughter at the doors of the Bull Court, and the chink of gold. It was not cheap, to buy your way in there after dark. In came Alektryon, swift and glittering, his kilt stitched with plaques of pearl and his hair stuck with jasmine. He had a necklace of striped sardonyx, and a rolled kid belt covered with leaf gold. He strode among the dancers, flirting with this youth or that, talking of the odds and the newest bull, like any young blood who follows the ring. But I saw his seeking eye, and went toward him.

"Theseus!" he said, making eyes at me and tossing back his hair. "I vow you are of all men the most fickle. You have forgotten my feast and eaten in the Bull Court! You have crystal for a heart. Well, I will forgive you still, if you come now for the music. But hurry; the wine is poured out already."

I begged his pardon and said I would come. "The wine is poured" was a signal agreed on between us, for something that could not wait.

We went out into the Great Court, which, since it was still early, was full of lamplight, and of people with torches passing to and fro. He caught my eye, then leaned upon a column in a Cretan pose. As someone passed he said, "How can you be so cruel?" and fingered my necklace and drew me near. Then he said softly, "Minos has sent for you. The way is marked as before. You must go alone."

He spoke as if he had learned it off. But I had never had word from the King, except through the Goddess. I stared, trying to read him. His Cretan looks, his finery, his foppish ways, all made him doubtful to me, once I began to doubt. I knew nothing of his standing among the warriors. My eyes met his. He took me by the arm, a grip tender to look at but strong and hard. "I have a token for you. Watch out, and take it like a love gift." He opened his hand saying, "I was to tell you it has been cleansed with fire," and then, as someone came past us, "Wear it, my dear, and think of me."

The ring in his palm was of a pale gold, very old and heavy. The carving was in an antique style, pointed and stiff, but the worn device could still be read: a bull above the shoulders, a man below.

He slipped it on my hand. Under his warning eye I smiled, turning it this way and that. I had seen it once before. So I leaned on his shoulder, as I had seen youths do in Crete, and whispered, "It is enough. What does he want?" He put his arm around my waist and said, "He did not tell. It is something heavy." Then he looked past my shoulder and murmured swiftly, "One of Asterion's people. We mustn't look too well in together. Quick, give me the slip." I shrugged him coyly off me, and went away. Though I felt a fool, I had no more doubts of him.

Down in the vaults, I found the second thread tied ready, and a clay dark-lantern. I had never been this way alone. It is natural, when with a girl, to expect boldness of oneself; but now I found these ancient warrens eerie and awesome, haunted, it seemed, by the dead who had been crushed there when Earth-Shaker was angry. The bats that came winnowing round the light were like souls kept from the River. When at length I came to the Watchman, looking at me under his moldering helmet with the caves of eyes, it was like meeting a comrade; one knew what he was, and that he belonged to a god. I made the sign of propitiation, and it seemed he said to me, "Pass, friend."

When I reached the door above, I doused the lantern and stood silent, listening. No one was on the stairway. I shut the door behind me, and saw (for there was a moon this time) how it closed flush with the wall and the painting hid it. There was a little hole to hook one's finger in, and work the catch. White moonlight fell on the stairs beyond, but the tall throne was in shadow. I trod softly through, and saw faint light under a door. Going up to it I smelled the incense. So I scratched the panel, and his voice bade me enter.

He sat in his high-backed chair, masked as before, his hands laid on his knees. Yet it was not the same. The room was clear of litter. The incense burned before a stand on which stood some symbol or image. And there was some new thing about him; a stillness, and a power.

I touched my breast in greeting and said softly, "Sir, I am here."

He beckoned me to stand in front of him, where he could see me through the mask. I waited. The air was close and fetid, the smoke stung my eyes. They were heavy for sleep; I remembered that tomorrow was the bull-dance.

"Theseus," he said. His muffled voice sounded clearer than before, and deeper. "The time is come. Are you ready?"

I was troubled, wondering what had miscarried in our plans. "We are, sir, if need be. But the day of the burial would be better."

He said, "The day is proper, and the rite. But the beast of sacrifice is not enough. Something is needed of us, Shepherd of Athens; me to suffer it, and you to do it." He pointed with his bare right hand to the stand behind the smoke. Then I saw the holy thing that stood there. It was a two-headed ax, fixed upright on its shaft in the polished stone.

I stood still. I had not thought of so solemn a thing as this.

"The gods can send a sign," he said, "when our ear hears them no longer. They sent a child to lead me."

For a moment I wondered whom he meant. But though Alektryon was three and twenty, he would have known him from his birth.

The curved crystals of the mask were turned toward me. I looked at the ax wreathed in blue smoke. What he asked was seemly, and good every way. Yet my hand hung down. This was not Eleusis, where I had fought a strong man for my life. I felt myself shiver in the close air. I had thought, "He is old enough to be my father."

"These two years now," he said, "every breath I have drawn has fed my enemy. I have only lived to keep my daughter from him. Not one of the Kindred dared to offer for her; not one dared stand between him and the Gryphon Throne. Now I have found a man, why give him one day longer? Take care of her. She has her mother's blood; but her heart will rule it."

He stood up. He was taller than I by half a head.

"Come," he said. I heard a soft laugh within the mask; it made me start like the bats in the vault below. "He has had a good run, our long-horned Minotaur. But he cannot be Minos till the priests have seen my body. And they know who owns the Guard. I wish I might watch his face, when the blood-guilt comes homing back to him. Come, Theseus; nothing is left to stay for. You have the ring already. Labrys is waiting; take her from her bed."

I went to the polished stand. The ax was shaped like the one they use in the bull ring. Its haft was bronze worked with serpents; but when I looked at the head, I saw it was of stone, the edges of the blades hand-flaked and ground, the neck drilled for the shaft. Then I raised my fist in homage, knowing that this was Mother Labrys herself, the guardian of the house since the beginning.

He said, "It is two hundred years since she took a king, but she will remember. She is so old at her trade, she could almost do it alone."

I lifted her from her bed. Dark shadows beat about me,

like stooping ravens. I answered, "If the god says so. We are only watchdogs, to hold or let go when they call our names. But it is against my heart."

"You are young," he said. "Never let it trouble you. You are breaking my prison."

I felt the ax in my hand, and it balanced well. "Speak for me," I said, "beyond the River, when the Avengers ask whose hand you fell by. If I live I will see your tomb well found with all a king should have; you shall not go hungry or scanted in the paths of darkness under the earth." He answered, "I will commend you there as my son, if you are good to my child. If not I shall require it of you."

"Do not fear," I said. "She is like my life to me."

He knelt before the image of the Earth Mother, and turned his back; then he drew off the mask and laid it down before him. His black hair had broad streaks of white, and his neck showed through it like the bark of a dead tree. He said without turning, "Have you room?" I lifted the ax, and said, "Yes, for a man of my height there is room enough." "Do it, then, when I invoke the Mother."

He was a short while silent; then he cried aloud to her in the ancient tongue, and bowed his head. My hand was still unwilling; but it was due to his honor not to keep him waiting. So I swung down the ax, and it came strongly with my arm, as if it knew its business. His head lolled down, and his body sank at my feet. I drew back from it, my flesh shrinking in spite of me. But when I had put Labrys back to lick her chops after her long fast, I turned to him again, and saluted his shade as it started on its journey. His head lay turned toward me; and though it lay in shadow I saw what stopped my breath; he had not the face of a man, but of a lion.

I ran out through the curtain, and stood panting in the fresh night air. My limbs shuddered and my hands were cold. But in a little, when I could think, I was glad for him. I saw the gods had set upon him a mark of honor, now he had made the offering at the people's need. Thus they may turn to men at last, after long silence; after blood and death, and the bitter grief for what can never be undone, have closed the listening ear thicker than dust. So may they do at the very end, even with me.

A flake of moonlight struck the coping of the sunken shrine. I looked about me, and saw against the wall the tall white throne of Minos, with the priests' benches either side, and, painted behind, the guardian gryphons in a field of lilies. An owl hooted, and somewhere in the Palace an infant cried till its mother stilled it. Then all was silent.

There was danger here, and I should have been gone already; but this place seemed set apart only for me, and for its watching gods, and the ghost waiting for the ferry on the sighing shore. It seemed unworthy of what had passed, that I should scramble off like a thief. I felt he saw me. So I crossed the painted floor and sat in the seat of Minos, laying my hands flat on my knees and my head against the throne-back, sitting upright and thinking my thoughts. At last I heard beyond the doors the voices of the Guard calling their rounds. So I rose up softly, and went back through the dark maze along the path of the thread.

9.

I WOKE heavy-headed, with all the teams astir before me. As I fetched my breakfast yawning, I saw Amyntor eying me. Presently he asked how I had slept.

I was not used to rebukes from Amyntor. But I remembered how I had gone off last night, and that he was an Eleusinian. "You fool," I said, "do you think I went courting? I was sent for. Minos is dying. By now he must be dead." It was best for his own sake he should know no more.

"Dead?" said Amyntor. He looked about him. "Not yet; hark, no one is wailing."

It was true. After the mystery performed in silence and dark night, I had forgotten to wait for clamor. There was no doubt I had dealt a death-blow. Labrys had split his skull. I said, "Well, he is sinking fast; I had it for certain." Surely, I thought, by now someone has found him.

"Good," said Amyntor. "This must bring things to a head. Meanwhile there is the bull-dance; you had best get some more sleep."

"I am not tired," I said, to keep him from fretting; he was always trying to nurse me. "Besides, they'll never hold the dance with the King lying unburied."

"Don't sell the calf before the cow gives birth," Amyntor said. He had been the rashest of the Companions, before he came to Crete; it was being a catcher that had steadied him.

I went back to my pallet to keep him quiet, telling him to say nothing to the others. It would only put them on edge; and it might be noticed. I shut my eyes; but I was wide awake behind them, listening for the outcry that proclaims the death of a king. Now and again I saw under my eyelids some Crane tiptoeing up to look at me. They were afraid of my coming to grief in the ring, so near our time. Hours seemed to pass. I grew too restless to keep still, and got up again. Noon came and our food; and the Cranes ate slenderly, as one must before the dance. For an hour we rested, playing at knucklebones; then we heard the pipes and tabors, and it was time to go.

The sun shone. There were scents of warm dust and sharp spring leaves. We touched for luck the altar to All the Gods, which stands by the dancers' gate. Round it in the dust sat the sacred cripples, bull-dancers who had walked out of the ring on their feet after a goring, but would never dance again. Some of them were old bald men and crones, who had sat here fifty years. They scratched and chattered in the sun, threatening to ill-wish us unless we gave them alms; we put our gifts into their bowls, hearing the music, and getting our bodies ready to dance in.

The sand was hot from the sun; the women's stands tittered and buzzed, the gamblers called the odds. We came before the shrine, and I looked up, trying to read in her

face if she knew her loss. But through her ritual paint one
could tell nothing.

We spread and made our circle in the ring, and I took
up my place facing the bull gate. Before it was lifted, we
heard a bellow behind it. I could feel, all round, the Cranes
pricking like dogs. It was the same with me. You could tell
by the sound that something was wrong.

The gate chains rattled. I got ready to watch him when
he paused to look about him. On his bad days he would
come in with his head held low, and stand fidgeting his
forefeet. The gate rose clattering; and I raised my arm to
him in the team leader's salute. It seemed to me that I was
still waving when he was on me. Without looking to right
or left, or pausing to draw breath, he had shot straight out of
the bull gate and across the ring, like a boar from covert,
like a thrown javelin aimed at my heart.

My mind was slow for lack of sleep; but my body thought
for me. I flung myself sideways; his horn struck my thigh
glancing, and knocked me down. I rolled away and scrambled upright, spitting out dust and blinking it from my eyes.
Hot blood ran down my leg. There was a screeching as if
all the women in the stands were being ravished at once.

I flung my hair from my eyes. Hippon was riding the
bull's brow, clinging like a monkey in a hurricane, while
Amyntor and Menesthes wrestled him by the horns. That
could not last long, the way he was going. His eye was
bloodshot, and on his mouth I saw a yellow foam; he moved
as if he were mad. I looked at the mill about his head, not
liking it much; but there was only one thing for it. When
he was straight a moment, I grasped the horn-tips and
vaulted over all three of them, to land upon his neck. I
twisted round and straddled him, holding the horns low by
the head and drumming my heels into his dewlap. It took
his mind from the others, and they got away. He charged
on with me, as fast as a war chariot. There was a noise too
like the roar of battle, and I heard ten thousand open throats
bawl "Theseus! Theseus!"

I looked through my hair and saw Amyntor tearing along

beside the bull, waiting to catch me when I let go. All the Cranes were wheeling round, too near. He was not ready for them; though I felt shaken half to pieces, I could not leave him yet. "Open out!" I shouted. "Let me ride him!" I locked my feet under his throat, trying to squeeze his windpipe and slow him for want of breath.

He charged onward, tossing and bucketing till my very teeth seemed loosened in my jaws. And the Cranes for the first time had disobeyed me. They were scrambling everywhere. When Herakles dragged a moment, I saw Melantho and Chryse trailing on the horns, then they were gone, I could not see where. Flecks of foam flew backward on my face and arms; and in my nostrils was a·strange acrid smell.

The shouting faces were coming near. He was making for the barrier. Now I must leave him, or he would batter me off. I loosed the horns; Amyntor, through everything, was waiting. As he set me down, I knew I was done, a sitting bird when the bull came for me. Amyntor was all spent too; I could hear his sobbing breath. The Cranes were coming up, but they were breathless and slow, from doing more than they had been told to. I waited for Herakles to turn at the barrier and come back. But instead came a great crash, splintering, and shouting. He had charged it head-on.

It was made of cedar-wood as thick as your arm; but he shook it. It rained down nuts and sweets and fans, and even a lap dog. One horn was stuck in it; he wrestled it free, and then he turned. But for me, all the bull ring was slowly turning. Only one thing I knew: that I had been gored, and if you lie down then, your blood is for the Mother.

I stood, panting and swaying. Beside me Amyntor was exhorting me with curses and Minyan love-names, and calling on the gods. It is forbidden to hold up a victim. The bull came on. He seemed as slow as a dream. I thought I must be lightheaded. He seemed coming for ever. His big eyes, bulging and bloodshot, looked into mine. I gathered my last strength, watching which side he would gore. His head went down. It bowed, and sank, and touched the sand. His forelegs folded. He heeled over like a wrecked ship, and lay down in the dust.

There was a hush, and a wavelike sound of awe and wonder. Then the cheers began.

My eyes were clearing, though I felt weak and sick. I saw that my wound though bloody was not deep. The ring was like a garden, as people threw in like mad whatever they had with them, fans and scarves and beads and flowers. The Cranes gathered about me, filthy, grazed and bruised, dust in their hair, their grimy faces streaked with sweat. Phormion was limping; Chryse owed him her life, as she told me after. As she came up, hand in hand with Melantho, I saw her face was scored along the cheekbone so that blood ran down; she would never more be the perfect lily that had sailed from Athens. Helike was joking with Thebe; as happens also at war, she had been taken out of herself and lost her fear just when there would have been sense in it. Amyntor's grin was silly with weakness; mine was as weak, and doubtless no less foolish. Telamon offered me his shoulder, but I waved him off. My girl in the shrine had been scared enough; at least I could salute her on my feet.

She stood bolt upright on her dais. Her paint stood out like a doll's, but she performed the ritual unfaltering. I was proud she had commanded herself, so as not to betray us; though she had not the Sight nor the Hearing, I thought, she would make a queen.

Old Herakles lay where he had fallen. A bunch of windflowers, thrown from above, had spilled over his head. As I looked he gave a heave and twitch, and the flies settled on his eyes. And from above, where the upper stands were dark with the native Cretans, came a thick solemn buzz, as from men who have seen a portent.

We went out to the gate. I was tired, but not too tired to think. I remembered the guard about the sacred bulls; no common man could enter even the compound. I looked up at the empty box of Minos, and then at the box beside it. There sat our patron, receiving compliments upon his team. But I saw his eyes, when he did not see mine.

Once out of sight, I was not too proud to be carried. In the Bull Court the wise woman washed me and dressed my leg, and gave me a hot spiced cordial, while Aktor looked on whistling through his teeth. Our eyes met. He looked at the herb-woman, shook his head for silence, and walked away.

Thalestris stood by my pallet, one hand on her hip, the other scratching her black hair. I beckoned her nearer. She bent and looked at me, not like a woman at a hurt man but like a warrior watchful in an ambush, waiting the word. I said to her softly, "The bull had medicine." She nodded. I said, "Are the arms well hidden? Asterion must know something." I was wondering, as I spoke, how soon he would send for me, and what death he would make me die.

She said, "He can't know much. Or the arms would be gone already. Yes, they are safe. Don't trouble yourself; you will be good for nothing till you are rested." I saw her shoving off the dancers who were coming up to speak to me. She was no fool; she knew if I did not rest now there might be no time later. I lay thinking of her words, my mind slow with weariness and with the herb-woman's drugs. "He can't know I killed Minos, or he could put me openly to death. He can't know of the arms, or they would be gone. But does he know about the Mistress? Or whom she meant by her oracles? Has he put Perimos to the question, or his sons? What does he know?"

So I thought; but I was growing drowsy in spite of myself. I heard again the buzzing of the Cretans, who thought the god had killed the bull at my feet. "Well," I thought, "sure enough he has been with us." And it seemed I felt his presence still about, solemn and brooding, so that the sounds of the Bull Court seemed too loud, and made me uneasy. But even as I thought it I fell asleep. I dreamed of my childhood, of serving the island shrine in the hush of noonday, and listening to the spring.

When I awoke, the lamps were being lighted, and the dancers were sitting down to eat. Amyntor, who must have been waiting for my eyes to open, came over and asked

what he should bring me. I sat up, though I was almost
too stiff to do it, and asked if there had been any news
of Minos' death.

He looked about him. But there was no one near; the
dancers were all eating. "No, Theseus. Who told you of it?
Can he be trusted? There is quite another rumor going about
today. It is said that when the fleet set sail for Sicily, before
the gales, Minos went with it, but it was kept secret. They
say he went to take the island by surprise, and that was why
it was kept dark. It has been denied from the Little Palace,
which makes one think it may be true."

He brought me soup, and a barley-cake, and a piece of
honeycomb. I ate, lying on my elbow, and wondering how
long it would be before we got the news that Minos was
dead in Sicily. Truly, I thought, it is a beast that thinks; and
quickly too. It had been clever to deny it; I had to own I
should not have thought of that myself.

And then I thought, "But he must still need time. This
proves it."

The wise woman came, and felt me over. She oiled and
worked my limbs, kneading and knuckling and slapping;
looked at my wound, muttering charms, and said it would
heal clean. At the table the dancers were sitting over their
twice-watered wine, in the last hour of talk before the girls
were fetched away. I stretched out under the old woman's
hands, feeling my sinews loosened and my blood run sweetly.
Nothing was left but the smart of wine on my graze, and
a heavy drowsiness. I turned, when she had gone, to sleep
again. Then I saw Aktor the trainer standing by my pallet.

"Well," he said, "so you have come to life again. I will
write it on the door of the Bull Court, and save my legs.
You have slept sound enough. When you lay there through
the earthquake, with all the outlanders who never felt one
bawling to their gods, I looked if you were dead; but you
were sleek as a baby."

"Earthquake?" I said staring, and then, "Why yes." I remembered the feel of the brooding god; I had been too tired
even to know a warning when I had it.

"It was nothing much," he said. "A shelf of pots gone in the kitchen. Well, the Cranes will have to catch another bull." He looked at me. This time no one was in hearing.

I said, "What did they give him? I smelt it in his steam."

"How should I know?" He looked round again. "I should think what the dog fanciers give their beasts before a fight. The dogs mostly live, but it would be guesswork, the dose for a bull." He had been stooping, but now he got down on the floor beside me, to speak lower. "One we won't name must have a hole in his pocket now. If he still needs a talent of gold, he must wait till summer when his ships come in."

"Gold?" I said, thinking my cordial must have had poppy in it. I still felt slow.

He said, "A ghost is talking"; a Cretan saying for what one will not stand to before witnesses. "He has got something on hand that is emptying the strong room. All day his agents have been scrambling about Knossos calling in revenues, chasing rents, selling up debtors, borrowing from the Phoenicians. Well, you know your odds. Even money three months ago, now it's six for eight, and still the bookmaker's headache. Go to any one of them and try if you can back Theseus to live; they won't touch it; if you bet on the Cranes you must bet on points. But this morning, so I hear, all over Knossos there were bets laid on a kill, at a hundred to one, or longer; quietly, here and there. And all about the same time, to keep the odds from shortening. What do you make of that?"

"Make of it?" I said. "What should I make? I'm only a mainland bull-boy. In my village we're simple folk." My brain was spinning. Aktor looked down at me scratching his head, then said, "Sleep out your medicine, lad, you're fuddled still," and went away.

My eyelids felt like lead; sleep lay upon me closer than a lover. But I thought that if I closed my eyes, I would believe after that I had dreamed all this. I saw Amyntor hanging about near by, and beckoned. "I have something to tell you. Bring Thalestris too."

They came and hung over my pallet, eying me like something that may fall apart. "Be easy," I said to them. "The Minotaur knows nothing. He did this for gold."

If I had spoken in Babylonian they could not have looked blanker. I did not blame them.

"Minos is dead. You can take that for certain. He is hidden somewhere in the Labyrinth, bundled away without rites like a dead robber, to give Asterion time. He needs to buy troops, and friends; but he can't claim the treasury till the death is known. Stuck between the horns, as you might say. So he backed the bull for a kill, to raise the wind."

They stood drop-jawed, like village idiots. It almost made me laugh.

At last Amyntor said slowly, "He did it for gold? But we are the Cranes. We have danced a year for him."

Thalestris flung back her head. "Mother of Mares!" she cried. And indeed she looked a true daughter of Poseidon Hippios, her strong dark mane tossed out behind her and her nostrils flaring. She planted her fists upon her hips, and showed sidelong like a wicked colt the blue whites of her black eyes. "What are these Cretans? They and their baths, and their talk about barbarians. Hollow as sucked gourds! If you shook them they would rattle! Theseus, why do we wait?"

In the old days at Eleusis, it would have been Amyntor who spoke first. But nowadays he would take his time. He had been standing with his black brows joined above his hawk-nose, fingering the place where his dagger should have been.

"Theseus," he said, "how this man has despised us!"

I nodded. "Yes," I said. "He has always held us light."

"Vengeance is the right of any man who is not a woman. If he had done this knowing there were arms hidden in the Bull Court, I would have liked him no better, and thought of him no worse. But all he knows of us is our honor; and he has sold us off like the spare goats in a lean year. By Black-Horned Poseidon, Theseus, it is enough! For this we will have his heart."

10.

IN THE morning the old woman came again with her warm oils. I had slept like a log; my leg wound was drying cleanly, and not much deeper than a scrape. The muscles I had thought were torn were only strained; all I needed now was to move about. Tonight I would go up to the sanctuary, and find whether Ariadne knew that Minos was dead. If they had locked up his door, she would have no remedy, without betraying the secret way. But, I thought, even when she knew, what could she do, or Perimos, or Alektryon, or any of us in the Bull Court? Whoever owned knowledge of the death would be charged with the killing. Yet every day we waited, Asterion would gain strength.

After I had limbered up at exercise, I felt well enough; yet all this weighed on me. I stood with the Cranes, and Thalestris, and another team leader, young Kasos of the Sparrowhawks, a Rhodian pirate's son, enslaved when they hanged his father. They were eager for some action, and I put on cheerfulness, ashamed to feel so low when nothing was wrong with me. Across the Court, the Dolphins had got a cockfight on. The mounting noise went through my head, and I longed for it to be done. At last I cried out in spite of myself, "Make them stop that din!"

"What is it, Theseus?" said kind Thebe. "Does your head still ache?"

"No," I said, for I had that moment understood myself. "It is a warning. The earth is going to shake again. I think it won't be much. But noise is bad, when the god is angry."

They hushed their voices. I saw Kasos glance at the great ceiling beams, and fidget his feet. "It doesn't feel," I said, "like a bad one." For it did not press hard on me, but only prickled. "But make them be quiet, and stand off from the walls."

Nephele had gone over to the cockfight; the team came running, while the cocks by themselves bounced up and down, pecking and spurring, then stopped and stood with bunched wings, looking uneasy, as if the god had warned them too. My head tightened, and every trifle made me angry; there were pins pricking my feet. Just then up came Aktor, whom someone, I suppose, had passed on the warning to. "What is the matter with you, Theseus? Why don't you get back to bed, if you still feel shaky, instead of setting the Bull Court by the ears?"

I could have struck him. "Get away from that column," I said softly. I could not bear to raise my voice. Just as he opened his mouth to answer, the earth rumbled and jarred, and a big molding from the column-head burst into bits beside him. Pots crashed in the kitchen; the Palace beyond echoed with shouts and squeals and invocations. Around us the dancers called on the hundred gods of the Bull Court, outlanders lay on their faces shielding their heads, lovers clutched each other; and Aktor looked at me with his jaw so wide that you could count his teeth.

Something caught my ear. I put up my hand for silence. Then I heard it, low and far down, the thing I had heard tell of: the great muffled bellow of the Earth Bull in his secret cave. Every sound else was hushed. Friends reached for each other's hands. The earth settled, and the sound died slowly. My head felt better, and I could speak aloud.

"Wait!" I said. "While the god is here we will pray to him." I stretched my hand palm downward over the earth. "Earth-Shaker, Father of Bulls, you know us all. We are your children, your little calves who danced for you. You have heard our feet, you have tasted our blood in the dusty sand. We have taken the bull by the horns; we have leaped for you and not run away; we always gave you a show. Wrong has been done here, but we did not do it. We have lived in your hand. Hold us up now, when we have need."

So I prayed; and those not in the secret thought I was

asking him to spare us in the ring. But he knew my meaning.
I felt my words sink deep, through the flags of the Bull
Court, and the vaults below, down through the rubble of
the ancient Labyrinths, through the virgin earth and the
living rock, down to the sacred cavern where the dark lord
stands in his bull shape, long-horned and curly-browed, with
great eyes glowing red as embers in the night.

The House of the Ax fell quiet. In the Bull Court, people
stood about looking at me and whispering; then the talk and
the games began again, the ruffled cocks were matched, the
bull-leapers swung themselves over the wooden bull. As for
me, I took Aktor's advice after all, and went to bed. I did
not feel myself yet, and wanted to be let alone. Yet when
I was there I did not like it; my pallet was uneasy to me
and I wished to be on my feet. I got up and watched the
next cockfight, and played Five Fingers with the Cranes.
But my head ached, just as if the earthquake had not cleared
it; my spirits were oppressed, and sudden sounds went
through me, so that I wondered if I was going down with
fever. I felt my wound, but it did not throb nor burn, and
my brow was cool. I had not been sick since I was a child,
and could not remember much of it. I thought, "Have I
been poisoned?" But no dancer was served with food in the
Bull Court; we took our own from the common dish. Neither
my chest nor my belly pained me. My limbs did not shiver.
Yet a kind of horror crawled on my skin, and my eyes saw
thick darkness mixed with the light.

Supper came, and I played with a mutton bone; I did not
want the other bull-leapers to see me off my food a whole
day after a shaking in the ring. The Cretan servants cleared
the food and brought the wine, and the dancers gossiped
with them in the way of the Bull Court. I heard them with
half an ear talking of that night's festival; the spring moon
was full, and the women would dance on Daidalos' Maze
by torchlight. But the darkness would not lift from me. I
thought, "It is the shade of Minos, complaining of his wrong.
I am the nearest thing he has to a son; he wants me to

bury him, and set him free to cross the River. Be patient, poor King; I have not forgotten."

The weak wine went round. People were laughing. I was angry with them, that they could be merry. In the high windows the sky was pink with torchlight; I heard the music of flutes and strings begin, and wished it away. The old steward, who had served the tables of the Bull Court fifty years, came for the wine jars; and Melantho asked him what the people were saying about Herakles' death. I roused myself to listen.

He answered softly, "They don't like it. They misliked it yesterday, and today they like it less. They're saying he was doctored, to beat the book. They don't name names, they know better; only yours, Theseus, for the man who saved their bets. But they're saying today no good can come of it. They say the Earth Bull won't stand still to have his tail twisted, not by the greatest in the land. Two shocks since it happened; no great harm done, but they take it for an omen. And now there's the harbor."

I jumped round on the bench, saying, "The harbor? What do you mean?"

"You should be keeping your bed," he said, "by your looks tonight."

"The harbor! What is it there?" I felt suddenly maddened; I could have shaken it out of him with my hands. And yet, something in me dreaded to hear.

"Gently, lad!" he said. "You've had a bone-shaking and no mistake. I can't speak for my own eyes, but the runner from Amnisos says the sea's sunk down to half a fathom there, and all the ships are aground. People are saying it's a warning of bad luck."

The Bull Court spun and went black. There was a wine-cup shoving at my mouth, and the old man's voice saying, "It will do you good." I was standing bolt upright, grasping the table. The honey-sweet taste of neat wine was on my lips; all round were staring faces, open eyes and mouths. I flung the cup away and heard it break on the flagstones. People caught at me, as if I needed holding up; I felt as light as fire. My skull seemed open and streaming with blue flames. I gasped for air, filled my chest wide with it, and let go. A cry like a wolf's filled the echoing Bull Court, and the voice was mine.

Faces closed in on me, and hands and arms, which I fought away. My fist was up to hit again, when my eyes half cleared and I saw the eyes before me. It was Chryse with her scarred cheek, clinging to my shoulders. I dropped my arm, and heard the sound of my own panting, while some shred of sense in me thought by itself, "She has grown again. She is as tall as I." Then I heard her saying, "Theseus! Speak to us. Tell us what it is. You know us, Theseus; we are the Cranes. We will not harm you. See, we are your people."

I struggled with the frenzy, though I felt it must tear me in pieces. Somehow I must hold together; no one could save them now but I. I kept myself whole, though I shuddered all over, and it seemed my very soul would burst and be lost in darkness. And after such a struggle as made the fight with that other bull seem like children's games, I grappled the madness, and felt that I could speak. But first I took Chryse's hands and held them fast in mine; they seemed to link me to myself.

"Chryse," I whispered, "call the Cranes."

Voices shouted, "Look, we are here." I kept hold of Chryse's hands and my eyes on hers.

"A warning!" I said. But it came out like the croak of the dying, and they cried out, "What?"

"Hush!" said Chryse softly. "It is the god in him." They waited, and I tried again.

"It is a warning. Great and terrible. It hangs like the shadow of a mountain; I have felt it through those others, it falls far ahead. Poseidon is coming in black anger, stamping on the cities, we have not seen such anger since we were born. Not yet. But soon. The god is coming. I feel him in the ground."

There were voices somewhere gabbling; but Chryse's hands of a bull-girl, steady and hard, were warm in mine and her voice said quietly, "Yes, Theseus. What shall we do?"

I had seemed to myself only a burning shell; yet at these words something within me thought. I said, "The house will fall. We must break out or die." I blinked, and shook my head, trying to clear it. "Is Thalestris here?"

Beside me her deep boy's voice said, "Here I am." I said, "The arms; you must get the arms."

She said, "Look, they are fetching the girls to bed. Most of us are shut in already. We are the last." I could hear, now, the scolding voice of the priestess. "The doors are bolted outside," Thalestris said. "How can we get back?"

I was giddy, but someone was holding me up. It was Amyntor, the good catcher, ready as in the ring. I said, "The fancy-boys; where are they?" I was past choosing words. Hippon and Iros said, "Here, Theseus. We know what to do." I suppose they knew I would not have insulted them in my right mind. I said, "Leave the girls just time to arm. Have you something to give the guard? Thalestris, have the girls all ready to rush the doors. Waste no time; if anyone stops you, kill them out of hand. When you come we will fight our way out together. Hurry, hurry, the god is nearer."

I stopped with a gasp. Holding the madness off had been worse than holding a boar upon one's spear. I heard through a daze the priestess promising to birch the girls if they would not leave romping like trulls with the boys and come away.

They ran off; and the voices of the youths dinned in my ears, shouting questions and asking each other what I had said; for most of them had only heard a single cry. Chryse was gone and the noise tormented me; the warning surged and roared and crashed through my head, or withdrew leaving a dreadful hollow hush filled with the tread of the approaching god. The awe and terror which it is man's nature to feel before the Immortals goaded and spurred me to fly for my life. And when I held my ground, the madness burned me up, and the warning would not be contained within me. I shook Amyntor off and leaped on the table among broken winecups, and shouted it aloud.

"Poseidon is coming! Poseidon is coming! I Theseus tell you so, I his son. The sacred bull was killed and the Earth Bull has wakened! The House of the Ax will fall! The House will fall!"

Then there began a clamor that went through my head like hot black spears. People ran about calling on their gods or for their lovers, snatching up their jewels or other men's, trying to run away or to head off the runners, fighting and grappling on the floor. They only felt the fear I told them of. I felt the fear itself. I had drawn a great breath to shout again, when through the tumult a far, clear voice, like a singing bowstring, seemed to say within me, "Know yourself. Do not forget yourself. You are a man, a Hellene."

I paused, and knew that those who fled in panic without arms would be trapped within the Labyrinth. I took a long bull-leap off the table and hurled myself among them, cursing them and telling them to wait. But even as I spoke, thick shouting sounded along the Court, and in came the two guards from the inner door. They must have been drinking in the guardroom, it being a feast day, and slow to heed; there was always noise in the Bull Court, and their work was only to keep the door. Now they stood bawling and staring, asking if everyone was mad. They were full-armed, with seven-foot spears.

The sight of them almost brought me to myself; but I was giddy still. As I walked forward, I heard Telamon, who was always level-headed, say, "The boys have been drinking; someone gave them some unmixed wine. It's only horseplay." One of the guards said to the other, "The trainer can deal with this. Find him; he must be at the dancing." Then he broke off and said, "What's that?"

The sound drew nearer; a yelling and screeching like mountain cats in moonlight. A horde of girls rushed in, their arms full of weapons; bows and daggers, quivers and sawndown spears. In the van, their arms bloodied to the elbows, were Iros in a woman's skirt and scarf, and Thalestris stark naked, her bow and quiver at her back, her hair like black war-smoke streaming behind her. The girls had stripped to their bull-dress to free their limbs for fighting; I suppose in the scrimmage the weak link of her belt had gone. She took no notice, which among Amazons is the modesty of the field.

They ran up the Bull Court shrieking their war cries; and at one look the door guards flung down shield and spear, and fled. But they might as well have run from the hounds of Artemis. Swift feet outran them; a twisting heap of slender limbs engulfed them; bright-honed bronze flashed up and down. When the girls scrambled up from the prone bodies, not only the Amazons had breasts dabbled with blood.

Now the boys ran at the girls, demanding weapons, snatching and shouting, treading the dead men underfoot. And all of myself that was myself was in a rage with the panic I myself had made. I had meant to plan our breakout like a war, with stealth and coolness, and the time fixed with our friends outside. But it is not for men to see as far as the gods. I stood half crazed before my troop of madmen, knowing nothing clearly but the god's wrath gathering and brooding, like the dense air before a storm. And yet there was a soul within my soul, free of the madness, which stood apart and whispered, "You are the King. Remember your moira. Do not lose yourself; you are the King."

I pressed my hands to my brow. With covered eyes I prayed to the Sky Gods, to King Zeus and to Serpent-Slaying Apollo, for wit to save my people. Then I looked about me. I did not feel much better; yet I was answered, for I knew I could do what I must.

I stood before the mob, and shouted for silence, and my voice was like my own again. So they heeded me and stood still, those who were saner calming down the wildest. Then I could hear far off, from the northern terrace, the sound of the flutes and strings; for all this had passed swiftly, since first I had cried aloud.

I went among them, making those with spare arms share with those who had none, and thinking where we should go. I knew all the ways from the Bull Court into the Labyrinth, but those would not serve us now; we must reach the open beyond the walls, and soon, for my head was bursting with its burden of dread. There was only one way: to storm the great outer gates of the Court, which we had never seen opened; they looked to have been locked and barred for a hundred years. There was no knowing if they would be guarded, or even walled up on the other side; there was no key. They must be broken down.

I looked for a ram. The benches and the table were lighter than the doors; there would be long battering, great noise. The time was passing, the god was near. Then I saw the Bull of Daidalos, his oaken platform set on solid wheels, and his horns of bronze.

Among us we pointed him at the door. Then, shouldering and heaving all together, we brought him to a crawl, to a lumbering run. His platform struck the doors; they shook, and gaped, and burst right open. Out we ran, the bull nosing before us, into a pillared portico; flaking frescoes showed in the moonlight. The Bull Court must once have been a hall of state, in another age of the Palace. There was no guard.

We tumbled past the great red king-column, and down the steps. Before us was a tangled garden, with tall black cypresses; beyond, torchlight and music. Now we were out it sounded loud and wild, with cymbals clashing, and I saw why only the guard had heard our noise. As we ran across the garden, and put three or four spear-casts between us and the walls, I heard the Cranes around me cry out with relief. But I was tighter than a lyre-string, for I knew the god was near.

We looked about us, grasping our weapons. Amyntor beside me said, "Where are all the Cretans? There were servants in the Bull Court, when this began." Someone said, "I saw them run for it. I suppose the rest are watching the women dance."

I struck my hand against my head. Truly and indeed the god's madness had possessed me utterly. In all this while since it seized me first, I had not once thought of her.

The ragged garden was sweet with the scents of spring. Behind us the great pile of the Labyrinth, bright with lamp-

light, stood against a cloud-flecked sky where moon and stars
ran like driven ships before the wind. Before us the cypress-
tips leaned against a rose-red glow of torches. Hands and
drums and cymbals beat, flutes shrilled, a thousand voices
were singing. And it was a horror to me; for in the midst of
it was Minos' daughter, the Mistress of the Labyrinth, her
little feet striking the angry earth, her ears hearing the pipes
and lyres, but deaf to the voice of the warning god. The
sky was pressing on my head with its flying moon and all its
stars, as heavy as a king's burial-mound. The ground under
my feet sent thrills of fear up through my sandals, shuddering in my belly and my loins.

"Amyntor," I said, "Thalestris, Kasos. Keep everyone together, there in that grove. Hide in the bushes. Then do not
move; it will be soon. I will come back quickly; pray to the
god and wait."

They asked questions; but there was no time. "Wait," I
said, and ran toward the torches.

I came up unheeded behind the crowd. High wooden
stands enclosed the floor three sides; the fourth was open,
but blocked with standing men. They were Cretan peasants;
not many; there were few Cretans anywhere, but I had other
things to think of. I had just heard the Palace doves fly up,
and all the birds of day rise chattering from their roosts.
The god was breathing on my neck, so near that I feared
neither Cretan nor Hellene, man nor beast, but his coming
only.

The Cretans let me through. They were used to being
pushed aside by fair-haired men. Here and there one knew
me and called out my name surprised. I reached the coping
round the dancing-floor, and sprang upon it, and stared
about to find her.

A thousand torches, set on high poles, were streaming sideways in a rising wind. The smells of burning pitch and dust,
of flowers and perfume and warm flesh, swam through my
head. I saw before me the great paved maze of Daidalos, its
magic pattern inlaid with black and white stone, smooth
and bright and wide between the columned stands with their

glittering people dressed for the feast. The women sat with their jewelled boy-dolls in their arms. On the edge of the floor was the music, the tambours and the cytheras, the cymbals and Egyptian harps, the skirling pipes from the aulos to the little flute of ivory whose fine sound flickers like a snake's forked tongue. The music shrilled, wounding the deathly silence in which the dark god stood waiting. And in the midst of the maze, strung along the crooked path of scoured white marble, hair and skirts and jewels swinging, arms entwined and slim waists swaying to the beat, was the wreath of women, weaving and twisting and turning on itself, like the house snake who sloughs his winter skin and is made new again. It bent about and came toward me. I saw her face, gay and flashing, touched by no dread, no shadow, leading the dance.

I saw her; and all my soul and body, scourged by the god's anger and ridden almost to death, longed for her breast and her warm arms as a child flies to its mother from the terrors of the dark. I leaped out from the parapet upon the checkered floor; and even as I leaped, the mighty voice of the god cried to me, "I am here!"

The earth lurched beneath me, grinding and shuddering. The marble flags I ran on tilted endways, flinging me down on hands and knees. There was a mighty crashing and roaring, shrieking voices, cracking wood. My fingers grasped an edge of paving that worked to and fro like a living thing; I was rocked and tossed about as the strong-laid floor of Daidalos broke like water and surged in waves. And deep below, as he tossed the groaning land upon his great black horns, the Earth Bull boomed and bellowed, louder than the shouts of terror, louder than the thunder of falling column and floor and wall.

There was someone with me sobbing and crying like a woman as she gives birth. The sobbing shook me; it was my own. I had been with child of this great doom; now it was as if I myself had brought it forth with tearing of my body and the sweat of agony. As the broken marble settled under me I clutched it gasping and trembling. Everywhere around me the things that man had raised above the earth returned to it again, shaken back to their beginnings by the furious god. Shouts and moans came from the broken stands; from the Palace a wild howling of dogs and women, the squeals of children mad with pain and fear, men calling each other or crying for help, loosened blocks rumbling and crashing. I lay in the storm of this infernal noise; and felt flooding into me, as I lay, a strange white empty bliss. For I was delivered of my warning. The great hand of the god loosened about me, his madness cleared from my head. I was weary, bruised, and fearful, but neither more nor less than man. While flying feet stumbled over me and the greatest of all kings' houses fell about my ears, I gave a great sigh of ease; it seemed almost that I could have slept.

I raised my head. The wind blew dust and grit into my eyes; a woman rushed past me shrieking, with her skirt on fire. At that I remembered why I was here, and got upon my feet. I was sore and aching, as after a great shaking in the ring; but the giddiness had left me, my head was clear. I looked about me.

The dancing-floor was like a sea-strand where a wreck has carried. The drunken torches leaned on their poles, or guttered on the ground; the tilted flagstones were strewn with a rubbish of garlands and trampled harps, shoes and scarves and bloodstained fans, broken dolls and the ordure of men in terror. The fallen stands were loud with cries and curses and splitting wood. One of them was on fire, where a torch had fallen. And in the middle of the maze, all cowered together as bright birds huddle in thunder, were the dancers.

I ran toward them, picking my way in the mess and rubble. Some were kneeling and beating their breasts, some swaying with covered faces as they wailed, some waving their arms and crying for their menfolk. But in the midst I saw a girl standing alone, with wild bright eyes, silent, staring about her. She was mine, looking for me; against sense and reason knowing I would come for her.

I reached her and caught her up. Her arms gripped me, her face thrust at my neck, her breast crushed upon mine panted and thudded with her beating heart. I ran with her off the floor, picking my way over prone bodies wailing, sputtering torches, trampled flowers, my feet slipping in I knew not what. We ran into the gardens, where the thorns of roses tore us as we fled. Then there was soft earth with sharp spring flowers in it. I put her down.

I had had no thought but to save her. But men are straws in a torrent, when the mighty gods move on the earth. We learned then what it means, when they say that Earth-Shaker is husband of the Mother. We lay a moment in staring stillness, clinging and gasping; then we fell on one another like leopards coupling in the spring.

The passion, being god-inspired, was healing. The earth was moist and sweet; the wrath of Poseidon had stirred its scents like the gardener's spade, but now it was quiet, a friendly bed. There we lay, I suppose not long, drawing in strength from the Mother's breast. Then we got stumbling to our feet. She looked at me with dazed, swimming eyes and cried, "My father!"

"He is dead," I answered. "A good quick death." She was too stunned to ask me how I knew. "You must mourn later, my bird. My people are waiting, let us go."

We shook the earth from us, and I led her by the hand. As we came out of the garden-close, we almost fell over a pair lying as we had lain. They did not heed us. Then we faced the Labyrinth, and saw what the god had done.

There where the tiered and terraced roofs had marched one above the other, lifting their proud horns to the sky, was a broken line as ragged as mountain rocks. The columns of the colonnades had fallen, the windows which had been soft with lamplight were black empty caves, or blinking eyes of fire. You could see, through the broken porticoes and through arches from which balconies had crashed away, the flames from the spilled lamp oil running along the floors, leaping up curtains and canopies, eating the wood of bed and chair and fallen rafter, roaring already and crackling as the strong wind swept it on.

Women passed us flying and wailing. One of them carried

the child Phaedra clinging about her neck. Ariadne called, but they rushed by unheeding. I hastened on to where I had left the dancers.

They were all there. Some were still calling on the god as I had told them to. They saw us and came running. The grove was bright with firelight now, and I saw tumbling out from under the flowering thickets those whom Mother Dia had stricken with desire. People called to each other that I was here, and ran up, and caught at me. Amyntor indeed embraced me; all this seemed natural, at the time. Not one had been harmed in the earthquake, beyond some grazes when they were flung down.

I said to them, "The god has heard our prayers. Now we will go down to Amnisos, and seize a ship to get off in when the gale eases. But first, look here! Here is the Mistress, Minos' daughter, spared from Poseidon's anger. Help me to care for her; she will be my wife. Look at her well and know her. Here she is."

I swung her up on my shoulder; in the Bull Court one learns the knack. I wanted to be sure they knew her face, lest she should be lost in the tumult, or ravished by the young men; it was a time of wildness. So I lifted her, as one lifts one's standard for one's troops to see and remember.

They cheered. The noise amazed me, that so few mouths could make it. And then I saw that all around us, in the mounting glow of the fires, the walks and lawns were black with Cretans. They came swarming and clambering up the slopes, from the open places where they had fled to abide the wrath of Poseidon. The servants in the Bull Court had heard my warning, and run out to warn their friends. All through the Palace, Cretan had told Cretan; they had put down broom and pot and lamp and trencher, and slipped away. They did not hold the gods so light as the courtiers of the Labyrinth.

They had fled and lived. Now they beheld in ruin the proud house of Minos, where they had known heavy labor and slight esteem. They saw the broken doors, the smashed chests and closets spewing out silks and goldwork; the tilted wine jars, the tables spilling their feasts; the precious cups and rhytons they had filled and carried, always for the lips of other men.

So they had crept near, meaning to make themselves the heirs of Labrys. Then just as they reached the upper terrace, I had lifted up before them the Goddess-on-Earth.

She stood to them for the prayers King Minos had answered; for the oracles that had sweetened their coarse bread with mystery and hope; the little Cretan goddess, whom tall fair-haired Pasiphaë had been ashamed of bearing. She was their own, their stake in the glories of the Labyrinth. She was the heart and kernel of the old religion, nearest to the Mother who takes men to her breast and soothes them like whipped children after her husband's wrath. She was the Thrice Holy, the Most Pure, the Guardian of the Dance; and, seeing her, they remembered the sacrilege done before her in the ring, which had waked the Earth Bull to ravage Crete.

They thronged about us, roaring like the sea. They had seen who held her, and remembered the oracles, the ring in the harbor, and the warning that had brought them out. Some of them began shouting the marriage cry, whooping and dancing. But most were pointing to the Palace shaking their fists, or waving sticks and knives. As they pressed forward, sweeping us along with them, a voice howled, "Death to the Minotaur!" and a hundred answered, "Death!"

Amyntor and Telamon closed up beside me, locking their arms across my back. All together we bore up the Mistress; we dared not set her down, lest she should be trampled in the milling press. Remembering the wrecked stands by the dancing-floor, I thought it ten to one Asterion was dead; I was angry at all this hindrance, thinking only how to get my people away. And then, of a sudden, just like the oil flames running along the Palace floors, I felt a fire leap from the Cretans to the bull-dancers around me. A spark of it fell on my soul, and it burst into a blaze.

We thought of our distant homes, our parents weeping when we were snatched away; some of us had been courting, some betrothed, some in love with a craft or with the good land of our fathers, some with our hearts set on renown; from all these things, from the places and the customs of our kin, we had been torn away to die for the sport of the painted Labyrinth. We thought of the haughty envoys coming for tribute who had held our people light. But those of us who by now were bull-dancers to the bone remembered before everything how Asterion had made merchandise of our courage and our blood. The gods were held cheap in the House of the Ax; but we had been brought from places where gods are honored. Though we were slaves, yet we were a proud people, the little calves of Poseidon. We did not take kindly to being any man's cattle.

High above the shouts of the Cretans rose the Amazon battle scream. Closer, about my ears, Amyntor and Menesthes were yelling, as they had yelled at the Isthmus and at the storming of Sounion Head, "Ares Enyalios! Ah-yah-yah-yah Enyalios! Hai-ai-ai Theseus! Theseus! Theseus!"

I threw back my head, and gave the war cry.

We began to move faster. I remembered my dive in the muddy harbor, crawling among ships' garbage to find the ring. I remembered how he had bought me like horseflesh, after I had defied him like a warrior; how he had shown me at his feasts like a dancing dog; how he had made me sing. And I said within me, "Let him dare to die before I come! Wait, Minotauros, wait. Wait for the mainland lad in the leather breeches; the mad bull-boy good to turn somersaults and nothing more! Ares of the Battle Call, Father Poseidon, keep him for me!"

I could feel Ariadne's fingers clutching my hair, as our charge bore her forward. Presently we came to some carrying-chairs, which had brought nobles to the dancing; we throned her in one of these, and the Cretans lifted the poles. As she rose above the mellay, I looked to see if she was frightened; but she was leaning forward, grasping the chair-arms, her lips parted as if she drank the wind.

A roar broke forth like spring snows rushing down a mountain; but the spate streamed upwards, and was made

of fire. The flames had found an oil store. As they met the
breath of the gale they were flattened, and blown streaming
to the north. By this huge cresset the House of the Ax was
lit like day, and I saw that one block still stood entire. It
was the western wing, where the great stair led down to the
sunken shrine and the white throne of Minos. I thought, "If
he lives, he is there."

They had found a second chair, and tossed me into it,
lifting it shoulder-high. I made them turn it round, so that
I could stand as in a chariot, with the high back for a rail.
I did not want the bull-dancers to lose me. On I rode like
a ship on a tossing sea, the Cranes close around, the Cretans
cheering. To them I was Theseus the bull-leaper, whom the
Mistress fancied; the odds-on favorite who had saved their
bets. But to myself I was once more Kouros of Poseidon,
Kerkyon of Eleusis; Theseus son of Aigeus son of Pandion,
Shepherd of Athens, riding to my enemy. "Ahai! Ahai!" I
shouted, as one leads the battle line. The war calls answered.
My blood sparkled and sang.

As we came near and the fire-glow warmed our faces, I
thought of Minos, for whom the god himself had raised a
burial-mound and fired the altar. Minos had sent the tribute-
galleys forth. Under his seal the mainland cities had been
assessed: so much corn and wine, so many mares in foal, so
many bull-dancers. I would have ripped his soul from his
breast upon a battlefield, if our threads had crossed there.
But it is a king's work to rule, to widen his lands, to win
spoil for his warriors and feed his people. And he had
greeted me by my title, though I was a slave. Asterion had
offered me gold; he had put wine and dressed meat before
me to the sound of music. But he had made my standing
mean, and hurt my pride in myself when it was my whole
estate. It is what any man will have blood for, who is half
a man.

We came in from the east, and saw a place that was not
burning. It was the Bull Court. The lamps had been
smothered by the falling roof; the shell still stood, and one
or two columns; in the portico the Bull of Daidalos kept his

sturdy feet, with painted plaster up to his hooves. I made them put me down, to lead the way.

We climbed over the fallen roof beams, and the prone inner doors. In the passage beyond lay the floor from above, broken chairs and women's paint-pots, and a child's body curled upon a toy. Fiery sparks floated over us on the wind, and the air rippled with heat. Behind me ran the bull-dancers, who had kept with me while the Cretans looted; working together was in our blood.

Presently we came out on a wide space of ruin. It was the Great Courtyard, where on smooth pavement cool to the feet nobles and envoys had walked among pots of lilies, and flowering lemon trees. Three of its sides had fallen in on it, the south right to the ground; to the east were leaning floors with flames licking along them. But the west wing stood. One of its balconies had fallen; the crimson pillars had smashed through the flagstones, and painted flowers stood bare upon the wall. But in the lofty entrance porch the huge king-column upheld the lintel above the stairs, and at the top of them I saw armed warriors.

I was going to shout for the charge, when I heard groaning. Though the air was full of screams, from people trapped in the ruins, this caught my ear. It was quite near; as I looked about, a heap of rubble moved, and I heard my name.

It was Alektryon. He lay with his curled black lovelocks white with dust; his gaping mouth was scattered with flakes of plaster. So had the boy-dolls of painted clay, which the Cretan ladies deck in springtime, lain on the dancing-floor trampled and unstrung. One hand hung limp; the other moved and fluttered over a great column-drum that lay across his belly. A rag hung out from under it; yellow silk stitched with turquoises, but it was mostly red. As I looked down, two Cretans shouldered each other to snatch his jewels.

I flung them off him, and knelt down, with half an eye for the porch where the troops had seen us. His grimy hand gripped my arm. "Theseus," he said. "Don't leave me for the fire."

I looked at the great column; then at his eyes. We understood each other. I brushed the rubble from his breast; he was slender, and weakly as it beat one could find his heart. "This will be quick," I said. "May the Guide lead you kindly. Shut your eyes."

He put his hand on my wrist, and panted as if he would speak again. I paused, and he jerked his head to the west wing, saying, "The Minotaur." Then he shut his eyes as I had told him to. Seeing him bite his lips with pain, I left him in it no longer. He caught his breath and died; and I turned away, for there was much to do. So I never saw who got his necklace and earrings.

Men were coming down the steps, holding up shields against the stones the Cretans were throwing. Forth stepped Phoitios, with his boxer's nose, and standing before the king-column called out in Cretan, "Be quiet, good people. You have a king to mourn for. Minos is dead in the earthquake. How he sinned against the god, and incurred this vengeance, you will be told when there is time. But first the new Minos must be hallowed, who can make our peace with Earth-Shaker and avert his anger. Now while I speak to you the sacred rite is being done; the time is too desperate for public shows." There were boos and howls of anger; but Phoitios was a man who could face out a lie. He flung up his hand palm out; he was a man used to command, and the sign had power. "Take care! He is in the presence of Mother Dia! It is sacrilege for men unpurified to approach the shrine. Have you not had enough misfortune? Stand back, and escape the curse."

They drew back muttering. They were not warriors, and had good cause to fear the gods. Then in the pause, a high clear voice sang out across the courtyard. "Who are you Phoitios," it said, "to curse for the Mother?"

She stood on the platform before her chair, her right arm raised, the flame-light flickering on the dress she had led the dance in. Phoitios' mouth set, and his men looked at each other. I too gazed in awe. Never before had I heard her speak with power; it made me shiver.

She said, pointing toward the sanctuary, "In there is the curse upon the Labyrinth! I call all gods to witness, he has murdered Minos! There is the killer, in the holy place, un-cleansed of blood-guilt, standing before the Mother. And you speak of sacrilege!" There was a dead hush, but for the rush and crackle of fire. She stretched both hands out over the earth and cried aloud, "May the Mother curse him and all gods below, and may Night's Daughters hunt him down into the ground! And on the hand that sheds his blood let there be a blessing."

The silence broke in roaring. The Cretans surged forward. I cheered them on; a warrior does not forget the battle. But my mind was troubled. I thought, "She does not know who struck down Minos. Will her curse fly home to me?" And then I thought, "No, for Minos himself freed me of it," and then again, "But she would have known who killed him, if she had spoken in the power of any god." Then I felt better. As to Asterion being her own mother's son, there is no holier duty than to avenge one's father. One could only praise her, if she wanted to see his blood.

The Cretans were hurling stones again and pressing nearer; behind us was the fire, and before the enemy. I jumped up where the bull-dancers could see me, and gave the call of the bull ring, when everyone is needed to turn the bull.

A boy's shout answered mine. Thalestris scrambled up the rubble, the firelight turning her strong limbs all to gold. She reached back over her shoulder to her quiver, and nocked an arrow to her string. It spoke, and Phoitios fell.

"Well shot!" I called, and turned to smile at her. But she did not look. She was giving at the knees, and sinking back-ward, with a javelin standing up under her breast. She fell; the blood of her wound was bright as scarlet, and there was a rattle in her breath. A red-haired Amazon who had fought at her left hand knelt down beside her wailing. Thalestris pushed her away, to struggle up on her elbow; she scanned the battle line, and pointed out the man who had thrown the javelin. The red-haired girl leaped to her feet again. Under the glowing sky her eyes seemed to glitter with tears of fire; she blinked them away, and steadied her hands to aim. The man clutched his throat, and I saw the flight of her arrow between his fingers. Then she turned back; but Thalestris' stare was set, and she lay still, with her black hair spilled among the crocks of a painted vase.

The red-haired girl gave a scream that drowned all the din of the burning Labyrinth, and rushed toward the spears. I shouted my war call and sprang ahead. I liked her spirit; but I was not going to have a woman get there before me.

The bull-dancers came swarming over the broken stones. Our feet were light, from dodging bulls in the thick sand of the ring; and the weapons in our hands were like food in famine, to us who had flirted with death unarmed. The troops on the steps had spears and shields; but Cretan bulls have long horns, and stronger fronts than a plated war helm. We were used to unequal matches; it had been our life.

They were still hurling javelins, and ours could not be thrown; they had all been shortened, to smuggle into the Bull Court. Amyntor was by me. We grinned at each other, with the love of men in battle who know each other's minds. Each of us picked his man, and waited till a stone made him throw his shield up; then we ran in and grappled him round the middle. Each of us came away with shield and seven-foot spear.

We pressed up the wide stairway. Not far off I saw the red-haired Amazon, with Phoitios' arms and helmet. The guards upon the steps had locked their shields; but we bore them back and back, past the painted frieze of noble youths bearing gifts to Minos, up and back toward the hall above. Sometimes they would trip as they felt for the stair behind them, and pitch down into our hands. The steps grew slippery, but it was worth it to get their arms. I saw some at the back beginning to steal away, and raised a yell to put the rest in fear.

Suddenly, like water from a sink, they trickled back into the shadows. They had gone to hold a narrower pass. We gave a loud triumph call. Among all the voices, there was

one that made me turn. It was Ariadne, borne high by the
cheering Cretans, her hair dishevelled, her eyes wide, crying
us on to the kill.

As we tore up the stairs, I looked at the red-haired
Amazon, whose spear arm was dyed now with a crimson
wound; and my heart hid from its own thought. For war
frenzy is honorable in a warrior girl, who sheds her own
blood and risks her own life beside you. I know, who once
had such a comrade, no man better than I, how as a bright
torch it lights the battle. But in a house-woman with soft
hands, whose painted feet have scarcely felt rough ground
beneath them, it is not the same.

"Well," I said to myself, "wrong has been done her, and
worse wrong threatened. She has a right to vengeance. And
it is a time to do, not think."

At the top of the stairs was a hall, and beyond that an
entry where light showed through from a staircase open to
the sky. But while they held the outer steps, those I thought
had fled had been building a barricade, of fallen stones and
chests and such heavy stuff. It looked good for a long while.
They shouted at us from behind it, bidding us begone, and
leave Minos to his sacred task.

I said to Amyntor, "Sacred task! There is only one thing
the gods still want from him. If he were half a king, he
would offer it himself, not leave us to take it." Then I looked
through at the staircase, and remembered the place below
and how the land lay there; and I had a thought.

"Kasos," I said, "keep up the attack here. Press them hard;
don't let them think you are playing for time. There is a way
I know; but it may be blocked by the earthquake. If I get
in, you will hear my war call." I looked for the Mistress, and
saw her safe among her guardian Cretans. Then I rallied the
Cranes to me, and said, "Follow me."

I led them down the steps again, and along the courtyard, toward the northern block beyond which was the Bull
Court. There was a little warren there of kitchens and still-
rooms and paint stores and blending rooms for oils and

scents. There too was the old lamp room, with its trapdoor to the vaults.

The face of the block had fallen, and the upper floors had caught the fire; but below were thick walls and pillars, and at ground level one could get inside. I must own I did not like it. Poseidon's great rage might have deadened me for a lesser warning; and the place looked ready to fall if one only breathed. Before we entered, I prayed him for a sign if he was still angry. Nothing stirred but the fire above us; so we went in.

The lamp room stood. The shelves had fallen, and the lamps lay smashed on the floor. There were oil jars broken too, and we looked at each other, knowing fire might close the way behind us. But below were the strong pillars of Cretan Minos, which had withstood two great earthquakes. I thought it was a chance worth taking; and the Cranes trusted me.

Below, all was thick darkness. We made wicks from our garments for two lamps which would still hold oil; there was no lack of kindling. I found the secret thread still tied about its pillar. I took it in one hand, and a lamp in the other, and led the way.

The place had changed. We had to paddle in wine and oil, in lentils or in sesame, where the shock had thrown down the cysts and shelves. And once, as we crossed the ancient armory, we saw beyond it, through a narrow chink, wild tossing torchlight, and heard the shouts of men fighting like beasts. I guessed the vaults of treasure lay there. But the Cranes kept with me, sure and silent. Our minds were single; we did not take that sickness.

At last we came to the Watcher. Great stones had fallen from the pillar by him, and he had risen a little out of the ground. You could see his jaw now and his fine strong teeth; he must have been young. The Cranes started, but he was an old friend to me; I saw no malice in his grin. It was his shaky pillar I did not care for; I put finger on lip, and we trod cat-footed.

At last we saw before us the upward door, and under it a

crack of light. We crept up softly; and laying my ear to the
wood, I heard a sound of chanting.

I tried the door, fearing to find it jammed out of the true.
But it opened smoothly, still oiled from the last time. We
grasped our weapons, and slipped within. The anteroom was
full of a flickering glimmer. We crept across it; beyond was
the great stairway, all dusky red with light thrown back from
the burning sky. But there were lamps below, and mixed
with the smoke a swirling cloud of incense. I signed for silence, and looked through.

I saw before me a rite scrambled up out of fear and
wreck: priests and priestesses in their daily clothes, with some
rag or scrap as symbol of sacred raiment; rich pedestals bearing lamps of common clay, a boy with a dirty face holding
the fretted censer; cracked vases of precious work laid leak-
ing by, and the holy oils in pots from the kitchen. The white
throne of Minos stood empty between its gryphons. The
daggled crowd faced the other way, to the sunken earth
court. White-faced hierophants stood round it, their gold-
stitched robes torn and soiled, like mountebanks in rich
men's cast-offs bought from chamber grooms. Their incanta-
tions, shaky as the plaints of beggars, filled the place with a
gabbling drone; sometimes they coughed, as wind-blown
soot caught their throats.

Down in the earth court a man was standing, naked down
from the neck; broad-bodied, thick-legged, thatched with
black hair on chest and groin and shins, a-straddle before the
sacred Labrys. His trunk glistened with the chrism a shaking
old man and woman smeared on him with half-palsied hands.
From the neck down he was man, and base; above the neck
he was beast, and noble. Calm and lordly, long-horned and
curly-browed, the splendid bull-mask of Daidalos gazed out
through the sorry huddle with its grave crystal eyes.

Above the chanting, half muffled by the walls, I could
hear the fight still raging; the clatter of weapons and of
stones, the shouts of men, the Amazons yelling. Our friends
had kept faith with us. Now it was time. I gave the war
whoop, and rushed out among them.

The celebrants screamed and scattered. There was a rush
for the staircase, old men and women knocking each other
down, while those who were stronger trod them under.
From outside came the shouts of the defenders, as they
heard they had been taken from behind. A few wild-eyed
guards, who had been stationed about the Throne Room itself, rushed in disordered. I thought the Cranes could hold
them. As for me, I had one thing to do.

He stood at bay, against the high wall that carried the
stairway above the pit. It was too deep for him to climb out
of it except by its steps. I stood at the top of them, and
called his name. I wanted him to know me. The gold mask
turned, and the curved eyes faced me. Fixed with that kingly
gaze, which lent majesty even to what hid within it, I lifted
my arm, and gave the salute of the team leader to the bull.
Then I leaped down to him.

For a moment he stood with the wall behind him. Then
his arm shot out grasping. A shape like a black thunderbolt
whirled round him in the air. He had snatched up Mother
Labrys from her stand, the King-Eater, the ancient guardian.
On the stairs above us, a priestess screamed.

He had denied me my warrior's standing; so I had been
ready to kill him unarmed as one kills wild beasts. Yet it
stirred my heart, to see there would be a fight. I danced
about him, feinting with my spear, while he waited, half
crouched, with the ax laid back to his shoulder. And it
seemed wrong to me that either of us should be armed, save
he with his long horns, which presently I must grasp and
vault on, while the gamblers called the odds, and the people
shouted in the painted stands.

The old priest and priestess had scrambled out; now the
small space was clear. I lunged, to make a quick end. But
fear had quickened him too. Down came the stone blade
upon my spear shaft, a foot from the head, and it drooped
like a switched grass stalk, cut half through. Then we two
were alone in our little bull pit, as in the days of the primal
sacrifice; the armed beast and the naked man.

I heard his heavy grunting in the hollow mask, as he came

forward lifting the ax to strike. There was strength in those
fleshy shoulders. Above in the Throne Room was a battle
raging; there could be no help yet. He had worked round
me, to head me off from the steps, and was driving me back
against the further wall. Then, when there was nothing more
to do, my body thought for me, as it does in the dance. I
stood up against the wall, and when the ax came at me,
dropped like a stone. As it struck the wall where I had been,
I seized his leg and threw him.

He fell heavily, on the hard glazed floor of the earth
court. I heard the muffled clang of the gold mask striking;
and when I grappled him and saw it askew, I knew he was
fighting blind. He still had the ax; but now we were in-
fighting, and he could not swing it. He shortened his grip
and, as we rolled and twisted, beat me with it as one might
with any stone. But I hampered his arm, so that it did me no
great hurt. And I thought, "Labrys will never fight for him."
She was old, and used to dignity; and once again she had
fed upon a king. She would not like to be taken lightly.

And I was right. If he had let her go, and used both hands
to wrestle, he would have had a chance; he was twice my
weight, and had not labored that day like me. But he was
no wrestler, though Cretans are well taught; he could not
give up the hope of cracking my head. So as he raised the
ax blade, I had time to grab my dagger out of my belt, and
drive it home with all the strength left in me. It had a long
way to go, through his thick carcass; but it reached his life.
He doubled up with a great grunting cry, clasping his midriff. I stood up from him, with the ax in my hand.

A cry went up from the people on the stairs; but more of
awe than grief; and a deep hush followed it. Looking up, I
saw the Cranes all safe, and the guards already fled away.
Before me he lay writhing, scraping the noble mask of the
Bull God on the floor. I drew it off, and held it up to the
people.

Now I saw his face, grimacing with bared teeth. I stepped
up to him, to hear what he would say to me. But he only
stared at me as at some shape of chaos, seen in a dream

where nothing makes sense. He who had thought to rule without the sacrifice, who had never felt the god's breath that lifts a man beyond himself, had nothing to take him kinglike to the dark house of Hades. And yet, mixed with the blood and sweat that smeared his breast, I saw the oil that had made him slippery while we grappled. He had been anointed, when we broke in. So after all there was a rite still to do.

I lifted the mask of Minos, and put it on. Through the eyes of thick curved crystal, everything looked little, far and clear; I had to pause awhile, to get the feel of it and judge my distance. Then I swung Labrys back, and brought her down, my head and shoulders and body coming round with the blow. The force of it tingled through my hands; and the voice at my feet was silent.

From the Throne Room above I heard the cry of the Cranes; and from the porch the din of rout, as the news reached the defenders. But I stood still, seeing through the crystal a small bright image, such as a god may see who looks down from the sky, far down and back for a thousand years to men who lived and suffered in ancient days; and in my heart was a long silence.

BOOK FIVE

NAXOS

1.

WE SAILED from Crete, at last, in a ship we found in an olive field.

Not only the earth had felt Poseidon's trident. The ebbing sea, that had grounded the keels at Amnisos, had rushed back with the earthquake. It had broken the mole, and dashed the ships upon it, and flooded the lower town, and killed more people than a war. But a few ships had been carried inshore and stranded softly, like this among the olives. We rolled her down to the water on the trunks of the broken trees.

We mounted guard on her day and night, till the weather let us get away. All Crete was in turmoil. As soon as it was known the House of the Ax had fallen, the native Cretans rose up everywhere, to tear down the strongholds and sack the palaces. Sometimes the lords were killed with all their household; sometimes they fled to the mountains; a few whom their people loved were left in quiet. Rumors came in every hour; and men would send to me, asking me to lead this band or that. To all these I gave the same answer, that I would come back soon. It was not as a freed bull-dancer leading freed slaves to plunder that I meant to reign in Crete. I would come as a king, to Hellenes and Cretans both alike. Now there would be no lack of ships; if I could not get enough in Attica and Troizen and Eleusis, I should have Hellene kings elbowing each other to share the enterprise; more than I wanted, if I was not quick. From this day on, the mainland would rule the Isles. Never again, in any Hellene kingdom, would boys and girls take to the hills at the sight of a Cretan sail.

The bull-dancers who came from the Hellene lands took

ship with us, and the Minyans from the Cyclades. Only two girls stayed behind to marry Cretans; men who had loved them from the ringside, and sent them gifts and letters, but never met with them till now. But they were from other teams; even now when our hearts looked homeward, the Cranes were one kindred still.

We had no great trouble to man our ship. Many men had killed old enemies in the rioting, and wanted to get away before the blood-feud caught them up. We built a shelter near the place, and did not let the girls go far alone, even full-armed. It was a lawless time.

When at last the wind was fair and steady, we met on the shore and killed a bull to Poseidon, and poured him libations of honey and oil and wine, thanking him for his favors and praying him to bless our journey. Also we did not forget Peleia, Lady of the Sea. Ariadne made the offering. Her dress was frayed, and her train of priestesses two poor old crones we had found huddled over a fire of sticks. But her beauty still held my breath, as it had from the gilded shrine above the bull ring.

The fires were quenched with wine; the ship ran down the rollers, and lightened as she felt the sea. I picked up the Mistress in my arms and waded through the water, to set her feet on the deck that would bear us home.

Once more I stood in a ship of Crete, looking at the wine-dark restless sea, and seeing the towering yellow cliffs stand with their feet in foam. But Ariadne was weeping for her homeland, and while I talked to her of Attica the last landmarks sank away.

Next day we saw a great smoke ahead of us. Toward evening the pilot said to me, "It is on Kalliste, where we should lie tonight. A forest is on fire, or there is war."

"Of that we have had enough," I said. "Watch out, and if the town is burning, run for Anaphe."

We sailed onward, and the smoke hung in the sky like a great cloud black with thunder. As we drew nearer, an ashy dust began to fall on us, darkening all the ship, and our flesh and clothes. Presently the lookout called to the pilot, and I

saw them chattering on the beak. Going up there I found
their faces pale. The pilot said, "The land itself has
changed."

I looked at the gray landfall; and it was true. My belly
crept with awe and fear. I drew into myself, to listen for the
god; some dreadful wrath seemed written on the very sky.
He sent no warning; but for the black cloud, all was peace.
So I said, "Go nearer."

We came on. A fresh following wind streamed off the
smoke to the northward; the late sun shone pale and clear.
And then, as we stood in to westward of Kalliste, we saw
the dreadful thing that the god had done.

Half of the island was clean gone, sheared off from the
hilltops straight down into the sea; and in place of the smok-
ing mountain there was nothing. The god had carried it all
away, all that great height of rock and earth and forest, the
goat pastures and the olive groves and the orchards and the
vineyards, the sheep pens and the houses, gone, all gone;
nothing was there but water, a great curved bay below huge
sheer cliffs, where wreckage floated; and outside the bay, by
itself on a horn of land, a little mound pouring out smoke,
all that was left of Hephaistos' lofty chimney.

The sea around us was strewn with burned branches and
dead birds and lumps of half-charred thatch; a thing like a
white fish swimming was a woman's arm, drifting alone. I
shuddered, and remembered how the place had made me
uneasy on the voyage out. Surely some great impiety must
have been done there, a thing to make the gods hide their
faces in the midst of heaven. I saw it as it had been last year,
all dressed with fruit blossom, as harmless to look at as a
smiling child, only for that doomed brightness. We went on
quickly, for the sailors would not stay. They reckoned that
in such a spot even the sea and air must be charged with
the god's anger, that it would stick to a man and eat the
marrow out of his bones. Some of them wanted to sacrifice
the ship's boy to keep Dark-Haired Poseidon from pursuing
us. But I said it was clear the god had taken his due, and it
was not us he was angry with. So we left that place, and

gladly too; the rowers labored faster than the rowing-master gave the stroke, to put it behind them. Sunset came down, such as none of us had ever seen, splendid and awesome, great towering purple clouds in a sky of crimson and green and gold, dyeing all heaven and slow to fade. We took it for a sign that the gods had ceased their anger, and were still our friends. With a little breeze we made Ios by midnight, and sheltered there. Next morning the wind was fair. We steered for the tall shape of Dia, that fertile island whose city they call Naxos.

Before evening we were in the harbor, looking up at the hill-slopes rich with olives set in green corn, with orchards and with vines. So well the Mother has loved Dia, no wonder they named it with her name. It is the greatest of the Cyclades, and the richest too. From afar we saw the royal Palace standing among vineyards, a high bright house in the style of Crete. Ariadne smiled and pointed; I was glad the place was homelike for her. Kalliste had quenched her spirits.

Two or three of the bull-dancers had come from here. In the arms of rejoicing kindred they told their tale. We were the first ship straight from Crete, since the fall of the Labyrinth; till now the Naxians had had only wild talk third-hand. They cried out that they had seen dreadful portents; a noise like a thousand thunderbolts, and a shower of ashes, and the night sky lit with fire over Kalliste. It had happened, as we learned, the very day and hour when the House of the Ax was stricken.

Our news filled them with awe and wonder. Time out of mind, Minos had been High King of all the islands; they had traded by his laws and paid him his tribute. From Dia it had been very great, because the land was rich. This year it had been due again; now they would keep for themselves their olives and corn and sheep and honey, and their wine, than which there is none better; and all their boys and girls would dance at home. There was a feast tomorrow, of Dionysos, who himself planted the vine there, when he came sailing from the east as bridegroom of the Mother;

and they would keep the day as it had never been kept before.

But it surpassed all the rest for them, when they heard who Ariadne was. The people are mixed in Dia, but Naxos and its royal house are Cretan, the ancient stock without Hellene blood. They have the old religion, and a reigning Queen. So when they saw the Goddess-on-Earth among them, it was a greater thing than if Minos himself had come. They set her in a litter, lest her foot should touch the ground, and bore her up to the Palace. I walked beside her, and the rest followed behind.

At the porch of the Palace they set her down, and the steward brought a greeting cup. They led us off to the bath, and then into the Hall. The Queen sat in her place before the king-column, in a chair of olive-wood inlaid with pearl and silver; her footstool was covered with a sheepskin scarlet-dyed. On a low seat beside her sat a dark young man, with strange shadowed eyes, whom I took to be the King.

She rose and came to meet us; a woman of about thirty years, handsome still, and a true Cretan, with dark crimped hair in serpent tresses, breasts heavy but round and firm, and a little waist tightly cinched in with gold. She held out to Ariadne both her hands, and gave her the kiss of welcome. The Palace women had dressed her richly from the Queen's own store, in a deep-blue gown that twinkled with silver pendants, and her eyes, new-painted, glowed in the lamp-light.

The tables were laid, with food and places for all the dancers, though we were near twoscore. The Queen was gracious, and pressed us to eat and drink before we told our tale. Ariadne sat on her right hand, at the head of all the women. When I had said I was her husband (we were to marry in Athens, but I did not want her to lose standing here) I was put on her left, beside the King.

He was a handsome youth, about sixteen years old, lively and graceful; all made, you would have said, for gaiety and women's love. He did not look strong enough to have fought for his kingdom, and I wondered how he had been chosen; but I did not care to ask him. There was something about him I could put no name to, a daimon in his eyes; not that they wandered, like men's eyes whose wits are troubled; rather they were too still. Whatever he fixed his gaze on, it was as if he would drain it dry. When they put his golden cup into his hand, he turned it round till he had seen the whole of the pattern, and for a long time stroked it with his fingers. To me he was very civil; but like a man who from courtesy hides his straying thoughts. Once only I saw him look toward the Queen, with a grief that I could not read, for it seemed mixed with darker things. Though there was no need yet to talk, beyond the civilities of the table, something oppressed me in his silence, and I said only to break it, "You have a god's feast here tomorrow."

He raised his eyes to my face, not with any message, but as he had gazed at the winecup, or the women, or the flame of the new-lit lamp. Then he said, "Yes." That was all; but something woke in my mind, and of a sudden I saw everything. I remembered Pylas saying to me in the mountains above Eleusis, "I know how a man looks who foreknows his end."

He read it in my face. For a moment our eyes met, seeking to speak together. It was in my mind to say, "Be on my ship before cocklight, and with the dawn we will be away. I too have stood where you stand now; and look, I am free. There is more in a man than the meat and corn and wine that feeds him. How it is called I do not know; but there is some god that knows its name." But, when I looked into his eyes, there was nothing in them that I could say it to. He was an Earthling, and the ancient snake was dancing already to his soul.

So we drank our wine; and I did not wonder he took plenty. We did not speak much, for I had nothing to say that could be said; whether he knew that I was sorry, whether it comforted or angered him, I do not know.

When we had done eating, the Queen asked for our tale. So Ariadne told how the Labyrinth had fallen, how I had

had my warning, and who I was. Speaking of me before
people made her blush, and me to wish for the night. But I
could see that the Queen pitied her, when she heard the
Mistress was going to a Hellene kingdom ruled by men. As
for the King, he listened with wide dark eyes and the lamplight shining in them; and I saw that if it had been a tale
of Titans or the old loves of the gods, it would have been
all one to him, as he looked on night and feasting and the
light of torches for the last time.

Ariadne finished her tale, and I spoke too when the Queen
invited me. "Alas!" she said when she had heard. "Who can
be called fortunate, till he has seen the end? Lady, you have
known a change beyond the common lot." Then she remembered the courtesies, and bowed toward me, saying, "And
yet the Fates have relented to you after." I bowed, and
Ariadne smiled along the dais. But I remembered how she
had said in Crete, "You are a barbarian; my nurse told me
they ate bad children." And I thought within me, "Will she
always see me in her heart a mainland bull-boy, even when
I am a king?"

The Queen was speaking still. "Now you must take heart,
and forget your griefs. You and your husband and your
people must stay for our feast tomorrow, and honor the
god who makes men glad."

When I heard this, I did not look at the youth beside me.
All my wish was to be gone with the first of day. I tried to
catch Ariadne's eye with mine; but she was speaking her
thanks already. Outside a little wind was getting up, which
might keep us in port tomorrow; if after slighting these people we could not get away, it would be a sorry business.
The times would be confused now Crete had fallen; one
might have need of friends. So I put a good face on it, and
looked pleased.

After we had heard the harper, the Queen wished us good
rest, and got up from her chair. The King also bade me
good night and rose. Once again my eyes met his, and my
heart felt bursting with what I wished to say; but it fell

away from me, leaving me silent. As they reached the stair I saw her take his hand.

The tables were taken out, and the men's beds made in the hall; the women were led away, to the grief of those who had become lovers since we left the Bull Court. Of these were Telamon and Nephele. But from what I had heard of the rite tomorrow, it was only a fast before a feast.

Ariadne and I were given a fine room on the royal floor. This was our first night in a great bed. So although the wind had eased, I did not say much of the delay, except that to be at home would be still better. She answered, "Yes, but it would be a pity to miss the festival. I have never seen it as they do it here." As no one had told her what I knew, I said no more, and soon we slept.

Early next morning, the singing woke us. We dressed and joined the others, and went with the people down to the shore. Already they were dancing, and the jars of unmixed wine, dark and strong, sweet as ripe grapes, were going from hand to hand. People greeted us; we caught fire from the wine and laughter, and began to feel that oneness with the feast which is Iakchos' magic gift.

Everyone looked seawards; soon shouts of rapture greeted a sail. The ship came round the point toward the holy islet just off-shore; and all the women began to slip away. The Naxians took our girls along; and Ariadne too was drawn from my side. I saw no harm in it, knowing the honor they held her in.

The ship approached, all bound with green boughs and wreaths; the mast and oar blades and the beak were gilded, the sail was scarlet. Young girls were singing on the deck, playing the tabor and the pipes, and clashing cymbals. Standing in the prow, girt with a fawnskin, crowned with green ivy and young vine-shoots, stood the King. He was very drunk, with wine and with the god; as he waved to the people, I saw a mad gaiety in his shadowed eyes.

On the sacred isle his train and his car were waiting. They waded to the ship and pulled her in, and lifted the King ashore to a crash of music.

Soon the car was coming through the knee-deep ford. Men drew it wearing leopardskins and the horns of bulls. They pulled on the ropes and yokes; those dancing round them wore strapped to their loins great leather phalluses that bounced as they sprang along. They sang and clowned and called out broad jests to the people. Then came the gilded car, and round it the women.

They came beating the cymbals, or bearing long garlands twined among them, or waving the sacred thyrsos on long poles. As they danced they sang, but the song was wild and blurred, for the maenads had on their masks already. Above smooth shoulders and wreathing arms and dancing breasts were the heads of lions and leopards, of lynxes and of wolves. Their dark Cretan hair flowed free behind them. I thought that one could not have picked out among them even one's own sister or one's wife. The King stood up in the gilded chariot, laughing wild-eyed, and swaying tipsily as it bounded on. Sometimes he would take a handful of corn from a bin beside him, and scatter it on the people, or jerk his gold cup to sprinkle them with wine. Then they would leap for the blessing to fall on them, and the women would scream, "Euoi! Euoi!" The men who drew the car began to leap and run, pulling toward the hill road. As they went the King's arm waved the cup, and I heard that he was singing.

The people began to stream up from the shore toward the hills; and I felt one with the feast, for that is the magic of the god. But I waited for Ariadne to come back from the island, now the rite was done, so that we could go up together, and share the madness and the love. The car and the music were far ahead, and I grew impatient, but I waited still. I did not want her running about without me. One must not be angry at what women do in Iakchos' frenzy; the way to keep your girl is to have her yourself.

Some lads were dancing to the double flute; I danced with them till they cried, "To the hills!" and ran after the rest. Still she did not come. A few women waded the ford to shore, but they were old, or great-bellied with child. I asked one such if she had seen her. She stared, and said,

"Why, she is with the Queen and the maenads, following the god."

You do not last long with the bulls unless your wind is sound, and I soon caught up with the crowd. Alone upon the road I felt angry and anxious; but some of the Cranes were drinking and dancing in an orchard all in flower; they held out their hands to me, and I was one with the feast again. The farm people brought out their best wine in honor of the god, and it would have been boorish to rush away. But presently we went on, up to the goat pastures where the hills are high. I had seen already that on the tops there was snow.

We came out far above tilled land, among thyme and heath and smoothed gray boulders, rain-scoured and hot with sun, where lizards basked and darted. From these tall mountains one sees sea and sky all one, a great round ether of shimmering blue, and the gray isles floating weightless in it. With the young men I threw myself on the springing turf, panting and laughing and drinking. We had picked up somewhere a big wine jug painted with wreathing squids and seaweed. Amyntor and I and some youth from Naxos aimed the wine stream into each other's open mouths, shouting and spluttering. Then the Naxian looked past us and jumped up and ran off. I saw him chasing a girl among the boulders.

It is on the lower ridges that the women begin to fall away from the god's maenad train, those whom the madness does not wholly possess. They throw off their beast-masks, leaving the mystery to those it calls, and wander dreaming or half wild about the hillside, and give themselves to love.

"Now," I thought, "for certain I shall find her." She was only a guest, and had done all that was due. The rest she would be glad to miss. So I went upward with the others. I was full of wine now, and one with the feast, and last night's grief had left me. It was Earthling business, and nothing was asked of us strangers except rejoicing. A long way off, somewhere beyond the ridge, I heard a thin shrilling, like the cry of birds, from the maenads still about the King. But it was far away. Soon I should find my girl; "or," I thought as we reeled up singing toward the snowline, "a girl at any rate."

We linked arms in a line, and sang and shouted and passed the wine along; I and the Minyan next me leaned our heads together and bawled our life stories in each other's ears and swore eternal friendship. Soon we came to the first snow, lying in pools and lakes among the green-brown mountain grasses lush with its moisture. We knelt and flung it on our faces to cool them from the climbing and the wine.

I stood up, and saw above us the snow pools broken. There was the track of many feet, a crushed vine-shoot, and a broken flute. They must have left the car when the ground got stony. Not far off was a streak of scarlet; a scarf, I thought, dropped by a girl. But when I got nearer, it was, or had been, a fawn. There was not much left to know it by, but further on I saw the head. I stood silent, staring; for a moment the dance of my blood was stilled and chilled.

As I stood there, something cold struck my neck, and I turned round. There was a little pine wood just above, in a fold of the mountain; laughter came from it, and a girl ducked behind a tree. Putting up my hand I found a snowball in my hair. So I gave a shout, and ran.

The pines were thick, the mats of the needles soft and dry. She squealed and dodged among the pine boles, half frightened and half not. I caught her at the edge of a little hollow, and we rolled in a tangle to the bottom. She was a Naxian girl, with long sloe eyes and a nose tip-tilted. I don't know how long we stayed there; the time of Dionysos is not like the time of men. After a while I heard a giggle, and saw another girl watching us from up above, and climbed up to make her pay for it. In the end we stayed all three together, and time was lost again. All the strain and stretch of danger was loosened out of me, the fierceness of war and the care of kingship. This seemed the only good, to be one with the living mountain, with her birds and goats and wolves and her sunning snakes and flower-bells, drinking the strong honey from her thriftless breast, living each breath just as it came.

Once, while we were lying half asleep, watching the pine tufts weaving against blue sky, and hearing them sough softly, the breeze brought from far off a high, wild, birdlike scream; a long shrilling upward and upward, falling away to silence. But by now the wood was all murmurs and kisses and little scuffles and shrieks, and they filled the stillness quickly. I too reached out for the girl beside me. It was no use to think. There had been nothing in his eyes a Hellene could speak to.

The magic time of Dionysos slipped by unreckoned; and the sun riding homeward clothed the hills with gold. Those who were soberest called out that dark would overtake us on the mountain if we did not go. So we went down under the great sky arched clear and yellow over the purple islands; singing old songs, tipping the bottoms of the wine-jars, and holding our girls' hands till the farms began and they slipped away.

Already down in Naxos the lamps were burning. The long walk had sweated out my drunkenness; my limbs were full of youth's kindly weariness, my eyes heavy for sleep. I looked down at the Palace bright with torches, thinking that when I met Ariadne there, I would ask no questions and answer none, and then we should keep friends. She would be in her bath by now; I thought pleasantly myself of warm water and sweet oils.

When dusk was falling, and the evening clouds were touched with fire below, we were on a farm road which twisted through the olive groves. The girls had all gone home, and the songs were dying away. As we walked in twos and threes, the youth beside me pulled my arm, and went off the road into the field. Everywhere the men withdrew into the shadows; and, looking back, I saw a white flitting, as of ghosts, come slowly down the hillside, winding half hidden through the groves. The men sat down, in places under the trees that were not sown with barley. I looked at the youth who had signed to me; but he only said under his breath, "It is better not to meet them."

I sat, and waited, watching the road through the twilight;

no one had said it was forbidden to look. Presently they came in sight, wavering here and there, stumbling and wandering as if in sleep. Some had their masks still on; from lolling necks and shoulders, fierce faces of lynx and leopardess stared wide-eyed; but sometimes they hung by a loose string, and one saw the parted lips drooping with weariness, the half-closed eyelids. The pipes and cymbals trailed from their limp hands; their long hair hung forward, tangled with heather and matted thick with blood.

They were stippled with blood like the spotted panther; their bare arms, their breasts, their clothes. Over their feet it was powdered with pale dust; their hands were dark with it, clotting the fingers and streaked above the wrists. The poles of the thyrses, which dragged behind them like the spears of wounded men, were dabbled all over with blood-stained hand-pri-ts. I covered my mouth with my hand, and turned my eyes away. The Naxian had been right; there could be no luck in looking nearer.

They seemed a long time passing. I heard the dragging feet, the stones kicked blindly, the little gasps as those who tripped caught hold of others. Then the sound drew away, and looking again I saw them melt into the shadows at the bend of the road. I was getting up when I heard wheels coming, and waited to see.

It was the gilded chariot, going home empty. It was lightly made, and two men pulled it easily, one each side the pole. They had taken the heavy bull-horns from their heads, but still wore their leopardskins, having no other garment. They plodded along, muttering shortly sometimes to each other, like men after a long day's plowing; two dark-haired Naxians, a youth and a bearded man.

The chariot passed, and no one followed; that was the end, and I rose to go. Then, when I was on my feet, I saw into the back of it. It was not empty after all. A body lay on its floor, jogging limply with the jolts of the rough road. I saw a torn blue skirt, and a little arched foot rouged at the toes and heel.

I ran out from the trees, and seized the rail of the car;

the men feeling my weight on it stopped and turned. The
younger said, "It is not lucky, stranger, what you are doing."
The elder said, "Let her alone till morning. In the sanctuary
she will not come to harm."

"Wait!" I said. "I will see her, lucky or not. What has
been done to her? Is she dead?"

They stared at each other. "Dead?" said the young one.
"No. Why dead?" And the elder, "She will take no hurt,
man, from our Naxos wine. It is all good, and we keep the
best for today. Leave her be; her dream ought not to be
troubled. While her sleep holds, she is still the bride of the
god."

From his way of speaking, I guessed he was a priest. I
guessed too, I don't know how, that he had had her on the
mountain. I turned away from him, and leaned into the
car.

She lay curled on her side, against the bull-horn head-
dresses which the men had taken off to ease their brows.
Her tumbled hair was like a sleeping child's, but for the
sticky points it ended in. Her eyelids lay smooth and full
and glossy over her eyes, and against the dark lashes her
cheek bloomed softly. By those I knew her, and by the
tender breast cradled upon her arm. I could not see her
mouth, for the blood all over it. It was open, for she was
breathing heavily; I saw her teeth, even, crusted with dried
blood. As I bent over her, its stale reek met me mixed with
the smell of wine.

After a while I reached out, and touched her shoulder
where her torn bodice bared it. She sighed, and murmured
something I could not hear, and her eyelids fluttered. She
stretched out her hand.

It had lain closed on her breast, like a child's who has
taken her toy to bed with her. Now when she tried to spread
it out, the blood on it had stuck between the fingers, and
she could not part them. But she opened her palm, and then
I saw what she was holding.

For almost a year I had sat by the Cretan ring, and
watched the bull-dance when I was not dancing myself. I

had watched the death of Sinis Pinebender, and kept the face of a warrior. But now I turned away and leaned upon an olive tree, and almost threw the heart up from my body. I heaved and shivered in the chill of evening; my teeth chattered, and water poured from my eyes.

At last I felt a hand upon my shoulder. It was the bearded priest. He was a well-made man, brown-bodied and dark-eyed; his limbs were scratched and bruised from running about the hills, and stained with wine. He looked at me sadly, as I had looked at the King last night, not knowing what to say to me. Our eyes met, like the eyes of men at sea who would hail each other, but the wind carries the sound away. I turned my face, ashamed he should see me moved.

Presently I heard something, and looked round. The youth with the pole upon his shoulder was walking off with the chariot. I took a few steps after it on the road. My belly felt cold, and my legs were made of lead. The priest walked with me, and did not hinder me. Then when I paused he stopped, and stretched out his hand.

"Go in peace, Hellene guest. It is grief to a man to look on mysteries he does not understand. To yield unquestioning, not to know too much; that is the wisdom of the god. She is of our blood; she understands it."

I remembered many things: the bloodied horns of bulls, the voice in the burning Labyrinth. She had told me in our first night she was all Cretan. Yet not all; she was Pasiphaë's daughter too.

The car with the young man pulling it passed the turn of the road, and glimmered through the olive trees. A bright spring moon was rising, making everything pale and clear, casting dark shadows of leaves. The priest's spotted pelt and dappled limbs seemed one with the tree trunk where he leaned watching me. He thought his thoughts, whatever they were, and I thought mine.

The sunset was fading, and the moon's face lifted above the sea, making a white path which shone between the moving boughs. I saw the moon and her brightness; but the place had changed for me. My life which was I stood upon a lofty platform, gazing on a great rock's shadow flung across a plain. Clear and brilliant was the starry sky, spanning the amber mountains; and the high Citadel too shone of herself, as if her stones breathed light.

"Indeed and truly," I thought, "it was not lucky when I looked too near too soon. A cold bed, and a cold shadow on my fate, this looking will bring me. For what I must do now, dead Minos will not forgive me in the house of Hades. So much the worse for me. But better for the strong house of Erechtheus, which stood long before me and will stand long after. I will not go back to that light with my hand full of darkness; not even the darkness of a god."

I looked at the priest. He had turned his face to the moon, which glittered on his open eyes; his body was quiet as the olive tree, or as a snake upon a stone. He seemed like a man who knew earth magic, and would prophesy in the madness of the dance. And then I thought of the great Labyrinth, which had stood a thousand years; and how Minos had said the god's voice called them no longer.

"All things change," I thought, "except the gods who live for ever. And who can tell; after a thousand ages, they themselves in their house above the clouds may hear the voice that calls home the King, and make the offering of their immortality—for do not the gods' gifts excel the gifts of men? —and all their power and glory will rise like smoke to a higher heaven, and pass into a greater god. That would be death into life, if such a thing could be. But this is life into death, the madness without the oracle, the blood without the listening ear and the consent that frees the soul. Yes, that is death indeed."

My mind went back to the room behind the sanctuary, where she had called me a barbarian. I felt her fingers touching my breast, and her voice whispering, "I love you more than I can bear." And I saw her waking tomorrow in such another room, washed from the blood, perhaps with the madness all forgotten, with wondering eyes looking about her, and seeking me. The chariot had passed out of sight down the hill road. I could hear no longer even the sound of wheels.

I turned to the priest, and found his eyes already on me. "I have done an unlucky thing," I said. "Perhaps it has displeased the god. This is his feast day. It will be better for me to go."

He answered, "You have done him worship; he will forgive a stranger's ignorance. But it will be better not to stay too long."

I looked toward the road, empty and pale in the moonlight. "A royal priestess, called to this mystery; she would have honor here in Dia?"

"Do not be afraid," he said. "She will be honored."

"You will tell your Queen, then," I said, "why we go like this by night, without thanks or farewell?"

"Yes," he said. "She will understand it. I will tell her in the morning; tonight she will be weary." There was silence, and I searched my heart for another message, where there was more need of it. But there was nothing to say.

At last he said to me, "Grieve no longer. Many-formed are the gods; and the end men look for is not the end they bring. So it is here." He stepped out from the tree, and walked away through the grove. Soon he melted into the fleckered shadows, and I saw him no more.

The olive field was empty; my companions were long gone. I went alone down the road, and came to the sleeping harbor. The watch was still by the ship, not all blind drunk; and some of the crew had come to sleep on the shore. There was a night breeze, blowing from the south, enough to fill the sail; if they were sluggish at the oar, it was no great matter. I told them it was dangerous to stay, that they must find the others and bring them quickly. They hurried off; it is easy to wake men's fears in a strange land.

When they were gone, I told the pilot's mate to fetch in the dancers. Then for a while I stood by the sea alone. I pictured her next day on the holy islet, looking out to sea, seeking our sail; thinking perhaps that some girl at the feast had made me forsake her; or that I had never loved her, but only used her to help me out of Crete. So she might think. But the truth would be no better.

As I paced to and fro, hearing the ripples suck the shore, the crunch of my feet on shells, and the night guard's drowsy song, I saw a pale form wandering by the water, and heard a sound of weeping. It was Chryse, her gold hair, loosened on her shoulders, pale in the moonlight, crying into her hands. I took them from her face. There was no stain on them, but of dust and tears.

I told her to be comforted, and weep no more, whatever she had seen; that what was done in the god's frenzy was best not thought of after, being a mystery hard for Hellenes to understand. "We are sailing tonight," I said. "We shall make Delos by morning."

She looked at me dimly. I remembered her courage in the bull ring, and how she had brought me to myself when I was mad. She swallowed, and put back her hair, and wiped her eyes. "I know, Theseus. I know. It was all the frenzy of the god, and he will forget tomorrow. He will forget, and only I will remember."

It was a thing I had no help for. I might have said that everything passes, if I had had time to learn it myself. As I shook my head, I began to see some of the dancers running down to the ship. The watchman's cresset showed their faces; among the first was Amyntor. His mouth was open to question me, but then he looked again. He turned to Chryse, shyly, and hanging back; I saw he was in fear of her anger. Their eyes met, peering in the uncertain torchlight; suddenly he ran across, and took her hand. Their fingers folded together, in a knot as close as a goldsmith makes upon a ring.

I did not trouble them with reasons, for they would have heeded none, but said they must help to get in the rest of the bull-dancers; we should set sail at midnight. They ran off, still handfast, toward Naxos, where the lamps were being quenched for the night.

The moon made its twinkling pathway on the sea. A dark shade broke it, the little island of Dionysos; I saw the sanctuary roof with its Cretan horns, and one small lighted window. They had left her with a lamp, I thought, lest waking in a strange place she should be afraid. When midnight had passed, and we put out into the strait under the sinking Pleiads, I saw it was still burning. It shone steadfastly until the sea-line hid it, keeping faith with her sleep while I fled away.

2.

WE REACHED Delos with the light of morning; as we drew in, the sun was standing over the holy hill.

On a bright day in Delos, the very stones, which twinkle with sparks like silver, seem to flash and glitter under the kiss of the god. Water and air are clear as crystal. You can count every pebble as you wade ashore; and when you look toward the stairway that leads to the sacred cave, it seems you could count every flower upon the mountain. From the hilltop above the sanctuary, the plume of the morning sacrifice uncurled in a deep sapphire sky.

There was a joy here beyond laughter; and for us who were Hellenes, even though our feet trod Delian soil for the first time, a homecoming beyond tears. As I walked up to the lake and the sacred grove, along the warm sparkling causeway, the sharp white sunlight seemed to wash from me the earth-darkness of Dia, the rotten glow of Crete. All here was lucid, shining, and clear; even the awe of the god, the secret of his mystery, hidden not in shadows but in a light too dazzling for human eyes.

Before we sacrificed, those of us who had shed blood asked to be cleansed of it, so that no angry ghosts should follow us home. We bathed in the lake that looks up to heaven with its round blue eye; then we climbed Mount Kythnos, and up there with the blue sea laughing all round below us, Apollo cleansed us and the Avengers were sent back to their own place.

When the rite was done and we were walking down the long stair from the sanctuary, my mind went back to the harper who had sung in Troizen, and at Eleusis had re-shaped the Mystery. I turned to the priest, who walked near by me, and asked if he had been back to Delos again.

The priest told me they had had word that the bard was dead. He had perished in his own native land of Thrace, where he served Apollo's altar. The old religion is very strong there; as a youth he had sung for its rites himself, and the priestesses had been angry when he made Serpent-Slayer a shrine upon the mountain. But after he came back from Eleusis, whether that his great fame had led him into hubris, or he had had a true dream from the god, he went forth to meet the maenads at their winter feast, and tried to calm their madness with his song. Everyone knows the end of it.

Now he was dead, said the priest to me, the songs and the tales were growing round his name; how great stones had risen at his voice, to make walls and gateways, how his ears had been licked by Apollo's serpent, and he knew the speech of birds. "They say the Dark Mother loved him, when he was young, and set a seal upon his lips and showed him her mysteries beneath the earth. He crossed the river of blood, and the river of weeping; but Lethe's stream he would not drink of, and seven years passed over him like a single day. When the appointed time drew near, for her to let him back to the upper air, she tempted him to speak while he was still in bonds to her; but he would not break the seal of silence, nor taste her apples and her pomegranates that bind a man for ever, because he was vowed to Apollo and the gods of light. So she had to set him free. All the way up to the mouth of her dark cave she followed him, listening to his harp as he sang upon his way, and crying, 'Look back! Look back!' But he did not turn till he had stepped forth into the sunlight; and she sank into the earth, weeping for her stolen secrets and lost love. So people say."

When this tale was done, I said, "He did not speak of it. Is it true?"

"There is truth and truth," said the priest of Delos. "It is true after its kind."

We came down from the hillside into the grove, and made our sacrifice on the altar of pleached horns. And seeing the Cranes stand all about me, I thought how soon we should be scattered to our homes, and our close bond loosened; nevermore should we be limbs of one body, as we had been in the ring. It was not proper that so dear a fellowship should be lightly tossed away into the drift of time; it should be dedicated in its passing. So I said to them, "Before we go, let us do our dance for the god."

So we called for music, and did him the crane-dance, which had drawn us first together, and made us a team. The priests reproved us, when they saw the girls stand up to dance with men; but when I told them why, they said there could be nothing shameless in a thing so blessed by the gods. Once more as we danced, gulls flashed and cried above us, and round us was the sea's unnumbered laughter. For a deck we had the greensward by the lake; and for a mast the sacred palm tree that Leto pulled on in her labor, when the god was born. We plaited and wove our line by the glancing water, making fast the memory of what we had done in the strength of trust. When it was over, most eyes were blinking. But Amyntor and Chryse outshone the Delian sunlight, like people who have no loss to grieve for, but are taking all their harvest home.

Next day, when we had rowed out of the strait, we met so good a wind that it lifted us as far as Kios. And in the clear evening light, we saw a low gray cloud upon the skyline. It was the tops of the Attic hills.

Then from impatience we would not coast round to the port, which would have put some ten miles on our next day's journey; we found a sheltered beach south of the island, and made our camp there. We were fewer now; all through the Cyclades we had been dropping off bull-dancers as we passed near their homes. Now, Iros said, the Cranes were like the old friends at a feast, who stay to gossip when the rest have gone.

We had eaten, and in the falling night our fire was sinking to embers, when Amyntor pointed and said, "Theseus!
Look."

Far off to northward, at the dark meeting place of sky and
sea, there was a faint changing flicker, too low and red
for any star. Telamon said, "The first light of home," and
Menesthes, "It is a watch-fire. It must be on Sounion Head."

We all showed it to each other, and lifted our hands to
thank the gods. Then in a while we lay down to sleep. The
night was calm; nothing sounded but the slap of ripples
on the rocks, and the crickets thinly shrilling. Now for the
first time I felt Crete fall quite away from me. I lived again
in Athens, riding her plains and hills, talking with her people, fighting among her warriors, walking her rock. I lay
looking up into the thick-starred sky, thinking of time to
come.

I thought of the fleet I must raise, and soon, to bring
order into Crete, or it would become another Isthmus. I
wondered how many ships my father would have built, if
Helike's brother had got his message through. If other
Hellene kings had not been ready to venture against Crete
while Minos ruled the islands, one could not blame them;
I wondered what I should have done in his place myself.
"Built my own ships," I thought, "and waited on the gods
for a lucky day. And sent to Troizen, where I would be sure
of help. But I am young; my father is weary with his long
wars and troubles. They have made him a careful man."
Then I thought of Attica, with its warring tribes and vil-
lages, and wondered whether I should ever bring him to
try my plan for the three estates.

I got up from where I lay, and stood at the sea-edge looking northward. The fire still burned, and was brighter than
before; a watchman must be feeding it. And then I knew
it was my father's beacon. Perhaps it had burned there each
night since I sailed away; or perhaps there had been rumors
from Crete already. I pictured him standing on the Citadel,
watching these same flames; and my heart hurt me, as it
had when he gave me the chariot on my feast day.

I thought of our leave-taking when I was led away to
Crete; I seemed to feel his hand on my shoulder, and his
parting words were in my ears. "When that day comes, mark
your ship's sail with white. The god will have a message
for me."

"What did he mean?" I thought. "He is a man grown old
too soon. He meant more than he would say before the
people. A message, he said; a message from the god. It
was for his sign that he meant to take it. For sure, if I paint
the sail, I shall never look again on his living face."

My heart beat thickly. I was afraid. There was no surety
for his purpose, nor, if one knew it, for his holding to it
still. He was a man grown weary. How could one guess his
mind?

From the grass inshore I could hear my comrades snor-
ing, or sighing in sleep; and two lovers whispering. I wished
I had only their cause to wake. It was a heavy choice to
bear alone.

I stood on the beach, pressing my palms into my eyes
till flowers of red and green burst out behind my eyelids.
Then I looked out again, and saw the watch-fire shine. And
a thought came to me. I stripped off my clothes, and waded
into the cold spring sea, and struck out from the shore.
"Father Poseidon!" I said. "I have been in your hand, and
you have never told me wrong. Send me your sign now,
if I am to go on with our dark sail. If you keep silence, I
will do as he bade me, and make it white."

The sky was clear; but a little breeze ruffled the water.
As I swam out from the shelter of the shore, the wavelets
lifted me up and down, and sometimes a small crest splashed
upon me. As I turned on my back, to lie upon the water, a
wave came bigger than the rest, and tipped down my head.
I floundered before I could right myself, and began to sink.
The sea closed over me. And then I heard plainly in my
ears the sign of the god.

I ceased to struggle, and the water floated me upward.
I swam back to land, my heart at peace now; for I had laid

the choice upon the god, and he had answered plainly, putting me out of doubt. The thing was lifted from me.

So I said then, and still say in my heart, when on great days of sacrifice I stand before the gods, offering for the people on the High Citadel, Erechtheus' sacred stronghold. The great Horse Father who came to my begetting, Earth-Shaker who held me up and spared my people even when he was angry, would never have led me into evil. I saw for my father a little sorrow, and then joy unlooked-for. How could I guess that he would so reproach himself; that he would not even wait till the ship reached harbor, to see if the sail told true?

Or perhaps it was not that. In a private grief, would he not have gone like a common man, by falling on his sword, or by strong poppy which steals the soul in sleep? But he leaped from that same balcony above the rock, where once I had been afraid for him, and pulled him back from the edge. Surely it was the god who sent the sign to him, as loud and clear as it came to me? We were both in Poseidon's hand; it was for him to choose.

Man born of woman cannot outrun his fate. Better then not to question the Immortals, nor when they have spoken to grieve one's heart in vain. A bound is set to our knowing, and wisdom is not to search beyond it. Men are only men.

AUTHOR'S NOTE

By CLASSICAL times the Theseus legend (a brief outline is given below) had so fabulous a garnish that it has sometimes been dismissed as pure fairy tale, or, after Frazer, as religious myth. This briskness was not shared by those who had observed the remarkable durability of Greek tradition; and the rationalists had their first setback when Sir Arthur Evans uncovered the Palace of Knossos, with its labyrinthine complexity, eponymous sacred axes, numerous representations of youths and girls performing the bull-dance, and seal carvings of the bull-headed Minotaur. The most fantastic-seeming part of the tale having thus been linked to fact, it becomes tempting to guess where else a fairy-tale gloss may have disguised human actualities.

That the early heroes were men of gigantic stature was an axiom with the classical Greeks. Bones of a Bronze Age warrior, unearthed in Skyros by Cimon, were unhesitatingly hailed as Theseus' on the strength of their size alone. But a youth accepted for the bull-dance can only have had the slight, wiry build which its daring acrobatics demanded, and which frescoes and figurines all portray. And indeed, the main elements of his story bear this out. Men who tower over their opponents have no cause to evolve a science of wrestling; and Theseus is conventionally shown in combat with hulking or monstrous enemies, living by his wits. The tradition that he emulated the feats of Herakles may well embalm some ancient sneer at the overcompensation of a small, assertive man. Napoleon comes to mind.

If one examines the legend in this light, a well-defined personality emerges. It is that of a light-weight; brave and aggressive, physically tough and quick; highly sexed and

367

rather promiscuous; touchily proud, but with a feeling for the underdog; resembling Alexander in his precocious competence, gift of leadership, and romantic sense of destiny.

It would be in the levelling fashion of our day to conceive Theseus as a nameless adventurer who came to Athens by way of successful banditry in the Isthmus, and coerced the King of Athens into making him his heir. But, apart from this being a suicidal step for Aigeus to take unless a close blood-tie protected him, Theseus' voluntary departure for Crete points to a man bred and trained for his role in the archetypal tragedy of Achaean kingship.

There is no doubt that the royal sacrifice was on occasion self-imposed, and was practiced down to recorded times. The semi-historic Kodros stage-managed his own death in combat with the Dorians, on hearing that the Pythia had predicted defeat for them if he fell. Leonidas of Sparta is said by Herodotos to have made his stand at Thermopylae, after dismissing his allies, in response to a similar oracle. Even as late as 403 B.C., the soothsayer of Thrasybulos' liberating army, possibly by right of his priesthood the highest in formal rank, predicted them victory if they charged after a man had first fallen, and himself leaped forward upon the enemy spears.

It has not to my knowledge been suggested before that Theseus was endowed with the earthquake-aura, an instinct well attested among animals and birds. Even today, such a gift would be precious in any Greek town or village; to Bronze Age men it would surely have appeared divine. The Earth-Shaker's favor and protection are stressed throughout the legend; and it is noteworthy that the death-curse which was his gift to Theseus was answered by a giant wave. The passion of Poseidon for Pelops (Theseus' great-grandfather in the legend) suggests a hereditary trait. So seismic an area is the Peloponnese that the statues in the Olympia museum all stand surrounded by deep sandboxes, ready to break their fall.

From the Knossos finds it is clear that the Cretan bull-ring equalled that of Spain in popular esteem. It is not inconceivable that a leading *torero,* enjoying perhaps the combined prestige of a Manolete and a Nijinsky, might become a princess's lover, and play some part in the downfall of the regime. Archaeologists agree that the Palace was burned, plundered, and wrecked by earthquake, though whether concurrently or consecutively is not known. The contemptuous nicknames given to the Cretan serfs are suggested by the Knossos Linear B inscriptions. A small living room was found close to the Throne Room, in which the King had apparently spent some time, perhaps for religious reasons. In the Throne Room itself, there were signs that a ceremonial anointing had been violently interrupted.

The legend contains many apparent improbabilities which, when examined, reside only in some nonessential detail. For example, Theseus cannot have brought his female impersonators from Athens in disguise, since bull-dancers were almost naked; but the ruse with the door is likely enough. And with the poisoned cup, it is only incredible that Aigeus should choose a public banquet to commit the grave crime of murdering a guest. Given Theseus' meteoric career of conquest, nothing is more likely than the attempt itself. The episode must have been a favorite in the Greek theater, where the inevitable presence of the chorus may have influenced the tale. As for his concealment in Troizen, the theme of the heir hidden away till old enough to defend himself is world-wide, and current in the folk tales of Africans today. It is a commonplace of insecure societies; a stratagem so natural that even animals practice it. In considering any very old tale, it is as well to remember that primitive people have a strong sense of drama, and apply it to their lives. We shall mislead ourselves if we withhold belief from such events only because they seem highly colored by the standards of an Admass society.

There is no evidence for the word Hellene in Mycenaean times. I have used it because it conveys to many people a less localized concept than Achaean.

THE LEGEND OF THESEUS

KING AIGEUS OF ATHENS, dogged by misfortune and childless through the enmity of Aphrodite, established her worship in Athens and went to consult the Delphic Oracle. It enjoined him not to untie his wineskin till he reached home again, or he would die one day of grief. On his way back through Troizen he told his story to King Pittheus, who, guessing that some notable birth was portended, led Aigeus while drunk to the bed of his daughter Aithra. Later in the same night, she was commanded in a dream to wade over to the island shrine of Athene, where Poseidon also lay with her. When Aigeus awoke he left his sword and sandals under an altar of Zeus, telling Aithra, if a son was born, to send him to Athens as soon as he could lift the stone. This feat Theseus achieved when only sixteen; he was then already a youth of heroic size and strength, skilled with the lyre, and the inventor of scientific wrestling.

Choosing to travel to Athens by the Isthmus Road, in order to prove himself against its dangers, he overthrew in single combat all the monsters and tyrants who made its travellers their prey. In Megara he killed the giant sow Phaia, and in Eleusis slew King Kerkyon, who slaughtered wayfarers by forcing them to wrestle to the death.

When he reached Athens, the witch Medea, his father's mistress, divined his parentage, and to secure her own son's succession persuaded Aigeus that this formidable youth was a threat to his throne. Aigeus prepared a poisoned cup to give him at a public feast; but Theseus displayed the sword in the nick of time. Aigeus dashed the cup from his lips and joyfully embraced him; the witch escaped in her chariot drawn by winged dragons.

Aigeus adopted Theseus as his heir amid public rejoicing; Pallas, the former heir, and his fifty sons, were killed by the young prince or driven into exile. Theseus won further honor by taming a wild bull which was ravaging the Marathon plain. Soon after, however, the City was plunged in mourning by the arrival of the Cretan tribute vessel, with a demand for the boys and girls regularly sent off to be devoured by the Minotaur.

King Minos of Crete had been provided by Poseidon, in answer to a vow, with a magnificent bull for sacrifice, but had kept it for himself. As a punishment, Aphrodite visited his queen, Pasiphaë, with a monstrous passion for it, which she consummated within a hollow cow made for her by Daidalos the master-craftsman. Their offspring was the Minotaur, a being with a man's body and bull's head, who fed on human flesh. To conceal his shame, Minos had an impenetrable Labyrinth made by Daidalos, where he withdrew from the world, and, in the heart of the maze, concealed the Minotaur, introducing a supply of human victims into his den.

The quota from Athens was seven youths and seven maidens. Among these went Theseus; according to most versions, by his own choice, though others say by lot. At his departure, his father charged him to change the black sail of the sacrificial ship to a white one, should he return alive.

On his arrival at Crete, Minos mocked his claim to be the son of Poseidon, and challenged him to retrieve a ring thrown into the sea. Theseus received from the sea nymphs not only the ring but the golden crown of Thetis. His exploit caused Minos' daughter, Ariadne, to fall in love with him; she gave him in secret a ball of thread with which to retrace his steps through the Labyrinth, and a sword to kill the Minotaur.

This deed accomplished, Theseus gathered the Athenian youths; but the girls were imprisoned apart. Theseus had prepared for this in Athens by training two brave but effeminate-looking boys to take the place of two girl victims. These unbarred the women's quarters, and all the victims escaped to Athens, taking with them Ariadne, whom, however, Theseus abandoned on the island of Naxos. Dionysos, finding her there, became enamored of her and made her the chief of his maenad train. Coming in sight of Athens, Theseus forgot to change the mourning sail for a white one, with the result that Aigeus in grief leaped off the Acropolis, or off a high rock into the sea. Theseus thus succeeded to the throne.

During his reign he is said to have unified Attica and given laws to its three estates of landowner, farmer, and craftsman. He was famed for his protection of ill-used servants and slaves, for whom his shrine remained a sanctuary down to historic times. Pirithoos, King of the Lapiths, raided his cattle as a challenge; but the young warriors took to each other in the field and swore eternal friendship. Theseus took part in the Caledonian Boar Hunt and the battle of the Lapiths and Centaurs, and is said to have emulated the feats of Herakles. In a foray against the Amazons he carried off their queen Hippolyta. Later her people in revenge invaded Attica; but Hippolyta took the field at Theseus' side, where an arrow killed her. Before this, however, she had borne him a son, Hippolytos.

After her death, Theseus sent for and married Phaedra, King Minos' youngest daughter. Hippolytos was now a strong and beautiful youth, devoted to horsemanship and to the chaste cult of Artemis, his mother's tutelary deity. Soon Phaedra was seized with a consuming passion for him, and begged her old nurse to plead her cause. Upon his shocked refusal she hanged herself, leaving a letter which accused him of her rape. Theseus, convinced by the fact of her death, drove out his son, and invoked the death-curse entrusted to him by his father Poseidon. As Hippolytos drove his chariot along the rocky coastal road, the god sent a huge wave, bearing on its crest a sea-bull, which stampeded his horses. His battered corpse was brought back to Theseus, who had learned the truth too late.

Thereafter, Theseus' luck forsook him. While helping in Pirithoos' attempt to abduct Persephone, he was confined in the underworld in torment for four years, till Herakles released him. On his return he found Athens sunk into lawlessness and sedition. Failing to restore the rule of law, he cursed the city and set sail for Crete. On the way he stopped at Skyros, where through his host's treachery he fell off a high rock into the sea.

SELECT BIBLIOGRAPHY

Plutarch: *Life of Theseus*
M. Ventris and J. Chadwick: *Documents in Mycenaean Greek*
L. R. Palmer: *Mycenaean Greek Texts from Pylos*

                                 Achaeans and Indo-Europeans
J. Chadwick: *The Earliest Greeks*
A. J. Wace: *Mycenae*
                                 The Mycenae Tablets
J. D. S. Pendlebury: *The Palace of Minos, Knossos*
C. Zervos: *L'Art de la Crète, Néolithique et Minoenne*

I. Thallon Hill: *The Ancient City of Athens*
Ed. S. Radhakrishnan: *The Principal Upanishads*
R. Graves: *The Greek Myths*
Eranos Yearbooks 2:   *The Mysteries*
W. F. Otto: *The Homeric Gods*
G. Glotz: *Ancient Greece at Work*
M. I. Finlay: *The World of Odysseus*
L. Cottrell: *The Bull of Minos*